MEDUSA

Also by Skye Kathleen Moody

Fiction

K Falls
Rain Dance
Blue Poppy
Wildcrafters
Habitat

Nonfiction (as Kathy Kahn)

Hillbilly Women
Fruits of Our Labor

MEDUSA

Skye Kathleen Moody

St. Martin's Minotaur
New York

This is a work of fiction. The characters, incidents, and dialogue are products of the author's imagination and are not to be construed as real. Any resemblance to actual persons, living or dead, is entirely coincidental.

www.minotaurbooks.com

Library of Congress Cataloging-in-Publication Data

Moody, Skye Kathleen.
    Medusa / Skye Kathleen Moody.—1st ed.
       p. cm.
    ISBN 0-312-26678-2
    1. Diamond, Venus (Fictitious character)—Fiction. 2. Government investigators—Fiction. 3. Women environmentalists—Fiction. 4. Northwest, Pacific—Fiction. 5. Drowning victims—Fiction. 6. Serial murders—Fiction. I. Title.

PS3563.O5538M66 2003
813'.54—dc21

                                            2003041263

First Edition: August 2003

10 9 8 7 6 5 4 3 2 1

For
Mr. Ford
ti voglio bene

Beauty is that Medusa's head
Which men go armed to seek and sever.
It is most deadly when most dead,
And dead will stare and sting forever.

—*Archibald MacLeish*

PART ONE

She was nine years old, mean as they come. She hated her brother, yet he was the only person she trusted. She got a kick out of playing wicked pranks on Henry and his detestable best friend, Tim Diamond. Whenever they teased her—and they teased her mercilessly—Pearl made them pay. She could be a witch when she wanted to, and she had no conscience about making Henry cry. Sometimes he deserved it, like when he called her "hair ball" in front of her schoolmates. Pearl actually enjoyed punishing Henry, making him bawl like a baby. Tim Diamond never cried, hard as she'd tried to make him. Still, she was determined to break him, too. Meanness was her nature. She didn't know why. But Pearl had never—ever—been mean to Rupert.

She liked ice cream—chocolate raspberry crunch swirl. Rupert kept a gallon carton in the small fridge, in the galley of the main salon. She liked Rupert's little rooms, the captain's quarters, tucked behind the pilothouse. Rupert's rooms were cozy, full of warmth and pleasure, except when Rupert went away and left her in there. Then, sometimes, she felt frightened and would cry out for Rupert to come and rescue her. From what? She wasn't sure what to call it, only that she didn't like it when Rupert left her in the captain's quarters. She liked Rupert, though, and if he weren't an adult, she might even have trusted him. He wasn't like the other adults Pearl knew. Nothing like her parents. They ignored Pearl and Henry. Why did they even bother having kids if they were always too busy to give them any attention? She hated her parents, and she wished they were dead.

When she was a good girl, when Pearl wasn't being mean, Rupert rewarded her with ice cream and other treats. She was happy being a good girl for him. But sometimes, at home with her family, she worried that she might give their secret away—hers and Rupert's. Not because she would ever tell on him, ever report him, or make up lies or exaggerated stories. No. Because Rupert loved her and she wanted to tell everyone, including her stupid parents, who were never home when she needed them, who never cared whether she was happy or sad, never even cared if she lived or died. She wanted to tell them how good Rupert was to her. But that was forbidden, and, above all, her word to Rupert was sacred. They had made a pact.

Her brother knew. But Henry had his own secret friend, who rewarded him when he was very good. Henry was often good. Sometimes when she and her brother were alone, out of their parents' earshot, Henry would say to Pearl, "I wish Larry was my real father."

Pearl would always answer, "Well, someday I'm going to marry Rupert." To that remark, Henry would inevitably cock his head to one side and pretend to think it over; then he'd break out into a fiendish grin. "Hell no," he'd say, "you're wa-a-a-y too ugly." And then Pearl would know that everything was normal, that she had no reason to fear, either for Henry or for herself.

This morning, shortly after dawn, Pearl lay in her bed at home. The gentle baritone of foghorns had crooned her awake. The house was quiet as she rose and went into the bathroom. She showered and washed her frizzy mop. Looking in the mirror, she saw her owl-shaped face and curled her upper lip at it. Rupert kept assuring her that her homely face didn't matter. Still, she held out hope that one day she'd be as pretty as her mom. As pretty, but not as cold. By 6:30, Pearl was dressed and ready to go. Henry took a little longer to get dressed, so they didn't get started until almost seven o'clock.

They left by the side door, as usual. This summer morning, a thick fog blanketed the city, and they couldn't see more than three feet in front of them. In the public park adjacent to their house, Tim Diamond was waiting for them, standing beneath a dewy madrona, barely visible in the fog. Tim was carrying a plastic trash bag full of something, but Pearl couldn't tell what. Pearl and Henry followed Tim down the steep, rocky path to the beach. The dinghy had already arrived. They could see its prow poking through the fog.

Rupert was on time, as always, waiting in the dinghy beside the little makeshift dock that Rupert and the three children had built the previous summer. As she stepped into the dinghy, Pearl noticed that Rupert wore a worried expression. She had seen it only once before, a few days earlier, after Rupert and Ziggy had had an argument aboard the *Caprice*. Pearl didn't know what they'd been arguing about, but afterward, Rupert had had this horrible frown on his face that reminded her of a pissed frog. Like he looked this morning. Pearl didn't dare ask him what was wrong. When the three children had boarded the dinghy, Rupert throttled the Evinrude down and the boat purred, because he kept the motor in tip-top condition. They plowed through the fog. Five minutes later, they were climbing up the ladder onto the *Caprice,* Tim's stepmother's yacht. All famous movie actresses had big yachts, Tim had told Pearl. And Pearl had believed him.

As soon as they boarded, Rupert led Pearl to the captain's private quarters, where she was expected to do her lessons before she could play. Once inside the cabin, Rupert smiled, and Pearl felt much better, because for some reason his terrible frown had frightened her. Then Rupert cracked a funny joke, and she laughed, a giggle, he said, that reminded him of a waterfall. Then, as usual, he explained her lesson for the day. They spent almost an hour in Rupert's private quarters, Pearl working on her lesson; then Rupert left her alone and went forward to steer the *Caprice* away from the dock.

Pearl had a particularly tough lesson, but she just kept thinking about chocolate raspberry crunch swirl ice cream, and finally she completed it. She donned the mandatory life vest and rode the yacht's elevator down four stories to the main deck, where Henry and Tim stood waiting for her. Both Henry and Tim wore life vests, too, but what's this? Pearl wondered. The two boys were dressed as pirates. Henry had a bandanna wrapped around his blond hair and he'd drawn a fake tattoo on his forearm. Tim must be Captain Hook, she realized, because he wore an eye patch and his right hand was missing, replaced by a coat hanger's hook. Tim's one visible eye twinkled menacingly. Tim was Asian or something. Maybe Chinese. And he was smaller than Henry, even though the two boys were approximately the same age—twelve. Now Henry stepped forward, the only person she'd ever trusted, and she wasn't prepared for what came next. Henry gripped Pearl's arm so that it hurt and said, "Pearl Pederson, today you die."

He said it like he meant it.

"Tie her hands," yelled Captain Hook, aka Tim Diamond, through a thick, unrelenting fog. "That way, she can't save herself."

"Front or back?" the pirate hollered through the gloomy mist.

"Back, idiot. Over that fat butt."

Henry Pederson, aka Pirate Henry, obeyed Captain Hook's command.

"Tighter," growled Hook. "We don't want her breaking loose."

Pirate Henry cinched the yellow nylon rope tighter around his sister's wrists. Prisoner Pearl cried out, cursing Henry and Hook. Henry removed the pirate's bandanna from around his head and blindfolded his sister.

Pearl cried, "Let me go, rat face, or I'll tell Daddy you watch his *Playboy* DVDs."

"Shut up, icky prisoner."

"Now read off her crimes," Hook commanded.

The boys had prepared meticulously for this moment, having come to the *Caprice* the night before to set the stage for "Pearl Fright." They had placed a wood plank on the *Caprice*'s aft railing and secured it with duct tape to the vessel's rear starboard side. They situated it behind a lifeboat, so that it couldn't be seen from the pilothouse. That way, Captain Scree couldn't see them terrorizing Pearl. The duct tape and the nylon rope Hook had given Henry to bind Pearl's hands were the only concessions Hook had made to modern technology. He wanted everything else just as the original Captain Hook would have had it, right down to the teak plank, left over from a recent remodeling of the *Caprice*'s galley. It made a perfect execution stage.

Their plan was simple and seemingly foolproof. They would scare the pants off Pearl, but at the last minute,

Captain Hook would show mercy and Vinegar Tongue would be granted one last reprieve, one last chance to make up for all the nastiness she had perpetrated upon her brother and her next-door neighbor, Tim Diamond, Captain Hook. At last, Pearl would come under their control, her evil ways reined in, her menace stanched.

Nils Pederson, Pearl's and Henry's father, the city's most popular businessman, was a chunk of charm, and smart besides. Their mother, Ingrid Pederson, was an ice princess, who had once been crowned Miss Ballard. Unfortunately, being the Pedersdottir-Pederson offspring did not guarantee comeliness, and although Henry was developing into a Norse god, Daddy's spitten image, Pearl had lost at genetic roulette. Mom and Nils had overcompensated for Pearl's genetic misfortune, and for their chronic neglect, by lavishing gifts and privileges upon her and generally allowing her free reign. If Pearl wanted something that belonged to Henry—say Henry's favorite DVD—Henry was expected to relinquish it. If Pearl wanted lima beans for dinner, Cook was obliged to comply, never mind that Henry had to endure the green fester on his own dinner plate. If Pearl wished to scream at Henry, or at Penny and Pepper, the poodles, or at Loon, the family's pet duck, or if Pearl wanted to play nasty tricks on her next-door neighbors, the Diamonds, she could play her cruel hand and not fear punishment. The Pedersdottir-Pederson parental unit completely ignored Pearl's hatefulness, and that was why Henry and Tim believed she had to walk the plank.

"Pearl Pederson, you are charged with the following crimes." Henry held up an elaborately designed document. " 'First and foremost,' " he read aloud, " 'you are a menace to society. Your constant screaming, your lying and cheating and tattletale behavior have caused grave damage to your brother'—that's me—'and to your next-door neighbor, Captain Timothy Hook. Furthermore, you are fat and sloppy, and you fart in public.' "

Pearl screamed, "Rupert, help! Help, Rupert!"

But the *Caprice*'s skipper didn't come to rescue Pearl.

"Now walk," commanded Captain Hook.

"I don't want to."

"I said, 'walk.' "

Pearl inched a few tentative steps forward along the wood plank that jutted out portside from the *Caprice*'s stern. The plank bounced, nearly throwing her off balance. She cried out, her normally acidic tone of voice now whiny, quivering, pleading, a condition that pleased both Captain Hook and Henry.

"Please let me get down," she begged, and then began hiccuping sobs.

"Go on, scum, all the way to the end," said Henry cruelly.

"Oh please. I can't. Let me down. Please. Please let me down." Pearl's little legs trembled as she struggled to keep her balance at the edge of the long wooden plank that jutted out into the fog. They could barely see her now through the thick mist, but they could hear her sobs and cries. Then Captain Hook spoke.

"Will you promise to obey us?"

"I promise, I promise. Let me down. I'm afraid."

Captain Hook made a strategic decision. All along, he had intended to frighten the prisoner until she agreed to his reasonable conditions. Right along, he'd had every intention of granting a reprieve. Now Hook and Henry exchanged glances.

"I say, Girl overboard," declared Henry.

But the benevolent Hook raised a hand and signaled to his pirate in their secret coded, a gesture that meant "Spare the prisoner."

"Oh hell," grumbled Henry, and he walked away, complaining about chickenshit games. Hook saw Henry's back-

side as he walked toward the aft cabin. Because of the thick
fog, he didn't actually see Henry go inside, but he heard the
cabin door slide open and then shut again.

Pearl was sobbing. Taking pity, Hook climbed up onto
the plank, scooted to the end, removed Pearl's blindfold,
and then untied the nylon cord that had bound her wrists.
Pearl squinted, rubbed her wrists, and got down on her
knees to crawl back aboard. Hook scooted back along the
plank and stepped into the boat. He was adjusting his eye
patch, he would later tell the police, when he saw the tentacles. And then everything happened so fast, too fast to
recall every little detail later on, when details were crucial.

"Help!" cried Pearl as she went overboard.

Tim sprang into action. Leaping onto the plank, he
reached out for Pearl, but too late. Pearl screamed and disappeared underwater. Tim dove into the deep, frigid
waters, but Pearl was gone. He dove and dove but couldn't
locate Pearl. On the fifth dive, he came back up with her life
vest, but no Pearl inside. Where was she? Searching across
the water's surface, Tim saw the big jellyfish float by, riding
the outbound current. He shouted Pearl's name. Nothing.
He called again and again, but Pearl didn't answer. He
shouted up to the pilothouse, "Man overboard!"

He meant "Girl overboard." He meant Pearl.

That's what Tim Diamond told the police.

CHAPTER TWO

Waikiki
June 29

Tragedy gives no ground to bliss. A lighthearted spirit expects nothing dark to invade its idyllic world, so when tragedy intrudes, all good humor that came before acquires the frivolous mantle of bittersweet foreshadow. This, looking back, is what Venus Diamond felt on that late-June afternoon when Bart called. Even then, she had no idea how dark things were to become.

In the three weeks she had spent at the Coral Reef on Waikiki Beach, Venus had polished her scuba-diving skills and had learned to play mah-jongg. Her normally pale complexion had acquired a lobster glow, and the gruesome nightmares had begun to recede. She did not know the exact name of the medication her physician had prescribed after the "incident," only that it came in little white capsules with black belts and that it delivered a noticeable punch. Over time, the brain-altering chemicals had salved her psychic wounds and overlaid them with a cloud of memory. That was the point of being sent to the Coral Reef, after all, to "get better," as the boss had put it.

From all outward appearances, the Coral Reef, in Honolulu, looked like any other posh tropical resort, its broad strand of Dixie Crystals beach merging with translucent turquoise waters inhabited by breathtaking marine life, much of it in human form. There were luaus, hula-hula dancers, scuba school. All in all, doing time at the Coral Reef could be a sublime experience, and the best part was, your stay at the rehab center was never recorded in your employee file.

Oly Olson, her boss at U.S. Fish & Wildlife's Pacific Northwest regional office in Seattle, had banished Diamond to the Coral Reef after determining that she had used poor judgment on the job. Olson had promised that since this was the first incident of its kind, if she agreed to get treatment at the rehab center for undercover federal agents, he would allow her to return to work with the same responsibilities as before. Poaching big game was on the rise in the Pacific Northwest, and he needed her, but he didn't need a mental case. And so it was agreed that she would be confined to the Coral Reef in Honolulu until she had demonstrated full recovery from a diagnosed "post-traumatic stress disorder," which had triggered an act so mortifying, she still could not call it by its name. Thankfully, most of her coworkers had been kept out of the loop, and her family also had no idea what she'd done. Only Olson and her fellow agent Louie Song knew of her transgression, and she hoped it would stay that way.

This morning, on the beach in front of the Coral Reef, at the dive equipment–rental stand, Venus checked out a single oxygen tank and a face mask. She had taken her medication an hour earlier and was feeling better than average; in fact, for better or worse, she felt invincible.

Plunging into the crystalline waters, she wore the oxygen tank, oval face mask, a string bikini the color of seaweed, a new scuba belt complete with speargun and a new pair of flippers, which matched the turquoise sea in which she cavorted like a native. If she weren't careful, they'd catch her and serve her up as puu-puu. Her blond hair waved around her face like a sea dandelion and her vivid green eyes terrified the more timid inhabitants of Honolulu Harbor. She gripped an underwater digital camera in her left hand, while her right hand worked as a flipper paddling forward. Swimming through sunlit depths, she followed a school of electric blue fish. They had yellow lips and orange tails. They were pancake-shaped, uniform in size, about six inches in circumference, had tiny red eyeballs, and probably had a name like Hamehameluauluauhamehameluauhame. When she aimed her camera, the fish instantly turned their tails to her. That's the trouble with shooting wildlife. You always end up capturing the butt shot.

She was following the school, when suddenly a giant manta ray confronted her. The huge devilfish had been watching her from its coral-reef hideout. Now it undulated toward her.

For a split second, the manta ray's terrible face stunned her. Then she broke into a thrashing spin, confusing it, but even as she sped away, she knew the big boy wanted revenge. She was no bigger than an hors d'oeuvre, hardly worth the effort. Still, he pursued her. She swam faster. When she felt his tail whipping at her flipper, she shook it off, gladly relinquishing it. When she felt his jaw nudge the second flipper, she gave that up, too, thrashing upward.

Now he appeared beside her, on her left. His eye met hers and he turned to face her. Moving in for the kill, he lunged, but she flipped over. He bit into her oxygen tank. She unbelted it and let it go. He spit out the tank and swam upward, then dove down again from above. She propelled herself toward the water's surface, in the direction she thought was shore. A hundred yards or a hundred feet— she couldn't tell. Then he was back at her side. She whirled and, raising the camera, popped off a frame.

The flash momentarily stunned the ray and he froze long enough for her to reach the speargun in her belt. The next time he attacked, she was ready for him. She tossed the camera and he caught it in his jaws. Face-to-face with him now, she aimed the weapon and fired. The spear's barbed tip struck neatly between the eyes and blood oozed out, forming thick red clouds. As the devilfish sank, she grabbed its jaws, reached in, and pried out the camera.

When she surfaced on the beach in front of the Coral Reef, she shucked off the diving mask, handing it to a uniformed attendant. His name was Al and he was maybe fifteen years old, of Hawaiian descent. Al checked the face mask for damage.

"See anything interesting?" he asked.

"Sure did."

"What?" Al looked up.

"A school of pancake fish."

Al laughed scornfully. "You psychos get all hot over a bunch of scavenger fish. Where's your tank?"

"Lost it."

"You pay," Al said menacingly.

"I pay." She showed him her new porcelain teeth.

"How can anyone lose a strapped-on tank?"

"Something bit it off." She flung her hair off her face. Water droplets hit Al's shirt.

Al picked at his shirt and mumbled, "Not another *Moby-Dick* tale."

She walked away, moving across the comforting sand as she made her way up the beach. Al called after her, "Next time, bring your own gear."

At the top of the beach, where the Dixie Crystals met

the Coral Reef's emerald velvet lawns, she claimed her favorite umbrella and chaise, wrapped a sarong around her hips, and, nestling into the lounger, fished a book out of her beach bag. *Advanced Diving Techniques*. She'd checked it out of the loony bin's library that morning and was already halfway finished. She cracked the book's spine, relaxed, and read two sentences before her cell phone rang, deep inside her beach bag, and her life took an awful turn for the worse.

CHAPTER THREE

It was Bart, her brother, calling from Seattle. She had told him three weeks ago, when he'd dropped her at the airport, that she was heading for Honolulu, on the first leg of an around-the-world adventure.

"You'd better come home," Bart Diamond said now. "There's been some trouble."

"What trouble?" Venus covered the phone and looked around. No security guards or other eavesdroppers lurked.

"Pearl Pederson has drowned."

"That little brat who lives next door to Mother?"

Bart said, "She went overboard into Elliott Bay. From Mother's boat. Just off the marina below the house. They haven't recovered her body. Sis, the cops are holding Timmy under house arrest. They say he intentionally pushed her overboard, then dove in and held her underwater until she drowned."

She set the book down underneath her beach umbrella. A uniformed attendant came by with her medication and a mango cocktail to wash it down. She was just beginning to feel comfortable with the daily routine at the Coral Reef, all the broken pieces of her body and her brain beginning to recover. Two months earlier, during a poacher bust on the Olympic Peninsula, she had taken a bullet in the jaw. It had punctured her cheek, shattering half of her lower jaw, which had had to be reconstructed. The surgery had been successful, but the stress had encouraged a malaria relapse, which had nearly dropped her into a permanent coma. The hole in her cheek where the bullet had entered hadn't yet healed. It would in time, though. It was the posttraumatic rage that still needed tending—a rage that had triggered the ugly incident, inappropriately aimed at her colleague Louie Song, her truest ally, instead of at the poacher who had shot her.

The attendant went away. "Bart," Venus said, "is this some kind of dim-witted joke?"

"This time, I'm not joking. The detective in charge of the case says once they recover her body—if they recover it—the prosecutor plans to charge Timmy as an adult."

"He's twelve years old, for chrissake. You can't try a twelve-year-old as an adult."

"That's what I said, but the detective says the prosecutor's out for blood. You know, Nils Pederson's daughter and all."

"Nils Pederson might be a rich and powerful businessman, but that doesn't justify charging Timmy as an adult."

"Remember the recession? How Nils invested in King County when Boeing deserted?" Bart waited for her to comment, and when she didn't, he added, "The county owes Nils. It's usually age thirteen, but the prosecutor's making an exception in Tim's case."

She could feel the pills sliding down her esophagus. She said, "Where's Timmy now?"

"Mother bailed him out. He's at home, confined to his room. They put one of those electronic anklets on him, so he can't run away without being tracked."

She found her towel beneath the beach umbrella, mussed her damp hair. The Hawaiian sun had bleached it nearly snow white. She said, "Timmy didn't push Pearl."

Bart sighed. "Henry was with them, Pearl's brother. Henry claims he saw Timmy push Pearl overboard and then dive in and hold her head underwater. Apparently, they were playing some game. Henry claims Tim said beforehand that he wanted to drown Pearl. Of course, Tim claims that Henry's lying."

"Oh God." The sun beat down. Venus covered her eyes. Her jaw ached and the new tooth implants felt alien.

"I know," said Bart. "Tim's the chronic liar. And according to Mother, that little Henry Pederson is a child saint. They'll take Henry's word over Tim's for sure."

"Look, Bart. I really can't come home now."

"You have to. Timmy trusts you. He'll talk to you. We can't get through to him. He snaps at everyone, and he's refusing to cooperate with the police. The kid needs you, Venus, and hell, so do I. Between Timmy and the Red Queen, I can't handle this much longer by myself."

The Red Queen was their mother, Bella Diamond, the actress. More actress than mother. She had recently played the role of the Red Queen in a noir version of *Alice*. Ever since, her children had called her the Red Queen, or R.Q. for short. She knew, but she didn't care. The Red Queen was all-powerful.

"It's just not convenient now. Really, Bart, I can't possibly get back home for . . . well, several weeks. I know that sounds cold and heartless."

"Think how it will sound to Timmy."

The sun beat brighter, hotter. Venus reached up and unconsciously rubbed the hole in her cheek, the wound still healing, still obvious. She could feel Bart's anxiety all the way from Seattle. In spite of the tropical heat, she shivered. She packed the book and towel in her beach bag and began walking toward the Coral Reef. "I'll take the red-eye," she said. She checked the time on her cell phone. "Tell Timmy I'm on my way."

"I'll tell him. And Sis?"

"What, Bart?"

"I think I should warn you. Timmy's telling everyone who will listen that Pearl was taken underwater by a giant jellyfish."

"They do grow big in Puget Sound."

Bart laughed thinly. "Yeah, well, Mother's a total wreck," he said "She's incapable of handling this. I plan to stay with her and Tim, but I need your help. You know how inept I am at handling crises."

"Like I said, I'll be home by morning."

"Where are you now?"

"Honolulu."

"You've been there for three weeks now. I thought this was going to be a circle-the-globe safari. Why are you hanging out there?"

She massaged her eyelid. "Surf's up. Nice waves. I'm having a ball."

She went inside the Coral Reef, walked up to the desk. Ted, the secretary, was finishing a bag-lunch. She told him she wanted to check out. Ted scowled, set his sandwich aside, worked his lips, silently, and finally said, "You're checking yourself out?"

"That's right."

He sighed wearily and recited his mantra. "You understand that if you check yourself out of this facility before the date set by your agency, we are required to report this

information to your caseworker. Furthermore, you understand that if your agency so orders, we will send federal
officers to find you and bring you back to the facility?"

She nodded.

"You realize that a federal court may at any time decide
to locate, detain, and possibly, again at the discretion of the
judge, punish you for disregarding your agency's orders?"

"Yup."

Ted snorted, made a long entry into the computer, and
then handed her some papers to sign. She did so with a
flourish that she hoped exuded self-confidence and control.
He snatched the papers back and said, "You'll be back. I'd
stake my life on it."

She went up to her suite, showered, packed, and made
a flight reservation. She took a long, restless nap, rising in
time to make the red-eye flight. She dressed, tossed the
camera into her carry-on bag, and disconsolately fondled
an orchid lei a hula-hula girl had placed around her neck at
the Coral Reef's weekly luau. She went down to the library
and turned in the diving book, then to the clinic, where she
tried, unsuccessfully, to stock up on the magic pills. By
11:00 P.M. she was sitting in the backseat of a taxicab, Val-
halla shrinking in the rearview mirror.

CHAPTER FOUR

Seattle
June 30

Bart was waiting at the airport in Bella's Jaguar, top down. Tan and fit, wearing summer whites, Bart turned heads wherever he went, and now wasn't an exception. A couple of Asian women standing at the curb stared at Bart, palpitating like two overheated wrens. Women drooled over Bart, but he barely noticed. He just went about his bachelorhood playing a broad field, all knockouts, and whenever the subject of commitment reared its demonic head, Bart bailed. He played sax in a strictly cool retro jazz band, and he also played at sculpture, for which he was handsomely compensated by his exclusive clients. Like Venus's other siblings, Bart had inherited their mother's lean, long-boned good looks, unlike Venus, the family anomaly, the miniature person, the elf among titans. Maybe that was why she had turned out the grittiest of them all.

Venus tossed her carry-on bag into the back and slid into the passenger seat. She wore a madras Patagonia shift and Danish clogs. She didn't look like a refugee from a loony bin.

"You look like a goddamn lobster," said Bart. "Where's your luggage?"

"That's it."

"I thought you were going around the world." He pulled away from the curb and entered a traffic lane. "You need more than carry-on to circle the globe."

"I travel light," she said. "How's Tim?"

"Miserable. Mother has confined him to his room. No television, no computer, no nothing. Actually, the homicide detective took Tim's computer. Evidence. And Mother refuses to speak to him. The kid's deeply upset." Bart indicated the glove compartment. "Morning paper's in there."

Venus opened the glove compartment and fished out a newspaper. The headline read NILS PEDERSON'S DAUGHTER MISSING, PRESUMED DEAD. In smaller print, the subheading said, "Bella Diamond's Adopted Son May Have Pushed Pearl Pederson Overboard from Actress's *Caprice*."

"High scandal," said Bart drolly. "Our family is hamburger in the news media's grinder. Mother's house and the Pedersons' house next door are surrounded by reporters demanding interviews with everyone from Tim to Nils to Mother's chef. The media calls us—by 'us,' I mean the Diamond family, not the Pedersons—'a dynasty of spoiled, selfish, hoity-toity, rich parasites who think we can get away with murder.' Of course, they don't bother mentioning that Nils Pederson is worth twice what Mother is worth and that he made his fortune by exploiting his employees and buying off city councilmen and county commissioners."

"Hey, the man's daughter just drowned. Cut him some slack."

Bart snorted and said, "I've never liked that SOB. Ever

since he demolished the old Schwartz house and built that ostentatious barn next door to Mother's house, he's been a pain in the ass. He epitomizes the definition of nouveau riche."

"Can it, Bart. Anyway, I don't understand the news media. They've always loved the Red Queen. They've coddled her, for chrissake, made her their local icon, the darling of contemporary noir film. How can they turn on her like that?"

Bart shrugged. "Mother can't understand it, either. Hell, she expects nothing less than adulation from the press. But this time's different. They want to cut us until we bleed, and they're attacking her through her children. They've even dredged up some old records of my grade school arrest for selling grass to the nuns. If you have any deep dark secrets, you better be prepared to see them exposed."

Her heart stopped, then kicked back in.

She said, "They'll lose interest soon enough. Meanwhile, how's the Red Queen holding up?"

"Confined to her private quarters. This is her finest role yet, the betrayed stepmother. She's playing it to the hilt. She won't eat, won't speak to anyone, except Stephen, of course. I think Stephen is gradually gaining control over the family."

"He's her personal assistant. That makes him powerful."

Bart continued: "Mother's latest film is being shot in Curaçao, so it took her awhile to get home. I had the honor of being first on the scene. The homicide detective in charge of the case, a chap named Rocco, turned Tim over to me, but not before he clamped on that electronic ankle bracelet."

"Tell me what happened."

Bart related the details, at least the few he knew. The

three children, Timmy, Henry Pederson, and his sister, Pearl, had been playing a game on the *Caprice*'s stern. Pearl screamed and then went overboard. Henry insisted he saw Timmy push Pearl overboard, then dive in and hold her underwater. Timmy claimed that Pearl lost her balance and fell overboard and that a huge jellyfish reached out with its tentacles and grabbed her, pulling her underwater. He said he had dived in to try to rescue her. Pearl's body still hadn't been recovered, although death by drowning seemed the only logical conclusion. It had been forty-eight hours since the event. No sign of Pearl. The news media was favoring the "boy murderer" angle.

By the time Bart had finished relating what he knew, they had reached downtown.

Venus said, "Take this exit."

Bart took the Seneca exit off I-5 and came up at Sixth Avenue.

Venus said, "Let me off here."

"What are you, crazy?"

"Pull over. I have an errand to run. I'll meet you at Mother's for dinner."

Bart pulled over to the curb and Venus stepped out onto the sidewalk.

Bart said, "Seven sharp. Say, how's the malaria?"

"Fever's gone. Does Rocco have a first name?"

"Detective."

"Thanks heaps." She disappeared into the city streets as Bart pealed off into the traffic.

Detective Rocco stood when she entered his small office on the sixth floor of the Public Safety Building. He held out a hand. "If it isn't Venus Diamond, the Renaissance woman," he said. "I wondered when you'd show up."

He had a nice handshake, not too showy. Venus sat

down and so did Rocco, his desk the safe zone. On his desk, a brass nameplate read DETECTIVE ROCCO. No first name. Venus self-consciously checked the drape of her shift. He was that handsome.

Rocco said, "I've heard about you. Saw you on CNN when you rode the space shuttle with a bunch of earthworms."

"Actually, it was butterfly larvae."

"Oh, yes, the CNN program mentioned that you're a lepidopterist."

"I have the butterfly bites to prove it."

Rocco nodded. "Well then, and what else? My buddies here in Homicide tell me you're a famous poacher detective. U.S. Fish and Wildlife's biggest troublemaker. I understand you've butted up against my colleagues on more than one occasion. In fact, I was warned that you'd come swiftly to your stepbrother's defense."

She opened her palms. "And here I am."

Rocco rubbed his clean-shaven chin. "Yeah, and what else? You're the politically correct Diamond, the family rebel with an attitude. Sure, I know a thing or two about you. I'll bet you're a registered Green and support ecoterrorism."

"Tell me what happened and I'll get out of your hair." She didn't feel like making small talk.

Rocco licked his dry, fleshy lips and said, "Yeah, okay. I'll tell you as much as you're allowed to know. But this is an ongoing investigation. I'm sure you understand, being a federal agent."

"So give me what you can, and no holding back just to be coy."

Rocco said, "Let's get out of here."

They walked up the hill, past an open square where a concession van was parked and volunteers were handing out sack lunches to a line of homeless people standing in the hot sun, waiting for their simple dole. As they passed, she handed a beggar a fiver.

Rocco said, "Oh no, not another bleeder."

"But for grace and good fortune . . ." she said, then, "Where are we going?"

"McHugh's Pub proletariat enough for you?"

Rocco had his favorite table. A waiter materialized. Venus ordered a single malt neat, double shot. Rocco asked for a beer. "Nothing fancy," he told the bartender. "But make it light. I'm on a diet. I gained twenty pounds during my vacation in Italy. Sicilian food is my downfall."

"For a cop, you sure volunteer a lot of information."

"Hell, every bartender in the joint knows I'm on this diet. I just say it for myself."

When the drinks came, Rocco watched her caress the glass holding two fingers of scotch. She didn't drink immediately, waiting for the scotch to warm.

"It's bad luck all the way around," Rocco said, pouring his light beer into a frosted mug. "Nils Pederson lost his only daughter. Your stepbrother's headed to kiddie prison for the rest of his destroyed adolescence. At the very least, he'll be locked up in a juvenile home, but the prosecutor's going for the harsher penalty, prison. And he's decided to raise the bail amount. Flight risk. They have kiddie prisons. Did you know that?"

"I track poachers. Very few of them are children. This is the first I've heard of kiddie prison." Venus sipped the scotch.

"Tim can do himself a huge favor by confessing. If he'd just give us the real story, the prosecutor might show some mercy. But as long as he maintains the science-fiction alibi, I'm afraid he's cooked."

"Why do you call it science fiction?"

Rocco grinned. "You're a wildlife agent. You know as well as I do that jellyfish don't grab people. I don't care how big they are; they don't have brains and they don't attack, except maybe in self-defense." He reached up and loosened his tie.

"What about Pearl's brother, Henry?"

Rocco shrugged. "He's clearly a witness, nothing more. Not a suspect at this time. Henry swears he saw Tim push the girl off the plank, then dive in and hold her head underwater. He's a good kid, a very credible witness. By the way, I'm sorry about all the negative media. Not that I control it or anything. Your mother's such a popular celebrity, even more so after that Red Queen role. I'm sure this has been a blow to her, especially with the big bash she and Nils had planned on her yacht." He shook his head. "Newspeople, God love 'em, are a fickle tribe. But don't they say in show biz that bad press is better than no press?" He watched for a reaction. Venus stared at him.

"Like I said, it's bad luck all the way around."

"My family isn't concerned about negative press. My family is concerned about Tim."

"Sure, of course. I was just referring to the upcoming election campaign. The big vote-raising bash on your mother's yacht. Rumor has it your mother and Nils Pederson are pooling their fortunes to back a surprise mayoral candidate." He winked.

Venus looked confused.

Rocco said, "You know, your mother's role in Pederson's grab for political office."

"What are you talking about?" A familiar sinking feeling swept over her, the same feeling she had every time she was about to learn of one of her mother's real-life dramas. Inevitably, the famous actress's entanglements, political or romantic, affected the whole family. Celebrities shouldn't have children.

Rocco said, "Oh, hey, maybe I'm speaking out of turn. You better ask your mother. It might still be hush-hush. On the other hand, the whole thing might have been canceled, seeing as how, at least I've heard, that Nils and your mother are not speaking to each other, so your mother may now be excluded from the plans in any case. Sorry, I'm thinking out loud."

"Bad habit for a cop."

Rocco said, "You married or otherwise attached?"

"Was, by a hangnail. Then the hangnail fell off and I got walking papers."

He grinned. "Married people always say more than they want to. It's a particular form of guilt complex, known only to the tethered." He checked his watch. "In forty-eight hours, I'll be a free man."

He made it sound like he was untangling from a spool of string.

"Say, Rocco, have there been any other reports of big jellyfish sightings in Elliott Bay?"

Rocco shook his head. "Anyway, the thing Tim described to me is a total impossibility."

"Anything at all out of the ordinary?"

"Since Pearl went overboard, the SPD's been inundated with reports of weird sightings. You know how it goes. Overreaction to media hype. Hysteria. Bogus paranoiac hallucinations. Everybody wants in on the action."

"So what can I do to help Tim?"

"Convince the boy to confide in me."

"Maybe if you were more forthcoming . . ."

"Hell, Venus, you're a cop. You know my situation. I can't share certain details of an ongoing investigation with a suspect's family. You know the rules."

"Break them," she said, meeting his gaze.

Rocco paused, as if thinking it over, and passed a hand across his face.

"Can't do it," he said finally. "Wish I could, honestly."

"We do it all the time. So do you."

Rocco shook his head. "Not me. I'm a tight-lipped SOB." He polished off the light beer. "I may want to call you in for a statement," he said. "Can I reach you at your office?"

"I'm on holiday. You can reach me at the family home."

She gave him a card with her cell-phone number. "If you feel like sharing, give me a call." He nodded. Before she left, she asked, "Who at Harbor Patrol is on the case?"

Rocco said, "Nobody. It's my case. You want anything, you come to me."

"How long have you been a cop?" she asked.

Rocco said, "Nineteen years. I guess that dates me." She nodded. "What about you? How long have you been chasing scumbag poachers?"

Her hand went up and touched the place on her cheek where the bullet had left the gaping hole. Rocco kindly averted his eyes, and that made her feel even more self-conscious. She dropped her hand and said, "Ten years. More or less."

Rocco smiled. "We're all scarred," he said kindly. "Inside or out. Someday I might show you my bullet hole."

"Why don't you start by telling me your first name?"

"I never use it."

She caught a cab to Belltown, where she owned a condominium, the booby prize in the divorce settlement. She showered and changed, then slid behind the wheel of her Audi convertible. It purred as she rolled out into traffic.

The *Caprice* was Bella Diamond's latest toy. Two hundred forty feet bow to stern, 35 feet port to starboard, four levels of opulent staterooms and salons. The oceangoing vessel had been owned by some Saudi prince before Bella had nudged the price downward, then grabbed it at a Sotheby's

"Fine Marine Vessels" auction in Liverpool. Moored in Elliott Bay at a marina just below Bella's home, the *Caprice* had become quite a curiosity on Puget Sound.

Venus parked in the marina lot, walked to the gate leading onto the docks, and punched in the security code. The gate opened and she stepped onto the main dock. Several boat owners ambled by, coming and going from their boats, and she knew most of them by name. Usually, they greeted her, but now they ignored her when she spoke to them, staring right through her, as if she were invisible. Suddenly, being a member of the Diamond family had lost its caché. Nobody wanted to rub up against a murderer's family.

The *Caprice* stood in the water, an icon of the extravagant lifestyle her mother led, a lifestyle Venus had cut her baby teeth on and had ridden into adulthood, then abandoned for a more Zen-like existence, partly in self-defense. A certain jealousy and intolerance are heaped upon those born to wealth, as if you could choose your ancestry. She had felt it as a child when other kids teased her about being the spoiled daughter of a titled British heiress turned American movie star. Venus had hated the attention, and the judgmental way people had treated her. She had grown to despise the money, as well as all the trappings of wealth and social standing. Her natural instinct had always been to avoid the ubiquitous spotlight constantly illuminating her mother. And too, she was an undercover cop. She couldn't afford publicity, unlike the Red Queen, the star, for better or for worse, a media magnet.

The *Caprice*'s exterior, its white hull and four stories of cabins and salons, had recently been painted, the teak trim burnished to a rich glow. Someone had spent hours on the brightwork, and the yacht's chrome and brass fixtures gleamed in the afternoon sunlight. An ambitious police officer had tried to draw yellow police tape along the ship's length but had given up at the first porthole. The gangplank was down, indicating someone was already aboard. Venus walked up to the main deck.

"Rupert?" she called out.

No response from Rupert Scree, the *Caprice*'s skipper.

She walked across the wide deck, peering inside windows as she passed various salons and private quarters. Nothing. She entered a passageway and pushed a button. An elevator opened. She rode it up four stories, got out, and walked aft along the top deck. Rupert Scree lived on the top deck, his quarters a small stateroom behind the pilot-house. Venus wasn't spying, but she happened to glance into his window as she rounded the stern. The drapes were open and she saw Rupert Scree inside, lying on his bed. He was naked, and so was the woman on top of him.

CHAPTER FIVE

Muffled voices escaped from inside the skipper's cabin. Cries of passion. Venus backed off, stepped to the portside railing, and whistled self-consciously into the soft breeze, but she could still hear the lovebirds. She walked forward, returning to the passageway, rode the elevator down to the main deck, and punched Rupert Scree's number into her cell phone.

He answered on the fifth ring. Ten minutes later, Scree appeared on the main deck, accompanied by a dark-haired beauty who must have been conceived during a screening of *Snow White*. She wore short shorts, which exposed the whitest legs Venus had ever seen, sandals, and a terry-cloth jacket with a hood that covered her head. A few locks of coal black hair fell across her face. She carried a cheap aluminum roasting pan that had been badly scorched on one side and was empty except for some leftover crumbs.

She kept her head bowed, eyes cast downward, the strand of hair teasing her nose and her full cherry-colored lips. She said something to Scree in a soft murmur and then hurried down the gangplank and along the pier toward the parking lot.

"Who's the hot babe?" said Venus.

Scree was tall and thin, with scruffy sun-bronzed hair and salt-parched skin the shade of tobacco. He came forward to where Venus stood near the railing, held out his hand, and shook hers. He said, "Her? Oh, that's your mother's new chef. She brought me some food left over from last night. Apparently, your mother isn't eating."

They went through a teak door leading into the main salon, a huge ballroom-size area with hardwood floors and curving leather couches the color and texture of butter. This was the Red Queen's party room during her impromptu voyages to nowhere, on which she was usually accompanied by a coterie of film celebrities. Venus sat on the couch that faced the dance floor. She'd sat here before, whenever the R.Q. demanded her presence at one of her posh sailing parties, Venus choosing the seat nearest the door so she could escape when the Hollywood gang's revelry reached fever pitch. Unlike her mother, Venus wasn't a party girl.

Scree went over to the wet bar, fiddled around, and came back with two glasses—rum and Coke, with a lime wedge. "Where should I start?" he asked her.

"From the beginning. You decide what that is."

Scree sprawled casually across a couch. Venus noticed that his white deck pants were spotless and perfectly creased. She didn't know much about Rupert Scree, only that he was an experienced sailor and an ex–Coast Guard rescue diver and that he had once been honored by the Coast Guard for rescuing the crew of a fishing vessel that had caught fire at sea. He had earned his captain's license at a respected local maritime academy. Where had he come from just before Bella hired him to skipper the *Caprice*? She wasn't privy to this information, but Bella's capable personal assistant, Stephen, always ran security checks on potential Diamond in-house staff. Surely he'd run a check on Scree. Scree had been the *Caprice*'s skipper for what, fourteen, fifteen months? No less than that, because Venus recalled the retirement party for the previous skipper. She had first met Rupert Scree at that party. Yes, fifteen months ago. By now, he must be used to the Red Queen's quirky whims and impulsive voyages.

"I knew the kids were on board, of course," Scree began. "Your mother and the Pederson kids' mom had given them permission to sail with me that day. I was taking the *Caprice* up to Friday Harbor to meet with a marine architect. Your mother's having her stateroom renovated. The architect lives in Friday Harbor."

Venus said, "Why couldn't the architect just hop a floatplane down to Seattle? It only takes forty minutes."

Scree jerked his thumb northward, accurate as a compass needle. "All his equipment is up at Friday Harbor, some major software and a computer design system that he doesn't like to move. So your mother said to just take the boat up there." Scree swigged the rum and Coke. "Course, that never happened," he said regrettably. "We never made it out of the bay here. There was thick fog. Then the girl went over. . . ."

Venus said, "So you had left the marina in the fog. What time?"

"Early. About nine o'clock. My log has the exact time. The police have my log. Anyway, close to nine o'clock." Scree sipped more rum, sucked in some ice and rolled it over his tongue. "The kids were aft. I didn't actually see what happened."

It was still early, he recounted, and the thick morning fog had obscured the bay as the *Caprice* prepared to sail.

The yacht had just left its moorage, when a container ship appeared on radar. Scree steered to port to allow the larger ship a wider berth. Scree and his crew couldn't see the cargo ship except on radar, but they heard its horn, and then a tugboat accompanying the ship poked through the fog. Scree got on the radio, tuned into Channel 13, and heard the vessel transport operator make a Rule 10 announcement, made when conditions warrant special instructions. Scree asked the VTO about area traffic and then contacted the container ship to make passing arrangements. Because of the poor visibility, Scree chose to stay well clear of the larger vessel. Suspecting a long siege, he had ramped down the *Caprice*'s speed and idled a quarter of a mile offshore from the marina, the yacht's bow facing northwest, toward the mouth of the bay and the shipping lanes, now shrouded in the impenetrable fog.

Up in the wheelhouse, Scree had heard Pearl's screams vented through a raspy speaker system and had sent his engineer aft to investigate. After a few minutes, the screaming stopped and the engineer had returned, saying glibly, "The boys are making Pearl walk the plank."

Scree remembered that he had grinned and said, "Kids," and the engineer had grunted agreement. Scree had asked the engineer, "They wearing life vests?"

"Sure, they each have one on," the engineer told him.

Scree then turned on the radio to hear a weather update. The cloud cover was thicker than ever now—no heavenly bodies, no landmarks visible to the naked eye: "So I sipped coffee and sat back, waiting for the cargo vessel to negotiate the fog. A few minutes later, I ran my routine scan of security video cameras aboard the vessel.

"One of the cameras is in the rear main-deck salon. As I was scanning the video, I saw Henry Pederson step inside the salon. Then, a few seconds later, I heard Timmy's voice shouting for help. I yelled to Ziggy to go aft and check things out, but he'd already gone back. The girl's screams must have worried him. When he saw she'd gone overboard, he went into the water. But by then, it was too late to save Pearl."

Venus noticed tears welling in Scree's eyes. He blinked and they spilled onto his face. With the back of his hand, he wiped them away. "Sorry," he said softly. "She was a sweet little girl."

"Who's Ziggy?"

"Ziggy Nelson, my engineer. It was just the two of us crewing. As I said, Ziggy went aft, but it was too late. Pearl had gone under and Timmy had dived in after her and was still in the water. Ziggy dove in, but he didn't find her. Only thing he found was her life vest."

"So it was Ziggy Nelson who went aft the first time to check on the kids?"

"Uh-huh. And then he returned when Pearl's screams got louder and more hysterical."

"Where can I find Ziggy Nelson?"

Scree shrugged. "He stays with his wife on their boat over at Shilshole. The *Dirty Blonde* is the boat's name. He gave a statement to the cops. He's a good man, a good sailor. Ziggy tried his damndest to save her, but he couldn't dive deep enough fast enough. She sank fast." Scree rubbed his five o'clock shadow and seemed to focus inward, like he was deciding if he should say something more or clam up. Finally, he said, "If Tim had wanted her to drown, why did he dive in after her? To support a story about accidental drowning?"

"Henry told the cops that Tim dove in and held her head underwater."

Rupert shook his head. "I don't buy that. I don't think Ziggy does, either, but you'd have to ask him." He hesitated, then added, "Zig told me something truly weird."

"What was that?" she asked him gently, because he still seemed reticent.

"Zig said her life vest was cut off her. By something sharp. Both shoulders slit through, so it would easily slip off her."

"Any idea what cut it?"

Scree shook his head. "Naw. Zig told the cops, though." He put a hand on his stomach, as if it hurt.

Venus said, "You feeling all right?"

Scree winced. "Bit of a sour stomach. I'm okay."

Venus said, "Did you save the video of Henry?"

"Sure. In fact, I told the officer—what's his name? Rocco. I told Detective Rocco about seeing Henry inside the cabin just before I heard Timmy's shouting, and Rocco asked me for the tape. I gave it to him."

Why hadn't Rocco mentioned the videotape to her? And the life vest?

Scree's cell phone rang. "Sorry," he said, and stood up, still holding his stomach, still obviously feeling discomfort. He walked across the salon, maybe seeking privacy, and answered his phone. Whoever had called Scree was screaming so loud that Venus could hear it across the ballroom.

"For chrissake, Natalia, calm down," Scree shouted into the phone. "I'm coming right now. Just stay where you are and wait for me." Scree clicked off and turned to Venus. "Sorry, I have an emergency. Can we finish this later?"

"Anything I can do to help?"

Scree said, "Naw. A friend's in trouble. I can handle it. But I need to go help her. She's . . . she's sick." He seemed agitated.

Venus said, "How about you? Are you feeling okay?"

He said, "Sure. Just a little indigestion. Must've eaten something bad."

They left the *Caprice* together. In the marina parking lot, Scree slid behind the wheel of a battered blue 4×4. Venus watched him peal off onto the road.

Rupert didn't like her. Something about her smallness bothered him. He likes big women. Tall, rangy women, with something to latch onto. And too, she has those green eyes that bore into him like a couple of laser beams. Like she can see right through him. How much does she know? Maybe the boy had talked. That had been a bad mistake— Pearl letting Tim Diamond in on the secret. Tim should have drowned, instead of Pearl.

What was her name? Venus. He'd met her, seen her a few times aboard the *Caprice* during the big Hollywood bashes. He knows she's a federal undercover agent. Fish & Wildlife. The sons of bitches who board ships and search for wildlife contraband, tear your cargo to pieces, leave it for you to clean up. Rupert hadn't had firsthand experience with U.S. Fish & Wildlife, but he had friends whose vessels had been confiscated for smuggling wildlife contraband. He knew of a dude over at Lake Union Marina, ex–wildlife cop, who lived on a ninety-foot tug that had been confiscated in a wildlife contraband bust. His "reward" for catching the perps. Goddamn corrupted government agents. They probably steal the jewelry off corpses, too, like the Seattle fuzz.

Natalia had been incoherent on the phone. Whatever the hell had gone wrong, she needs Rupert there fast. But 15th Avenue West is socked in with rush-hour traffic and Rupert is stuck in the long, snaking line of vehicles heading north toward the Ballard Bridge. He has little patience for traffic jams. He shoots into reverse, backs up five inches, jerks the wheel of his 4×4 as far as he can to the left, backs up again a few more inches, repeating the process until he can pull out of the line of idling engines, then force his way into the oncoming traffic lane, drive twenty cars forward, and cut back into the line. Several drivers curse him, but Rupert could give a hot damn. Once off the Ballard Bridge, traffic eases up. He zigzags through Old Ballard's narrow cobblestone streets, avoiding Market Street traffic. When he finally reaches Shilshole Marina, he sees the *Dirty Blonde* moored in her slip.

Natalia, Ziggy's wife, stands at the bow, watching Rupert hurry down the dock. From inside the boat come cries of lamentation, loud sobs interspersed with Russian epithets. Lina. The cousin from Saint Petersburg. Wailing like a caterwaul. Lina, the large lady. Rupert's kind of gal. Natalia waves frantically now, and Rupert hurries faster along the dock. A man steps out of a Chris-Craft moored in the slip next to the *Dirty Blonde*. He says something in Russian to Natalia and she calls back to him in Russian. He stands on the Chris-Craft's deck and listens to the wailing pouring forth from the *Dirty Blonde*'s cabin.

"Tell her to shut the fuck up," Rupert says to Natalia as he boards.

Natalia says, "I tried. She's hysterical."

"Where's Ziggy?"

Natalia goes down below in front of Rupert. "He didn't come back. He hasn't called me, anyway. I've had the cell phone on all the time. He hasn't tried to call. I don't know where he is, but he might be in bad trouble."

Lina's in the forward portside berth. Rupert goes in and shouts, "Shut the fuck up, will you? You'll have the whole world on our ass."

Lina rolls over, a whale on bedsheets. She stops wailing, but she continues to sob quietly. Over and over, she says, "The liddle boy."

"Where is he?"

Lina points to the V berth. Rupert slides open the door

to the V berth, looks in. The boy's body lays across the bed. He's about twelve years old, maybe as old as fourteen, but no older. He's naked. His face is blue, swollen. He has welt marks across his torso and legs. His right hand has been severed and is missing. He's dead.

Natalia comes up behind Rupert. "It was an accident," she says.

"Like hell." Rupert turns away from the boy's body.

"What shall we do with him?" says Natalia.

"Where the hell is Ziggy?"

"I told you: I don't know." Natalia lights a cigarette, inhales. A deep phlegmy cough rises in her throat. She says, "We have to get rid of him."

"How did it happen?"

Natalia shakes her head. "Lina wasn't here. She went shopping. When I got here, I found him. Then Lina came in right after me, just before I called you. I don't know how he got here or where he came from or who he is. I don't know nothing. Just that he's in there and I want him the hell off my boat."

Rupert cocks his head toward the berth where Lina lays prone and heaving sobs. "Why's she so goddamn hysterical?"

Natalia rolls her eyes. "She cries about everything. It's how she is." Natalia shouts something in Russian that only makes Lina wail louder.

They wait until sundown. Wait until the sun has set behind the Olympics and complete darkness cloaks the Sound. Then Rupert unties the *Dirty Blonde* from the dock and they motor out into the Sound and enter the shipping lanes, Rupert watching out for cargo vessels. Once in a shipping lane, he idles down and turns the wheel over to Natalia. He goes aft, to the V berth, and wraps the boy's body in black trash bags and knots a rope around the bags, to which he attaches a small anchor. He drags the package up onto the deck, lays it in the stern. He returns to the wheel and steers the boat toward the middle shipping lane, then he returns aft and with Natalia's help, slowly slips the anchor and its attached package over the stern's port side. With a soft splash, it breaks the water's surface and then sinks swiftly.

Rupert looks at Natalia. Through the darkness, he can see the whites of her eyes. They glint. Rupert says, "Don't you ever involve me in this shit again."

CHAPTER SIX

The news media swarmed outside Bella Diamond's estate, and the Pederson property next door, their satellite-equipped vans clogging Magnolia Boulevard. The gated entrances to the two estates stood side by side, an ancient cedar tree regally dividing them. Nils Pederson routinely kept security guards at his gates, and now, Venus noticed that the Red Queen had hired her own uniformed guards to fend off the Fourth Estate and looky-loos. Several satellite vans had telescoped their light poles above the walls that surrounded the Diamond property on three sides, spotlights aimed into the garden, poised to flick on at nightfall in case something dramatic occurred. Maybe the boy killer would attempt an escape under cover of night. Might be a Pulitzer in here somewhere.

Venus drove up to the gates. The news reporters mobbed the Audi. A perky blond woman shoved her face in the open driver's window, her nose nearly touching Venus's face. "My name's Kimberly Forget," she said. "For-zhay. It's French. I'm a junior investigative reporter for KIRO, the CBS affiliate. Can I talk to you?"

Venus said, "Not here. Not now," and started to raise the window.

Kimberly Forget shoved her business card at Venus. "Call me anytime, day or night," she said. "I might be able to help you."

"That's what they all say." The window rolled up, buffing out the media noise. Venus looked at her Swatch. Six-thirty. At this time of year, total darkness wouldn't fall until 10:00 P.M. The mob rocked the Audi. She gunned the engine and they fell back like dominoes. She heard Kimberly Forget's voice shout, "Remember For-zhay. KIRO television."

Bella's gates were locked, and on the other side stood two security guards who didn't know Venus from Eve. She called the house on her cell phone. The Red Queen's personal assistant, Stephen, answered. "Oh, it's you," Stephen said coolly. "You needn't have come. I thought you were on vaca—"

"Buzz me through, Stephen."

Silence.

"Stephen, I said, 'Buzz me through.'"

"Your mother does not wish to see anyone."

"Open this gate now, Steve-o, or I'll raise so much hell out here that Mother will be mortified."

After another brief pause, the gate opened soundlessly. The guards jumped back. She drove through, reporters swarming, but they knew enough to stop at the property line, and the security guards had drawn their Glocks. She pulled into a vacant space on the circular drive, parking between the Red Queen's Jaguar and a little cherry red Jetta.

As she strolled up the long path between manicured lawns and topiary bushes to the front door of her mother's home, Venus's childhood home, she was suddenly aware of a lovely buzz, a feeling that all was well in the world, and this startled her, because she knew it wasn't true. And then she realized that the Coral Reef's medication had finally kicked in big time. She let herself into the family home, using the key she'd had since childhood. Why in all these years hadn't the security-conscious Stephen changed the locks? She made a mental note to broach the subject with the Red Queen.

At the end of a long corridor, Stephen stood sentry near the door to Bella's private suite. "Your mother does not wish to see you," he said acerbically in his usual clipped authoritarian tone of voice. Stephen was thirty-three, in great physical condition, a deliberate fussbudget, and he could be a sanctimonious royal pain when he wanted to be, which, in Venus's case, was all the time.

"Just me, or anyone?"

Stephen's eyes flickered. He was thinking it over. His folded arms pressed against his muscle-man T-shirt. Venus noticed how tan Stephen's arms were compared to his pale face. He was a golfer. On the course, he always wore a cap that had been soaked in ice water. He was that kind of guy. Cautious, walking a paranoiac ledge.

"Anyone."

"Come on, Steve-o, I'm her daughter, remember?"

"I have asked you at least a dozen times to stop addressing me by that hackneyed pseudo nickname." He dug his heels into the lush carpet.

"All right then . . . Stephen. Please stand aside. I need to speak with the Red Queen."

He didn't budge, only said, "How dare you refer to your mother with such a disparaging label?"

"Hey, she played the role. And the title fits her better than her real name. Now get the hell out of my way."

Stephen bristled. His neck flushed crimson. He said smugly, "I have my orders." Stephen relished wielding power over Bella Diamond's affairs, especially over her family's access to her. He had that inheritance-hungry aura. The Red Queen was far from croaking, the picture of youthful fifties, a thoroughly healthy specimen. But life's a crapshoot, and Stephen had his luck invested in the long haul. The Red Queen adored him, and he was here to stay.

Venus said, "You should visit Turbo Tan. That way, your face and arms would match."

"I shall not dignify that with a response."

"Come on, stand aside."

"I told you: I have my orders. This is your mother's house. If you do not care to honor your mother's wishes, then please leave this house at once."

"You're getting a tad uppity, aren't you?"

"You heard me." He wasn't budging. "Under no circumstances are you to knock on this door or in any other manner attempt to disturb your mother."

"You can't stand here all night."

Stephen didn't reply. Instead, he shifted his gaze over Venus's left shoulder, focusing down the hall. Venus turned around. A bulldog in a security guard's uniform approached. Stephen said, "Perfect timing, Sid." Sid the bulldog and Stephen exchanged places. Stephen jerked his head at Venus. "This is the daughter I warned you about. Under no circumstances is she permitted to disturb Ms. Diamond." Sid checked her out and curled his lip at something he found unpleasant.

Venus followed Stephen into the long hall. When they had reached the foyer, she said, "Whose Jetta is that parked outside? The red car."

Stephen said curtly, "More than likely, it is the vehicle of the child psychologist sent by the police. She is interviewing Timothy."

"What about a lawyer? Shouldn't an attorney be present when Timmy is being interviewed by the police?"

"I am sure that isn't necessary. Dr. Lane is what is known as an advocate. Her sole purpose in interviewing Timmy is to help him cope with the trauma. And I really think you should just stay out of this altogether. You are nothing but a troublemaker." Stephen turned on his heel. She watched his back as he strode toward the kitchen.

She found Bart in the living room, drinking wine and staring out the big picture windows as if the solution lay somewhere in that beautiful night vista. Bart was a dreamer, a totally right-brained artistic genius, and now it seemed that he had retreated into his fantasy world to escape the dreadful reality. They talked for a while; then Venus went to her room, a quiet sunporch on the villa's lower level. It had been her bedroom years earlier, when this house had overflowed with the activities of five spoiled brats and two love-struck adults who sometimes behaved like parents, but not often. The good old days. What had been good about them? What? Laughter. Playfulness. Her father. He had been the best part of her childhood. After he died, the house had seemed to lose its soul, had, for Venus anyway, become a less friendly place, a place she did not enjoy visiting. Suddenly, she wanted to be back at the Coral Reef, in its gently authoritarian clutches, a ward of the feds, where, for the first time since childhood, she had felt coddled and secure.

Venus rummaged through her carry-on bag, fished out the digital camera and a small book. As she headed back along the hall toward Timmy's bedroom, she saw the backside of a woman who had stepped out of his room and was walking toward the stairs leading up to the house's main floor. The woman carried a large briefcase by its handle and had a handbag tucked under her arm. She walked swiftly, efficiently, as if she had a destination in mind.

Venus ducked her head into Timmy's room and said, "Hey, sport."

The boy flicked a limp hand at his stepsister. His normally café au lait complexion had sallowed. Stress, and lack of sunshine. She couldn't see his eyes, only veils of coal black lashes. But she knew he'd seen her enter his bedroom, because the corner of his mouth jerked sideways, dimpling his cheek, a dark, sardonic expression lately conferred on all of his visitors. He was allowed to keep the door ajar but was not permitted to leave his room without the express permission of his stepmother. He scooted over on the bed, making room for Venus.

Timmy was twelve, give or take a year—no one knew his exact age—and Venus had hit thirtysomething. They had been step-siblings for five years, ever since the Red Queen had adopted the Asian orphan with a mysterious past.

"How's Mother?" Timmy scratched his ear.

Venus said, "Still confined. Stephen delivers meals, but she hasn't touched food for three days."

"Maybe she's on a diet," Timmy offered hopefully.

"She's in shock. She's never had to deal with a murder. That is, with one of her kids being charged with murder."

The boy said hotly, "You don't believe me."

Venus reached over and stroked his arm. He pulled away.

"Hey, Timmy, I'm in your corner."

"Take your hand off me."

She did. Timmy said, "You can't be in my corner unless you believe me."

Venus sighed. He was right. Virtually no one believed his story of how Pearl had drowned. It was too fantastic, too sci-fi. Even Venus had nagging doubts. Now she chose her words carefully. "It's not so much the monster jellyfish part, Timmy. It's the fact that prior to this incident, you had made something of a name for yourself as a weaver of tall tales."

"You're calling me a liar."

Venus stretched her neck. "I wouldn't put it that harshly. 'Chronic fabulist' works for me."

"Same thing." Timmy folded his small arms over his tiny chest. Across the room, his Famous Astronauts wall clock made tiny clicking sounds, marking time. Six-fifty-five P.M. June something. What? He didn't know and he didn't care enough to inquire.

Venus noticed that on his wrist he wore the matching astronaut watch she had given him last Christmas. He had told her then that it was his favorite gift.

Venus said, "I understand a psychologist just came to visit you."

Timmy laughed sharply. "Dr. Lane. Yeah, she just left. She's a cop and a manipulative bitch."

"What did you tell her?"

"Same damn thing I've told everyone else. She wrote it all down; then she called me a liar, and then she left. She's got monkey breath and no ass."

Venus said, "Detective Rocco said the prosecuting attorney's office has decided to raise your bail amount."

The boy laughed harshly. "So now I'm a flight risk."

"Apparently, pressure was applied to the prosecutor."

"Yeah, and we know who applied it."

"Mr. Pederson wields a lot of power. Anyway, that's not what I wanted to talk about."

She handed him the digital camera. He accepted it reluctantly, his limp hand indicating disinterest. As he studied the images from Hawaii, Venus noticed his eyes flicker. She had succeeded in diverting his thoughts from his dilemma.

He said, "This is a manta ray, right?"

"I was that close." She recounted the struggle, how she had killed the manta ray before it'd had a chance to kill her. At first, Timmy seemed interested, even slightly proud of her, his eyes glinting at her vivid description of the underwater encounter, but that light quickly faded from his expression.

"I doubt they'll ever find Pearl's body," he said glumly. "Anyway, jellyfish don't leave fingerprints, and I doubt they'd find DNA. So why didn't Mother tell me about the bail being raised? Why did she have to send you in her place? I've been in here for two solid days now, and Mother hasn't come downstairs to see me yet."

Venus ruffled the boy's silky hair. "Mother didn't send me. I came home on my own, as soon as Bart called me with the news. I spoke to Detective Rocco a little while ago and he told me about the bail being raised. And Mother loves you, Timmy. Remember that. She's just a bit off her feed over this. Give her some more time."

"Hell, she's had plenty of time. I want a divorce from this whole stupid family. You know what? I used to think that Henry and Pearl had the world's worst family. They hate their parents and their parents hate them. But now I think my family's even worse than the Pedersons. Just because Mother's a famous actress and rich as hell, you all think you're better and smarter than everyone else. Well, you're not. I'm ashamed to be part of this family."

He was livid, his face red, his small fists clenched tight. Venus said, "You're wrong there, Timmy. We're human, like everyone else. A little loopier and a lot more privileged than most, but I didn't choose my genetic makeup or my ancestors, just as you didn't ask for yours. Anyway, you're one of us now."

"Huh!" Timmy shrugged as if he were shedding something, maybe his adopted family.

He stood up and paced the room like a caged beast. Venus watched him pace, first across to the Famous Astronaut clock, then to the windows, then over to the French doors that opened onto a wide flower-festooned terrace, then to the bed where Venus sat, but not too near, then retracing his steps. While he paced, he fidgeted, alternately rubbing his chin and scratching his chest. Maybe signs of puberty. He didn't look old enough for puberty. But then sometimes he resembled an ancient vizier in a child's body. His teachers worried over Timmy's small stature and over his amazing intelligence. He was an anxious, impatient, argumentative student, prone to correcting teachers, inclined to what they termed "inappropriate behavior." By this, the teachers meant that Timmy frequently challenged their pedagogical techniques. It's not easy being a child with an adult's brain but not the maturity, an orphan with an unknown past, a kid with only the dimmest memories of his real mother, no memory at all of his father, and a native culture that eluded his soul. Five years ago, Venus had rescued Timmy from a terrible fate, and since then they had been thicker than blood.

"Listen," she said. "I've got some official time off. I'm going to help you get through this thing."

"'Thing,'" Timmy said, and scoffed. "That's a funny word for being framed. I am being framed, you know. I did not push her. And I stick to my story." Timmy glanced up at her and added, "Anyway, I know you were in the loony bin. And that you escaped."

Panic surged through her. She said, "I didn't escape. I checked myself out."

"Sure. And when they catch up with you, your ass is grass."

"Who else knows?"

"Nobody. I've kept it quiet."

"How did you find out?"

"About the Coral Reef?" He smiled cunningly. "I have my sources."

"Do you know why I was sent there?"

He shrugged. "Maybe. Maybe not."

So he probably didn't know the exact nature of the incident.

She said, "Can we perhaps keep the Coral Reef as our little secret?"

Tim cocked his head, thinking this over. Maybe a little leverage would come in handy.

"Come on, Timmy. My future's on the line here. Promise me you won't tell anyone."

Tim considered his options. On the one hand, what he knew about her might serve as good bribery material. And yet, she was his favorite living person, the only real ally he'd ever had. He cocked his smart-ass head and said, "I'll think it over. Meanwhile, I won't tell anyone."

She couldn't let it go. "So how did you find out about the Coral Reef?"

"I told you: I have my sources. Now, if you get me out of this mess, maybe I'll share them with you."

"Then be straight with me. Did Pearl fall overboard, or . . ."

"I've already told everyone," he said through clenched teeth. "She was on her hands and knees. Either she lost her balance or something pulled her overboard. I didn't actually see her go overboard, just heard the splash. Then the jellyfish dragged her under."

"How could a jellyfish be so strong?"

He turned his back to her. "Get out," he said.

She persisted. "Just tell me one thing. Why didn't Henry see this jellyfish, or whatever it was?"

Tim was harboring his rage, doing his best not to explode at the only adult he might be able to trust. After awhile, he turned around to face her. He looked straight into her eyes and spoke in a deliberate clipped manner. "Henry is lying."

Venus winced. The boy's story would never convince a jury. He certainly hadn't convinced the prosecutor. The fact that the prosecutor was considering charging Timmy as an adult meant that he was convinced Timmy had drowned Pearl. The fact that, even if Pearl's body was never recovered, Henry Pederson would be the star witness meant that the prosecutor believed Henry's version of events. After all, Henry Pederson had a reputation as an honest boy, the sort of boy who never told a lie.

Timmy said, "You still don't believe me."

Venus reached out, placed an arm around him, and drew him close. He didn't resist. "Timmy, I'm in your corner. Believe me when I say that I will defend you to the end. Mother's attorneys are the best—"

"They don't believe me, either."

"Listen to me. We'll find a way out of this, I promise."

He turned his back again. He said, "The only reason they're doing this to me is because her dad's so powerful. If her dad had been a homeless person or a cokehead or something, they'd just drop the whole thing."

"We need to focus on what's happening, not what might have happened under different circumstances."

"Damn Mr. Pederson. Damn Henry. Now I really do feel like murdering somebody."

Venus grabbed his chin and made him look her in the eyes. "Listen here, young man. You can say that to me, but to no one else. I know it's just a figure of speech. I know you don't mean it, but other people might take you seriously."

"I am serious."

"Do you understand me?"

Timmy nodded.

"And curb the profanity. It's a sign of weakness, and it

won't help your case." She sighed. "Anyway, the police have a video from the *Caprice*'s security camera. I haven't seen it yet, but apparently it supports your contention that Henry went inside the cabin and so couldn't have seen anything."

" 'Contention.' " He stared blankly at the wall.

She said, "What do you think about Detective Rocco?"

He said, "He's a cop. That says it all."

Venus fished a book out of her pocket, then handed it to him. "Read this book, and when I come back this evening, I'm quizzing you on it."

Timmy glanced at the title. "*Pacific Coast Pelagic Invertebrates: A Guide to the Common Gelatinous Animals.*"

He said, "Where'd you find this?"

"Airport bookstore. Sea-Tac."

He said, "Did you know, by the way, that jellyfish are particularly strong indicators of the ocean's health? When jellyfish blooms proliferate, as they have in recent years, this is an indication that ocean waters are growing warmer, thus killing off certain species that under normal conditions would feed on algae blooms. Jellyfish thus have more food and so their numbers increase. They are indicators. Jellyfish are the pigeon of the sea."

She said, "Okay, wise guy, thanks for the education. Still, I want you to read this book. I'm telling you, when I come back later this evening, I'm going to ask you some important questions."

He started to say something, hesitated, then said, "Do you know anyone who owns a tugboat called the *Earline*?"

She thought it over. "No," she said. "Why?"

He shrugged. "I'm thinking . . . in my head . . . that a tugboat named the *Earline* might have something to do with why Henry's lying through his teeth."

"You're not making a lot of sense. I think you're hiding something. What are you hiding?"

Tim shook his head but didn't reply.

Venus tried one last time. "Give me more to go on," she said. "You can trust me. I can't help you unless you're completely candid with me. I need to know everything you know."

"Go away," he said with a weary sigh. "I've already told you too much."

She slipped out of the room, leaving the door open a crack. Through the crack came Timmy's small, angry voice.

"She wasn't a nice girl."

CHAPTER SEVEN

Venus stepped onto the kitchen's broad outdoor dining terrace. The second-story terrace overlooked the Pedersons' elaborate gardens next door. A simple wrought-iron fence divided old money from nouveau riche, Bella Diamond's inherited fortune from Nils Pederson's more recently acquired business fortune. Investments. Apparently, he'd ridden the crest of the dot-com debacle, cashing in at its peak, just before the crash, his opulent property and ostentatious mansion bearing a day trader's soul.

Both properties had sloping Hollywood lawns that rolled gently to a steep bluff shored up by the root systems of ancient madronas, delicate bark peeling from their thick red trunks exposing fresh green bone beneath. So far, no reporters or looky-loos had scaled the bluff, where a sheer two-hundred-foot cliff rose from a narrow beach strewn with barnacle-infested boulders. Both estates' gardens were meticulously maintained by Japanese gardeners, the privet shrubs, camellias, Japanese maples, and Fuji cherry trees all expertly sculpted, the lush flower beds heady with proliferating hot-pink and yellow rhododendron bushes. Wisteria wove along a portion of the wrought-iron fence separating the two gardens. On the northwest corner of the Pedersons' property, past a lackluster city-built cyclone fence, was a small wooded public park full of old madronas and cedars, which the city had wisely chosen to preserve. Venus had played in that park as a youngster, had always felt that a strangely sinister atmosphere clung to its trees and grass, as if it hid some dark evil, or some frightening secret, in its cool shadows.

Southeast of the park, where the Pederson property began, the Pedersons had constructed a swimming pool. The pool's surface now reflected whimsical clouds forming in the deepening twilight. Venus remembered that Ingrid Pederson, Nils's wife, enjoyed nocturnal bathing, and for this purpose they had installed the pool, twice the size of the Red Queen's indoor lap pool, placing it outdoors because Ingrid liked it cold. Closer to where Venus stood on the upper terrace was a small cedar grove that marked the upper edge of the property line, providing a natural screen between the two houses. Here in the cedar grove, the wrought-iron fence curved and meandered to accommodate the tree trunks. The iron fence, a monument to neighborliness and the need to mark territory, however inaccurately, reached as high as the lowest cedar branches, ten feet from the ground, delineating two incompatible architectural styles: the Pedersons' showy, overwrought contemporary Swiss chalet with its telltale naïve touches and the Red Queen's classical Italianate villa and gardens.

Even the grove had changed. Since the Pedersons had acquired the next-door property, the fecund ground beneath the cedars in this dividing grove had been superficially sown with fine gravel, which was periodically raked and cleared of the occasional stray slug. Until a few days ago, this graveled cedar grove had marked the world's friendliest border. Now a child's death divided the victim's family from the disgraced family of the accused. Her family.

Venus recalled her life here as a child, when another house had stood on the Pederson property, when there was no iron fence between the properties, when the Pederson property was owned by the Schwartzes, who had lived on that land in an elegant English Tudor. Venus and her siblings had played with the Schwartz children, and they'd made constant trips through this grove, which back then was carpeted in fertile black soil that harbored giant ferns, mushrooms, lady slippers, and wild poppies. Back then, the children had named this grove "The Land of Thrush." Here in Thrush, all children were free to do as they pleased and no child would ever harm another; in fact, no harm would come to a child at all. Here in Thrush, only good magic occurred, like the fairies that came out from beneath the mushroom, seeking magnolia petals filled with morning dew, their favorite beverage. At night, the fairies held grand balls as the children watched from their bedroom windows. But when the Pedersons bought the land in the booming nineties, they had razed the old Tudor house and constructed their statement home, and then they had graveled over Thrush and installed the meandering iron fence.

To be fair, installing the wrought-iron fence had been the joint decision of her mother and the Pedersons. Theirs had always been a friendly, neighborly relationship. The actress frequently included the Pedersons on her invitation lists. Nils and his pretty wife would make cameo appearances at Bella's star-studded affairs, Nils basking in the afterglow of Russell Crowe and Whoopi Goldberg, Ingrid coolly batting her eyes at Anthony Hopkins. Nothing is quainter in the eyes of a movie star than the local yokels showing up to ogle the stars. And the Pedersons were always anxious to show off their most famous neighbor to their friends. The actress had been presented at numerous charity functions hosted so capably by Ingrid in their garish home. Ingrid, the social gadfly, creeping her way upward. Truly, Bella Diamond and the Pedersons had become fast friends, the best of neighbors. The Pederson children, Henry and Pearl, had played with the actress's stepson, Timmy. Henry and Timmy had been especially close, Pearl their common enemy. Henry had frequently spent the night at Timmy's, and although the fastidious, finicky Timmy had declined reciprocal invitations, the boys had always been solid.

On the second story of the Pederson home, a broad artificial-wood deck was now deserted except for a single security guard who lounged in a patio chair, gaping at the sun setting behind the Olympics. In the evening dusk, Venus saw a light snap on inside the Pederson house, in a room with towering windows and sliding glass doors leading onto the terrace. Maybe the living room. Venus had never been inside the Pedersons' home, but she had climbed the meandering fence once before, last summer, when Pansy, her mother's shar-pei, had tunneled under the iron rails and terrorized the Pedersons' toy poodles. Venus had taken the shortest route to fetching Bella's dog. Now she climbed the fence again and had reached the crest, when the security guard on the Pederson's terrace yelled, "Hey!"

"It's okay. I'm the neighbor." She came over the Pederson side of the fence and held her hands up. "I'm harmless. Are the Pedersons home?"

"Who the hell do you think you are?" the guard complained. "None of your effing business if they're home or not. Now, go back where you came from or I'll personally take you there."

Venus made a praying gesture. "Please just call indoors and ask if one of the Pedersons will see Venus Diamond, Timmy' stepsister."

The guard grumbled but made the call. After a short standoff, Henry Pederson slid open the glass door and came across the deck. He was tall for a twelve-year-old, Swedish as a lingonberry pancake. His yellow hair hung in bangs trimmed just above his glacier blue eyes. His skin had the pallor of a polar bear and he had those thick pale lips that drive women to shoot collagen. He wore a blue cotton-knit shirt, white shorts, and Nikes without socks. Venus walked up a flight of stairs to the deck, where Henry and the guard stood watching her warily.

"What do you want?" Spoken as if she were a total stranger, not the cool big sister of his best friend, who had taken Henry and Timmy to numerous Mariners games and bought them all the junk food and souvenirs they craved.

"How are you holding up, Henry?"

Henry came forward and looked her directly in the eye. She noticed for the first time that Henry Pederson was now taller than she by several inches.

"I said, 'What do you want?'"

"Are your parents home?"

"They are not." Crisply enunciated.

"When they come home, would you tell them that I'd like to speak with them?"

"About?"

"Pearl," she said. "I'm sorry about your sister."

Henry chewed his lower lip.

"I'm sure you miss her."

Henry sighed. "You'll have to make an appointment, like everyone else. You can call my dad's office and give your name."

He then turned to go.

Venus said, "Just one thing, Henry."

Henry turned halfway around. Venus stepped forward. The guard moved in to defend the boy. She sidestepped him and caught Henry's gaze in hers.

"Timmy says you're lying. If you are lying, you'll be doing everyone a big favor by admitting it. Timmy's going to prison, Henry, unless you tell the truth."

Henry stared at her for a few seconds, then said in a controlled voice, "You are mentally deranged." Then he turned and walked slowly across the deck and through the sliding glass door. She heard the door slide shut and a lock snap into place.

Rupert Scree wasn't answering his phone. She left another message, her third since their afternoon meeting. She wanted to ask him again about the life vest, to clarify exactly how it had been cut off Pearl's body. Rocco's service answered his office phone. She left a message that he could phone anytime, day or night, saying she wanted some answers and she wanted them now. She went down to the villa's lap pool, swam, thrashing the water until her mind separated from her body, until the fuzzy alcohol and meds combo surrendered to sheer caloric burn, until her mind could work on its own without distraction. Half an hour later, she stepped out of the pool and went into the shower. When she came out of the shower, a towel wrapped around her, she saw Bart in the pool.

"Stephen still won't let me visit the Red Queen," she said to Bart.

Bart kept swimming and said, "Her orders."

"Everyone, or just me?"

"Everyone." He sped up, and she left him midlap.

She dressed, then went to Timmy's door and knocked. No answer. She opened the door slightly and peered inside. The room was dark, but a thin ray of late-evening light shone through the blinds. She could see that Timmy had fallen asleep, the jellyfish book splayed across his chest, the electronic anklet marking his shame. She shut the door silently. She was headed for the kitchen when her cell phone rang. It was Olson, her boss, calling from a tavern in Ballard. The chief had recently acquired a lady friend, a "Swedish gal," he liked to say, and she owned this small pub, where Olson now spent most of his off-duty hours.

"I'm just betting you're in Seattle and not Honolulu," he said.

"You bet right."

"Welcome back," said Olson, sardonically. "Sorry about the rotten news."

She thanked him.

"So I guess this means you are AWOL from the Coral Reef. That your rehab plan has gone to hell."

"Apparently."

"I guess you know that Song has asked for time off."

She didn't know. She hadn't spoken with Louie Song since the incident. They were involved, whatever that meant. The incident had occurred the day she was released from the hospital after the jawline reconstruction. Louie had been the recipient of her wrath, the wrath she should have visited upon the poacher who had shot her. Afterward, Louie had stopped speaking to her, understandably. Then one day, he'd called her at the Coral Reef. He had wanted to visit her. Except Song had no idea that she was checked into a loony bin. He thought the Coral Reef was a resort. She had demurred, explaining that she preferred to take her world tour solo. She traveled best solo. Song had been royally ticked. She hadn't spoken to him since then.

Olson said, "He's requested the leave so that he can be with you right now."

"Did you grant it?"

"Negative. We have the Tran trial on the calendar. Since you and Song broke the poacher ring, and since you are on"—he cleared his throat—"medical leave, Song needs to sit in every day of the trial. At least until you come back. It promises to go six weeks or more. Presumably, your makeup time at the Coral Reef will be completed before then."

She felt relieved. She didn't need complications. "Okay," she said. "Tell Louie I'll ring him up soon."

"Tell him yourself. I'm your boss, not your social secretary."

"How's Helen?"

Helen was the taverness.

"Sweet as ever. I'm thinking of popping the question."

"Oh God, no."

"What's wrong with my remarrying?"

"It's the unknown element, Chief. Will you turn all mushy and soft, or will you turn into a gruffer version of yourself? It's the unknown that scares me."

"Go to hell," he said, and hung up.

Stephen wasn't anywhere in sight. Probably in his room hooked up to the computer. He was a regular on several golf chat lines. Venus went into the dining room and sat on a window bench, where she watched the sun melt into the horizon behind hordes of reporters outside the gates. How convenient for them that the victim's house stood next door to the house of the accused. Any minute now, they'd switch on those spots, bathe the two estates in hot lights, see what they could see. When they did, she saw the KIRO reporter, Kimberly Forget, her pale face and blond hair bathed in the spotlights. She was watching both homes, scanning them slowly, as if drinking in all their opulence, expecting that any minute something really newsworthy would happen.

Venus went back into the kitchen. It was still deserted. She remembered the woman Rupert Scree had said was the Diamond family's new chef. She wondered what had happened to Jurgens, the chef who'd been around for years. The woman must be a new employee on the staff. Like Scree had said, the new chef. Venus hadn't met her yet. The door to the live-in staff's quarters was shut. Stephen had never occupied these quarters, preferring to take over a guest suite adjacent to the lap pool. The guest suite Stephen had chosen offered a panoramic view of the Sound and the Olympic Mountains. He'd charmed his boss into this arrangement. Venus imagined that if Stephen wanted to sleep in the Red Queen's own bed, he could probably charm her into that arrangment, too. Nothing untoward— good heavens, no. The R.Q. wasn't lusting after Stephen, nor he after her. At least, Venus didn't think so.

Out of curiosity, Venus knocked on the door to the staff quarters. Jurgens had made his home there. But if Jurgens had left, replaced by the new chef, was anybody occupying these quarters now? No response. Venus tried the knob, but the door was locked.

From a bowl on the counter, she plucked a ripe Bosc pear. She was headed for bed, when she remembered something. She went into the dining room and peered through the window. The news media's spotlights still washed over the front garden. The Jaguar was parked in the circular drive, in its usual spot. The red Jetta was gone.

She ate the pear, fixed herself a wee Dalwhinnie, and climbed into the same bed she had occupied as a child. She lay on her side, the healing jaw facing up. Just before she fell off to sleep, she wondered what the Coral Reef had served for the evening's snack. Tonight was luau night.

The next morning, she went down to Timmy's room. He was seated at his desk, the jellyfish book open. The space where his computer should have been seemed ominously empty. He'd been waiting for her.

"Here it is," he said, pointing to a color photograph in the book. "Scyphomedusa. Family Cyaneide. Common name, 'lion's mane.' I'm sure this is it."

He handed the book to Venus. She read the description. " 'A swimming medusa. Looks like an eight-pointed star at the end of its power stroke. Bell two meters. Eight thick lobes on margins. Eight clusters of up to 150 tentacles arranged in several rows, arising from horseshoe-shaped regions between the lobes. Eight rhopalia. Oral arms short and highly folded, forming a blocky mass. Life span, up to one year. Animals larger farther north. Unpleasant sting. Common to waters of the Pacific Northwest.' "

Venus tucked the book under her arm. She said, "I want you to draw me a picture of what you saw—from memory. Everything you can remember. Make it in color."

Timmy said, "I can do that."

"Do it now. I'll see you in half an hour. I'll be in the pool if you need me."

She swam ten laps, then showered, dressed, and returned to Timmy's room.

"This is what it looked like," he said, "from the angle that I saw it. I saw the top of the dome and I saw some of the tentacles and oral arms."

"Show me the oral arms." Venus peered over Timmy's shoulder. He was sitting at the desk, his sketch pad with the jellyfish drawing lying on the desktop. He pointed at the tangled mass, out of which came the tentacles, the mass every bit like a lion's mane.

"These squiggly protuberances—they're the oral arms," he said.

"Give me a general idea of its size."

Tim stood up and paced the length of his bed. "About this long," he said. "Not counting the tentacles' reach. With the tentacles' reach, I'd say about half the size of this room. It was a big sucker. She might have been stung to death, instead of drowned."

Venus estimated the size of Timmy's room at twelve by fourteen feet. She said, "Are you sure about the size?"

"Positive. Also," he said, sitting back down, "I could see its stomach through the dome." He pointed to the dome in the sketch. "See that space in there? That's the stomach. It takes food in with the oral arms, the stuff that looks like a lion's mane. Its mouth is on the bottom. It stuffs food up there into the stomach, which is almost transparent, and it digests the food. It spits out whatever it doesn't like." Timmy turned around and looked and her, then said frankly, "I doubt that it would like the taste of Pearl."

"You only saw one of these things, right?"

"One was enough."

"So, it wasn't a group of these lion's mane jellyfish . . ."

"Aggregation," he stated, correcting her unfinished question. "More precisely, an aggregation of prototypical medusae and a smack of jellyfish. By the way, I would prefer that from now on, you address me as Tim. Timmy is a boy's name. I am no longer a boy."

"What are you?"

"A young man."

"Okay, Tim." She paused a beat, then said, "Do you think Pearl drowned, or do you really think she might have died from a jellyfish sting?"

"Why do you ask?"

"The book says a lion's mane's sting is uncomfortable, but not deadly."

Tim stood and went over to a bookcase. He searched until he found the book he wanted, then pulled it out of the shelf, opened it, and said, "Have you ever heard of the Indo-Pacific box jellies?"

"Er . . ."

"For example, the Australian box jellyfish has a deadly sting. It can kill."

"We don't have Australian box jellies in this part of the world."

Tim closed the book and said, "So they say."

Dr. Lane, the child psychologist, sat primly on the couch in the Pederson home, her knees pressed together, her summer linen skirt tucked around them, concealing any hint of thigh flesh. Her skirt ended halfway down her slender, pale calves and she wore nylon stockings and sensible shoes. Her black hair was caught back in a headband and her face free of makeup except for a swath of red lipstick neatly drawn across her Cupid's bow mouth. She had remarkable black eyebrows and skin the shade of fresh cream, with little rosy blushes across the cheeks. Her eyes glittered like finely cut aquamarines, and now they observed Henry Pederson as he wrung his young hands together and wept crocodile tears.

"It's okay, Henry," she said softly. "It's all right to cry."

Henry glanced up at the woman, grateful and entreat-

ing. "Why do they question my story?" he complained
plaintively. "I . . . I-I'm telling the truth."

"Of course you are telling the truth, Henry. And we all
believe you."

"The police don't. The police don't believe me!"

"Calm down, dear. The police are just doing their job.
They have to be certain that every detail fits together. They
are just doing what they are trained to do. Now, tell me one
more time about the rope, about what you saw Tim do with
the rope."

Henry pressed his wrists together. "He made Pearl put
both her hands like this and then he tied rope around her
wrists really tight."

"What kind of rope?"

"I already told you. Nylon cording. The stuff they used
for running fender lines. Yellow nylon cording."

"That's good, Henry. Always give the most detailed
description you possibly can." Dr. Lane wrote something
down in the small notebook. "And then what happened?"

"Then he made her walk to the end of the plank. . . ."

"No, I mean just before that. Remember how we
talked about the life vest?"

Henry looked at Dr. Lane. He seemed confused.

"I mean, about the life jacket. Pearl's life jacket."

"Oh. He took it off her and tossed it overboard."

"You saw him do this?"

"I saw him. I did!"

"How did he take the life jacket off if her hands were
tied behind her back?"

Henry breathed deeply and concentrated. "He cuts it
off. I can see him cut it off and toss it overboard."

"And why," said Dr. Lane very gently, "have you not
mentioned this before today? Before just now?"

Henry buried his face in his hands. "I forgot about it.

Until just now. Until you asked me about her life jacket. Then I remembered."

Dr. Lane nodded, apparently satisfied with Henry's statement. At this moment, Ingrid Pederson poked her head around the corner and said, "Will you stay for lunch, Dr. Lane?"

Ingrid looked haggard and worn-out. She hadn't slept in days, except in fits and starts between horrific visions of her baby girl going down, down, into the depths of Puget Sound, her little body sinking, her wrists bound, helpless against the pull of the sea. Since the moment she had learned of Pearl going overboard, it was all Ingrid could do to get dressed each morning and face the throngs of police investigators and family and friends, sympathizers all, that came and went through her home. Nils had kept her shielded from the news media, so she didn't have that to suffer. She could barely focus on anything except that awful picture of Pearl drowning. Still, the least she could do was to offer the child psychologist a little bite of lunch.

"No thank you, Mrs. Pederson," said Dr. Lane. "I have another appointment in . . ." She consulted her wristwatch. "My goodness, the time has flown."

Henry raised his head from his hands and said, "I'll bet you're going next door to see Tim Diamond. To get his side of the story."

Dr. Lane smiled pleasantly and stood up. "You are right, Henry," she said, smoothing her linen skirt. "I have been appointed to treat both of you boys, at least through the grieving process and the trial stage. That is, if it goes to trial."

Ingrid came into the room. Wringing her hands, she said to Dr. Lane, "We appreciate your kindness, Doctor. I still find it so difficult to accept the reality of . . . of things."

Dr. Lane patted Ingrid's shoulder comfortingly. "I'm here for you, for all of you. Don't hesitate to call on me anytime, Mrs. Pederson."

"It's Pedersdottir, really. Or it was. Oh. I don't know. You see, I was a Pederson before my marriage to Nils. We had the same last name, so many Nordic people do. But the correct title for a daughter of a Pederson is *Pedersdottir*. And I have always gone by my maiden name. Until Nils decided to run for mayor in the upcoming election. Oh dear, I wasn't supposed to talk about that. He's going to be a surprise candidate." She smiled apologetically, adding, "Then Nils thought it best we use the same surname. All of us. Even . . . even Pearl."

"Oh," said Dr. Lane. "I didn't know. . . ."

"Most people don't, unless they are Scandahoovian."

Ingrid's little attempt at humor fell flat. Dr. Lane patted her again on the shoulder and said, "Anything I can do, anything at all . . ."

Henry, recovered from the arduous interview and his weeping spell, spoke up. "I thought you were a child psychologist."

"I am, Henry," said Dr. Lane, smiling at the boy.

"Then how can you help my mom and dad?"

Dr. Lane said, "All the psychologists in our program are trained to help the entire family of crime victims. Even though I am a child psychologist, I am trained to work with every family member."

Henry said, "Well then, why do you work with Tim Diamond? He's not a victim's family member. He's the criminal. Tim murdered Pearl."

"Henry!" said Ingrid sharply.

"That's all right, Mrs. Pederson," said Dr. Lane comfortingly. "Henry has suffered a terrible, terrible shock. That's all right."

"It is not all right for my son to speak ill of others. Shock or not, Henry is forbidden to call Timmy that."

Henry skulked out of the living room. After he had gone, Dr. Lane said to Ingrid, "He's so fragile right now, Mrs. Pederson. Give him as much slack as possible. I know that you all are suffering terribly just now, your whole family's in shock. Let me take care of Henry. You concentrate on yourself and your husband."

Ingrid dissolved into tears. "Thank you, Doctor. I'm ever so grateful."

"Call me Cherry," said Dr. Lane, and she let herself out through the front door and fought her way past the news reporters, making her way around the big cedar tree to the gate of the Diamond family home.

At first, when Stephen showed Dr. Lane into the boy's bedroom, Tim refused to speak to her. "I don't like your attitude," he told Dr. Lane. "And I told you not to come back."

"Here now, Timothy," Stephen said curtly, "this is no way to behave. Now get off that bed, stand up, and greet your guest like a gentleman."

Tim rolled off the bed, stood sullenly, his head cocked to one side, and mumbled, "Hello, Dr. Lane."

Dr. Lane smiled and held out her hand as she entered the boy's room. Tim stepped forward and shook the doctor's hand limply. Dr. Lane made herself comfortable in a chair by the terrace doors. The doors were slightly open, and she could smell the fragrant perfume of a lilac bush that grew near the house.

Tim pulled out his desk chair and sat facing Dr. Lane, his hands resting on his thighs. He didn't know why she had even bothered to come back to see him. His story was the same. It would never change, no matter how many times she asked him to tell it.

She took her time opening her briefcase, fishing out a small notebook and a tape recorder, which she set up on Tim's desk. Before turning it on, she looked at Tim and said in a gentle voice, "Timothy, I need you to tell me the details just one more time. From start to finish. Please try to recall every last detail, down to the smallest thing, even if it seems unimportant. Try to recall everything. Can you do that for me?"

Tim crossed his arms over his chest and mumbled, "Yeah."

He hated her, like he hated all the stupid police, but he was smart enough to realize that cooperation might work in his favor.

"All right now, dear," said Dr. Lane. "Everything, just as you remember it."

The Coral Reef's black-belted pills had worked like a charm. Venus felt better than she had in months. But sooner or later, without a supply, the accumulative effects would dwindle, and then what? She called and made an appointment with the family psychiatrist. Doesn't every family have its psychiatrist? Dr. Wong couldn't see her until the following week. Maybe the euphoria would last until then.

Her jaw no longer ached as much. The bullet hole had shed its healing scab and now bared itself for all to see and ponder over. It wasn't something you could cover up with the concealing arts, or wish smaller. It was a hole on her face, and it gaped. When the surgeon had rebuilt her jaw-line and implanted the new porcelain teeth, he had promised she'd look better than ever once everything healed. But everything hadn't healed yet, including the bullet hole, which would require plastic surgery, and her memories were as vivid as ever.

Tim refused to speak to anyone except Venus, and then only in clipped non sequiturs. Bella refused all food and visitors (at least Tim was eating). Dr. Lane had called Bella to set up another appointment with Tim, but his step-mother had refused to speak with her, so Stephen had made the arrangements. He hadn't bothered checking with Venus or Bart. Stephen was a proactive kind of guy.

Next door, the Pedersons came and went under cover of thick security. Venus had called the Pederson home and left messages, which weren't returned. She'd called Nils's office, and the diplomatic secretary had said she'd give Mr. Pederson the message, but Nils had not returned the call. Rupert Scree wasn't talking, either. Twice, Venus had gone down to the marina, and both times she'd found the gang-plank drawn up on the *Caprice*. She'd gotten no response when she called Scree's cell phone, just his curt message to leave a name and number. Rocco had called her back to say he had been in divorce court for two days, and he'd made the effort to announce that as of now he was a bachelor again. That didn't bother her at all. Several times, when she had stepped out onto the terrace seeking fresh air and pos-itive energy, she had noticed Henry Pederson on his terrace, pacing, almost as if in a trance. He'd pace for a while, then pause and gaze over at the Diamond property, in the direc-tion of Thrush, the in-between land, then pace some more. He'd pace for nearly half an hour, then disappear into the house. Every few hours, he'd repeat the routine. Then he'd go back through the sliding glass door, and Venus would hear the door slide shut and the lock click.

The engineer, Ziggy Nelson, who had, according to Rupert Scree, attempted to save Pearl, was the only other eyewitness. She wanted to talk to him, to hear his version of what had happened. She had gone to Shilshole Marina to look for the *Dirty Blonde*. She had flashed her badge at the harbormaster, and he'd let her in the gate, but when she'd located its slip, the *Dirty Blonde* wasn't in its berth. In the next slip was an old Chris-Craft 48, its occupant a burly man about sixty, with a thick Russian accent. He told Venus the *Dirty Blonde* had sailed and wasn't expected back for a week or more. He wasn't friendly.

On the third morning since arriving home, Venus came to the breakfast table, set out on the terrace, to find Bart pouring coffee for a wiry, hyperactive man whose mustache was wider than his face. Bart introduced the man as Guy Foss, the film director.

"Mr. Foss is going to try his hand at Mother," said Bart.

"Good luck," Venus said to Foss.

Foss leaned over a small plate holding a single macrobiotic muffin. Plucking at it like a bird, he said, "I'll talk her out of her rooms. Have to. Film's behind schedule, way behind. Have to. I'll get her out of there."

In the end, Foss failed in his mission. He went back to his hotel to rest before the next attempt. After Foss left, Venus said to Bart, "Have you met Mother's new cook?"

"You mean 'chef,' darling. And he's not new. Jurgens has been Mother's chef for five years."

Venus said, "I thought Jurgens had been replaced. That is, Rupert Scree told me that Mother's new chef is a woman. In fact, I saw her. . . ."

Bart shook his head. "Ask Stephen. Stephen knows I'm right."

Stephen materialized then, as always, on cue. She asked him about the chef. Stephen said, "Jurgens hasn't gone anywhere."

"Why haven't I seen him around?"

"Chefs get time off, too," Stephen said coolly. "Jurgens has been visiting a relative up in Snohomish for several days. I've been doing the cooking. Jurgens returns this afternoon."

Venus went into the kitchen, where she rummaged around, searching for the roasting pan she had seen the girl carry off the *Caprice*. Nothing in Bella's kitchen resembled the pan she'd seen the girl holding. "Then who was the girl visiting Rupert Scree on the *Caprice* two days ago? She was carrying an aluminum roasting pan, and Rupert told me she was the Red Queen's new chef."

Stephen winced. "We do not use aloo-*min*-ium in this kitchen. Never have and never shall. This is strictly a copper and stainless facility. And I assure you, Jurgens is the only chef working in your mother's kitchen."

Over breakfast, Venus said to Bart, "Have you noticed how Stephen's persona colors the atmosphere around here?"

"Like I said, he's taking over the family." Bart wiped his mouth, stood up, and walked toward the kitchen, where Stephen lurked. Maybe waiting to clear off the breakfast dishes. "I'm going to my studio," Bart said to Venus. "Can you hold down the fort for a few hours?"

Stephen emerged from the kitchen, saying, "She doesn't need to stay here. I am quite capable of managing this house and caring for your mother."

Later that morning, without warning, the Coral Reef's medication suddenly lost its potency. Black demons stalked Venus's brain, trifled with her concentration. She tried swimming, but the demons would not retreat, only grew more persistent. And then, against her will, the incident reared its ugly head.

She hadn't meant to hurt him. Especially not to humiliate him. If she had ever loved anyone, she loved Louie

*Song. They had been cops together for more years than she
cared to remember. Hired together, trained together. They
had been through poacher wars and long, arduous stake-
outs. Tedious courtroom trials. When she had married
Richard Winters, Louie had done everything in his power
to interfere, willing the marriage to fail. Because she was
Louie's. That's what he had told later, after she had left
Richard. Now she lived alone, terrified of committing to
anyone, even Song. But why had she been so heartless? At
the time, she had convinced herself that she was being the
righteous one, the truth-bearer, the hero. Instead, she had
been the fool, and in the process, she had hurt him, perhaps beyond forgiveness.*

Guy Foss returned around 10 P.M. to try coaxing the
actress out of her confinement. No such luck. The film
would suffer another day's delay. Foss drank a couple of
glasses of Bella Diamond's gin and skulked back to his
hotel. At 11 P.M., a ruckus broke out among the reporters
on the parking strip in front of the Diamond and Pederson
homes, two reporters from competing television stations
quarreling over territorial rights to a patch of parking strip.
The dispute escalated to a fistfight. Others joined in and
finally Nils Pederson himself appeared at his gates and
ordered the melee to cease. While he was out there, in pajamas and robe, the cameras rolled and someone shouted at
him, "How can you stand living next door to your daughter's murderer?" Nils waved the question away. Kimberly
Forget, the KIRO reporter shouted, "Mr. Pederson, are you
calling for life imprisonment, or for the death penalty?"

Nils Pederson, looking suitably crestfallen but debonair
in his navy silk bathrobe, his blond-sliver hair perfectly
combed, peered directly into the cameras and said, "You'll

have to ask the prosecutor. I have no hand in that."

Somebody snickered.

At sunset, the tugboat *Earline* left its moorage at Pier 69 and moved at minimal speed into Elliott Bay, facing the mouth of the bay that opened into Puget Sound's shipping channels. Outside the bay, in the shipping lanes off Shils-hole, the cargo vessel, *Dolgota* plies the calm evening tides heading north by northwest, holding its speed to a mini-mum. Since dropping off its cargo of Asian imports at Har-bor Island, the *Dolgota*'s rusted hull sits high in the water. She flies two flags: the Stars and Stripes, and the Russian standard. Her decks are bare.

When the sun finally drops behind the Olympics, in the clandestine moment between dusk and twilight, the *Earline* increases her speed, continuing her steady journey out of harbor. By nightfall, the *Earline* has reached the shipping lanes and when the lazy summer daylight smeared across the low horizon finally fades, the tugboat *Earline* pulls up beside the *Dolgota*'s corroded hull.

A crane aboard the *Dolgota* groans into action. The crane raises an empty lift and then lowers it over port side. From the tug, two figures silhouetted against the star-studded sky attach several small crates to the crane. The crates are lifted aboard the cargo ship, and then the crane lowers a man from the *Dolgota* onto the *Earline*. Business is transacted in low voices. Laughter drifts up into the sweet summer air, a bottle emerges and the two sailors on the *Earline* drink with the man from the *Dolgota*, then the man steps onto the lift, ready to be raised back up onto the *Dolgota*. The crane moans, raising its human cargo, one man silhouetted in the soft light emanating from the *Ear-line*'s cabin, the only illumination needed for the figure on the *Earline*'s deck who points a gun at the man in the lift and fires. The gun's report echoes off the *Dolgota*'s hull as the man on the lift crumples, then rolls off, crashing into the Sound.

The crane is secured on the *Dolgota*. One blink of a signal light informs the *Earline*'s crew that all is well aboard the cargo vessel, perhaps better than ever before.

From the deck of the *Caprice*, Rupert Scree witnesses all of this activity through a pair of binoculars, then he enters the wheelhouse, ramps up the *Caprice*'s engines, and steers back toward moorage in Elliott Bay.

As the *Earline* swings to head back toward the harbor, another vessel appears at the mouth of the bay, a mammoth fish processor, *Spindrift*, a floating warehouse, rusting but still seaworthy. When the *Earline* passes the *Spindrift*, it signals the processor. The *Spindrift* signals back, and the *Earline* picks up speed, heading for its berth at Pier 69. The *Spindrift* turns to port and heads for Pier 91, adjacent to Elliott Bay Marina. Passing the dock where the yacht *Caprice* is pulling into its slip, the *Spindrift* maneuvers smoothly into its temporary slip.

A night owl might have heard a *splunk* when Rupert Scree slipped over the side of the pier into the frigid bay. On his back are strapped two oxygen tanks. He wears a black wet suit, a loaded cargo belt, and flippers. He carries a speargun and a flashlight switched onto low beam that shines a narrow path through the green crystalline saltwater. Diving deeper, he disrupts a school of herring as he dispatches fine bubbles upward toward the water's surface. Down here, anemones and jellyfish glow incandescent and crabs claw the mucky sea floor. At a depth of twenty feet, Scree checks his wrist compass, switches the flashlight to high beam and aims it straight ahead. He swims a hundred yards until he comes to a kelp forest. Penetrating the tangled mass, he pauses to check his position then dives downward. When he reaches bottom, Scree sees a littered seabed. Rusted boat hulls. Oil drums. Car fenders. Garbage. Eventually he comes upon a warren of wood pilings coated with bright red starfish that have protruded their stomachs onto some mussels and are sucking flesh out of their shells. Scavenger fish, bottom feeders, circle below. Now the hulls of boats appear and he swims toward the largest one. The *Spindrift*. On the subterranean pilings where the *Spindrift* is docked, clusters of brilliant blue-and-pink anemones wiggle tumescent fingers. Pushing to the surface, Scree brings his head above water and listens.

Beneath a waxing moon, a car drives onto the pier, then another, and another. Men scurry to and fro along the pier, moving catlike, silent shadows in the moonlight. The *Spindrift*'s cargo hold yawns open and swallows them, and the cars keep coming, until twelve are secured inside the hold. A flurry of activity, and then the hold's door screeches shut, then total silence. In the distance, the *Dolgota* sounds a resonant Klaxon, whose melody drifts across the bay to fuse with the click-clacking of a train headed north to Canada, full of passengers who saw nothing outside their windows except resplendent moonbeams on the water. The cargo vessel sounds its horn once more, this time a shorter note, and then it goes silent, having served its purpose in the night symphony.

Reaching into his belt, Scree pulls out an explosive charge. He secures the charge to the *Spindrift*'s hull. He's setting the timing device when something the size of a buffalo invades his peripheral vision. It glows in the moonlit depths, and when he turns, he faces what looks like a golden lion's mane waving a ghastly greeting. A night owl might have heard a splash as Scree struggled, bobbing to the surface once before the golden mane tangled around him. He struggled in the inky depths, and when finally he had untangled from the creature, neither species could claim victory.

So far, the Coral Reef hadn't tracked her down, but Venus wondered if they had actually contacted her caseworker. Her body told her that the medication had lost its power and she felt herself sinking back into that mental quagmire that had triggered the incident. Maybe Dr. Wong, the Diamond family's psychiatrist, would pre- scribe a few pills over the phone. She called his office and got his receptionist, Sun, on the phone. Venus told Sun about her dilemma, not in vivid holographic detail, cer- tainly not including the incident itself, just the necessary parameters.

"Doctor no help you," said Sun kindly. "Doctor see you first. Then give pills."

"What am I supposed to do until then?" Venus almost screamed at Sun.

Sun was accustomed to desperadoes. "Hang in there,

sweetie," she told Venus. "Time go by fast. You get suicidal, you call nine one one. They come get you."

"That's what I'm afraid of. Now, listen here, Sun, I need some medication and I need it now. Can't you let me speak to the doctor in person so I can explain my situation?"

"Sorry, sweetie. You come next week. Meantime, try drinking some *mouhma* in hot tea. One pot should help keep euphoric state until you see doctor."

"*Mouhma*'s illegal."

"Liu Ping has some. Go see Liu Ping." Sun hung up.

Liu Ping's Chinese pharmacy was in the heart of Chinatown, a block east and two blocks south of the Panama Hotel. Venus stopped by the Panama for a quick milk tea, then set out for Liu's Apothecary. Some local artists had created giant multicolored dragons, which now festooned Chinatown's telephone poles. They leered down at her, and when she crossed Jackson Street, and a saffron dragon hissed at her back.

Liu Ping stood behind the counter in his usual spot, as bald and coy as ever, his white goatee a little longer and thinner than the last time she'd seen him. Liu Ping had a long record of arrests for selling endangered animal parts, including fresh bear gall and paws. In the end, Liu Ping always turned state's evidence and so escaped prosecution, but just barely. He had a small dog, bone white, whom he'd named Zen, a brilliant, hairless creature who reputedly read Chinese text. She looked around the shop. Zen wasn't seated on his usual green silk cushion. Then she heard his growl and looked down just in time to save her ankle from a deep wound.

"Call him off, Liu Ping," she said.

"Zen," said Liu Ping, apparently amused, "over here. Come, Zen."

Zen loped over to Liu Ping and was sent to his cushion, where he burrowed into the silken threads and nodded off.

Venus said, "He used to like me."

Liu Ping said, "Zen too smart for that."

She told Liu Ping she wanted some *mouhma*. He acted like he'd never heard of the stuff. She said, "Central Asian. A tarlike substance merchants in Uzbekistan's bazaars will tell you comes from rainwater dripping down mountainsides. Actually, it is a potent tarry opiate that in minuscule doses in hot tea will cure the dangdest things. And you know what the hell I'm talking about, Liu Ping. O-pi-um."

"This some kind of sting," said Liu sourly.

"No way. This is for real." She told him about Dr. Wong's receptionist.

Liu listened, then said, "Sun way out of line. Not have that in my shop."

"Aw, c'mon, Liu, give me a break. How many times have I saved you from the big house?"

Liu made a sour face. "I save myself. You nothing but trouble."

She glanced over his shoulder at the tall medicine cabinet with a hundred small drawers, each marked with a Chinese character. One of the them reminded her of a jellyfish. Wasn't it true that some Asians eat jellyfish? "Say, Liu," she said, "what do you know about jellyfish?"

"Taste good."

"Yeah? Like what?"

"Like what they taste? Like . . ." He thought it over. "Like salty rubber chicken." He leaned his head back and cackled. Zen looked up from his pillow, checked out the action, then resumed snooze position.

"Who eats jellyfish? Japanese?"

"All Asian eat jellyfish."

"Really?"

Liu nodded, gripping the counter with his gnarled

hands. His fingernails were brown from tobacco burns, the nail on his left index finger about four inches long.

She said, "Are they expensive?"

He rubbed the crepey skin beneath his eye, as if to help him think. "Some jellyfish very expensive. Depends. Rare jellyfish cost big money. I have none in shop today. Out of stock."

She took Tim's jellyfish sketch from her bag, showed him the picture of the lion's mane.

"You ever get any of those in here?" She looked around for a fish tank.

Liu Ping laughed again. "No siree."

"Can you order me some?"

The old Chinese man leaned across the counter and spit his words. "You try another sting."

"Hey, calm down. No sting. I don't think harvesting jellyfish is illegal, Liu Ping."

"You stupid girl. I no stupid man. Go away."

She held up a placating hand. "No, no, no, no, no. Oh Liu, I give you my word of honor, no sting. I'm just curious about jellyfish. Truly. Please believe me. This is no sting. So forget about jellyfish. To be honest, Liu, I'm very desperate. I need something to keep me from blowing my brains out, and I need it fast."

Liu made a face. "Maybe you do it."

"Blow my brains out?"

Liu nodded and grinned, showing his yellow bric-a-brac teeth.

She held out a hand. "Okay. Give me a gun."

"Oh no you don't. Not in my shop. You go out in street. You go away from my shop. Then you use your own gun. I see your gun now. You can't hide it from me."

"All right, all right, all right." She was getting agitated, the desperation of her plummeting body chemistry taking over. "Give me anything—I don't care what—to keep me nonpsychotic until I see Dr. Wong next week. I'm begging you, Liu."

The old Chinese man chuckled. "What are you paying me back?"

"Whatever you want. Cash on the barrelhead. Just give me something."

Liu tugged on his long beard and then went into a little room behind some tattered silk curtains. While she waited for him to come back, she turned to the dog and said, "Hey, boy."

Zen looked up.

She said, "Where does he keep the *mouhma*?"

Zen growled, stood up, shook, and came forward, growling louder.

She held out a hand, its back side to the dog. "Calm down, boy, calm down."

Zen lunged at her ankle, gripped it between his iron jaws. She yelled and Liu came running.

She was on the floor, wrestling with Zen, when Liu beat the dog off her. She stood up, brushed off, and complained, "I was only being friendly."

Liu glared at her. "You ask him for contraband."

She shrugged.

Liu said, "Don't do that again. You do that again, I kill you. Then you won't have any problem, see?"

"I see." She sounded more humble than she felt, but right now, humble was politic.

Liu reached into his robe and fished out a tiny package wrapped up in brown paper. He handed it to her. "You take these pills one every two hours. You take with lots of water."

She palmed the little package and said, "What do I owe you?"

"You go away and never come back."

"You know I can't promise that, Liu."

"Give me back package." He thrust out his hand.

She pleaded with him. Finally, they struck a compromise. Liu Ping said, "You bring me that jellyfish in exchange for pills." She agreed. She'd agree to anything for the pills. Zen trotted out into the street to watch her fleeing with the tiny panacea.

"Just try to relax, Henry, dear."

Henry rested his head back against the couch. The afternoon sun beat down through the picture windows, striking Henry directly across the face. It gave him a headache.

"I can't," he said, frustrated. "That sun is driving me crazy."

Dr. Lane stood, walked across the Pedersons' living room, and drew the vertical shades across the huge windows. She returned to the couch where she usually sat while working with Henry.

"Is that better, dear?"

"Much." Henry relaxed a little. His fingers beat a soft tattoo on the couch cushion. "Okay, I think I'm ready now."

"Henry," said Dr. Lane gently, "I want you to imagine a wonderful lake. You are in a kayak, paddling across the lake's smooth surface. All around are evergreen trees. The lake is smooth and the air is still. There is not a sound except the sound of your paddle as it gently strikes the water. You are gliding, gliding. You are entering an enchanted cove and in this cove everything that has ever happened to you is recalled with perfect clarity. How do you feel, Henry?"

"Um-hmm," said, Henry, already dropping into a trance state.

"Good. Now you are in the cove of remembrance and you are recalling every tiny detail of the day your sister drowned. You are going to tell me every little detail, in perfect order, and it will all be just fine. And after you finish, you will feel very refreshed. Now you are growing sleepy."

Henry's head dropped to his chest.

"Now you may begin. Put the paddle aside. Look into the beautiful cove and tell me everything that happened on the day Pearl drowned."

"We were planning to scare the shit out of her," began Henry. "We hated her. She was the world's meanest brat. So we decided to scare her pants off. We planned ahead. We got the rope and the duct tape and the engineer gave us a wood plank he'd found aboard the boat. We set everything up the night before. Then when we boarded the boat that morning, we grabbed Pearl and marched her to the rear, back where we had attached the plank. Pearl got all snarly and tried to wrestle away from us, but we had her tight and . . ."

Henry paused. His index finger twitched a few times.

Dr. Lane said, "Can you hear me, Henry?"

"Yes," he said distantly, dreamily.

"What are you remembering now?"

"Pearl called Tim 'a Chink'. I smacked her butt with my pirate's sword."

He paused.

"Then what happened?" asked Dr. Lane gently.

Ingrid poked her head around the corner, but when she saw Henry's state, she quickly retreated. Best not to interrupt. She went into the kitchen, where her sister, Cora, and some friends had gathered to keep her company while Nils got on with his business. A financial giant can't shirk his duties, after all.

In the living room, Henry had gone deeper into the trance and was struggling to recall a certain detail.

"Take your time, dear. That's all right," said Dr. Lane gently.

"Ummmm . . ."

Dr. Lane checked her wristwatch and wrote something on a notepad. Her small tape recorder rested on the coffee table and she checked and verified that it was still on, the tape still rolling.

"So then we go aft," said Henry. "I can't see very well because there's so much fog. Tim is leading us, and Pearl is between Tim and me. I'm holding my sword against her back. The sword is made of wood. It pokes real good but won't really cut. Pearl is mad and she's whining like a little baby. I tell her to shut up. She keeps whining, so I poke her hard with my sword. She stops whining and then she farts. She does it on purpose, just to make me sick. Now we're near where the plank is attached to the side of the boat. Tim orders Pearl to climb up onto the plank. She won't do it. I have to do something to make her climb up there. I say, 'Get up there or we'll kill you.' So she climbs up onto the plank . . ."

Henry's voice drifted off. Dr. Lane said, "I can't hear you. What happened next?"

"Tim tells her to walk to the end of the plank. I get up there and tie her hands behind her back."

"Did you, Henry? Or was it Tim who tied her hands?"

"I did."

"Are you very sure?"

Henry breathed in and out, in and out. Dr. Lane said, "Don't you recall Tim had the nylon rope and Tim tied Pearl's hands at her wrists?"

"No, I . . ."

"Picture this. Tim climbs up onto the plank. He is tying Pearl's wrists together behind her back. You are standing on the deck, watching. The fog is very thick, but you are standing close enough to the plank to see Tim tie Pearl's wrists behind her back. Is it coming to you now?"

"I . . . yes. Yes, that's Tim tying up Pearl."

"Good. Now, what happened next?"

Henry seemed to struggle with his thoughts. Just then, a loud thud sounded from the kitchen. Ingrid had fainted and fallen against a counter, knocking off a stack of pots and pans, which clattered against the floor. Ingrid's sister, Cora, had caught Ingrid just in time, but the sound of pots and pans falling had jarred Henry out of his trance.

Henry blinked a few times and looked at Dr. Lane. "I'm hungry," he said.

Dr. Lane leaned over and clicked off the tape recorder. She placed it in her briefcase, stood up, smoothed her skirt, and said, "We're finished for today, dear. Go on and get something to eat. I'll come back tomorrow, and maybe then we can finish up the details."

"Okay." Henry headed for the kitchen.

"I'll just let myself out," said Dr. Lane, and she did, checking her watch. She'd be a bit early to the Diamond's, but that nice Stephen wouldn't mind.

Somewhere in Asia, they waited for his return. According to his research, probably Southeast Asia, or possibly Malaysia or Indonesia, or Singapore. When he stood close against the mirror and studied his face, he saw—what?

Café au lait skin. Vietnam? Korea? Bali? Bali, maybe. But there was something Chinese. Burma?

Something about his hands suggested Burmese. His fingers were unusually long and tapered at the tips, more like sharpened pencils than the fingers of other Asian body types. Even among Asians, the only time he'd seen pointed fingers like his own was once in Chinatown, at a dim sum restaurant, when Venus had introduced him to her friend Louie Song, who was part Chinese, part Burmese. Song had fingers like Tim's. Tapered Burmese fingers. He'd seen them in pictures, too, of Burmese dancers. But Song's face was rounder than Tim's face, more Chinese. Tim's face was small, with delicate, rather sharp features. When he studied himself in the mirror, he often thought he saw a grown man who had been shrunken down to child size.

Other features puzzled him. The slanted almond-shaped eyes, so black that you couldn't see the pupils dilate, could be from just about any Asian country. His mouth, he had observed, alternated between full and round or thin and severe, depending on his mood. A narrow mouth, in any case. The hair, too, might be Chinese or Japanese, the shade of rich dark chocolate, straight and thick and silky. It never curled.

His nose? Straight and chiseled like a northern Europe-an's. His nose was the biggest mystery of all. If you just took the shape of his nose, you might think he was a Swede with a deep suntan. Only Swedes didn't tan; they burned.

Somewhere in Asia, but where? Lately, Tim had pur-sued the theory that he was part Burmese and part Han Chinese. A DNA test could break the code. He was saving his money for the tests, and he almost had enough saved to solve at least this part of his origins, if not the whole mystery. Some parts he remembered as if they'd happened yesterday:

There was water, salt water, and a rocky beach. A blue sky. Very, very blue, with no clouds anywhere. The sun was at the top of the sky, and it was hot. The sun looked so big, so close, he could have touched it, burned his fingers. There was the smell of seaweed, and looking at the water, he could see wind moving. Some seabirds were diving for fish.

He had an old box, a drawer from a dresser. Dark brown wood, wet, waterlogged. He had found it on the beach up at the driftwood line that same morning. It hadn't been lying there very long before he found it, because it still had tidewater inside it, and the tide hadn't come up that high for a week until just the night before, the midnight tide. So the drawer must have washed up on the midnight spring tide. He turned it over, dumped out the seawater, inspected it for seaworthiness, and, finding it floatable, dragged it over the rocks and down to the shallow tide line. Then he searched the beach until he found two long driftwood sticks, long and straight enough to work as poles.

He stepped into the drawer and, with a pole in each hand, pushed toward the sea. The drawer didn't budge. It sat on the tide line's rocky bottom, taking in water each time a gentle wave lapped to shore. It sat with the weight of him, unable to move, though he pushed as hard as he could. He was only five or six years old, something like that—he wasn't actually sure, but he knew that he was very small for his age, even for his race, which was a small race— something Asian, though he didn't know what exactly. But even his small body was too much for the drawer boat, and it refused to budge.

He felt the seabirds watching him and he heard one of them laugh. He was making a fool of himself, trying to move that drawer boat off land and float it on the sea. Then he had the idea to push the drawer boat out to deeper water, and once it was afloat, he would climb in. Then he'd chase the seabirds away with his poles and laugh at them. He waded about waist-deep, the deeper water chilling his body. He felt that he had been cut in half, half of him sweating under the hot sun and the other half freezing in the cold water. His canvas shoes had rubber bottoms, which protected his feet from the seabed's rocks and barnacles, but his legs were bare up to the top and his short pants billowed around his butt. His chest, too, was bare. The water here was clear and he could see the bottom half of his body as he waded farther out, dragging the drawer boat behind him. He saw a school of sardines swim past his legs, and a few clear jellyfish floated by, and everywhere seaweed floated, many varieties, many shades of green and brown and amber, with glowing bulbs on their stalks. Now the boat was afloat, and all he had to do was climb up into it. This wasn't as easy as he had imagined, as each time he tried climbing into the drawer, it tipped over and water rushed in and it sank. He must have tried fifty times or more to climb inside the drawer boat, and each time he grew more frustrated, until he became angry and shouted at the seabirds who floated by, mocking him with that high-pitched gull warble. Finally, he gave up climbing into the drawer boat, abandoned his goal of sailing back to Asia—for he knew that Asia was on the other side of this saltwater ocean—and headed back to shore, dragging his vessel and dreams behind him. For about an hour, his return to the motherland had seemed imminent and he had imagined himself a young sailor coming ashore to be greeted by his own people, his own race. They would rush down to the tide line—their tide line, which looked different than the tide line of his embarkation—and greet him with open arms. They would bow to the returning prodigy, their hands poised in prayerful thanksgiving that he had at last returned to his place of origin, where he was loved and honored and where his dear family awaited his imminent arrival in their small house in the village. The crowd would carry him on their shoulders through the village, to his father's home. Children would line the streets and shout, "Welcome back,———!"

That was just the problem. He didn't know his name, his real name. Now he was called Timothy, his American name, his official adopted name, but this was not his real name. Nobody knew his birth name, nobody on this side of the ocean. But over there, they would know it as soon as they saw his face; they would know his name and they would shout it to the heavens, and his grandparents and his father, would hear his name being exalted and they would come running, arms spread wide, crying, "Son, son, at last you have returned to us! Son, son!"

He would be caught up in their embrace, nearly smothered with kisses, and have to fight off their fervent touch. Even by family, he didn't like being touched more than just a brief embrace, a shallow, fleeting kiss. But he could feel their love and their warmth, and he loved them, too; and once inside the family home, with villagers peering in through the windows, they would eat their first family meal together since the day he had gone away, however he had gone. He had been too young for wanderlust, just an infant, unable to walk or even crawl. So how had he been taken from this land of his birth? He might have been kidnapped by pirates, or by some adoption schemers. Or, like someone—he couldn't recall who—had suggested to him, he might have been on the run with his mother, just an infant in her arms when she escaped the ruler of their country, who had been his father, her lover, and the devil himself. He had heard this story and many others, most of them pure conjecture, and he didn't know what to believe. All that he knew for sure was that he had a biological mother who had loved him, and he could still remember her warm body, her pretty smile, her sad dark eyes, and he could remember her aroma, like cinnamon buns. He thought he remembered her body hair around the birth canal, how soft it felt. He didn't remember her breasts, but he knew he must have suckled there, the warmth of her body making more of an impression than the milk that had nourished him. He couldn't remember how they had been separated, but he'd been told by his first stepmother that he was found beside his mother's body on this rocky beach, very close to the spot where just that morning he had come upon the dresser drawer. She had died saving his life. The lady who had found him beside his mother's dead body then became his mother.

Carolyn was very pale-skinned, with blond hair and eyes so light that they hardly had color at all. Carolyn had loved him and raised him tenderly but her husband, Chick, was an evil man without a conscience, and he had been involved in some shady business transaction. Carolyn and Chick had given him the name Timothy. They'd lived near the ocean, near this beach where he and his mother had apparently washed ashore. Ozone Beach, Washington.

When he was around six years old, Carolyn had disappeared. Chick claimed that Carolyn had deserted them, run off with a man she'd met in a bar in the village, a stranger, a foreigner. Chick said that Carolyn had cared more for her own happiness than for him and Tim; that Carolyn was mentally ill and that she could be dangerous, maybe even harm Tim. Tim knew these were Chick's lies, and he wanted to believe that Carolyn wouldn't have run away without taking him along. She had loved him. She was the only mother he really knew, except for the glimpses he still retained of his real mother.

On the morning he'd found the drawer, the morning when he had first tried his hand at boatsmanship and failed, he'd been trying to escape from Chick. He had dragged the drawer boat back onto the rocks, up over the rocky beach, and placed it on the high side of the driftwood log line. He'd thought that there it would dry out in the sun, and maybe later on in the afternoon, he'd try it again. But he'd realized he had to get back to the house before Chick discovered him missing and came after him with a switch. Just to be sure that the drawer boat wouldn't be found by other potential sailors, he'd covered it over with sand and rocks and dried sticks, until it was almost invisible among the pieces of driftwood. On the way home, he'd felt a pain in his leg, and when he'd looked at it, he had seen a swollen red ring around his thigh, just above the knee. Like a big cherry Life Saver. When he'd touched it, the skin burned and the whole leg throbbed. The more he'd walked, the more it had hurt, but he'd made it home and put on a pair of long pants. Even though Chick was a doctor, he hadn't wanted him to see the strange injury he had acquired at sea. Some kind of jellyfish sting. He'd hidden the swollen leg beneath his trousers, and though it had ached horribly, he'd never complained. The next day, when he'd returned to try again to sail away, the drawer boat was gone. In its place was an abandoned campfire, its ashes still warm.

Later, after Tim had recounted his deeply personal memories to Dr. Lane, he wondered how she had dragged it out of him. He never talked about these things, not even to the people closest to him. Except for Venus. He had shared all his private thoughts and all his memories with her, back when he was younger. But now, since this terrible incident, he had closed up so tight that no one could pry him open. Until Dr. Lane. He realized then that he was becoming fond of her. Her gentleness, her patience. Her maternal ways.

CHAPTER ELEVEN

It was one of those brilliant midsummer evenings, a hot peach sky fading into lavender blue shadows on the horizon. Dusk seemed impossibly distant, and on the pier just west of the Orbit restaurant, where little alfresco tables perched at water's edge, numerous diners had peeled off dinner jackets and sweaters and were soaking up the warmth and charm of a fine ambience. It was one of those evenings made for camaraderie, for pleasantness, for lovers, and so it seemed almost unthinkable when the sweet, idyllic atmosphere was rudely punctured by a woman's shrill screams.

She sat near the water's edge, at a table in the northwest corner of the pier. Sparky, the maître d', was first to reach the woman, who by now had keeled over and fainted in her husband's arms. Sparky rushed to her side, carrying a dampened bar cloth, which he placed across the woman's forehead. The husband, more shamed by the attention of other diners than concerned for his wife's well-being, repeated over and over, "Alexis, stop this now. Now Alexis, you just stop this nonsense. Do you hear me? Stop it right now."

"She's fainted, sir." Sparky gently but firmly shoved the husband aside and gathered the woman's limp body into his arms. Gently, he placed her flat out on the pier, checked her pulse points, and listened to make sure she was still breathing. Her chartreuse gown billowed in the warm breeze, and the flustered husband tucked the skirt of it underneath her legs. A man approached, saying he was a physician and offering to assist. Sparky's ego wasn't so bloated that he needed to revive this woman to prove his manhood. He let the man have a go at Alexis. The physician knelt, bending over the woman. Loosening the tight bodice of her gown, he saw that her breast was rigid, as if she had gone into shock. Examining her, he found several fresh red welts rising on the inner flesh of her right leg, just above the knee. Even as he watched, the welts grew in size and the flesh swelled. Something had bitten or stung her.

"Call nine one one," said the physician.

"Oh, for crying out loud," said the husband.

The physician said, "This lady needs immediate medical attention."

"This is a woman who believes that her refrigerator talks to her," said the husband impatiently.

While the physician examined the woman, the husband smoked and paced the pier. Sparky held the woman's head in his lap. Waitstaff attempted in vain to soothe the other diners, insisting it hadn't been the Orbit's cuisine that had struck the woman down.

"She's a prima donna," said the husband, loudly enough for all the alfresco diners to hear. "She exaggerates everything. I'll bet she's as conscious as I am. She's faking it."

"Why don't you shut up and help the doctor, you bastard?" shouted one diner.

"Go to hell," said the husband, snarling. "I know my wife and I know she's faking."

"Does she have allergies?"

"Only to me."

"Your wife is coming around now," said the physician. "Here now, madam, you're going to be all right. I'm a physician. You're doing just fine."

The woman opened her wide blue eyes and stared up into the physician's face. She turned her head to the side and saw Sparky, whom she recognized.

"Is it gone?" she asked, and then she swooned again.

"What, Alexis?" asked Sparky, using her given name, which he had overheard the husband call her. "Is what gone?"

"You're going to be fine," repeated the physician.

Sirens approached the pier.

"The sea monster. Is it gone?" the woman asked in a faint voice.

"What sea monster?" asked Sparky. "I didn't see any sea monster."

The husband covered his eyes. In a jaw-clenching fume, he said, "She's overly sensitive. She saw in the news about Nils Pederson's daughter drowning and the boy killer's story of a monster jellyfish. She acts out everything."

The woman turned her head to one side, saw her husband's shoes, saw him pacing the pier, then saw the other diners, who averted their eyes, pretending to ignore her mortifying dilemma. Soon haughty irritation replaced morbid curiosity. The woman's behavior had trespassed upon the other diners' privacy. How could anyone enjoy this idyllic evening now that a woman had keeled over right in front of everyone's eyes, possibly from food poisoning? They felt they shouldn't have to pay their dinner bills. The

Orbit should apologize for the embarrassing inconvenience suffered by innocent diners. This might be grounds for a lawsuit. A lawyer handed out her business cards. Plates were returned to the kitchen, the food untouched. Other diners complained of dizziness and nausea. Sparky heard the diners grumbling, some into their cell phones, spreading rumors:

"Of all places, the Orbit. Who would expect food poisoning here?"

"She just keeled over. I thought she was dead on the spot."

"No, she didn't vomit, just, like, fainted, but it was dicey there for a while, until the medics came and took her away."

In the end, the Orbit's management served everyone complimentary baked Alaska. Alexis Anders went home that night with her grumpy husband, Bob, insisting that she had seen a sea monster and that the thing had lashed out at her. The doctors in Harborview's emergency room had administered megadoses of antihistamines, which gradually brought down the swelling of the welts on her leg. Alexis told everyone who would listen that the monster had grabbed at her with long, slimy tentacles.

"He was, like, just a blob at first," Alexis told her sister Joan over the phone. "Sort of a golden globe. He came up out of the water and he had this, like, mane of kelpy things. And he had the longest tentacles I've ever seen. Seriously. He lashed out at me with them. Anybody would've fainted. And I did faint. I wasn't faking like Bob claimed. Bob's stopped speaking to me again. He says I totally mortified him in public and that this is my last chance. I don't exaggerate, do I, Joan?"

"To be absolutely honest, darling," said Joan delicately, "you are a marvelous actress. You should have stayed in theater instead of pursuing antiques."

"But, I *saw the monster that bit me!*"

"I know, I know you did, sweetie, I know."

By the next morning, just twelve hours after she'd seen the monster, Alexis Anders felt emotionally isolated from her family and friends. No one believed that she'd seen the golden blob, the sea monster that had stung her. The official diagnosis had come back: Severe allergic reaction, probably to wasp venom."

Tim lay on his bed, reading a book. Venus peered around his bedroom door. When he saw her, he sighed wearily, set the book on the bed, and folded his arms across his chest.

"What do you want now?" he asked sullenly.

"May I come in?"

"You always do."

Venus stepped into Tim's room, pulled out the desk chair, turned it to face Tim, and sat down. "There's no room for sarcasm between us," she said.

"Why are you here?" he asked, still cool, guarded.

"I'm here, Tim, because I love you."

Tim focused on the ceiling and shook his head. "I don't know what that means. As far as I'm concerned, people use love as a weapon."

"No weapon," she said, showing him her empty hands. "I love you. From the heart."

He didn't say anything. They sat in silence for a while. It was early evening and the sun no longer shone on this side of the house. The French doors opening onto the terrace were open wide and a warm breeze floated into the bedroom. With it came the scent of lilacs. Venus looked out at the garden. A dragonfly nose-dived into a shrub, maybe scouting a place to pass the night. If it didn't like that shrub, it could fly on to the next, or even to the next garden, or the next town. Nice thing about having wings.

Venus often wished she had wings. Maybe that was why she had become a butterfly nut and then a lepidopterist.

Tim said, "What are you thinking about?"

"Wings."

He laughed. "Hell, I wish I had a pair of those."

"Where would you go?"

He sat up on the bed. "Asia," he said.

"Home?"

"Uh-huh."

The evening light grew dimmer. From a distance came the familiar sonorous sound of a ship's horn, and Venus wondered if it was a cargo vessel or a ferryboat. When the light had almost gone, Tim stood up and walked over to his desk. He reached behind Venus and switched on his desk lamp. Then he turned suddenly and threw his arms around her neck. They held each other as he began to weep. The weeping became sobbing. She felt his tears on her collarbone, and she held him closer. She didn't say anything, just held him, until finally the moment passed. He let go of her and backed away. Returning to his bed, he sat on the edge, wiping his eyes on his shirtsleeve. A moment passed; then he said, "I need to be alone now. I need you to get out."

She was shutting the door behind her when Tim called her name.

"Venus."

"Yes, Tim?" She poked her head around the door.

"I love you."

Venus elbowed Sid aside and knocked on the Red Queen's door. Receiving no answer, she knocked again. She was carrying a tray heaped with her mother's favorite breakfast items—crumpets, gooseberry preserves, cantaloupe, and a demitasse of espresso. The tray had been perked up by Stephen's addition of a bud vase holding a tiny American flag.

Sid grunted and pointed to a hall table. "Put it there," he ordered. "I'll take it from here."

From a distance came the chime of the front doorbell. Venus set the tray on the hall table and went to answer the door. It was Rocco, all fresh and snappy and monotone in a lightweight summer suit. "Happy Fourth," she said cheerily.

Rocco said, "You're looking bright-eyed and chipper today."

"I feel okay," she replied, lying. She felt stupendous. Whatever Liu Ping had given her had sent her spirits soaring. They should prescribe the stuff at the Coral Reef.

"I need to take a statement from the Elusive One," he said.

"Go on back, but you'll have to pet the bulldog."

Rocco went down the long hall to Bella's private quarters. He had a way with bulldogs and was inside the hive before Sid knew what had happened. Venus sat on a couch in the living room, perusing the latest *Town & Country*. A few minutes passed, no more than ten; then Rocco came back down the hall and into the living room, looking ashen and spent.

Venus said, "She can be a shrew, Rocco. I should have warned you."

"She's over the edge. You need to call her physician."

Stephen stepped into the living room then and begged to differ. "She doesn't need a doctor," he said. "She's fine, really, just a bit rattled. I know how to take care of her. I can manage her."

Rocco and Venus exchanged glances. Venus called the family doctor, then took Rocco back to the kitchen deck, where they drank iced tea and stared across the meandering iron fence at the Pedersons' house. The usual security guard sat sentry on the rear terrace. A pair of admiral butterflies flitted around the lawns, dipping into beds of peonies and African daisies. At 8:00 A.M., the sun had already heated the city to a sweltering ninety-four degrees. Rocco loosened his tie.

Venus said, "Thank you. That was bothering me."

"I don't like to slouch on the job," he said. "But it's hot as hell."

"Try this," she said. She plucked an ice cube out of her tea and dropped it down her shirt. It melted between her small breasts, making a dark spot on her shirt.

"Go on," she said to Rocco. "It won't hurt you."

Rocco loosened his tie and collar and dropped ice down his shirt. It slid down to his navel and melted there. "I have to admit I feel better," he said.

"Toldja."

"You really are chipper today," he said.

"Ya sure you betcha."

He looked at her. Her eyes sparkled, the pupils little pinpoint dots, bright green irises glowing like traffic signals. He hadn't yet mentioned the hole in her cheek. Hadn't wanted her to feel self-conscious. But it was too obvious to ignore. Now he said, "How's that wound healing up?"

"The one on my face or the one on my psyche?"

"I'm talking about the plug you took in the jaw. Last spring, on that raid over on the Olympic Peninsula."

She chewed her lip, shrugged, and said, "Gets better every day."

"You on painkillers?"

"Negative."

He said, "You're taking something. Nobody takes one in the face the way you did and two months later walks around acting giddy. It doesn't happen that way. It takes time to heal the wounds. All of them. That includes the psyche. And it doesn't bother me if you're taking medication. I just want to know what drops that starlight into your eyes. It's not natural."

She made a tsking sound and said, "Don't be such a busybody."

"Hey, I'm a cop," he said. "Like you, I'm trained to know when an individual is lying."

"More ice?"

"Don't try bait and switch on me. What are you hiding?"

"Okay," she said. "I'll be honest with you. I'm flat-lining."

"What the hell does that mean?"

"Operating at an emotional idle. It's the 'black leather jacket around the heart' syndrome. You hide 'em, you don't feel 'em. Takes a little practice, but once you've got it down, life evens out; the way is smooth, unfettered. You go around with this false glint in your eye and everyone thinks you've got to be on drugs."

Rocco said, "What are you taking?"

She made a face, shrugged, and showed him empty palms.

He snorted. "You're disgusting," he said, and then the door chimes rang.

Doctor Wong swept in, calm and efficient, and was granted entry into the hive. Being the family psychiatrist, Wong knew the Diamonds better than they knew one another. He stayed with the actress almost an hour. When he emerged, he said, "I've given her a sedative. She is very traumatized, very panicky about the boy's situation. She'll probably sleep the rest of the morning and into the afternoon. I'm sending my nurse, Mae, over this afternoon. Mae will take good care of her."

"What about us?" said Venus. "We can take care of her, if she'll just let us into her lair."

Dr. Wong shook his head. "She is in a kind of shock. She has requested that her family keep a tactful distance. Please remember that she is your mother, and a very proud lady, too. She does not want her children seeing her in this weakened psychological state. Please honor her wishes. It is our only chance to restore her health. Otherwise, she will have to be hospitalized."

On the way out, Dr. Wong said to Venus, "I'll be expecting you."

"What?" She faked surprise. Rocco looked at Venus, then Wong.

Wong, quick to comprehend, smiled conspiratorially and said, "The court psychologist dropped off a copy of Tim's file yesterday."

If she was lucky, maybe Rocco had bought the ruse.

Tim stared out his bedroom window. Robins had built a nest in the lilac bush, and now it was full of squealing chicks, their little beaks shooting heavenward, demanding food. Now the mother robin arrived with an earthworm in her beak. Tim watched as she swallowed it, regurgitated, and fed her chicks. He had been following the robins' progress from the day the male and female had begun building the nest. He had watched the male and female mating ritual, had seen the female robin lay her eggs, and had seen some of the tiny blue eggs hatch. Birth.

More than once, a well-meaning but ignorant adult, knowing of his mysterious origins, had suggested that Tim, being an orphan, must have been dropped accidentally by a stork into an abandoned nest. When he was younger, he had wondered about this. Had he come from a stork's egg? Impossible. Storks have storks. Humans have humans. But how? He had once considered the possibility that his mother, a human, not a stork, had swallowed an egg with him inside and then the egg had hatched inside her, and then—what? Then he had learned to read, and, upon researching, he'd discovered that he had not, in fact, "hatched"; rather, he had traveled along a mysterious birth canal inside a woman he could barely remember, and she had pushed him out into the world, where she had loved him with all her heart.

No photographs existed to prove that he had ever been an infant, that he had ever resembled a baby. No evidence of any kind existed to prove—or disprove—his origins.

For all he knew, he might have been sent to Earth in a space vehicle. But no, that couldn't be. Because he remembered the softness of his mother's breasts, and the birth canal, he remembered the birth canal, and her tender crooning.

CHAPTER THIRTEEN

There is more than a year between the ages of eleven and twelve.

There had been the arson incident. He had only intended to get Venus's attention. He hadn't meant to burn out her apartment. Sure, he'd lied about the fire's origins. Who wouldn't? He wasn't an arsonist.

Tim lay on his bed, his hands crossed behind his head. The terrace door was open and from a distance came the sounds of fireworks. Small rockets, mere harbingers of what would come at nightfall. It was still light outside, still preshow. If he weren't in this god-awful mess, he'd be down in Myrtle Edwards Park, scoping out a good viewing spot before the fireworks began. Henry and Pearl would probably be with him, Pearl whining over Henry's refusal to buy her cotton candy. God, he had hated her.

Who the hell cared about fireworks anyway?

When Bella Diamond had adopted him, Tim thought for sure that his life had finally turned around. He was what? Seven, maybe. Around that age anyway. Now it seemed like eons ago.

There is more than a year between the ages of eleven and twelve.

How old was he, really? Somewhere, somebody knew the answer to that. Unless they had all died and taken their memories of him to their graves. And where were those graves? Carolyn had told him that his real mother's body was buried in the little cemetery on the north edge of Ozone Beach. Carolyn had had a stone placed on his mother's grave and had taken him to visit it many times, ever since she found him sitting beside his dead mother's body at the edge of the tide line. She'd found him on the sandbar near the river that ran through Ozone Beach, where the river poured its freshwater into the ocean's briny gullet. The sun had been just high enough to cast shadows that played games with perspective. She thought she saw a driftwood tangle on the sandbar, but when she approached it, she heard his faint voice, and then she saw the woman's body and the baby it embraced.

He'd been less than two years old at the time, probably more like eighteen months. Only a thin cotton shirt protected him from the elements. He sat in the cradle of his mother's outstretched arms. She lay in a fetal position, her arms reaching out in front of her as if reaching for her child. The woman had been dead for less than twenty-four hours, and there were signs of a severe beating before she had drowned. Her infant had been tied to her breast with a heavy cotton cloth, a swaddle used by so many Asian mothers. She was Asian, maybe a mixture of Chinese and Burmese. On one wrist, she wore a twenty-two-karat-gold bangle, and one of her front teeth had been inset with a diamond. No jewelry in her pierced ears. Her age had been estimated at around nineteen.

There is more than one year between the ages of eleven and twelve.

In the distance, someone set off another rocket, and Tim listened to its whistling ascent and its screaming climax. Somewhere out there, a kid was watching that illegal explosive and muttering under his breath, "Cool." Tim tried to imagine being out there himself, setting off fireworks. The previous year, he and Henry had caught hell from their moms for planting a Roman candle in the little park beside the Pederson's property, setting the rocket off at the exact moment that their most elderly and infirm neighbor, supported by her caregiver, shuffled past the park in her walker. Scared the bejesus out of her. They had caught holy hell all right.

Carolyn had been a great mom. If she hadn't disappeared, she would still be his mom. And Chick would be dead, or at least in prison. But that's not the way it had turned out.

Bella was a great mom, too, as far as actresses go. She didn't act like other kids' moms. She treated Tim like an adult and never talked down to him. She wasn't much of an embracer, but that suited Tim. He abhorred gushy, pawing affection. Bella maintained a respectful distance, unless he wanted to be held, however briefly. And she respected his intelligence, encouraged him to excel and because of her, he did. He went to the head of his class and stayed there.

The lies had started about the time his stepmother began leaving him behind when she went off to make films. He had grown accustomed to traveling everywhere with her, but one day she said, "You are excelling in school, Timothy. I want you to stay at home and concentrate on your education. One day, Timothy, you are going to be famous.

Probably even more famous than I am." Ever since then, whenever she traveled without him, he felt a sort of panicked abandonment. The lies grew out of this fear, this need for someone to pay attention to him, to prove that he wasn't, once again, being abandoned.

Now he had the reputation of a chronic liar. Nobody believed anything he said. Why should he even bother telling the truth?

The sun hadn't yet set, but the interim between exploding firecrackers was clearly diminishing, people growing impatient, restless, preempting the big bang. Then the fireworks would explode over the night sky, and for those few moments all troubles and cares would be forgotten. Most anyway.

Tim sat up. An idea had formed in his mind. He listened. The house, at least on this level, was quiet. Stephen might be out with friends to view the fireworks. Bella was no doubt still pouting in her room, her dog, Pansy, at her side. Down here, all was quiet. He slipped off the bed, went to the door leading into the hall, and listened carefully. Silence. He opened the door and stepped out of his room. Walking with the electronic anklet was a little clumsy. He walked quietly, slowly, so not to disturb the dog, draw attention to himself. At the end of the hall, a right turn led to the garage. He opened the door carefully and went into the garage, where now no cars were parked. Stephen's car was gone. The Jaguar was always parked out in front of the house. He turned on the garage light, quickly orienting himself. The tool cabinet. Over there above the freezer. Inside, a pair of branch clippers used by the gardeners. He snatched them up and moved quickly back to his room.

In his room, he prepared carefully, writing a brief note, packing a few things he would need, including the astronaut Swatch Venus had given him last Christmas. It matched the clock on his wall. He had told her he planned to become an astronaut. He fastened the Swatch onto his wrist, strapped on his favorite brown leather sandals, and finished packing his small waist pack. Then he applied the garden clippers to the electronic anklet. One snap and the anklet fell off, landing on the floor. He picked it up, placed it neatly on his bed. He locked the door leading into the house and stepped out through the French doors onto the terrace. The back lawns were bathed in deep twilight now, a perfect time for shadow play. If he stayed close to the bushes, he could make it across to the cedar grove. He had to step carefully across the gravel in the Land of Thrush, so as not to make sounds that might alert the security guards on both properties. He paused here, removed a DVD from his pack and set it down on the gravel. Maybe she'd find it. He moved from tree to tree until he reached the other side of the grove, where the meandering fence marked the property line. He had climbed this fence a hundred times. He got over easily, landing behind the rhododendrons, and picked his way along the periphery of the Pedersons' yard. Once, he looked up at their deck and saw a guard sitting in a lawn chair, maybe dozing. He waited until he was sure that the guard hadn't heard him, then moved swiftly to the cyclone fence and bolted over it. When he landed in the public park, he heard the guard call out, "Who's there?" He ran, heading for the path leading down to the beach. He reached the path just as a bank of floodlights washed across the Pedersons' Hollywood lawn. Behind him, he heard the Pedersons' two poodles barking into the night.

The festivities had begun early in the day with live music, hot dog vendors and beer stands, dancing and cavorting, lines at the Porta Potties, and the occasional dope bust. This evening, from this park, from its paths and jetty, a spectacular over-the-water fireworks display could be viewed at nightfall. On the outdoor deck at Orbit, over-looking Myrtle Edwards Park and Elliott Bay, Venus swallowed some of Liu Ping's pills. In tandem with single malt, they produced enough buzz to ward off recurring visions of the incident, allowing her to forget that her face looked like hell. She was waiting for Rocco. They had agreed to meet here, where they'd have a good view of the fireworks on the shore of Myrtle Edwards Park while he picked her brain about Tim. She was touching the scar on her face when Rocco showed up. He folded into a chair beside Venus and said, "It's nine-thirty. Half an hour till the sky explodes."

They ordered drinks. All around them, diners were gearing up for the fiery show. The fireworks barge had been towed to a location directly north of the Orbit, just off the jetty at Myrtle Edwards. At ten o'clock, somebody would throw a switch and the first of the rockets would shoot into the sky, accompanied by patriotic music, whistles, and cheers. They had front-row seats.

Rocco said, "This morning I received information about a missing boy."

She looked at him. "And . . ."

"A twelve-year-old. He was last seen over at Hiram Chittenden Locks. His mom waited forty-eight hours before reporting him missing. He hasn't turned up."

"Name?"

"John Stark. Parents divorced. Dad abandoned family. No siblings. Mom's an occasional waitress with a bad crack habit. John attends Swede Heights Middle School. Everyone says he's a good kid, except for one thing."

"What's that?"

Rocco sighed. "His mom caught him on the Internet, making plans to meet an adult female. Mom had a decent moment and went ballistic on him, took away his computer. She smashed it with a clawhammer. We contacted the Internet service provider. Nothing of value showed up, so Mom might have been hallucinating. She told Sanchez—Sanchez is the detective assigned to the Stark case—that she'd threatened to beat John if she ever caught him meeting adults on-line again. Apparently, he ran away soon after and hasn't been seen or heard from."

"Where at the locks?"

"Was he seen, you mean?" Rocco shrugged. "It's not exactly clear. Witness was the lockkeeper. He couldn't recall the time exactly, but he remembered seeing a boy matching John Stark's description walking along the locks where a couple of boats were waiting to go through. He didn't pay much attention, didn't notice if the kid got into a boat or just left on foot. Doesn't recall what the boats looked like, or their names. We've checked around. None of the boaties remember seeing him."

Venus shifted in her chair, faced Rocco. "Why are you telling me this?"

Rocco scratched his ear. "Maybe it's not related. Just thought I'd toss it out, get your reaction. See, he disappeared on the same day Pearl drowned."

"Let's not jump to conclusions."

Rocco nodded his agreement.

Venus waited a moment, then said, "So, besides investigating the hell out of Tim, I presume you're also checking out my entire family?"

"Can't be helped." Rocco ordered a couple more drinks for them. They sat in silence until the waiter returned. He set the drinks on the table and went away.

Venus said, "So how's my family shaping up?"

"Don't ask questions unless you really want to hear the answers."

"I do." She popped one of Liu Ping's pills, washed it down with scotch.

Rocco ran a hand across his mouth. "It's too soon. I'm

not ready to talk about it. And, by the way, you drink too much."

She ignored this. She was wondering what he had discovered about the Diamonds. Had he uncovered any family secrets she didn't know about? What had he learned about her? Did he know about the Coral Reef? About the transgression that had landed her there?

Her hand was resting on the table. Rocco placed his hand over hers and said, "Look. I know some things about you that you probably wish I didn't. I know about your failed marriage; I even know about your boyfriend over in Singapore and—"

"Reuben's a friend; that's all. I haven't seen him in two years."

"And about Agent Song."

She hesitated, then said coolly, "Louie's a colleague."

"And your lover."

Venus pulled her hand from under his. She said, "What are you getting at?"

Rocco shrugged. "I don't know exactly. Just that I found myself peering into your life more closely than necessary under the circumstances. You fascinate me. You've led a fairly exotic life. Me, I'm just a cop."

"With a failed marriage."

He laughed. "It does seem to go with the territory, doesn't it?"

The sky had turned deep blue, a tinge of crimson daylight draining fast behind the jagged Olympic peaks. From where they sat on the Orbit's deck, Venus could see the crowds in Myrtle Edwards Park. Excitement pervaded the atmosphere in the park and on Orbit's deck, people gearing up for the show. The preshow music had temporarily stopped, the lull lending drama, heightening anticipation. People had gathered along the jetty. A boy about Tim's age shoved his little sister aside to get a better viewing spot. The little girl screamed and shoved back.

Venus watched the two children tussle and thought to herself, God help Tim, if he really pushed her.

"My marriage was annulled," Rocco said. "I'd like to tell you about it."

She glanced at her Swatch. "You've got five minutes. Then you'll have to shout."

He turned his chair toward her. In the evening light, she noticed that his eyes were green like hers, only darker, the color of good jade. He said, "There's something about you that's an enigma. Mysterious. I haven't figured that out yet. But there's something else. You're a cop, like me. You know what my life is like."

Venus said, "I'm an undercover wildlife agent. That's a little different."

He shook his head. "Hell, Venus, you've seen it all, and you've seen it often enough to know what kind of night-mares I have. You have them, too." He paused, seeming to struggle for words. Finally, he said, "Oh hell, just forget it."

"Sure," she said, and pointed. "Now pay attention to that barge out there. Something's about to happen."

CHAPTER FOURTEEN

At ten o'clock, the city exploded in light. Fireworks splashed across the cobalt sky, a study in fleeting pointillism. From barges on Lake Union and on Elliott Bay, great rockets of light soared into the night and, ever expanding, burst forth in blossoms of red and blue and silver, yellow and pink and shimmering gold. People sat in Gas Works Park and along the shores of Myrtle Edwards Park, embracing their lovers and cold beverages, shouting to the exploding heavens, and somewhere in Myrtle Edwards, a speaker blared Springsteen's anthem to America. The city's fireworks displays had grown increasingly elaborate, and tonight, freedom's proclamation was noisier than ever. Old geezers plugged their ears. Terrified dogs scrambled for hiding places. The sound was deafening. The city glowed.

On the north end of Elliott Bay, at Pier 91, a massive

cruise ship, the *Norwegian Sky,* dwarfed the bay. From the cruise ship's perspective, Elliott Bay looked like a bathtub. The ship's passengers had gathered on the promenade to view the fireworks. From one side of the vessel, they could see the fireworks shooting up over Lake Union. From the other side, they could see the Elliott Bay fireworks. The whole display lasted about twenty minutes and demanded complete attention.

West of Pier 91, the private marina was nearly empty of boats. They had gone out into the bay to locate choice fireworks-viewing spots and then dropped anchor. In the bay, yachts and outboards, cruisers, sailboats and tugs, great hulking ferries, and cruise boats crowded together to view the fiery spectacle. The marina was almost deserted. Only two vessels remained moored at the marina, the *Caprice* and the hulking seafood processor, *Spindrift,* which had been moved five hundred yards from Pier 91 to the private marina, its hull still wearing a tiny big surprise. The *Spindrift*'s hold door had been opened, revealing a dark, yawning, empty cavern.

From the Magnolia Bridge overpass, one by one, at discreet distances, fifteen Mercedes-Benzes drove toward the marina exit, with plenty of vehicles in between each of them, then up the bridge, down the ramp, around the loop, underneath the bridge, and into the marina parking lot. Now human silhouettes emerged. They scurried into the parking lot, where they worked methodically and fast. The fifteen cars were moved from the parking lot to a place across the road, then driven slightly north to the marina. One by one, they were loaded into the *Spindrift*'s hold; then the door slid shut. At 10:14, as the festivities approached a climax, the *Spindrift* eased away from the dock and pointed its prow toward the mouth of the bay, its departure cloaked in dazzling curtains of fire.

Rupert Scree sat on the *Caprice*'s upper deck, marveling at his rival's stupidity. If he hadn't wanted Rupert to witness events, he should have loaded the cars over at Lake Union, before passing through the locks into the Sound. Rupert lit a cigarette, then pulled on it, inhaling deeply as he watched the *Spindrift* sail into the bay, cloaked in dazzling colored lights, its engines muffled beneath the sounds of fireworks.

She moved swiftly, but it didn't matter. At 10:17, the *Spindrift* exploded, making the biggest fireworks of all.

PART TWO

CHAPTER FIFTEEN

On a transparent dawn of awful surprise, resplendent sunbeams crept over the Cascade Range, burning citrine furrows into snow melt chasms, the fervid glow broadcast from alpine slopes to the sea. Chasing curdled mist, the sun singed clots of fog and, though the tatters, illuminated the city that clung to rocky shoals on a deep saltwater bay. Here on this dog-day dawn, the frigid bay waters pitched and rolled on a brisk southeasterly, uninviting, unless you were a harbor seal or an ocean-raised salmon heading home to spawn, or a spineless jellyfish.

Or, like little Pearl Pederson, of Nordic extraction. Had Pearl lived, she might have swum to shore, but alas, fully seven days had passed since the girl had last been seen going down into this saltwater bay. And now, on a sultry July morning, Pearl Pederson's waterlogged body rode a flood tide onto the boulder jetty at Myrtle Edwards Park, making landfall bruised and battered and bloated.

No wonder. Her corpse had tossed and languished in the depths of the bay for seven days, skittering in spite of itself across the treacherous sea floor until caught and tangled in the kelp forest bordering the jetty at Myrtle Edwards Park. Tangled, that is, until the kelp twitched and set her bloated remains afloat on cold, clear saltwater waves that broke against the boulders, where a harbor seal preening in the stark sunshine witnessed the awful spectacle tossed up onto land. The sleek, spotted ocean slug, flippered and whiskered, waddled over to Pearl's remains and sniffed. Then he slid into the water and splashed off.

Above the jetty, joggers trotted along a winding path that hugged the shoreline south to north. Pearl's remains had struck land at the park's northernmost jetty, above the fishing pier and the Happy Hooker Baite Shoppe, landing on slime-coated boulders, in plain view of the early-morning athletes. In all likelihood, one or more of them noticed the corpse tossed up on the jetty. But noticing and paying attention are traversed only by curiosity, an old-fashioned trait unfamiliar to most cosmopolites. Nobody paid any attention, until the jetty rats discovered Pearl, and they were already big as spaniels. Then finally a curious human came along the jetty rocks, and the spaniel rats scampered into their holes, because curious humans can throw sticks and stones and break rat bones. So when this snoopy human drew bravely forth from the joggers' path across the narrow strip of crab grass and over the driftwood logs down onto the granite jetty, all was quiet and serene around the remains of the former little Miss Pearl Pederson.

The curious human had a name and an address and, fortunately for everyone, a strong stomach. Thus, when Moses Freeny, a man of color, pierced and tattooed across his broad chest, detected a horrid odor as he jogged near the park's south end, a ghoulish itch spurred him to pursue the scent onto the jetty. There he came across Pearl's remains. Moses Freeny unfolded his Motorola StarTAC and called 911.

Once he heard sirens, Moses made himself at home on a driftwood log and placed a brief business call. Moses was a flesh piercer, a body artist, and he owned his own piercing and tattoo salon.

Moses' assistant answered. Moses told her he would arrive late at the salon this morning. No, nothing was wrong, really; he was just . . . well, delayed. He instructed her to tell everyone to go on as usual, Moses or not. And to reschedule his appointments.

Moses stared at the corpse. He thought it resembled bad helium-balloon art, and then he immediately regretted the metaphor. No matter who it was, this was no time for tongue-in-cheek jocularity. This was death. Maybe even murder. He suspected he knew who she was. Or had been. Her name and photograph had dominated the news during the past week—not that she was especially recognizable just now in her gaseous state—Pearl Pederson, daughter of Nils Pederson, the owner of a huge financial empire, a big shot around town. This was the little heiress. Girl overboard under her older brother's watch. Yet unconfirmed media gossip held that it wasn't Pearl's brother, Henry Pederson, whose negligence had caused her demise, but the Pedersons' next-door neighbor, Timothy Diamond, who had murdered Pearl Pederson. Moses had seen numerous newscasts portraying Timothy Diamond as a chronic liar who had once set fire to his stepsister's apartment, a boy who was always in trouble at school. He had pushed Pearl off the boat and then jumped in and held her head underwater until she drowned. That's what the news media was promoting anyway.

Moses Freeny wasn't convinced, though, and as he sat

waiting for the rescue squad, he pondered over the truth. If only Pearl could talk. Moses Freeny believed that some- where in Limbo, up in Brat Sister Purgatory, Pearl knew something that the authorities didn't when they had detained Timmy Diamond and announced the boy might be tried as an adult for the heinous crime of forcing poor Pearl to walk the plank. As for young master Henry, a little black lie got him off scot-free. Up there, Moses mused, Pearl knows there's more to the story, but even in her limbo state, she delights in keeping her tawdry secret. For seven days, how Pearl went overboard had been the subject of much debate. A self-conscious city, riding recession, raw from financial contraction, appreciated the diversion of Girl Overboard, and so cafés and cocktail lounges had made Pearl Pederson their topic du jour, a little divertissement from workday woes. Moses himself had participated in what was now popularly termed *Pearlizing*—that is, conjecture over how the nine-year-old heiress had gotten into the deep. While most of Moses' friends and acquaintances favored the "walk the plank" murder theory thrust forward by the news media, Moses voted for the "big tentacled jellyfish" hypothesis. In other words, Moses all along had sided with the accused, Timothy Diamond, who had insisted that a monster jellyfish had reared up out of the deep and taken Pearl down. Moses championed the friendless.

As the sirens grew louder, Moses experienced a pleas- ant thrill. Maybe now truth would surface, all bloated and rotten like Pearl—nonetheless, whichever Pearlizing theory prevailed, truth by autopsy.

Moses turned around and saw the rescue squad rushing across the park. He waved, and when they drew near, Moses pointed and said, "Down there. It's Pearl Pederson. She's wearing those distinctive Nikes, so it's Nils Peder- son's daughter all right."

The *Spindrift*'s violent destruction had temporarily over-shadowed the story of Pearl Pederson's controversial death. Little remained of the vessel and its crew. It must have had a crew, though its regular crew was not aboard that night. The regular crew was apparently accounted for, celebrating the birthday of *Spindrift*'s registered owner, Icyfrost Seafood magnate Tom Moran. On the night of July 4, Moran and his crew were reportedly all wearing silly flag-themed outfits and tossing back Bombay gin at five hundred feet in the air, at the top of the Space Needle, during a combo birthday/ Fourth of July fest. The *Spindrift* had returned from Alaska for repairs on its refrigeration and cannery systems. It had been docked at Pier 91 temporarily, waiting for a slip in the south bay so that repairs could be undertaken. The ship had unloaded its last cargo and should have had an empty hold. Icyfrost Seafood officials suggested that the vessel had been hijacked. The public knew only that the fish pro-cessor had exploded and that officials were remaining tight-lipped, saying only that it appeared to have been an accidental explosion caused by a fuel leak. Kimberly For-get, KIRO's rookie investigative reporter, was already assigned to the Pederson murder case. She was not assigned to the *Spindrift* story, much to her displeasure, but she fol-lowed it closely and knew as well as any other decent reporter that the fuel leak was only conjecture. Nobody really knew, yet, what had caused the *Spindrift* to explode.

Moses Freeny straddled the driftwood log and watched as Pearl's remains were handled and wondered over. The res-cue squad bagged up the corpse then placed it on a litter or stretcher, or whatever they called it, and carted her off. By this time, a couple of squad cars had shown up, and now the cops were photographing the scene and had drawn yellow crime-scene tape around that spot on the jetty. Moses snickered to himself. What else did they expect to find here? Fingerprints? A smoking gun?

A crowd of joggers had formed, now suddenly curious, the way people get when sirens go off. They stretched their necks to see, some holding cell phones to their sweaty faces, just like Moses had when he first came upon the scene, which had put a kibosh on his normally serene jog south to north, then back, thrice a week without fail. Until today. Now the sweat had dried upon Moses' ruddy features, and he sat on the log—best view in the house—and listened while the spectators bragged into their cells about being right at the scene.

Everyone had his own version of events. But as far as the cops were concerned, only Moses Freeny had any information of value to offer, and one of the plainclothes detectives, a cop named Rocco, suggested Moses might like to accompany him back to the police station. Moses didn't mind. A business owner can flex his schedule, and Detective Rocco promised to deliver him to his shop after he gave a statement. So he went along to the police station, never guessing how deeply he would become involved in this tragic tale.

By 9:00 A.M., word had spread and all the local television stations had placed cameras on the jetty in Myrtle Edwards Park, as if there was something to see besides granite boulders, kelp bulbs bobbing on the water's surface, the occasional gull scavenging along the shore, and the camps of homeless people. Moses himself was chased down by a flock of reporters, who eventually found him hiding under a gurney at his shop on Elliott Avenue West, the stampede led by KIRO's own Kimberly Forget, who burst into the private piercing room, and said, "Here's the witness, in here." Moses skulked out from under the gurney and reluctantly granted Kimberly an interview.

At 10:00 A.M., Moses Freeny's mug was splashed all over the television, and any hope he'd harbored of hiding from unpaid parking tickets was dashed in an instant. On KIRO, Kimberly Forget was spitting out the news from her strategic spot in Myrtle Edwards. By 10:12, Moses noted an incoming phone call from the Dept. of Motor Vehicles, which he didn't pick up, and by 10:20, a call from Bart Diamond, the accused boy's older stepbrother, which he did answer, but with trepidation.

Bart Diamond wanted Moses to meet him that evening. Moses suggested the Orbit's bar at five o'clock. It was near his shop.

That afternoon, Bob Anders, a deeply depressed failed day trader, shouted at his wife, Alexis, "Ever since that night you faked fainting at the Orbit, I have been unable to trust you. What sort of wife would humiliate her husband like that in public? No, Alexis, I've had it. Either you shut up about monster jellyfish, or you ship outta here."

Her courage bolstered by a secret savings account, Alexis yelled, "This is it, Bob. I am leaving this condo and never coming back. I'll send Joan for my things. Here I go, Bob. Don't try to stop me." He didn't. Alexis slid into her BMW and pealed off.

She could have gone to her sister Joan's house, but she decided that she wanted to be alone to lick her wounds. Maybe pamper herself. She drove to the Olympic Four Seasons, checked into an extra-large room with lots of light, signed up for spa treatments, then went up to her room and indulged in a long nap. Wasp venom, indeed.

CHAPTER SIXTEEN

When she went overboard, Pearl had been wearing a red-and-white-checkered seersucker shirt and matching shorts, red Nike runners with silver stars, navy anklets, and a pair of Hello Kitty panties. When her remains washed ashore, all of her clothing was intact, though torn and strained from the body's bloating. One of her Nike shoes had been chewed on, possibly by a shark. Her wrists showed no signs of abrasions and no rope was found attached to her body. The initial search of the *Caprice* turned up a length of yellow nylon rope, which Tim had told police was used to tie Pearl up, and which he insisted that he had removed before she went overboard. DNA tests on the length of rope had proved inconclusive. When she washed ashore, her wrists had not been bound, but the rope might have worked free underwater and been lost. Thus, the answer to the question of whether or not Pearl had been bound at the wrists when she went overboard would depend on whose story you believed, Tim Diamond's or Henry Pederson's.

According to initial toxicology results, Pearl had died almost instantly of anaphylactic shock due to a toxin known to exist only in the Australian box jellyfish. The jellyfish was not a native resident of Puget Sound. In fact, according to the police toxicology laboratory, none of the native Puget Sound jellyfish was considered poisonous. Some species delivered a rude sting, but nothing fatal. But the toxicologist's report about death by jellyfish sting was cast into doubt by the medical examiner's initial results. The ME had discovered what he believed was a more credible cause of death. His initial perusal of Pearl's body, albeit a superficial examination, revealed that death might have occurred by strangulation. By what, he couldn't say.

Ten A.M. Venus sat at Rocco's desk reading the toxicologist's report. While she read, Rocco watched her. He was noticing her fine features and her vivid green eyes and he was thinking that her lips needed the kind of soft bruising he could give them if he kissed her. He tried to switch his glance from her face to some papers on his desk, but his eyes wouldn't cooperate. When she finished reading the report, Venus looked up at Rocco.

"Are you staring at me?" she asked him.

Rocco said, "I was lost in thought. I didn't mean to stare. Sorry."

"Toxicology's initial report supports Tim's story of the jellyfish," Venus said.

Rocco snorted. "Look at the ME's initial report. Then wait till we get the final results from the autopsy before you jump to conclusions. I seriously doubt that she was killed by a jellyfish."

Venus said, "Tim calls them 'pigeon of the sea.' "

Rocco said, "Why's that?"

"Something about being the last of the scavengers, I think. You'd have to ask him."

Rocco said, "Maybe she got tangled up in a kelp bed. Strangled by kelp."

"Oh ya, sure, you betcha."

Rocco stood up. "Let's look at that videotape."

She followed him into an evidence room, where he signed out the video that Rupert Scree had given him. They went into an adjacent room, where Rocco pulled a screen down from the wall. He fed the VCR and the tape rolled.

Venus saw the interior of the *Caprice*'s rear salon. She could see that outside the salon windows a thick fog hung low across the boat's decks.

"Here it comes," said Rocco.

The door to the salon slid open and fog rolled into the cabin. Then Henry Pederson slipped inside. He wore a life vest and a sour expression. He was unhappy about something. He slid the door shut and walked across the salon to a built-in bar, opened the door of a small refrigerator, and began rummaging around. His back was to the camera, but it appeared that he fished something out of the reefer, held it for a moment, and then slipped it underneath his life vest. At that point, he apparently heard something, because he turned his head quickly, stood up, and ran to the sliding door. He opened it and stepped outside onto the deck, leaving the door ajar.

"That's it," said Rocco, turning on the lights.

"I don't like it," said Venus.

"But it appears to support Tim's statement."

"Except for one thing."

Rocco nodded. "I know. Henry went back outside fairly soon after entering the cabin. Maybe soon enough to have seen something. But why didn't he admit to going inside in the first place?"

"Maybe he was in shock and so he forgot about it."

"That would look bad for Tim."

"Yes," she said. "What about the missing boy? John Stark?"

"Nothing new. Still missing. For all we know, he could just be a runaway. Sanchez said he'd split, too, if he had a mom like Stark's."

Venus went to her condo in Belltown. She needed a break from the family drama. Checking her phone messages, she was surprised to hear Tim's voice. The caller ID indicated a nonlisted number. She listened to the message. Tim said, "You need to check out the *Caprice*." And then he'd hung up. Venus made a mental note to ask Tim about the call. She had been home less than twenty minutes, had made coffee and was stepping into the shower, when the phone rang.

It was Rocco. "I have some very bad news," he said.

"How bad?"

Rocco said, "Your stepbrother is missing."

Venus looked at her wall clock. It was 11:00 A.M. on July 5. Rocco was saying that he had received a phone call from the King County Jail dispatcher. The dispatcher had reported that sometime during the night or early morning, Tim's electronic anklet had signaled a malfunction. Rocco said, "Apparently, the night dispatcher was distracted by an unruly inmate and wasn't paying attention. No one at the jail noticed until just now, when the dispatcher received a call from your brother Bart. Bart said that when he attempted to deliver Tim's breakfast to his room a couple of hours ago, the door was locked. Each time he knocked, he got no answer. He thought the boy might be sleeping late, so he didn't want to bother him. That was stupid. Then, finally, a few minutes ago, Bart said, he busted down the door and discovered the boy's room deserted." Rocco paused and then added, "The electronic anklet had been cut off and left on his bed. Apparently, the room was neat as a pin, no sign of a struggle. And he left a note. Basically saying he'd taken off."

Venus said, "Where are you?"

"I've just left the office. We've put out a dragnet. I expect we'll pick him up before long."

"How long ago did he break out?"

"We can't say for sure, but the electronic cuff has a timer device, and it indicates that the anklet was removed from the suspect—I mean Tim—around nine-thirty last night. It must have been dusk. He left his desk light on. Anyway, he can't have gone far. I've dispatched a dozen patrol cars and we've sent out an all-points description of Tim. Don't worry, we'll find him."

"What about the boat? Did you check the *Caprice*?"

"Harbor Patrol just went by the marina," said Rocco. "Gangplank's up. There's no way Tim could have gotten aboard with the gangplank up. I tried Scree's cell phone, but he doesn't answer. I'm heading out to the airport. Someone called in a sighting of a boy trying to purchase a ticket to Mexico."

She said, "I want you to meet me at the *Caprice*."

"Why?"

She told Rocco about Tim's message.

Rocco paused, then said, "I told you: The gangplank's up."

"Meet me, Rocco."

He sighed. "I'll be there in ten minutes."

She said, "Make it five. Put your siren on."

She called Bart, told him to meet her at the *Caprice*, too. She dressed quickly, ran to her car, and sped through Belltown to Elliott Bay Marina.

The *Caprice* was docked in its usual position, hugging the end of the pier, the gangplank up and locked into the hull. Other mariners went to and fro along the dock. It was a beautiful day, the water calm, skies clear, a day made for leisurely cruising on the Sound. Some of the yachtsmen stared as the famous actress's children sprinted along the dock, but none dared call out to them, none wanting to taint themselves with infectious tragedy. Why invite trouble? Stay the hell away from those Diamond kids and their little Asian orphan stepbrother. You know, the murderer.

Bart said, "We'll need the gangplank."

Venus looked around the pier. Several luxury yachts, dwarfed by the *Caprice,* were moored in slips along the dock. A couple of fishing vessels had taken up temporary moorage, perhaps to unload their cargo.

"Stay here," she said. "I'll be right back."

Some clouds formed in the sky, robust and gray. Bart waited on the dock. Five minutes passed, then ten. The air grew cool and damp, and in the stillness came the occasional crack of fireworks—the leftovers. Then he heard an engine turn over, emitting a soft, smooth purr, and when he looked toward the Sound, he saw a yacht named *Betsy* edge away from the dock, then move back into its slip. Venus appeared on the *Betsy*'s deck and slid the gangplank down to the pier.

"Climb aboard," she called to him.

"Are you daft?" said Bart.

She waved him over to the gangplank leading onto the *Betsy.* He climbed aboard and Venus raised the gangplank.

"What the hell are you doing?" asked Bart. "You can't steal someone's boat."

"Just keep calm. No one saw me."

"They might have seen us coming aboard."

"They don't know who's skippering." She unraveled the ropes that moored the *Betsy* to the dock.

"What if the owner is out on the dock right now? Or comes while we're aboard?"

"This will take only a few minutes. We might get lucky."

The *Betsy*'s slip was four slips up from the end of the dock, where the *Caprice* was moored. Bart handled the ropes and fenders, and Venus took the wheel and steered the *Betsy* out of its slip. She pulled the boat alongside the *Caprice,* tied the *Betsy* to a cleat, and shut off the engine. They boarded the *Caprice.*

She used her cell phone to call Rupert Scree's cell phone. No answer, just the same curt message. They searched the main deck first—the salon and the staterooms, the sauna, the galley, the dining room. No sign of anyone. No indication that Tim had been here. They went below, searched the crew's quarters. Nothing. Venus opened the door to the cargo hold. The hold contained seven Porsche Boxsters, none of which belonged to the Red Queen.

No sign of the boy. They went up by elevator, searching each level of staterooms without success. When they reached the top deck, they went first to the pilothouse. It was deserted. A new log had been started, apparently on the day the old log had been confiscated by the police. The date of the first entry was the day after Pearl Pederson had gone overboard. Each entry was signed, "Rupert Scree."

Bart rummaged around on deck, checking lifeboats for stowaways.

Venus went aft to Scree's private stateroom. When she slid open the wooden door, she smelled trouble, and when she stepped inside, she saw it. Scree lay facedown in a dried pool of blood. A bullet had pierced his torso at heart level and another had struck his neck. A few inches from his outstretched hand lay a Gillette razor. His cheeks were caked with dried shaving cream. He was naked, his torso partly covered by a bloodstained bath towel that had apparently been wrapped around his waist and had come loose in the fall. Scree was very dead, very cold, and one leg had already gone into rigor. His right hand had been severed and was missing, and his eyes were open in an expression of disbelief, as if he'd never expected things to end this way.

Venus looked out the cabin door and saw Rocco's car pulling up to the marina.

Around four o'clock, Alexis Anders awoke in her Olympic Four Seasons suite. She bathed, spiffed up her hair and makeup, and went down to the cocktail lounge. Several elegantly dressed businessmen tried picking her up, but she wasn't ready for her first post-Bob fling just yet. She flirted but didn't deliver. It was during this cocktail hour that Alexis saw a television news broadcast.

She had stepped around to the loo. This particular loo had a television. The evening news was just starting. A news reporter named Kimberly Forget was repeating the story about the little girl's body being recovered that morning. Now Kimberly Forget was saying that the initial toxicology reports on blood taken from Nils Pederson's daughter's body indicated she might have died from a jellyfish sting.

That did it. Alexis seized her cell phone there and then and called KIRO news and asked for Kimberly Forget. "She's on the air," said the KIRO operator.

"Well, you tell Kimberly to call me back at the Olympic Four Seasons just as soon as she's ended her broadcast," said Alexis. "I have some information that could prove that boy is innocent." She left her name and said she'd be waiting in the bar.

An hour later, Kimberly Forget, and Alexis Anders were sitting across from each other at a cocktail table in the

Olympic's bar, a cameraman taping the interview. Alexis had been drinking ever since she'd seen the news report. She'd had too much merlot, and by the time Kimberly had arrived, Alexis was barely coherent. But Kimberly was a crack interviewer; she got her story.

CHAPTER SEVENTEEN

The note Tim had left read, "I am now a fugitive from injustice. I am not a liar, and I intend to prove it. Timothy Diamond."

For once, the news media proved an asset, as it hyped the story of Tim's disappearance. From her lair, Bella Diamond offered a fat reward for her stepson's safe return and issued a statement saying that she believed the boy had been kidnapped. Numerous Tim sightings plagued the police department's special hot line, but no potential clue panned out. If he had left the house before midnight, he now would have been missing at least fourteen hours, without a trace of evidence pointing to a kidnapping. As far as Rocco was concerned, Tim was a fugitive from justice and was digging his own legal grave by running away.

The police combed the property and interrogated the news reporters camped on the parking strip. They brought dogs into the neighborhood, then widened the search to include Interbay and the private marina, where the *Caprice* was now being guarded by officers. They scoured Pier 91. The behemoth *Norwegian Sky* had sailed that morning. They radioed for the cruise ship's crew to search the vessel, then ordered it impounded in Anacortes until a thorough search could be conducted by police officers. They had been twice to the airport on false leads and had scoured the Amtrak station and the Greyhound terminal. More than likely, Tim had fled on foot to a specific destination. He was a planner. He didn't do things willy-nilly. But when a child goes missing, even an intelligent child like Tim, every minute counts and every false lead wastes critical time. The longer a child is missing, the less chance he or she will be found alive—even runaways.

Venus swallowed a couple of Liu Ping's pills, then chased them down with scotch, searching her mind for clues to where Tim might have fled, and why he had taken such a risk. She got Rocco on the line. "Any sign of Tim?" she asked.

Rocco said, "No, not a hint of where he might have gone. Not yet."

She'd been combing the beach adjacent to the marina. More than once she had waded into the tide, a singular dread in her gut. Now she sat on the pier alongside the *Caprice*, guzzling scotch from a silver flask Louie Song had given her on her last birthday. Sure, she drank too much. Someday she'd do something about it. Now she said, "We've got to find him. I can't just sit around twiddling my thumbs. He's in danger. I feel sure of it."

"We'll find him. Don't worry."

"I worry, Rocco. He's my heart and soul. I've looked

everywhere I can think of, but he's just disappeared. If we don't find him soon, I'm going to lose it."

"Try to stay calm. I'm on top of this." Rocco hung up.

She called Olson, her boss. "We still haven't found Tim," she said.

"Bad sign."

"Don't say that. I don't want to hear that."

Olson said, "There's a rumor going around Fish and Wildlife about a woman who claims to have been stung by a giant jellyfish. Only we don't know her last name, or where to find her. It might be interesting to speak with her."

"Find her, Olson."

Olson said, "I have a friend at Harborview. I'll see if I can get the lady's last name and home address."

"Thanks," she said. "You're a gem."

"Don't flatter me. So what do you think about the missing hand?"

Venus said, "Scree's?"

"Did they find it yet?"

"Still missing, far as I've heard."

Olson said, "What about the Pederson girl's hand? Have they located that?"

Venus sat up straight. "Olson, what in the hell are you talking about?"

"Curt told me he heard from a buddy in SPD Homicide that when they recovered Pearl's body, her right hand was missing."

Curt Mandell was a rookie F&W agent.

Venus said, "Are you sure Curt wasn't pulling your leg?"

"Positive. The girl's right hand had been chopped off. Not chewed by some shark. Severed cleanly with a sharp knife. And then I hear on the news just now that Scree's hand was severed, too."

She got Rocco back on the phone. She said, "Ever find Pearl's hand?"

Rocco snickered. "You're a wily one, aren't you?" He paused, then, "We haven't found her hand, and I doubt we will."

"Nothing yet?"

"Sorry, kiddo. But Tim's a sharp one. He'll take care of himself. I bet he turns up sometime tonight with a guilty conscience and a lame excuse."

Venus said, "So how's the investigation going? I mean in general. No need to rehash all the gory details."

"Still waiting for initial autopsy results—on both Pearl and Scree. Media's latched onto the severed hands angle. And, too, the rumor about a toxic substance found in Pearl's blood. I can tell you right now, it wasn't the cause of death. But if it were true, Tim would stand half a chance at trial. But here's something disturbing: The ME says Pearl had raised welts across her legs and buttocks. As if she'd been whipped."

"You think her parents beat her?"

Rocco shook his head. "I hope to hell not. And would they cut off her hand? And there's Scree's severed hand." He paused, then said, "Tim ever cut himself, or anyone else?"

"Hell no. And don't ask such asinine questions again."

Rocco said, "Tim might have killed Rupert to cover up what happened aboard the *Caprice*. I admit it's far-fetched, but kids get hold of guns and kill. It wouldn't be the first time. But why cut off the hands? There's some connection between Scree and the kids."

Nine times out of ten, murderers are known to the victims, and often are family members. So, even though Tim was now officially charged with murder, Rocco was investigating the Pedersons, peering into the darkest reaches of their lives. Everyone, even a Swede, has a shadow, a dark silhouette of some prior sin, so well disguised in false memory that it seems harmless, or a secret longing that causes silent shame. Rocco was an expert. If the Pedersons were abusing their children, Rocco would uncover the evidence. Or if Henry Pederson had a history of telling lies, Rocco would find out. If his parents were protecting Henry from his part in Pearl's death, Rocco would find that out, too.

Venus said, "How are the Pedersons taking it?"

"They're pretty devastated. When we got to the morgue, I thought Ingrid would faint, and Nils was crying. Not exactly your stereotypically stoic Scandinavians. Who could blame them?"

Venus's other line rang. Olson, with a name and address. "Alexis Anders," he said. "Belltown Heights condos. Fourth and Broad."

When Venus hung up and told Rocco what Olson had said, Rocco remarked snidely, "Now how in hell is she supposed to fit into the picture?"

At 8:00 P.M., Venus sat across from Rocco in his office. She had given up searching the beach below the Diamond home, where no signs of Tim had turned up. A couple of halfheartedly munched sandwiches lay in their deli wrappers on Rocco's desk.

Venus said, "May I see Scree's preliminary autopsy report again?"

Rocco rummaged around, located the file, and tossed it across the desk.

The initial report confirmed that Scree had died of his bullet wounds. Both bullets had exited the body and were not recovered when the *Caprice* was searched. Scree had been dead less than three hours when Venus found his body aboard the *Caprice*. He was clean, no drugs in his system, at least according to initial toxicology results. The contents of his stomach revealed that his last meal was a grilled salmonburger, a green salad, and a glass or two of wine. The meal had been consumed early on the previous evening, the night before he was shot. He had been shot about 8:00 A.M. and death had occurred instantly. Scree's missing right hand had not been located. The autopsy was in progress; final results wouldn't come in for days.

Scree had no family to contact, only friends at the maritime academy. That afternoon, Venus and Rocco had dropped by the academy. None of the instructors or students knew much about Rupert Scree. Everyone said he was an expert sailor, a witty dude with a sardonic sense of humor, a little secretive sometimes, but didn't everyone have quirks? "What about his love life?" Rocco had asked. Scree had a reputation for promiscuity. According to one of his former instructors, Scree had slept with most of the women among his circle of friends, including the wife of one ex-friend. She had left her husband for him, only to be jilted by Rupert, who was fickle as hell. He had never been married and no one knew where his parents lived, or even if they were still living. Apparently, the most memorable thing about Rupert Scree was his heroic rescue mission when a fisherman's vessel capsized at sea. Everyone in the maritime community had admired Rupert for that, and the Coast Guard had presented him with a plaque marking his heroism.

Venus tossed Scree's file onto Rocco's desk. "What about records for his cell phone?"

Rocco shook his head. "He had deleted all the incoming phone numbers. I've asked Sprint to supply them. We should have the list before long."

She said, "This severed hand thing. It's got to be a mob hit."

"Which mob? We've got the Asian gangs in the International District and we've got the Russian Mafia down on the waterfront. Asian gangs have the rep for smuggling, Russians for protection rackets. So which one of them severs right hands as a trademark?"

A short, wiry man poked his head into Rocco's office. Plain clothes, dark pencil-thin mustache. Latin. Rocco introduced him as Detective Sanchez. Assigned to the Stark case, the missing boy, John Stark, who had gone missing the same day Pearl had gone down in Elliott Bay. Sanchez said, "Nothing yet. The mother's driving me crazy. I hate cokeheads."

Sanchez left.

"I hope they're not child-beaters." Venus meant the Pedersons. She said it more to herself than to Rocco.

Rocco said, "The arraignment's tomorrow at eight A.M. That is, if Tim shows up before then. I'm hoping he will, because otherwise, he'll face more charges, more kiddie prison time."

Venus said, "Assuming Tim does come back, where in the courthouse?"

"First floor. Room one oh three. Same judge— McGrath. He's ruthless. The prosecutor is definitely calling for first degree, asking that Tim be tried as an adult. You better go along. He'll need all the support he can get."

She nodded. What could she say? She'd be there for Tim. If he came back to face the music. And she'd be mad as hell.

Rocco must have read her mind. "And no shenanigans. McGrath will toss your little tush out of the courtroom so fast, you won't see the swinging doors. Behave. Keep that temper under wraps."

She looked at him. "How do you know about my temper?"

Rocco cocked his head. "Hey, I'm a homicide cop. I know these things."

The phone rang and Rocco picked it up. He listened for a few seconds, then put it on conference so Venus could hear. It was Kimberly Forget, the KIRO news reporter.

Kimberly said, "I might be able to help the boy's case. I mean Tim Diamond."

"Go on."

"I may have some credible information related to Nils Pederson's daughter's death. I interviewed a woman who claims to have seen the same sort of jellyfish the boy described."

Rocco said, "We know about Alexis Anders. Go on."

Kimberly said, "She was fairly credible when I interviewed her about the giant jellyfish. You should watch my report on tonight's ten o'clock news."

Rocco said, "Any idea where Tim Diamond might have gone?"

"I was hoping you'd tell me that," said Kimberly Forget. "Can we make an agreement?"

"I don't make deals and I don't play games," said Rocco.

Kimberly sighed. "I'm not playing games. I know something. I just want your assurance that if I am forthcoming with you, then you'll reciprocate, give me the first exclusive. Believe me, what I have to tell you is important. You'll care."

"I'm not interested in gossip," said Rocco.

Kimberly sighed again, deeper, more heartfelt. "Not gossip. One step removed from the horse's mouth. One very reliable step. I can't reveal my source."

Rocco looked at Venus. Venus rolled her eyes. Rocco said, "Okay, if it's really good, you get the first exclusive. What have you got?"

"The witness who found Pearl Pederson's body this morning. Moses Freeny. Do you know him?"

"Sure, we've talked to him."

Kimberly said, "Well, Freeny tattooed my boss a few months ago. And you know how they get all intimate during those rituals. So Moses Freeny tells my boss that he has this really great talent for hacking into computer files. So I asked him to check up on that child advocate person, that Dr. Cherry Lane?"

"And?" Rocco's leg vibrated impatiently.

"We couldn't find her listed in any employee file in the King County or Seattle judicial system."

"That's not unusual. We outsource some of that work. What else?"

"That stepsister of Tim Diamond's? Venus."

"Yep." Rocco's leg jiggled faster.

Kimberly said, "There's some bad juju on Diamond. I can't reveal my source, but it's credible. Someone thinks she's getting too snoopy. My source claims that she's as good as dead already."

Rocco and Venus exchanged glances. Venus made a face, as if to say, So what else is new? Rocco said to Kimberly Forget, "If you won't tell me your source, how will I know if I should take the information seriously?"

"You'll have to trust me," she said. "Like I trust you to keep your word. You can reach me anytime, day or night, at KIRO." She hung up.

Rocco sighed. "I never know what to do with hot tips from junior reporters."

Venus picked up a stack of police photos taken on the *Caprice* after Rupert's body had been removed. She riffled through them, found the photos of the hold packed with Porsche Boxsters. "So he was smuggling cars," she said. "But you can't carry cars overseas in a hold like that. They need to be in cargo containers. Besides, he could never have taken the *Caprice* away from its moorage for that long and gotten away with it."

"True."

An officer leaned into Rocco's office and handed him a fax, then went away. Rocco read the fax and said, "Ah."

"Phone numbers?"

Rocco handed her the fax. She read down the list of phone numbers from Scree's cell phone, most of them made locally. She said, "Mind if I have a copy of this?"

Rocco made her one. She tucked it into her pocket.

She said, "So that leaves just one other possibility."

Rocco looked at her, one eyebrow cocked. "Yeah?"

"The *Caprice* was being used as a shuttle. Carrying the stolen cars out to a container vessel. The cars are then loaded onto the container vessel and the *Caprice* returns to its port. The cars would be placed inside containers and the cargo vessel would then sail to its intended destination."

Rocco nodded slowly and said, "And where might that be?"

She shrugged. "What would be the most lucrative destination? A place where purchasing expensive vehicles is prohibitive because of high tariffs. Let's look at the economics. The vehicles are stolen. No purchase investment. They're shipped to their destination. Small investment for fuel and crew. The cargo vessel probably adds the cars on as a lagniappe. Its regular cargo pays for the trip. Once they've reached their destination, forged documents are provided to the purchasers—documents that make it appear the purchasers have paid the tariff. There's not a whole lot of up-front investment in this scam."

"Dangerous, though." Rocco passed a hand across his face. "If I had to guess, I'd say Asia. A tong could pull this off with finesse. Hell, those gangs smuggle people into our port all the time. They could easily operate this scam. And both Pearl's and Scree's killer left a signature. The severed hand could be a tong signature thing."

"Hong Kong and Shanghai are both excellent choices,"

she agreed. "And so is Russia. I'll bet if we check the shipping schedule for Elliott Bay, we'll find the cargo vessel."

Rocco picked up the phone. "Ask and receive," he quipped. He punched in an extension number and told the desk clerk to locate the shipping schedule for the previous ten days.

"What bothers me," Venus said while they waited, "is the woman on the *Caprice*."

Rocco frowned.

Venus told him about her meeting with Rupert and the woman whom Rupert had introduced as Bella's new chef. She finished by saying, "I'm telling you, Rocco, this lady who was leaving the *Caprice* is important somehow."

"How important?"

"She had an aura about her."

Rocco massaged his chin. He needed a shave. He didn't go for the scruffy look. He liked his face clean-shaven and smooth. He said, "What kind of aura?"

"Like Snow White."

Rocco laughed. "What kind of description is that, coming from a cop?"

"It's the only thing I can remember vividly. She was obviously shielding herself so that I wouldn't get a good look at her. She had a hood over her head and kept her head down, so I barely saw her face. And she lied. We know that she lied. Or else Rupert lied for her. Or maybe Rupert didn't know that she was a fraud. She was not employed on my mother's house staff. Jurgens, my mother's chef, and Stephen have both denied ever knowing her."

Another fax was handed around the door—the sailing schedules of cargo vessels entering and leaving Elliott Bay. They ran down the list. *Sea Bounty. Northern Star. Euripides. Prince William. Dolgota. Bright Sky. Southern Drifter.*

Several Cosco vessels, six Hanjin giants. The list went on and on.

Venus said, "Check both Russian and Chinese registries."

Rocco counted. "Five Russian, six Chinese."

"Who's in port now? Of the Russian and Chinese?"

Rocco read down the list. "No Chinese, far as I can tell. There's the *Dolgota*. It has Russian registry."

"May I see that list?"

Rocco handed it to her. She read it over twice, scrutinizing carefully, as if trying to interpret the Koran, to make it speak to her. In the end, she set the list on Rocco's desk and said, "So let's call the INS, share the wealth."

Rocco shook his head. "Hell, we don't know a damn thing they don't already know. And we're getting way off the beat here. We're looking for a twelve-year-old Asian kid who has run away from a murder charge and who may be armed and dangerous."

"Don't get me started, Rocco."

The phone rang again. Another Tim Diamond sighting, this time so phony baloney that Rocco was tempted to ignore it. But you never know, he thought. Got to follow up on every possible lead. "You want to ride along?" he asked her.

"You go ahead," she said. "I have an itch to scratch someplace else."

In the *Caprice*'s galley, Venus found the aluminum roasting pan. So Snow White had returned with it. Or else Rupert had brought it back and placed it in the galley cupboard.

She placed it in a plastic bag and locked it in the Audi's trunk. She drove to her Belltown condo, made a pot of coffee, and set the Sprint fax on the table. Sprint's records of Rupert Scree's calls included all phone numbers for incom-

ing and outgoing calls during the past billing period—
almost four weeks' worth of phone calls. She picked up her
phone and began calling numbers that had called Scree. She
got Ray's Boathouse, a restaurant near Shilshole Marina.
She checked off six calls from Ray's. She got a shipyard
where the *Caprice* had undergone its annual inspection.
Checked off that number. A couple of numbers that were
now out of service. Several calls from her mother's house.
Bella would have called Scree occasionally on boat business. And about thirty calls from one number. She dialed it.

A woman answered, her voice wary, tentative. "*Da?*"

She remembered then that Rupert had spoken to a
woman named Natalia on the phone. Russian name. On a
hunch, Venus said, "Natalia?"

"*Nyet.* Lina. You call for Ziggy?"

Ziggy Nelson? What other Ziggy could it be? Venus
said, "May I speak to Ziggy Nelson?"

Silence on the other end. Then the sound of the phone
receiver being dropped onto a hard surface. Venus could
hear the woman—or someone anyway—moving about.
Then in the distance, she heard Lina's voice say in a high
whine, "Natalia." Then again: "Natalia." another voice said
something in Russian and then two women held a heated
conversation in Russian. Venus listened, waited. Then Lina
came back to the phone. She said, "*Nyet,*" and hung up.

CHAPTER EIGHTEEN

Big buffalo clouds, dark and sodden, rolled across the fickle summer sky. The clouds opened and fine rain fell steadily, until eventually it gurgled in the gutters, its misty mantle warm and unrefreshing. Venus drove out of her condo's parking garage, turned right onto Western, and drove to Fifteenth Avenue West, the Audi's wipers softly urging raindrops off the windshield. She had to wait because the Ballard Bridge was raised to allow a two-masted yawl access to the locks. The yawl was a reproduction of an older ship, probably in town for the show of wooden boats the city held every summer. When the bridge came down, she drove across, rain still blurring visibility, and turned left, taking the shortcut through Old Ballard and then driving past the Hiram Chittenden Locks, where right now a million salmon were fighting their way up a fish ladder, back upstream to spawn and die in their rivers of origin. Where a boy named John Stark was reported as last having been seen near the locks. At Shilshole, she pulled into the parking lot and checked the waist pack where she kept her gun. She got out, locked up the Audi, and walked toward the marina.

In the office, the marina's harbormaster lounged in a tilt-back chair behind a puny battered desk, reading a paperback novel. She showed him her badge again and he rose wearily, went down to the dock, and unlocked the security gate. She walked along the dock to the very end. The *Dirty Blonde* sat in its slip, soft cabin lights glowing fuzzily in the falling mist. She was a Catalina 36, with a single mast and a fiberglass hull, poorly maintained. Venus hadn't expected to find the vessel in its slip; in fact, she had intended to visit the Chris-Craft next door, ask the Russian some more questions about Ziggy Nelson. But here was the *Dirty Blonde* herself, sails wrapped and covered to protect them against the weather, her fiberglass hull gently nudging its fenders against the dock.

Venus leaned down and knocked on a curtained glass porthole. She heard movement inside the boat, then saw a shadow. A hand reached up and pushed the porthole curtain aside. The woman's face that peered out into the night, seeking the origin of the knock, bore startled eyes, great flabby pink cheeks, and a nose like a lightbulb. Bleached-blond hair lay tangled across her forehead, and her twisted mouth seemed permanently scarred by fear. Venus waved her badge. Maybe the woman wouldn't read it carefully. The curtain went down and a few minutes passed in silence. The mist had grown chilly now, and Venus shivered from that or a fever—she didn't know which and didn't care. She knocked a second time, more insistently. The creature reappeared at the porthole window. Venus called out, "I'm a federal agent. Open the door, please. I just need to ask you some questions." False impersonation? Borderline.

This had the intended effect. Soon she heard the galley door creak open, and the figure popped up halfway out of the hold. In the faint light cast from a single overhead pole, Venus saw the woman. She was large with huge breasts, and limbs like gnarled logs. She wore a tight white turtleneck shirt, tight black capris, and a pair of canvas boat shoes. Her hair had been bleached white. When she spoke, Venus saw the gap in her teeth and heard the Russian accent.

"Vaht do you vant?" she asked suspiciously.

"May I come aboard, or do you want to come ashore to talk to me?"

The woman shrugged and nodded at the cabin. Venus stepped aboard the *Dirty Blonde* and went below, where the woman was now cleaning cigarette ashes off the galley table. A deck of playing cards was laid out—solitare. A single tumbler, which was full of clear liquid, sat beside the card game on the table. Looking at the shelf behind the seat cushions, she saw a bottle of Stoli and a small framed photograph of a man with lots of red hair, a bushy red beard, and Popeye biceps. The boat's interior had been sorely neglected, the wood trim moldy and rotting. Someone lived aboard. A sloppy person, or persons, who never put anything away, never found a home for pajamas or hairbrushes or soiled laundry. The dank cabin smelled like stale reefer smoke and boiled cabbage. The big woman indicated the seat cushions. Venus sat. The woman preferred standing in the passage that led to the forward berths. Venus introduced herself and said, "Do you speak English?"

"*Nyemnoga. Ya nygavaru po-angleyskki nyeh harascho.*" She paused, as if thinking, and added, "A liddle."

"What's your name?"

"Lina. Nyebolya."

"This your boat?" The woman nodded. Venus said, "Where's Ziggy Nelson?"

"Nut here."

"Any idea where I could find him?"

Lina reached into a pocket on the rear of her tight capris and fished out a crushed pack of Camels, then offered one to Venus, who declined. Lina found a Bic lighter on the shelf and lit up. She inhaled deeply. When she exhaled, she blew the smoke sideways, the way people do when they are conscious of irritating others with their smoke. She said, "I don't know nudding."

Venus said, "I'm looking for a boy. He's Asian, around twelve years old. His name is Tim. You know anything about him?"

Lina shook her head warily.

"You know a guy named Rupert Scree?"

Lina gazed through her cigarette smoke and moved back against the passageway, as if steadying herself against the doorjamb. She nodded once.

Venus told her about Rupert Scree. When Lina heard that Rupert had been shot and killed, she laughed sharply, reached for the tumbler, raised it to Venus, and said something that sounded like "Praise to Bog."

Venus studied the playing cards. She said, "You live here alone?"

"*Moshna?*" The woman's voice trailed an inflection.

Venus repeated the question. Lina nodded and said, "*Da.*"

"What about Ziggy? Where does Ziggy live?"

Lina tossed her arm wide, as if casting seeds. "The sea," she said.

Rupert had said that Ziggy Nelson had a wife. To Lina, she said, "Are you his wife?"

Lina shook her head.

Venus said, "Where can I find his wife?"

Lina's wary eyes snaked sideways.

Venus read the involuntary message. The wife was forward in one of the berths. Venus pointed and said, "Why don't you ask her if she'll speak to me."

Lina studied the tip of her cigarette, then backed into the passageway and, reaching behind her, slid open the door to the V berth. Soft Russian voices, then intensity in Lina's voice. Lina came back and jerked her thumb toward the V berth.

Venus found the woman prone on the berth, facedown, her head buried in her hands. Venus said, "Are you Natalia?"

The woman raised her head out of her hands, revealing a face swollen from crying. Even now tears poured forth onto her hands. They were wet, and she wiped them on the ratty coverlet. She rolled over on her side and said, "I am Natalia Derevyenka, Ziggy's wife. But you can't see Ziggy."

"Why's that?"

"Because he is dead." And she heaved and wept some more.

Natalia spoke better English than Lina. When she had recovered a little, she blew her nose into a tissue, wiped her hand across her eyes, and said, "They kill Ziggy. And then they kill Rupert. Now they will kill us."

"You and Lina?"

She nodded.

Venus said, "Who killed Rupert and Ziggy?"

Natalia sat up. She was a small, well-groomed woman with black hair and thick black eyebrows. The tender skin around her powder blue eyes was now scarlet from crying, and her black eyeliner had smeared, running down her face in dark rivulets that stained her cheeks. "I don't know who killed them," she said. "But whoever did works for Chekhov."

Chekhov! Venus stared. She said, "Larry Chekhov?"

Natalia nodded. "Yes. Larry Chekhov."

So the SOB was still alive. Larry Chekhov, the flashy Russian mobster Venus had wrestled off a floatplane's pontoon up in the San Juan Islands a few years back. Chekhov's boys had been smuggling endangered animal parts, bear paws and xiong dan, bear gall, from the United States to Asia. Chekhov had gone down into the icy San Juan waters and was never seen again, at least not by federal agents, who kept a warrant out for his arrest. Venus had always wondered if Chekhov had survived that frigid swim. Could anyone? She'd guessed not.

"Where's Chekhov?"

"I dun't know," said Natalia, raising up off the berth. She motioned for Venus to move into the main cabin. Natalia followed.

Lina had found two more tumblers and poured some Stoli into one of them and handed it to Natalia, who drank in large gulps, like a thirsty person drinking tap water. Lina held out the other tumbler toward Venus.

Venus felt her own forehead sweating. A little Stoli might help soothe the feverish brow. Still, she wasn't sure about these women. She shook her head. Lina put the glass down and lit up another cigarette. The three women sat at the table, Lina playing nervously with the deck of cards, now gathering all of them, stacking and shuffling them, slowly, slowly, then repeating the same routine as Natalia spoke.

"Ziggy worked for Rupert Scree," she began. "He was engineer on the ship Rupert skippered. A yacht named *Caprice*. After the little girl went overboard, the police interviewed Ziggy because he had gone down in the water to find her. He didn't find her, but he brought up her life vest from near where the girl went under. He gave it to the police, and then the police questioned him. After he gave his statement, a police detective told Ziggy he should not leave town for a few days or weeks, at least until they decided they had no more questions for him."

Natalia drank more Stoli. Venus stood up and leaned against the outside doorway. She felt hot and nauseous, claustrophobic inside the small cabin. Natalia continued.

"We live on this boat. Lina was just trying to cover for me. She is recently here from Saint Petersburg. She is Ziggy's cousin. She has been living on the boat with us for a few weeks. We were trying to find a way to keep her in America." She sighed, then blew her nose and wiped it. She said, "The day after the girl went overboard, Lina and I went shopping. When we came back, the boat was gone. We couldn't find Ziggy anywhere. We called around, but no one had seen him or the boat. Ziggy never called, never contacted me. That wasn't like Ziggy. He always called me. Lina and I stayed with a friend on a fishing boat in Salmon Bay. When we didn't hear and didn't hear, we finally got a ride back here to the marina. The *Dirty Blonde* was back here in the slip."

Natalia buried her face in her hands and sobbed. "They left his . . . They left his . . ." She struggled to get the word out. "Left his hand on this table. . . ."

Lina fell against Natalia and the two women held each other, moaning. Then Natalia looked up pleadingly at Venus and said, "Chekhov is the boss. They went against him. Chekhov had them killed."

Venus reached behind the women and picked up the framed photo of the redheaded man. Close-up, she saw his ruddy face, crudely handsome, his heavily tattooed arms, and his piercings—nose, ears, eyebrow. One silver ball stud protruded from underneath his lower lip. A real pincushion. She showed the photo to Natalia. "Is this Ziggy?"

Natalia's lower lip quivered. She nodded, then rested her head on Lina's big shoulder. "That was what he looked like," she said. "So pretty."

Venus was halfway along the slip when she reached Rocco on the phone; she told him to meet her at Shilshole. She stood on the dock in the misty rain, waiting for him. A single overhead dock light shone through the rain, casting a glow on the puddle at her feet.

Then she heard a silenced gun's soft report but didn't realize she'd been shot. She dropped sideways out of the light and crouch-walked into the shadow of the Chris-Craft. Another shot rang out. She felt warm liquid on her hand, touched it, saw the blood. Her arm was soaked. She thought the shots had been fired from the slip where the *Dirty Blonde* was moored. Peering around the Chris-Craft's hulky stern, she saw a figure running catlike along the slip, heading for the shore. She could see the hand holding the gun.

She backed up into the shadows and removed her gun from her waist pack. Blood poured down her arm, coating her shooting hand and her gun. She crouched, set the gun on the ground, and removed her shirt. With one hand and her teeth, she tore off a long sleeve and wrapped this around the wounded arm. She was almost finished, was pulling her shirt back on, when the figure appeared out of the shadows less than two yards distant and pointed a gun directly at her head. She saw the flashing teeth and the steady hand gripped around the gun. She backed up. The edge of the dock was about six inches behind her. She took a giant step backward and, as the gun went off, fell into the lake.

She had been in the water less than a minute when she

heard the sirens, and then Rocco arrived with an army of support officers. But now, all was silent and still, and the gunman seemed like a false memory. Except that her arm was bleeding. When she heard the officers' voices and saw the flashing blue lights, she raised up out of the bay and heaved herself ashore.

Bart said, "You okay?"

"Fine. Why?"

"Your forehead's sweating."

She wiped it off and kept reading. The bullet had only grazed her arm, leaving a shallow groove that required little attention. It was nothing compared to the jawline hit.

Earlier in the morning, she had navigated the news reporters and gone for a walk in the little park on the other side of the Pederson home. Just checking around, looking for anything. While she was gone, Rocco had dropped off the Russian women's printed statements. Bart had answered the door and placed them on the front hall table. When she returned home, she had to pass again through the barrage of newspeople, their cameras following her down the front walk, past the ancient cedar tree, and up to the gate of the Diamond estate. As a security guard opened up the pedestrian gate, she heard a voice call out, "Venus!" She turned and saw Kimberly Forget standing among the crowd of reporters. Kimberly waved at her and said, "Be careful, darlin'."

She walked up the drive and went into the house, where she found the reports on the hall table. She carried them out to the terrace and was now sifting through them with Bart, when Stephen came out onto the terrace, a telephone receiver in his hand.

"Police officer," Stephen said to Venus. "Asking for you. It's not Detective Rocco."

She put the phone to her face. She could feel the muscles in her rebuilt jawline tense. Her face felt hot, feverish. She might have an infection, she realized. When she identified herself, the female officer on the line said, "The ladies from the boat have asked to speak with you. The smaller one, Natalia, I think, says she has some information that might help locate your brother."

When Venus arrived at the Public Safety Building, the officer was waiting. She led Venus into a small conference room where Natalia and Lina sat at a small table, Natalia wiping tears, or sleep, off her face. Lina's large hands rested on the table, the fingers working on a cellophane-wrapped cough drop. Venus sat down across the table from the two women. Lina coughed, hacking, and asked for a glass of water. The officer brought a pitcher of water and three glasses, then stood near the door.

Natalia spoke, her voice lower and more controlled than the last time. She seemed to have recovered from the night before. Something about her demeanor was different, less phlegmatic, more determined. She said, "This is all Chekhov. I know him. I know what he can do."

Venus waited. Don't push too hard, she told herself.

Natalia wiped her face again. Lina hacked again and drank more water. Natalia shrugged her shoulders and said, "The detective promises us protection. Is that true?"

Venus said, "Detective Rocco has given you his word that as witnesses, you and Lina both will be protected by police officers around the clock and that you will be taken to a safe place where you won't be found."

Natalia said, "They took us to a motel. We're okay. They keep officers with us all the time. But what about tomorrow? What about the next day? And the next? How much longer will they protect us?"

Venus said, "Until you are out of danger. Presumably, that means until Chekhov is in custody."

"Ha." Natalia spoke to Lina in Russian. Lina echoed the "Ha." Natalia said, "We need a promise of total protection. Maybe give us new identities."

Was this some scam the two women had cooked up to procure a new identity for Lina as a legitimate U.S. resident? Or were the women really that terrified? Venus said, "I'll give you my word right now: You will be taken care of until Chekhov is in custody."

"Ha," Natalia said again. "He will escape. Chekhov never got caught before, and if now he is caught, he will escape."

"What do you know about my stepbrother Tim?"

Natalia spoke to Lina again. Lina nodded. Natalia said, "Lina saw the boy. He is Asian, no?" Venus nodded. "He is about ten or eleven, no?"

"Twelve. Small for his age."

Natalia nodded and spoke again to Lina. Lina launched into an animated, heartfelt monologue. She appeared very confident of what she was saying. Her hands drew air pictures, and then suddenly she clapped once and stopped talking, folding her hands on the table. Natalia looked at

Venus and said, "She saw the boy. She is sure it was him.
He had gone down to Chekhov's tugboat. Lina was on
board the boat. She had gone there to confront Chekhov
about my husband's murder. To tell the truth, Lina had
taken a gun with her and was planning to kill Chekhov. It's
a crazy idea, not possible, but Lina was out of her mind
from how they killed Ziggy. Lina had boarded the boat and
searched, but Chekhov wasn't around. When she was stepping off the boat onto the pier, she saw him."

"Tim?"

Natalia and Lina both nodded. Natalia said, "He was
standing on the dock. He spoke to Lina. But she didn't
understand what he was saying. She thinks he was asking
her a question, but she couldn't understand. She told him
she doesn't speak English and then he spoke to her in
Russian."

"In Russian?" Venus eyed the two women warily.

The women nodded in unison. Lina said, "*Da, pa-
ruskyi.*"

"Just a few words," explained Natalia. "He asked Lina
where was the tug's owner. Lina said in Russian that she
didn't know. Then the boy thanked her and walked down
the pier toward the end. She saw him walk behind a trash
container. Then she didn't see him again. She came back to
the boat and told me about what had happened. She was
supposed to be out at the market shopping for groceries, so
I was very surprised."

Something might be wrong with her story. Venus said,
"When did Lina got to the tugboat and see Tim on the
dock?"

Natalia stared. Two beats, then she said, "It was two
nights ago. The night of the fireworks."

Venus stood up. "What's the tugboat's name?"

"*Earline,*" said Natalia.

Earline. Where had she heard the name? Tim had mentioned it. Venus said, "Where's it moored?"

"Elliott Bay. Pier sixty-nine. Right downtown."

When Rocco's cell phone rang, he was just leaving the Greyhound station. Another Tim Diamond sighting. Dead end. Venus told him the Russian women's story. When she finished, she said, "I'm headed to the *Earline.*"

Rocco said, "I'll meet you there."

Alexis had awakened with a hangover and more nightmare memories, but as long as she didn't think about the monster jellyfish, her mood felt light. She had completely missed her own fifteen minutes of fame when Kimberly Forget went public with the "Lady and the Medusa" story on last night's news, Alexis saying into the camera, "That Diamond kid. The one they're all calling a murderer? He must have been telling the truth after all. Because that same thing stung me. I hope the jury believes him. Would I agree to be a witness for his defense? Absolutely. Because I have seen the big jellyfish." Alexis had missed it all. This morning, all she knew was that she had enjoyed a marvelous respite at the Four Seasons Olympic and it was time to head over to her antique shop to check on Frenchie, her assistant. When she entered the antique shop, she wasn't prepared for Frenchie's excited outburst. He shoved a computer printout in her face and said, "Look what I found on the Internet. The whole sea monster thing is spreading."

Alexis set her purse down on the counter and took the printout from Frenchie. It was a reprint of a story going around Frenchie's favorite Seattle chat room. On the first page, a headline read, "SEA MONSTER" DEVOURS BOATER IN ELLIOTT BAY.

According to intercepted police radio reports, the sailboat, *Kittilou* was crossing the bay from its marina, heading toward Alki Point yesterday afternoon, when, according to the skipper, a man named Blumenthal, a huge jellyfish broke the surface and startled his wife, who fell overboard and was attacked by the jellyfish.

Blumenthal who is in his thirties, witnessed the whole thing and suffered a heart attack as a result. He said the jellyfish was "bigger than a house." He claimed he saw the jellyfish use its tentacles to scoop his wife into its mouth and that he actually saw his wife inside the jellyfish, struggling in vain. Then the jellyfish went under with his wife.

Blumenthal was treated for shock and then admitted to a hospital, the location of which was not disclosed.

The Internet communiqué reminded readers that the skipper's description of the jellyfish matched the description given by the boy, Timothy Diamond, who was charged with murdering financier Nils Pederson's daughter. Diamond claimed a jellyfish had seized the girl. The author suggested that Blumenthal might have been hallucinating and/or imitating the Tim Diamond story in order to cover up the murder of his wife. No charges had been filed, but the police were investigating. Then, within hours of the incident, Blumenthal's heart suddenly stopped and he could not be revived. No other witnesses came forward, and after divers found no signs of Mrs. Blumenthal's body, the story never appeared in newspapers or on radio or television. The anonymous author of the report hinted that there must be some conspiracy.

"Well, that's just great, French," said Alexis. "If it's not dismissed as hysteria, now maybe people will listen to me."

People did. Around six o'clock that evening, when Alexis broke her promise to Bob and to herself by returning to their Belltown condo, just to gather a few fresh clothes, she parked her car in front of the building and walked to the front door. She had her key out and was just fitting it into the lock when a single bullet zinged across the street, striking Alexis Anders in the heart. She crumpled to the sidewalk.

"Look at this," Venus said, pointing into the water.

Rocco looked down. A late-afternoon sun pierced the clear green salt water that slapped gently against the pier. Rocco said, "Jellyfish bloom."

"Big jellyfish."

"Foot, maybe eighteen inches in diameter. None the size of Tim's bed."

They were at Pier 69. The tugboat *Earline* sat in the water, tied to pilings one pier south of the Orbit restaurant. They had checked the records. The *Earline*'s registered owner was listed as Icyfrost Seafood, but Tom Moran, Icyfrost's CEO, told Rocco he'd sold the boat to one of his employees. He couldn't seem to remember which employee, or even locate the bill of sale. They had searched the tug and had turned up one hopeful sign: fingerprints—Tim's. They had taken the fingerprints from the ignition. Had Tim tried to steal the boat? He had been on the *Earline*. A passerby had reported the sighting to the police. The witness had recognized Tim Diamond from television news broadcasts. The sighting was only an hour old. Now cops and civilian volunteers swarmed the pier. In Myrtle Edwards Park, the dragnet included every homeless soul who might have glimpsed the boy. It was assumed he couldn't be far away. A twelve-year-old accused murderer, maybe a double murderer, a fugitive from justice.

Rocco said, "You scuba dive?"

"Sure." She thought of Aloha Al. "Why?"

Rocco shook his head. "Never mind. You've got that wound."

"Hell, Rocco, it's only a graze. I can swim."

"I'm going to send divers down." Rocco got on the phone, ordered some divers from the Coast Guard's 9/11 team, and requested diving gear for himself and Venus.

Half an hour later, the sun still high enough to penetrate the water, they slipped into the frigid bay, coming alongside the *Earline*. Here lay a new world, once strange and lovely, now fouled with human refuse, the waste of ordinary activity on the steep hills of a sloping metropolis, fine and foul stuff that traveled in runoff drains down into this bay at the foot of the hills. Algae blooms coated rusted garbage with slimy green murk. The pier's pilings wore barnacle jackets, and a few sea anemones, yellow, orange, red, sucked at the barnacle flesh. Schools of herring swam amid the human trash, and jellyfish, mostly moon jellies and "fried eggs," floated everywhere in the sunlit bay. Rocco kept Venus close to the surface and let the more experienced divers go deep around the *Earline*'s hull, then down to the floor of the bay.

The tug's hull had recently been scraped clean of barnacles and painted. It shone smooth black underwater. They swam around it, bow to stern, port to starboard. Nothing peculiar. Just the usual sea scavengers. Nothing sinister. Rocco signaled time. When they surfaced, they climbed the ladder to the pier's deck, where a Coast Guard diver standing on the pier was holding one of Tim's brown leather sandals.

At nightfall, they lit up the sea floor with searchlights. The divers combed through Pier 69's pilings for signs of the boy. At 9:00 P.M., a diver brought up Tim's Einstein T-shirt. They continued searching.

The news media went wild. KIRO's junior reporter, Kimberly Forget, thick in the fray, saw her future unfold before her eyes. The biggest story of the year, and Kimberly was leading the pack. Still, they hadn't found a body down there. Kimberly stuck close to the scene.

The search continued through the night and into the soft light of dawn. Venus and Rocco stayed on the pier. Someone brought hot coffee, along with some sandwiches, which they didn't eat. Bart came down to the pier with Moses. They had been at Myrtle Edwards Park, searching the paths, coming up empty.

Rocco handed Venus a fresh coffee. He said, "Maybe you should go home."

She shook her head, warmed her hands on the coffee cup, and then drank.

"You need some rest," he said. He didn't like the way she was shivering. Rocco motioned at Bart, who came over and said, "What's up?"

"Take her home," said Rocco. "She's not well. She might have a fever."

"I'm not going anywhere," she said.

Bart slipped an arm around her. "Just a nap, Sis. Then I'll bring you back."

She tried fighting them off. She had to stay, had to be there if they found . . . something. She hadn't even noticed the fever creeping up on her, and by the time Bart and Rocco placed her prone in the back of a patrol car, she didn't know that she was delirious.

Bart had to explain to Rocco that she'd contracted malaria in Asia. Once in awhile, it reared its ugly head. This was malaria fever. She was sick and needed help. Bart got into the patrol car's passenger seat. The car sped to the University of Washington Medical Center, where a specialist in tropical diseases met them in the emergency room. Venus had tremors and delirium; her teeth chattered as if they would break. The doctor pumped her full of quinine-based intravenous fluids and anything else he could think of that might work. He said, "That's about all we can do. Give her the kitchen sink and hope for the best."

A hospital's intensive care unit. A small figure lying on a stretcher, tubes and wires stuck to her arms, her legs. Her ashen face jerking from side to side, her eyes starkly focused on inner turmoil, her dry, parched lips moving to an alien litany bearing witness to the current score: Parasites winning. Fever rising. Nurses checking monitors, IV bags, vital signs, whispering prayers and eulogies over their patient, whoever she was. More alien tongue-lashing. More jerking body parts. The bedside phone rings and rings and rings. Convulsion. Room crawling with white figures. Ice-cold bath. Patient yelling now. Another convulsion. Night falls.

An Asian man, very handsome, dressed in black leather, walks down the hospital corridor and then into the intensive care unit. Turns a corner, enters her room. He looks down at her. She's comatose, so he says, "Are you faking?"

She doesn't respond. He feels her forehead. No, she's not faking. He sits with her for several hours, willing her to wake up. Finally, he leaves her room, walks down the corridor to the cafeteria, buys a cup of coffee. When he returns to her room, the bed is empty, the IV lines dripping into the bedsheets.

In the early-morning light, more buffalo clouds thundered in off the ocean. The clouds open slowly, and by morning rush hour, a weeping rain fell over the city. Outside University of Washington Medical Center, Venus hailed a taxicab. She told the Sikh driver where to go and said to hurry. He took the Interstate at 90 mph. When she arrived at Pier 69, the divers were changing shifts.

CHAPTER TWENTY

July 7

She saw an evidence van, and officers wearing SPD vests scouring the pier. Had something else been brought to the surface? She saw news media vans, their searchlights streaming into the bay. She asked around. People shrugged or said they didn't know, just that a search was taking place. For the Diamond boy. She had been gone from the scene for—what? A few hours at most. Had they pulled out anything else? A grim-faced cop said he wasn't authorized to give out information. If she wanted information, she should find Rocco. She looked around, didn't see him anywhere.

The rain fell in a soft, steady shower. She wiped raindrops off her face. She called Bart. Twenty minutes later, he arrived with hot coffee and sandwiches, and he had Moses Freeny with him. They pushed through the news reporters camped on the pier, Kimberly Forget among them.

Venus and Bart stood, warming their hands around coffee cups, when they heard a commotion at the end of the dock. They sprinted. A crowd of divers, police officers, and medics had formed a tight knot on the pier. Where was Rocco? Someone said he'd gone for coffee. A minute later, she saw him break from the tight knot, move through the gentle rain, walking toward her, his facial muscles tight and strained, and he wasn't carrying coffee. He was carrying a clear plastic evidence bag. Inside, a watch. Tim's Swatch. The one she'd given him last Christmas. With astronauts on the face. Nothing else. He handed it off to an officer. He watched the officer go away, then looked at her, but though he tried to speak, nothing came out. She grabbed his shirt, pulled him close, and put her face up to his.

"What?" she said.

Gently, he removed her hand. He said, "Take it easy."

She grabbed him again, her fisted hand hard against his sternum. She shoved him backward against the pier railing. "What?" she yelled.

Bart said, "Stay cool, Sis."

Rocco exhaled. "Not here," he said. He tried to steer her off the pier, but she refused to move. He grabbed her hand.

"What's going on that I don't know about?" she said.

Rocco pressed his lips together. He gripped her shoulders. He didn't know what else to do. He said, "They found him."

A cold sickness clutched her guts.

Bart buried his face in his hands. "Oh God no."

Rocco said, "I'm sorry."

She pulled her hand away from his, made a tighter fist, held it closed, like a womb, a safe place where she held the last vestiges of hope. They stood at the railing and watched through the rain as Tim's body was raised up from the murky bay. He was placed on the dock and Rocco himself attempted to resuscitate him, but clearly he had been dead for a while.

Her fist opened and she exploded. She ran down the dock. When Bart started after her, Rocco pulled him back. She ran down the pier, heading straight for the bay. She crossed over to Pier 70, where the Orbit's tables and chairs were set out on the terrace. She threw chairs and tables, and soon the reporters went after her. Rocco threw them off, punching a couple who got too aggressive. He reached her at the end of the pier. She was still throwing tables. Rocco let her rage. He felt the same way. The girl's death had been bad enough. Now another child, this one definitely murdered. Rocco hadn't told her yet how the boy had died. Didn't want to tell her, didn't even want to know himself, but he did. He had seen the garrote marks when the body was pulled up off the sea floor. He hadn't been in the water long, maybe thirty minutes at most—before the divers went down the first time. The boy had been bound at the ankles and wrists. A filthy rag had been used to gag him. Some kind of rope had been used to strangle him. His upper lip was split open. He might have tried to bite the killer.

When she had exhausted herself, he led her to his car. Before opening the door, he held her the way he'd held so many other aggrieved relatives whose loved ones had died brutally at the hands of sick and evil men. What else can you do when you're the messenger?

Tim's body was taken to the medical examiner's office. Rocco drove her there and stayed by her side, and when she tripped and nearly fell on the slippery floor in the morgue, he caught her and held her until she steadied. She was cool now, as if frozen. Rocco had seen this in hundreds of people who had lost loved ones suddenly and violently. Usually, the frozen shock came first, then the rage. In her case, she got the nasty business taken care of first, and now, Rocco knew, because, like him, she was a cop, she would hold it together in public. No more outbursts, no more rage, nothing for the public to see. But inside, she would be a raving animal, and he knew that soon enough she would want revenge. Why did he know this about her? She was like him. If Rocco had lost a loved one, especially a child, he'd hunt down the killer and torture him to death. In about fifteen minutes, she would probably start thinking that way.

He steered Venus and Bart into the cold room, following the ME. The boy's body lay on a gurney just inside the room where the autopsy would be performed. Rocco held onto her arm as they drew near the gurney. He could feel her shivering, her taut muscles straining against the inner ravings. The ME slowly drew back the sheet. She looked down at Timmy's face. His eyes were shut and he seemed asleep, just like the other night in his bedroom, when he had fallen asleep with the jellyfish book splayed across his chest. She placed a hand to his cheek, lay her head on his small chest, and wept silently.

CHAPTER TWENTY-ONE

It's Venus, Mother. I'm on my cell phone, coming down the hall now. Tell Sid to let me in."

Silence, then: "I thought it was Echo."

Echo, the favorite daughter, Bella Diamond's pride and joy.

"No, it's not Echo. It's your least-favorite offspring. I want you to open the door and let me in."

Silence. Venus turned right down the long hall toward her mother's private quarters. Sid the bulldog snapped out of a doze and resumed his stiff blockade at the door. Venus waited a couple minutes. Still no sound from inside.

Sid said, "Budge off."

She looped her leg around his and threw him to the floor. She didn't have to take the key from him; he gladly handed it over.

The rain had passed, leaving the afternoon air already

sultry, and the sun beat straight into Bella's bedroom windows. The heavy drapes were drawn, but the French doors were open. Venus parted the drapes.

"I wish you wouldn't do that, Venus. I don't care for light just now."

She rested against bolsters and pillows in the very center of her canopied bed, a scarlet silk kimono wrapped around her perfect form. One limp hand lay across her normally razor-sharp eyes and in spite of her troubles, Venus noticed, she had applied lipstick and powder, and her hairdo looked fresh. Maybe her hairdresser was allowed inside the private hive. Beside her, snuggled against the scarlet silk, her aging shar-pei, Pansy, lay curled up asleep, panting softly. On the bed lay a tea tray with a pot, a cup and saucer, and a small plate of untouched cinnamon buns. Stephen must have brought breakfast in earlier in the day. No one had told her yet about Tim.

Venus drew the drapes open wider. A splendid vista appeared, the bright sun riding a blue-button sky, and the aquamarine Sound with little peaked whitecaps and sailboats like paper cutouts on the horizon. Venus said, "Aren't you hungry, Mother?"

"Pull those drapes about halfway shut, dear."

Venus adjusted the drapes. "It's a brilliant afternoon," she said. "How about we go for a walk in the garden?"

"Please correct your grammar. I do not feel like a walk."

"Well then, what *would* you like to do? You need some exercise."

Bella reached for her cigarettes and struck a match to one. She had given up smoking two decades ago, but since Tim's arrest she had revisited the habit.

"I get plenty of exercise on my treadmill. I don't need anything except to be left alone. And what have you done to your hair now, Venus? It looks absolutely dreadful. You remind me of a half-plucked dandelion caught in a wind tunnel."

"Never mind that."

"What you need is a decent hairstylist. You never could manage your hair. Now, if only Echo were here, she could show you what to do. Echo is so stylish."

"Mother, get out of bed and get dressed."

"How dare you speak to me in that tone of voice? I take orders from no one, particularly my daughters."

Venus sat down in a wing chair beside the canopied bed. "What if I brought Bart in here? Would you listen to Bart?"

"My sons have the good grace and manners not to attempt ordering me around. Unlike my daughters. Dagne has been phoning twice a day every day, and now she is threatening to visit. I don't need my children invading my home. Honestly, I have a good mind to change my will, to cut all of you children out, leave you with nothing, which is what you all deserve. Why don't you all just go away and mind your own business?"

"Timmy's dead, Mother. He was murdered."

She lay very still, one hand across her heart. With the other, she put the cigarette to her mouth and drew deeply. Tears welled in her eyes, and spilled over onto her perfect face. When she could finally speak, she said, "Get out of my house and leave me the hell alone."

Venus said, "Did it ever occur to you that Tim might have been telling the truth?"

"Not in the past three years. I want you to go away and leave me alone."

"All right, have it your way," she said. "Go on wallowing in your selfish humiliation. Stay in here in the dark until you pine away. Desert your family and friends like you deserted the boy who needed you more than he needed anyone else in the world. Break all of our hearts like you broke his. Go ahead, feel sorry for yourself. Have it your way. You always have it your way, don't you, Mother?"

She went out the way she had come, leaving the Red Queen to her cold tea and buns. And her denial.

A child's funeral is a terrible event. Two children buried on the same day brought the city to grief. Nils and Ingrid Pederson, accompanied by young Henry and several hundred mourners, gave little Pearl her first and last bouquet of roses at Good Shepherd Lutheran Church in Ballard. Uniformed police officers kept the news media at bay and private security guards hugged the small family circle: Nils, Ingrid, Henry, Cora, Ingrid's two brothers and their families, cousins from Minneapolis and Oslo. Friends, neighbors, business associates, city hall cronies, they all came to bear witness to a death whose means and motive they could not comprehend, to grieve for Pearl, the little girl who would never grow up, never grow out of her unfortunate homeliness to become Miss Ballard, never taste the victory of college graduation, the passion of opening up to a lover, or having children of her own. Little Pearl had been deprived of all that life might have offered her, the good and the terrible, the pain and the ecstasy. Her parents and her brother had been deprived of the girl's presence in their lives, for better or for worse, an only daughter, an only sibling. Inside that cherrywood casket, her remains were hidden from all the gentle and regretful gazes that fell upon its flower-festooned lid, where a simple silver cross marked her Christian burial. During the service, Ingrid and Nils held each other and wept into their embrace. Henry held his hands over his face, choosing not to share his innermost turmoil with anyone else. The advocate, Dr. Lane, had been asked to accompany Henry to the funeral, and now she sat beside the boy, calm and poised, there if he needed her. Once during the service, Dr. Lane passed a fresh linen handkerchief to Henry and indicated that he should pass it on to his mother, whose own hankie now was soaked with her tears. Henry had taken the handkerchief from Dr. Lane, inspected it as if it might contain a hidden object, and passed it on to Ingrid. Nils caught Dr. Lane's eye in apparent gratitude. In the rear of the church, Detective Sanchez watched.

At the cemetery on Aurora Avenue, the burial site had been cordoned off and the funeral procession allowed to drive right up to the grave site, which was located on a small knoll facing south toward the city and Mount Rainier. The sky was electric blue that morning, the softest breeze teasing the mourners' tear-stained cheeks. Nils knelt as his daughter's casket was lowered into the dark earth. Ingrid stood beside him, her hand on his heaving shoulder. Nils wept over the casket, his tears the last element to touch the burial box before the first fistful of earth, tossed by Henry, fell gently into the grave.

Afterward, two hundred mourners gathered at the Pederson home, where the wake was solemn and strangely silent, Lutheran-quiet. Mourners came and went, showing their engraved invitations and identification to security guards. On the parking strip, the major news networks and the cable channels focused on the local city celebrities arriving to pay their respects: police chief, judges, city councilmen, a well-known Swedish-American politician from the statehouse, the governor himself, and his family, including his little daughter, exactly Pearl's age, were Pearl still alive. They filed past the barricade that had been erected to hold back the news cameramen and reporters, and the looky-loos. The street was full of looky-loos, and there was more yet to look at, just on the other side of that giant cedar that marked the property line between two grieving families.

That afternoon, at Our Lady of Fatima Church in Magnolia, the ancient priest who delivered the eulogy at Tim's funeral recalled his own vague memory of the boy. "He was a dandy little boy," said the priest, "full of energy and enthusiasm. And a very bright boy. What may or may not have been going through his mind and his heart and his soul these recent days is not for us to know. We feel certain he was not guilty of the terrible act lately attributed to him. We know that he was basically a good boy, one who had suffered much loss from the very beginning of his life, an orphan rescued from abandonment and abuse, by a loving adoptive mother."

Venus sat beside Bella in the front pew at the center of the church. Bella had left her lair, and now faced the grim reality. No one blamed her for Tim's death. No one but herself. Now she wept silently behind her sheer black veil, holding a handkerchief not unlike Ingrid's against her mouth, as if to stanch the flowing pain. Her normally stiff upper lip had crumpled into an aggrieved grimace that no one dared stare at. On her right side, her son Bart held his arm around his mother's shoulders, and beside Bart sat his twin sister, Echo, and then Rex, the oldest brother, and Dagne, the firstborn of the Diamond children. They had all come from afar to say their farewells to Tim, their adopted brother, whom they little understood but whom they had loved and cherished. Besides the family, not many came to mourn the boy's passing. The last curse of the adopted is a funeral marked by empty pews. And also, he was an accused killer, a boy with a reputation for telling lies, some of them fantastic and wonderful, but lies just the same. He had killed and then had been killed. Speculation leaned toward a revenge murder, and the extended Pederson family and Nils and Ingrid's wide circle of friends now fell under the careful scrutiny of the Seattle Police Department. The sensational character of the boy's life and death attracted a crowd of the curious, who were kept at a distance from the actress and her family by a small army of private security guards hired by Stephen, who at this very moment was up at the house, supervising the caterers and servers who would work the wake.

The old priest droned on, hypnotized by his own monotonous voice, his vague and generalized eulogy growing more vapid as the minutes passed.

Venus sat stonily, her eyes dry, her face set into an unreadable expression. In truth, she was containing rage, but no one had to know that. Rocco knew. He sat in the pew behind Venus, turned slightly sideways, checking out in his peripheral vision the looky-loos. Among them, he saw a good looking Amerasian man. The Amerasian man's eyes met Rocco's. They shared something. So this was Louie Song.

During the family eulogy, given by Bart, Venus felt a hand touch her arm. She looked up. Kimberly Forget leaned across the pew and handed Venus a note, then turned and walked to the rear of the church. Venus opened the note and read, "Listen carefully. Watch out for Nils." The message was typed, not handwritten, and it wasn't signed.

At Communion, Venus noticed a woman dressed in a lightweight raincoat step to the altar. The coat's hood was pulled over her head, her face barely visible behind wide sunglasses. The only part of her exposed was her legs, pale legs, the shade of the deacon's surplice. The woman stood before the deacon, accepting the host, allowing the deacon to place it on her tongue. She made the sign of the cross— in reverse. Hands folded respectfully, she walked in front of the grieving family, looked directly at Venus, then walked to the rear of the church.

Those legs. From the *Caprice*. Venus remembered Snow White's pale legs. Venus turned around and saw the woman step through the side exit into the church parking lot. Venus followed, as the woman had intended, straight into her trap.

Outside, near the church building, the sun beat down on the big hearse. Venus looked around. The hearse was just behind her and to the left. The parish choir was singing "On Eagle's Wings," their melody reaching a crescendo. Venus heard a gunshot. The bullet zinged off the hearse's hood. She bolted, then saw the woman running toward a black Cadillac Seville, a gun in her hand. The woman turned and fired again, once, twice, three times, each shot barely missing Venus. Someone came out of the church and yelled, "What's going on out here?" The woman fired once more toward Venus, then jumped into Cadillac. Venus saw the car pull out into the street, but no one saw license plates, because there weren't any.

CHAPTER TWENTY-THREE

July 12

Venus had Rocco on the phone. "How in the hell did she get loose?"

Rocco sighed. "Calm down, for chrissake. You don't know that that was Natalia."

"Don't test my patience, Rocco. I'm sure the woman who shot at me is Natalia."

Rocco sighed wearily. "What makes you so sure?"

"Same height, weight. The legs I recognize from Snow White on the *Caprice*. So she knew Rupert. Natalia knew Rupert. And the sign of the cross."

Rocco scowled. "What sign of the cross?"

"At Communion, she made a reverse sign of the cross. Like a Russian Orthodox, not like a Roman Catholic. Rocco, you know damn well that was Natalia."

"I don't know anything for sure," Rocco said. "Any noncatholic might flub the sign of the cross."

"But she escaped."

Rocco held his head. He was tired and needed sleep. He said, "Calm down. We've already picked her up. They were at a gas station on lower Queen Anne. She was coming out of the rest room when we nabbed her. Her partner got away. We didn't see him, or her. The vehicle slipped through our fingers. Anyway, the gas station attendant says she drove away in a dark blue van. Not a black Cadillac Seville."

"Oh great. How the hell did she escape?"

"We had them stashed at a little Sea-Tac motel, a cheap joint out in the sticks. The department's economizing, and they'd only assigned one guard. He went out for food and Natalia just walked away. Lina said she didn't see Natalia leave the motel. They had adjoining rooms. Lina was no help at all, even through an interpreter. She just clammed up and buried her face in her knitting."

"Lina knits?"

"Maybe crochets. How would I know? Something with needles. Anyway, the women weren't under arrest; they were being protected. We couldn't legally prevent Natalia from leaving protective custody. We've moved them into the city, to the Edgewater Inn. They've got a twenty-four-hour guard and they're locked in."

"Natalia tried to kill me, Rocco."

"I repeat: You do not know the identity of the woman who shot at you. We have nothing to go on except a few bullet cartridges, which so far we haven't matched to any crime."

"Why don't you arrest her, throw her in the can?"

Rocco said, "We haven't found the gun. She swears that you're fingering the wrong person. I can't arrest her for having pale white legs."

"What about Chekov? You located him yet?"

"Hell, Venus, we're not Interpol. Cut us a break."

The malaria fever had taken its usual toll, but time and rest would eventually heal that malady. No medication would bring Tim back. Tim was gone, and with the funeral over, Venus believed it for the first time.

She found her mother's chef, Jurgens, in the kitchen. Jurgens had a face like a smashed pillow and little Santa Claus lips. He was tall, and now he bent over a huge pot of something exceptionally fragrant with aromatic herbs. She could identify rosemary and fennel, but that was all. "What's cookin'?" she asked him, trying to sound cheery.

Jurgens tossed some fine powder into the pot. "A bouillabaisse," he said. "One of your mother's favorite comfort foods. I hope this will wake up her taste buds. I'm worried about her."

Venus leaned against the kitchen counter, watching Jurgens work. He had a firm, sure hand, no hesitation, and he worked fast. Now he added the fish, reciting them, "Red snapper, pompano, fresh halibut, scallops, clams, mussels, and, ya, some very nice pieces of lobster. The trick here is to keep the fish morsels in two-inch slices and the smaller shellfish whole. I keep the clams and mussels in their shells. It gives a better presentation."

She waited until he brought the stew to boiling and set it at a rapid roil. She said, "How about some iced tea?" She made a pitcher of iced Darjeeling, fetched two glasses from the pantry, and carried them out to the terrace. Jurgens came out, wiping his hands on a fresh towel, then swabbing his forehead, moist from the bouillabaisse. He sat down across from Venus and drank half a glass of tea in one long swallow. They talked about Tim. Jurgens had been fond of the boy, and now he related his favorite memories of Tim, mostly kitchen capers that involved Tim snitching sweet rolls and Jurgens's special Danish sausage to hoard in his room. Most recently, when Tim had been confined to his room after the arrest, Jurgens had smuggled in special treats. Venus saw tears glisten in Jurgens's eyes. When he had finished reminiscing, she asked him about Snow White.

Jurgens shook his head. "Never had her working for me. I don't know who she could be, but she's never cooked in my kitchen, at least that I'm aware of."

"Let me ask you something, Jurgens," she said. "If you wanted to give someone food poisoning—I mean really raunchy poisoning—how would you go about it? What would you use?"

Jurgens folded his graceful hands. "Let's see now. First thing, I would choose a bacterial agent like *E. coli,* or botulism can kill, too, so that it would appear to be an accident caused by tainted food. But you can't just go down to the supermarket and order it. It's got to be growing on something like, oh, romaine lettuce. Or beef. I'd be more inclined to use the beef. But, like I said, first I'd have to get hold of some *E. coli* bacteria. After that, it'd all be easy."

"And folks can croak from botulism?"

"Ya, sure. Botulism often kills."

"But they don't always croak, right?"

Jurgens tilted his head to one side. "Ya, some of them live. But it makes them really sick. Horrible, horrible vomiting and diarrhea. You don't want to hear about it."

She traced a pattern on the sweating pitcher of iced tea. Jurgens poured them more tea. "Why do you want to know about food poisoning?" he asked. "Are you planning to kill Stephen?" He put a hand to his mouth. "Forgive me," he said. "I shouldn't joke about these things."

"We need to laugh, Jurgens. It helps ease the pain." She changed the subject. "This girl I asked you about, the one who reminds me so much of Snow White, I think it's possible that she tried to kill the *Caprice*'s captain by giving him food poisoning."

Jurgens made a face. "I thought Rupert Scree died from a gunshot wound."

"He did. But a few days before that, I was visiting him on the boat. That's when I saw Snow White—I think her actual name is Natalia—with the roasting pan. Scree told me she had brought him some food from Mother's kitchen, from here. He told me she was the new chef."

"Which, of course, was a lie."

"After the woman left, Scree and I had a drink and talked. About half an hour into our visit, he started holding his stomach, like it was bothering him. I asked him about it. He said he just had a little indigestion."

"What did you both have to drink?" She told him. Jurgens said, "Nothing wrong with that. Maybe it was indigestion. Indigestion can hurt, and it can give you mild symptoms of food poisoning, even though you haven't been poisoned. He probably just had a sour stomach."

Venus shook her head. "But something's wrong with this picture. For one thing, Scree lied to me about her. And then yesterday at the funeral, the same woman showed up and fired a gun at me."

"I remember all that commotion. I didn't actually see her fire a gun at you, but I remember seeing you leave the church and then hearing gunfire. And then she escaped in a red car without plates. I saw it on the news last night."

Venus said, "I have the roasting pan. But the food was all either eaten or thrown away, so there's nothing to test."

Jurgens raised an eyebrow. "Where did you find it?"

She said, "On the *Caprice*. In the galley. It didn't match any of the other kitchenware, but it was stuffed in the cupboard with other pots and pans. Maybe forensics could find something. I doubt it, though. It's been washed and dried."

"People miss corners and little crevices," said Jurgens. "That's where a lot of dangerous bacteria grows."

Song answered his cell phone the way he always had. "Talk," he said rudely.

She struggled with her anxiety. She had meant to call him sooner, but things had gotten in the way. Now she needed a favor. Song would think that was the only reason she was calling. Maybe it was. "I've been meaning to call you."

A little silence, then Song said, "Yeah, like I've been meaning to take up ballet."

"I want to see you."

"Why?"

"It's time I properly apologized. For the incident."

"Hell, Venus, you don't have to apologize for anything." Another silence, then he said, "I say we forget it ever happened, go on being friends, like always."

"Just friends?"

She heard him take a long, deep breath; then he said, "I need some time."

"I want to see you. Maybe in a day or two, when things calm down."

"God, Venus, I'm sorry," he said. "I loved Tim, too."

"I know." She paused. "I need a favor, Louie."

He might have responded with something cruel, said, You have a goddamn nerve asking me for favors after what you did to me. Instead, he said, "What do you need?"

She needed a roasting pan flown down to Fish & Wildlife's forensics lab in Ashland, Oregon. Delivered to Claudia Paganelli. Claudia was Fish & Wildlife's regional forensics doc. Venus had called Claudia, and Claudia had agreed to run some tests. Venus needed Song to fly the pan and a copy of a lab report down to Claudia by chopper.

Song said, "Where shall I meet you?"

"I have an appointment in Chinatown. Let's meet there."

"What kind of appointment?"

"Don't be a Nosey Parker." She sighed. "Okay, so it's with my shrink."

Half an hour later, she stood at the entrance of Dr. Wong's office building in Chinatown, watching Song ride up on his Harley. As he parked the bike and walked toward her, she felt her heart race. Song, dressed in black leather, his silken black hair, his almond eyes, this Amerasian vision of grace and beauty. He embraced her, held her close for a long time. When he let her go, he said, "I thought you were going to die."

"When?"

"In the hospital. I came to see you. You probably don't remember. You were comatose." He touched her face lightly. "God, I was scared. And then I came back and your bed was empty. And then, after they found Tim, I thought for sure you'd be a goner, that the fever would get worse and kill you."

"I'm okay. A little tired, a little weak, but okay."

She handed him the package and he sped off on the Harley, leaving her standing in the street, watching him fade into the distance.

Rocco hadn't expected her. When she brought the lab reports into his office later that day, he looked up from his computer keyboard and shook his head. "I don't want to see those," he said.

"Don't doubt till you hear me out."

"You sound like Johnny Cochran.

Venus tossed Claudia's lab report on his desk and said, "Read it."

Rocco looked up over his reading glasses and saw that she was serious.

Paganelli had found concentrations of a powerful toxic poison in the roasting pan's crevices. The toxicologist at Fish & Wildlife's forensics lab in Ashland, Oregon, had identified it as fentanyl, a powerful and deadly toxin.

Before Rocco could say anything, she dropped another lab report on his desk, this one an analysis of blood taken

at Harborview from Alexix Anders on the night she suffered a venomous sting. Venus had obtained the sample
through Olson's contact at Harborview. Paganelli's analysis stated that the blood sample contained an as-yet-
unidentified toxin, possibly jellyfish venom, but from
which species was not yet known.

"Alexis Anders appeared on television, claiming to
have been stung by a monster jellyfish at Orbit Restaurant
over on Pier 70. The day after her television interview, in
which she described the jellyfish and referred to Tim's jellyfish story, she was shot dead in front of her Belltown
condo."

"You don't have to remind me. Sanchez tells me we're
holding the husband. He hasn't been formally charged yet.
We have a good case against him, though."

"You might want to reconsider. Alexis Anders may
have seen something she wasn't supposed to see. In any
case, we can demonstrate that Snow White, whoever she is,
tried to poison Rupert Scree."

Rocco sighed, sat back, and folded his arms across his
chest. She edged into a chair, shook off a lingering chill,
and waited for him to speak. He said, "All of a sudden, I'm
thirsty."

They walked to the Proletariat Pub. Rocco ordered
light beer for himself and a Coke with lime for her. Rocco
poured out his beer into a glass and said, "Kimberly Forget
was right about the victim advocate, the so-called child
psychologist. We checked every county and city agency. We
checked our own victim advocates program. Dr. Lane
doesn't exist. At least not in any of our programs. I had the
department check all the private social service agencies in
the city. No one knows her. In other words as Forget suspected, she's a fraud. Fortunately, your nemesis Stephen,
recorded the red Jetta's license plate. It's registered to
Icyfrost Seafood Company. Same company that owned the

Spindrift before it exploded all to hell. The Earline, too, is registered to Icyfrost. The red Jetta's one of a fleet of vehicles they own. We're checking out the CEO now, guy named Tom Moran. So far, he looks pristine."

Back at the office, she said, "I want to go over there. I want to talk to this Mr. Icyfrost. But first, I'd like to see the videotapes from the *Caprice*. All of them." Rocco shrugged. He didn't care. He'd already seen them. They walked to the evidence room. Rocco checked out all the *Caprice* videotapes. They went to the conference room, where Rocco fed them into the VCR.

"Get out the popcorn," he said. They sat back and watched two hours of activity aboard the *Caprice*.

There wasn't much of interest on the security videos. A lot of jumpy camera angles of vacant rooms. Occasionally, a few frames of Rupert at the helm, Rupert in the main salon, pulling a beer out of the fridge, Rupert in the passageway, entering the elevator. Tedious stock-in-trade security videos. Watching them, Venus began to feel drowsy, but then near the end of the tape, something caught her eye. She grabbed the remote, put the machine on pause, then on rewind, and replayed the segment that had caught her eye.

"What'd you see?" asked Rocco.

It was a scene inside Rupert Scree's private quarters. "Watch the background here," she said.

The stateroom was in the foreground, its rear window in the background. Through the window appeared the face of a man. He had a beard, a red one, and red hair on his head. He wore a navy-and-white-striped sailor's shirt. He was peering into Rupert's private stateroom. Venus stopped the action.

"Ziggy Nelson," she said. "When was this segment taped?"

Rocco checked his notes. "The day Pearl went overboard."

Venus rewound the tape to the first frame. "Now watch carefully," she said. Rupert's stateroom appeared. She let the tape run a few frames, then froze the image. She said, "Look."

Someone exiting the stateroom. Only his backside visible. Wearing a navy-and-white-striped sailor's shirt.

Rocco shrugged. "So it's Ziggy again. So what?"

"Check out the left side of the frame. Scree's clothes cupboard."

Rocco looked. Half of Tim Diamond's face appeared around the door of the clothes cupboard. Rocco said, "What's he doing in there?"

"Spying."

Rocco's cell phone rang. The officer on the line said, "There's been some trouble at the Pederson home. Squad cars are on their way, but you need to get over there fast. An emergency," the officer told Rocco. "The Pederson boy, Henry, has gone missing."

The Edgewater Inn on Elliott Bay is an aluminum-plated tourist bunker, an architect's nightmare. Inside, down a dark corridor, a police officer stood guarding the Russian women's suite. When Venus showed him her badge, he knocked first and then held the door open for her. Lina and Natalia sat sprawled over a long couch, watching a television soap opera, Lina crocheting fervently and Natalia painting her toenails.

When they saw Venus, Lina reached over and punched the TV remote's off button. The northwestward-facing windows opened just a few feet above the bay. You could fish from the windowsill. Through the open windows, the

afternoon sun washed across the living room and through a
wide doorway, into a rear bedroom, Venus could see pools
of sunlight cascading across an unmade king-size bed.
Clothing was strewn everywhere. A cool breeze blew gently
off the bay, and the fresh air helped dilute an eclectic odor
of marijuana, perfume, and microwave popcorn.

Lina set her crocheting aside and heaved upward off
the couch. She mumbled something in Russian, plucked a
full ashtray off the coffee table, and lumbered into the tiny
kitchenette. Tap water ran as she washed out the dregs of
cigarette and reefer ash.

Natalia carefully finished painting a toenail, then
placed the brush in the bottle and screwed it tight. "We
weren't expecting you," she said, halfheartedly chagrined.
She got up and walked around, picking up stray objects,
the whole time keeping her toes curled upward so as not to
smudge nail lacquer on the carpet. "Can I give you tea?"
she asked Venus. Venus said, "No thanks, no tea just
now," and Natalia sat down again.

"Why did you try to kill me, Natalia?"

Natalia rested one foot on the coffee table and resumed
painting her toenails. Venus repeated the question. Natalia
glanced up from her toenails, the brush poised between her
thumb and index finger. Her full lips parted and she stared
at Venus. Smiling disingenuously, she said, "You are a crazy
girl." Then she bent back over her toenails, applying the
crimson lacquer.

Venus kicked the coffee table and Natalia's pedicure
went all wrong. "Now look!" cried Natalia angrily. "You
have spoiled my hard work."

Venus grabbed Natalia, wrestled her off the couch. She
was slightly taller than Venus, very athletic, with pecs like
little cannonballs, hard and solid. Venus said, "Why did
you try to kill me?"

Natalia pursed her lips. "Poof," she said, "I dun't know what you mean." She wriggled out of Venus's grasp. "Now leave me alone or I'll report you to the police. You have no right to harass me."

Lina came back from the kitchen without the ashtray, carrying a small Igloo cooler, and went directly into the bedroom. A minute later, she returned to the living room, empty-handed, and sat down in the impression she'd left on the couch. Picking up her crocheting, she said something in Russian to Natalia.

"She wants me to interpret what you are saying," Natalia explained, easing back onto the couch and starting the pedicure all over again.

"Tell me about Henry Pederson," said Venus.

Natalia shrugged lightly and interpreted for Lina. Lina shook her head. Venus said, "Ask Lina if she ever went to the *Earline* before the time she saw Tim."

Natalia and Lina talked. Natalia said, "Maybe a few times."

"Ask her if when she went to the *Earline* she ever saw a boy about five feet five, with blond hair and blue eyes."

Natalia spoke again to Lina. Lina listened, then looked up at Venus and grunted, "*Nyet.*"

Natalia said, "We don't know about this boy. Never heard about him."

Venus said, "What about a boy named John Stark?"

Natalia blinked. Lina groaned and started to speak, but Natalia shot her a sharp look and the big woman clamped her lips together.

Venus said, "Where's John Stark, Lina?"

Lina shook her head slowly. Natalia said something in Russian to Lina. Lina answered her tersely.

"She doesn't know nothing about any boys," said Natalia.

"What about Larry Chekhov? Does he like boys?"

"*Nyet,*" said Natalia. "I don't think Chekhov involves with that. The other boy maybe, because he was found by Chekhov's boat. But this other boy? I don't think so."

"Which other boy? John Stark? Or Henry?" Venus asked.

Natalia blinked her wide blue eyes, reached for a pack of Camels on the coffee table, lit up, and stared into the vacant middle distance between herself and the TV. Traveling in her mind. Finally, she said, "We don't know nothing. Why don't you leave us alone?"

Venus moved a chair on rollers closer to the couch, sat down. She rolled up her sleeve, showed the women her gunshot wound. "Who did this?" she asked them pointedly.

Both women stared, said nothing. Finally, Natalia made a face and shrugged. "Swear to God, we don't know about that."

"It happened the night I visited you on the *Dirty Blonde.* After I left the boat and had walked about halfway down the slip, someone tried to kill me. I think you both know who that was."

Natalia sighed and interpreted for Lina. Lina's face flushed pink, then crimson, the color of Natalia's nail lacquer. She crocheted faster, her beefy hands moving like two graceful swans mating. The afghan was black and red, already large enough to cover her wide lap. She focused intently on her flying fingers. When Natalia had finished interpreting, Lina suddenly threw down her crochet nee-~~dles~~ *hook* and tossed the afghan on the couch. She stood up and lumbered into the bedroom.

"You have made her upset," said Natalia quietly.

"Sorry about that, but you see, Natalia, I need to know who's protecting you besides the cops. Whoever shot at me meant to kill me after I had spoken with you two. If it had been one of Chekhov's men, I'm sure you'd agree that he or

she would have come after you next. That you were the
intended target. Otherwise, I'd have to guess that the person who shot me is a friend of yours. Or maybe it was you.
Maybe you tried that first time and failed. Maybe that's
why you tried again yesterday at the funeral."

Natalia's eyes opened wide, the whites drying before
she blinked. "Are you accusing me and Lina of shooting
you?"

"You know damn well what I mean, Natalia. But just
for your information, and Lina's, I don't think either one of
you tried to kill me that first time. I think it was Chekhov.
Or else Ziggy Nelson."

"Ziggy's dead," protested Natalia. She hiccuped a sob.

"So you say. Now let's see proof."

Natalia stared. "What proof? I told you what happened. I told you what we found."

"And tell me, just for clarity, what did you do with that
severed hand when you found it on the *Dirty Blonde*?"

Natalia covered her face with her hands. "I can't. I just
can't. We were so afraid."

"Go on."

"We came in. We found it on the table. Lina tossed it
over the side. We knew it was Chekhov's sign."

From the bedroom came a crashing sound. Venus ran
to the open door. Lina was nowhere in sight. The window
was wide open, hanging over the bay where Lina had
jumped into the water and was swimming like a crazed
whale, heading straight out into the harbor. Venus used her
cell phone to call the Harbor Patrol. Then she noticed the
small Igloo cooler on the bedroom floor. It was open and
the ice inside was fairly fresh, but that was all the Igloo
contained, ice. Natalia rummaged through the melting ice.
Whatever had been in there was gone. She flew into a rage.

CHAPTER TWENTY-FIVE

Lina plowed through the water, diving, then surfacing, blowing out great sprays of mist, her arms like flailing fins, driving her deeper into the bay. When the Harbor Patrol reached her, she came up without a struggle, but her hands were empty. Whatever she'd taken into the water, she'd left there.

The Harbor Patrol brought her back to the pier south of the Edgewater, where an ambulance met her. Venus stood on the pier and watched as two harbor cops held Lina underneath the armpits and lifted her up off the deck and onto the pier. She stood on her own power, her flowered dress plastered against her skin like a full-body tattoo. She was breathing hard. The medics tried to put her on a stretcher, but she swung at them and lumbered down the pier. Venus caught up with her.

"You okay?"

"Da," she said. *"Kaneshna,"* she added, indicating she certainly was.

They walked in silence for a few minutes; then Venus said, "Why did you do that, Lina?"

"Ya nyeh gavaru po-angliski."

"Look, Lina, you understand what I'm saying. Why in the hell did you go for a swim?"

Lina pushed her wet hair off her face. The exposed skin on her body had a bright red prehypothermia glow, but she wasn't shivering, didn't even seem cold. She said, "I want to drowned."

"What did you take into the water?"

Lina ignored the question. Venus repeated it, adding, "From the ice chest."

Lina repeated, "I want to drowned."

"But why?"

Lina quickened her pace. Venus kept up. When they had reached the Edgewater's entrance, Lina said, "The liddle boy."

"John Stark?"

"Da."

"His hand?"

"Pashaulsta?"

Venus showed Lina her hand. "Hand. The boy's hand."

Lina said, *"Da."*

Lina dripped all over the lobby and down the hall to her suite. The duty officer at the door of the suite had heard Natalia's screams when Lina dove out the window into the bay. Now several police officers met them in the hall. Lina pushed past them, into the suite, still dripping seawater. Venus followed. Lina went into the bathroom, peeled off the flowered dress, and stepped into the shower. Hot steam poured from the bathroom. She had left the door open. She didn't care who saw her. She had more important things on her mind.

Natalia sat on the couch, pressing her freshly manicured fingers against the bridge of her nose. She wasn't
weeping. Her mouth might as well have been sutured shut.
The living room was a mess. She'd been throwing things,
having a snit fit. Lina's big dive had enraged her.

Lina came out of the bathroom, a massive robe
wrapped around her body, a towel turban over her hair.
She said something to Natalia in Russian. Natalia didn't
reply, just sat still, pressing her fingers tighter into the
bridge of her nose. Lina went over and shoved Natalia up
against the back of the couch. Natalia squealed like a stuck
pig. Lina said something gruff and angry. Natalia kept
shaking her head, repeating, "Nyet, nyet, nyet."

Venus went into the kitchen, opened the fridge.
Heinekin greens. She fished out a bottle, found the opener,
popped the top, and drank. Sooner or later, the two Russian
women would calm down. Or maybe they were putting on
this show for her benefit. A charade, meant to make them
appear more important than they really were. Maybe they
worked for Chekhov. Anything was possible with these two
Stoli suckers. She found an overturned chair, righted it, and
sat down. She watched the rest of the show, which petered
out when Natalia, broken and sniveling, stomped off to the
bedroom and slammed the door. Lina took Natalia's place
on the couch, pulled out a roach from the bathrobe pocket,
and lit it with a little green Bic. She inhaled, held it in for a
couple seconds, exhaled. She did this a few times before she
said, "John was sweet liddle boy."

Venus waited. Outside the suite's door, the duty officer
was speaking to someone, possibly the hotel manager.
Arguing. Maybe an eviction notice. People weren't supposed to jump out of the Edgewater's windows into the
bay. True, the Beatles had fished from the Edgewater's windows, then filled a bathtub with smelly fish guts. Still,

nobody dives out of a window like Lina had done and gets to stay another night at the Edgewater.

Lina coughed. A dry hacking sound. When she had stopped wheezing, she said, "Pleeze. A beer."

Venus went into the kitchen, fished another Heinekin from the fridge, popped the top, and took the bottle to Lina. Lina whispered hoarsely, "*Spasiba*. Thenk you." She drank the beer in three long gulps, made a smacking sound, and said, "Pleeze. Anudder beer."

Venus went back into the kitchen, fished two more greenies out of the fridge, popped their tops. Out of curiosity, she reached up and opened the small freezer's door. Inside was one package, the size of a large fist wrapped in heavy plastic. Venus fished it out of the freezer. The package was labeled "Scree." She placed it back in the freezer and returned to the living room. Lina lay across the couch, her eyes bulging, blood pouring from the carotid artery she had just slashed. Venus shouted at the officer's in the hall and went to Lina's aid. The big woman fought, kicking and shoving until she grew too weak to resist. Venus applied pressure to the artery, held it until the ambulance arrived and took Lina away, hoping to save her life. But Lina had other ideas.

When she heard the commotion, Natalia appeared at the bedroom door. She stood leaning casually against the doorjamb, watching Lina being carted off. Before Lina was gone, Rocco arrived. Natalia flew to him, pressed her head against his chest, and sobbed. "Help me, Rocco," she cried. "This crazy girl tried to kill me."

Rocco, a look of mild confusion on his face, said, "I heard Lina jumped."

"Dived is more accurate," said Venus.

Rocco said, "She might live. If they can stop the bleeding."

Natalia moaned. "Such a stupid girl."

Rocco held her at arm's length and said, "Talk, Natalia."

Natalia tried to wrestle free from Rocco, but he gripped her tighter.

Venus said, "First, she tried to drown herself; then she slashes her artery. She really wants to die, Natalia. And you know why."

Natalia aimed her marvelous eyes at Venus. "I have no idea. Absolutely no idea why Lina would do that. She has never done it before, not since she came to live with Ziggy and me."

Venus said, "Tell us about the hand in the freezer."

Natalia scrunched up her face, acted confused; then a look of comprehension suddenly smoothed out her features. She said, "You mean Ziggy's hand? Maybe I already told you." Playing for time.

"I mean Scree's hand. The hand in the freezer is labeled with Scree's name, not Ziggy's."

Rocco peeled Natalia off his chest and went into the kitchen. Natalia burst into laughter. "You crazy bitch," she said to Venus. Rocco returned, his face ashen. Natalia clawed at Rocco's arm and said, "Don't listen to her."

Rocco called SPD, ordered an evidence unit to come fetch the frozen hand. Natalia protested, wailing. Rocco had had enough. "Get your purse or whatever you want," he growled at Natalia. "We're going out for a little while. And before this day's over, you might be living in a jail cell."

On the way out, Rocco placated the agitated hotel manager. If the Russian women could stay, the cops would take good care of the Edgewater. Besides, Rocco told him, the one woman might not survive and the other one might soon be arrested. The manager fretted, but in the end, he relented. The Russian women could stay as long as they didn't try any more funny business.

Rocco drove to the crest of Queen Anne Hill, parked outside the Five Spot Café. He'd treat Natalia to a hot lunch, then wiggle some information out of her. Venus went along. They went inside and ordered. Just as the food arrived at the table, Venus's cell phone rang. It was Bart.

"Moses found something in Tim's computer. I can't believe the cops missed this. You've got to see it."

Moses Freeny stood before Tim's bookcase, studying the titles. When Bart brought Venus in, Moses went over to Tim's desk, picked up a sheet of paper, and handed it to her. "After the police returned the computer this morning, Bart called and asked me to perform some file searches. I retrieved this file titled 'Personalized Dictionary.' "

Bart said, "Cops must have skipped over it, or they didn't read it all the way through anyway. It was mostly scientific definitions until we came to the end. To the 'Z's'."

Venus read what was on the sheet: "First they got Pearl. Then Henry. Then John. They'll never get me."

She looked at Bart and said, "Tim's computer was taken from him right after Pearl died. This had to be written before that day."

Bart nodded. "But it must mean something."

Tim's computer had been placed back in its usual spot on his desk. Venus sat beside Moses while he located the file on Tim's computer, called it up, and opened it.

"Let's print this whole file," she said.

"What's the point? The rest of it is all jargon."

Venus shrugged. "Let's do it anyway."

They printed out the file, sixteen pages of scientific words and their definitions. The only sentences that seemed relevant were those Venus had read: "First they got Pearl. Then Henry. Then John. They'll never get me." Filed under "Z."

Rocco had driven Natalia back to the Edgewater. In spite of his deft interrogation skills, Natalia hadn't crumbled. Venus met Rocco in the lobby. He had locked Natalia in the room, and a duty officer stood sentry at the door. He wasn't worried about Natalia jumping into the bay. She wasn't the type to risk her hairdo. Venus and Rocco went into the hotel's bar. Rocco ordered two India pales and they found a table on the outdoor deck. "No scotch for you," he said. Venus showed him the printout.

"Closest thing to a lead I've seen since Henry disappeared," he said. "And this almost certainly links the Stark boy to Tim and the Pederson kids."

She said, "Are you and I on the same page here?"

Rocco said, "I'm not ready to commit just yet. Let's just say things aren't what they seemed. There's more to this story than Scree's smuggling cars, possibly in competition with a similar operation run by the Russian mob. There's more than car smuggling here."

"That's what I'm afraid of," she said, and drank her beer. A minute later, she asked, "How did the parents check out?"

"Ingrid's clean as a whistle. Remote as hell, but clean. Nils has a dark side, but I think it's just Scandinavian angst. I don't think he'd ever harm his own children. He's been up to some financial shenanigans, though."

On the bar's deck, happy hour was under way, people shedding the day's tensions, unwinding, relaxing for the first time since they'd opened their eyes that morning. Rocco leaned back in his chair. The sun, now low in the sky, glanced across his face, dropping half of his face in shadow, lighting up the rest with a warm golden glow. Rocco's skin was swarthy, deeply tanned. His green eyes were watching her now. Sexy green eyes, intense. Or maybe more than watching. Maybe they were trying to say something. Then he blinked and the look was gone.

"Nils has a little scam going. Not exactly a mob connection, but near as they come without necessarily being mob-related. It has nothing to do with his securities investments. That all checks out clean. It's a restaurant-protection racket. You probably already know this, but Nils owns Pederson Security, that big company that provides guards to retail outfits, mainly restaurants. I did a little research, asked around. Then I checked against fire department records. Whenever Nils's company lost a contract, something bad would happen to the restaurant."

"Bad like what?"

"Bad like burned down. And one time, a burglary, during which the entire place was destroyed by what seemed to be vandals and the competition's security guard was shot dead. Then, lo and behold, when the restaurant recovered, they hired Nils's security guards, and now all's safe and serene."

"Protection racket. Petty stuff."

Rocco nodded. "Maybe not even related to organized crime. Maybe Nils's own petty little racket. Or, hey, maybe the tip of iceberg. We still don't know who his lackeys are. What interests me is his biggest client."

"Who's that?" She squinted into the sun.

"Nils has every city contract locked up. Pederson Security handles all of the city's outsourced security needs. If you wanted to get paranoid, you could surmise that Nils has the perfect setup to break into any city-owned building at any time after hours, when only his security guards are on duty. Nils could do a lot with that. I'm not saying he's taken advantage of the opportunities, just that he could anytime he wanted to."

The setting sun washed across Venus's face. She shaded her eyes with her hand. "What are we chasing here? Nothing you've just said leads to Henry."

"Correct again. Nils might be a scumbag businessman, but by all accounts, he's a distant but good father, a little too busy, more preoccupied with his work than his family, but an okay dad. Everyone we've interviewed says so."

Venus said, "Any news about the missing kid? John Stark?"

Rocco shook his head. "I asked Henry numerous times about John Stark. Henry insisted he'd never heard of John Stark. Henry's a hard kid to read. So far, it's a dead-end street. Sanchez is working that angle, too. And the ME identified the hand as Scree's. I don't have enough guys to work this case. We need more detectives. Hell, maybe Lina will talk. If she survives." He finished his beer, then ordered another. He said, "Nine out of ten times, it's a family member or a close friend of the family. The Pedersons come up clean. So do their family and close friends."

Venus said, "So I'm wondering what juicy bits you learned about my family."

Rocco laughed. "Hell, Venus, you know I can't talk about that. The rules, remember?"

"Break the rules."

He studied the back of his hand. The noise level on the deck had risen to a crescendo and offered no hope of diminishing. Rocco jerked his head and said, "Let's go for a walk."

They walked along Alaskan Way to Pier 69, where Tim's body had been pulled from the bay. The *Earline* was no longer moored there. She had been taken to a police inspection dock on Harbor Island. They walked down the pier to the place where Tim's body had lain when he was brought up.

Rocco said. "I tried like hell to make him breathe. Even though he'd been under water for hours. I tried to make him breathe."

She placed a hand on his arm. "Thank you."

They stood silently for a few minutes. Then Venus said, "About Tim? Are you finally convinced of his innocence?"

"Mostly."

"What's that supposed to imply?"

Rocco shrugged. "Those kids were playing walk the plank. Tim was Captain Hook. The real Hook's right hand had been severed. All I'm saying here is that it still looks bad."

July 14

Icyfrost Seafood owned six processors, two tenders, and a fleet of a dozen fishing boats. Their office was on the third floor of a four-story sixties-era office building on Industrial Way, the road running parallel to Hiram Chittenden Locks. When Venus and Rocco walked into the office, the only employee on the job was a brassy receptionist with a sour disposition and a foul mouth, which she tried hard to control.

"Mr. Moran's not here," she said. "I don't know where the eff he's gone to, but he better effing get back here in the next ten minutes or his ass is effed."

Rocco said, "Mind if we wait?"

"What the hell does it matter to me if you wait?"

She stood up, and Venus saw she was tall and rangy. She had the kind of arms that could haul crab pots, legs that could devour a man, or ride a deck in any storm. She loped over to the printer, snatched out a fresh document, and then loped back to her desk. She ignored them as she went about her work, posting invoices or something that Venus didn't understand. Eight minutes later, Tom Moran walked through the door, accompanied by two shipyard workers. Moran's face was beet red and he seemed pissed. He was bawling them out about a broken bilge pump. The two workers were smeared with oil and one of them had a wad of tobacco tucked into his cheek. When Moran finished the dressing-down, the beet flush faded and he morphed into an affable middle-aged businessman who had found success the hard way, on rough, swelling Alaskan seas, doing the world's most dangerous work.

Rocco showed his badge. Moran led Venus and Rocco past the loper, whom he called "Terry," into his private office. It had a window looking out onto the reception area. The two mechanics were out there making time with Terry. Moran sat down at his big empty desk and said, "If this is about the *Spindrift*, I haven't heard anything new."

Rocco said, "What do you think happened?"

Moran knitted his salt-and-pepper eyebrows and said, "I've had this discussion before, with the cops. According to the insurance investigators, she was hijacked off Pier Ninety-one and taken into the bay, where something went wrong with a fuel line and she exploded. They never found the crew. My best guess is that it was two or three ex-employees, maybe former deckhands. But the insurance investigators checked everyone out, all my former employees. They didn't find anything. And no one's shown up missing."

Venus said, "What about Ziggy Nelson?"

Moran's eyes flickered. Rocco said, "Word going around is that Ziggy Nelson was smuggling cars off the waterfront. Maybe on the *Spindrift*."

Moran's eyes flickered again. A shadow dropped into

them. He reached up with a broad hand and rubbed his face. His hand covered his mouth but not his eyes, and the darkness in them spoke more than words ever could. His other hand gripped his wide desk and he sat there for a moment as if paralyzed. In the reception area, Terry's spirits had improved. She was flirting with the two mechanics, and her throaty laugh drifted into Moran's office. Venus and Rocco waited while Moran apparently organized his thoughts, decided what to say. After awhile, his hand dropped from his face. He sighed deeply and said, "I heard Ziggy died."

Venus said, "That's the other word going around."

"You got any evidence of that?" Moran asked.

Rocco said, "Only the statements of two Russian women, one who claims to be Ziggy's wife."

"Ah. Natalia." Moran, smiled insincerely. "That little minx of a girl. Yes, she would say that. She would do anything for Zig. Lie, cheat, steal. Hell, she'd kill for Ziggy if he asked her." Moran shook his head. "I don't know. He might be dead. I sure as hell haven't seen him around my boats. He used to skipper the *Spindrift,* but I fired him off the boat. He was making too many mistakes."

Venus said, "What sort of mistakes?"

"Like always running a half a day behind schedule. Can't do that in the fish business. We got our clients to think about. So I fired him, but it was friendly. I don't stay pissed. Doesn't do any good in this business. Last time I saw Zig was—what? Two months ago. Hadn't seen him for six months, maybe more. Ever since he took the job on the *Caprice* and bought that Catalina he keeps over at Shilshole. *Dirty Blonde.* What a god-awful thing to name a sailboat. Yeah, it was about two months ago. He brought back the company car. I saw him for maybe ten minutes. We talked. We always talk baseball."

Venus said, "Ziggy drives the red Jetta?"

Moran looked at her as if she had surprised him. He said, "He used to. I let him hang on to it until he could pull together enough cash for his own vehicle. He paid cash for everything, ever since I knew him. So then, about two months ago, he finally bought a vehicle and brought the Jetta back to Icyfrost. That was the last time I saw Ziggy. He didn't show up at the big Fourth of July bash at the Space Needle. It was my sixtieth birthday and I took all my employees up to the Needle to celebrate and watch the fireworks. I even invited Zig and Natalia, but they never showed up."

Venus said, "What sort of vehicle did Ziggy purchase?"

Moran squinted, searching his mind, then said, "Ah, yes. An SUV. Ford Explorer. Souped-up job. Pinstripes, you name it."

Rocco said, "What color?"

"I seem to recall it was dark blue. Yeah, that's it. Kind of navy blue."

Venus said, "After Ziggy turned in the vehicle to Icyfrost, the red Jetta, what did you do with it?"

Moran shrugged. "Sold it."

"To whom?"

"To our security company. Pederson Security. Gave 'em a good deal."

Venus said, "Did you ever remember who bought the tugboat *Earline* from you?"

"The *Earline*." Moran blinked. "Hell, I used to own her. Sold her back four, five years ago. To a Russian guy. Don't recall his name. It was cash on the barrelhead. No bill of sale." He glanced up sheepishly. "The boat business is complicated."

Venus said, "Ever heard the name Larry Chekhov?"

Moran opened his mouth to reply but was distracted by noise from the reception area. An altercation. Then shouting. Venus looked through the window. A man wearing a face mask pointed a gun at Terry, shot her through the chest. She fell. Before the mechanics could react, the gunman shot them, and then he aimed at the window and fired. The first bullet hit Moran in the forehead, the second in the face as he fell to the floor. Rocco and Venus had their guns out. Rocco fired back through the window, but the gunman had turned and fled. Venus checked Moran's pulse. He didn't have one anymore. She followed Rocco out the door.

The gunman had fled west along the waterfront, heading toward the locks. They saw him running along the road's shoulder. A navy blue SUV pulled up, the gunman jumped in, and the SUV sped off. Rocco got on his cell phone and sent out an alert. By the time they got back to Icyfrost, the SUV was too far gone to chase.

CHAPTER TWENTY-SEVEN

Did she want to go on living? Lina did not, but life was being forced upon her by medical science, technologies that she could not fight. She wished to yank out the oxygen hose attached to her nose, but her arms and legs had been restrained. She had fought to die, but they wouldn't let her.

In Harborview's intensive care unit, Lina lay in her hospital bed, clinging to life. Beside her, Natalia sat in a high-backed chair, reading a paperback romance novel. Natalia, keeping vigil. Did she care if Lina died or lived? Would she prefer that Lina died and took her secret with her? Lina's secret was the same as hers. Or maybe Lina knew even more about John Stark, the "liddle boy." About Tim. And Henry and Pearl.

Venus stood in the doorway and said, "Mr. Moran sent his regards, Natalia. Just before he was murdered."

Natalia merely glanced up, as if Venus had told her the outdoor temperature had dropped ten degrees. No big thing. Not to Natalia. Maybe she was used to murder. Maybe it was a way of life for her.

Venus said, "Three other people were shot. All of them died."

Natalia set the romance novel gently in her lap, folded her hands over it, and tilted her head to one side, as if considering what she'd just heard. In the hospital bed, Lina moaned. One of her hands raised slightly off the bedcovers, beckoning Venus to come closer. Venus moved into the room, near to Lina's bed, leaned down, and put her ear close to Lina's mouth. Lina whispered, "The liddle boys."

Venus nodded. Natalia stood up, pointed at the door, and said, "Get out of this room right now. She can't be disturbed. It might kill her."

Venus took Lina's hand in hers. Lina squeezed it and her mouth moved, but the words weren't spoken, only formed on her parched lips as a silent proclamation, or confession. Natalia, enraged now, lunged at Venus, kicking and screaming, biting wherever she could. Venus wrestled Natalia to the floor and pinned her down. Natalia, breathing heavily, her blue eyes blazing, spit in Venus's face. Venus said, "Where is he, Natalia?" Natalia whipped her head to one side, defiant.

Venus shook Natalia hard. "Where's Henry?"

"Go to hell." Natalia spit in Venus's face. She struggled against Venus's hold, but in vain. Venus let her struggle until she tired, then jerked her up off the floor and shoved her into the chair. A nurse came running in.

"What's going on in here?" she demanded. "This is a sick lady."

"Not anymore," said Venus.

The nurse rushed to Lina's side.

Venus said, "She's a dead lady."

Stephen opened the door to Nils Pederson. Nils hoped not to disturb the family, he told Stephen, but he just wanted to check on a tiny detail. Several weeks ago, Henry had stayed overnight at the Diamond home, and apparently he had left behind a valuable family heirloom. A signet ring that Nils had given Henry for his twelfth birthday. It had belonged to Nils's grandfather. He asked Stephen if he would mind awfully if he had a look around Tim's bedroom.

"All right by me," said Stephen. "But I better check with Tim's stepbrother."

While Stephen went in search of Bart, Nils made himself comfortable in the living room. From the window of the Diamond home, he could see all of Elliott Bay, Mount Rainier, the city's skyline, and, in the foreground, his own property, the meandering iron fence, and the cedar grove that screened one house from the other. Nils would have liked to smoke a cigarette, but he resisted and seated himself instead on one of the actress's long couches, recalling the good times here, the gay parties with glitzy Hollywood stars, the way Kim Basinger had once caught his eye from across this very room and smiled at him, flirtatiously, Nils thought. Then Stephen came back and said Bart apparently wasn't at home and that Bella was indisposed.

"I imagine it would do no harm," said Stephen, "if you were to go down and look around Tim's bedroom. The police are finished in there."

Stephen accompanied Nils to the villa's lower level and left him to search Tim's bedroom. As he returned to the main level, Stephen's pager went off. Bella wanted to see him in the library.

Bella had faced the truth bravely, when it finally came, accepting the reality that she would never again hold Tim in her arms, never again tuck him into bed and remind him to say his prayers, always adding, "Don't forget my Pansy, dear." After the funeral, Bella had postponed work on the film in Curaçao. The director, Guy Foss, had taken the news gracefully enough. Now Bella had entered a grieving phase, the period of acceptance. Gone was her spark and verve, at least temporarily. She spent most of her time reading inspirational books, or just staring out across her gardens, lost in her sadness. She might sooner or later arrive at anger, but so far she had shown no evidence of anything beyond profound sorrow, and a regret that she had not done more to support Tim in his days of crisis. Eventually, largely unfounded guilt would surface to haunt her. And even after Venus apologized for her cruel remarks, the rift between them persisted, festering.

Stephen had taken on extra little chores to help smooth the healing process for Bella. He had shed his gloating, supercilious attitude and was taking pains to make Bella's life at least tolerable, if not contented.

She wore a black kimono and her blond hair was wrapped in a black silk scarf. She wore no makeup. She said, "Stephen dear, my Pansy needs to piddle. Would you mind terribly?"

Stephen fetched the shar-pei, leashed her, and, avoiding the reporters camped out front, took Pansy for a stroll in the villa's back gardens. Pansy took her time and Stephen kept checking his watch. He had things to do. He didn't have all the time in the world to accommodate a dog's whims. Pansy had trotted over to the Land of Thrush and was pawing around in the gravel, as if digging for a bone. The dog was lifting her leg on a cedar trunk when Stephen noticed something gleaming on the graveled ground. With his foot, he moved some gravel away until the thing revealed itself: a DVD inside a clear plastic box.

Stephen stooped over and picked it up. No label, but a typed note: "For Venus." Stephen waited for Pansy to finish

up her business, then went back indoors. He placed the disc
on the desk in his own room and was entering the hall
when Nils emerged from Tim's room.

Nils held up an open palm. In it was a signet ring.
"Thank you ever so much, Stephen," he said. "This ring
means a lot to me."

Natalia, handcuffed, sat in the rear of the patrol car on the
way back to the Edgewater. Venus sat in the passenger
seat, listening to the officer who drove allow as to how he
had always wondered what the rooms at the Edgewater
looked like. Venus could hear Natalia's heavy, slow
breathing, like she was trying to drop into a trance. She
wasn't crying over Lina's dead bones. And she still wasn't
talking.

Rocco was waiting in the suite. He removed the cuffs
and let Natalia freshen up, but first Venus scoured the bathroom for potential weapons: a woman's razor, some sleeping pills she might use on herself. Natalia came out of the
bathroom defiant.

"You can't arrest me," she said. "And if you don't
arrest me, you can't handcuff me. I want my attorney."

Rocco shrugged, said, "Go ahead," and handed her his
cell phone.

Natalia threw it back at him, cursing.

Rocco said, "Where's Henry, Natalia?"

"Go to hell."

Venus stood at the window, looking out into the bay
where Lina had gone berserk and tried to drown herself.
Had Lina taken John Stark's hand into the water? DNA
tests on the Igloo cooler might eventually provide an
answer. Whatever she had taken into the water, now it sat
at the bottom of the bay, where it would corrode, or
decompose, or just add to the sea floor's collection of

human refuse. God knows what else Lina had been hiding. At least Tim's hand hadn't been severed.

Venus turned to Rocco. "We're wasting our time," she said. "She's not going to talk. And I'm not going to stand around here all afternoon trying to rip the sutures from her mouth."

Rocco grunted. "Got any better ideas?"

"Maybe," she said. "I'll see you later."

When she entered Tim's bedroom, she felt his presence still there, as if he were standing over there by his bookcase, pulling a book off the shelf, the Australian Box jellyfish book. When she sat at his desk and turned on his computer, a knot of sickness visited her. The computer's hard drive had been completely erased.

Was it already too late for Henry? Or was he still alive, waiting, hoping to be rescued? But where? She was staring at the Famous Astronauts clock on the wall when tears pooled in her eyes, tears she hadn't shed in public. They came freely now, washing like rain down her face. She lay across Tim's bed, her body heaving sobs. She didn't remember how long it lasted, but when she finally raised her head off Tim's pillow, the sun had lowered in the evening sky and a soft twilight poured through the open terrace door, washing across Tim's bookshelves.

She went over to the bookcase. Beside the Australian Box jellyfish book was the book she had brought him. *Pacific Coast Pelagic Invertebrates.* On a hunch, or from macabre nostalgia, she pulled it from the shelf and opened it to the lion's mane medusa. A sheet of notepaper fell to the floor. She stooped, picked it up. She recognized Tim's handwriting: "Sometimes a lie is a necessary evil, to protect the vulnerable from a worse kind of evil." She turned the note over. On the back, also in Tim's handwriting were the words, *"Caprice, Spindrift, Earline, Dolgota,"* written as if he'd jotted them down for future reference. Or had he meant for her to find them?

Dolgota. Where had she heard that before? Then she remembered the shipping news. *Dolgota* was the name of a Russian-registered cargo vessel recently in port in Elliott Bay. But a check of vessels presently in port suggested that the *Dolgota* must have sailed.

At Icyfrost Seafood, she found a Russian sailor aboard one of the company's vessels. When she mentioned Ziggy Nelson's name, he reeled back and eyed her suspiciously. "What you want with Ziggy?" he said.

"Word is, Ziggy's dead," she said.

"Huh." Noncommittal.

She said, "Did you know him?"

"Ziggy?" He shrugged. "Who doesn't? He worked here, didn't he? Who doesn't know Ziggy?"

His name was Affanassi Kulagin and he came from Kamchatka Peninsula. He spoke a little English.

She said, "What does *Dolgota* mean in English?"

"*Dolgota?*" he said, and grimaced, as if trying to think. Then he smiled, showing all his rotten teeth and said, "Maybe I know. What's it worth to you?"

She handed the fisherman her credit card. "Whatever you want."

He shook his head. He had a better idea. "You take me to Immigration, make me legal," he said. "Then I talk."

The Russian fisherman wanted to strike a deal with U.S. Immigration & Naturalization. He told her he had information about boys who had been kidnapped. He'd fork over the info if INS would agree to give him a six-month visa. Six months would be long enough to land a lonesome American girl who'd marry him in a rat's hiccup. He'd be legal. He'd never have to return to Kamchatka Peninsula. Life would be good.

No such deal, but a promise not to prosecute him for his illegally entering the United States. Then maybe if he really cooperated, a short visa, maybe for ninety days. He was handsome enough. He could snare a wife in that little window of time.

He talked—little bits of information—then haggled. Then talked a little more.

So far, Venus had gleaned that Kulagin had delivered a load of salmon to a Russian cargo vessel, the *Dolgota*. The ship's captain, said Kulagin, through an interpreter had recently ordered the vessel's name repainted on its sides and stern. Now it was in English. *Longitude*. The *Longitude* was presently anchored out in international waters off the Olympic Peninsula. Something was going on aboard the ship, but Affanassi Kulagin claimed he didn't know the nature of what was happening. He'd heard about it from Ziggy's cousin, that big girl, Lina. Sure, sure, there was car smuggling. Everyone on the waterfront knew that. But something else, something that involved children. Boys mostly, according to Lina, but some girls, too. Befriended, taken to boats, brought aboard for a few hours, then let go. Some taken off to the *Dolgota* who never returned. Lina had told Affanassi that on the *Dolgota,* hands were collected. Affanassi said, "When Lina told me that, I knew who was behind this."

Venus said, "Who?"

Affanassi said, "Every Russian in this city knows that a cut-off hand is Ziggy's and Larry Chekhov's signature."

"You mean Larry Chekhov and Ziggy Nelson."

Kulagin tilted his head. *"Nyet.* I mean Ziggy Chekhov." Kulagin slapped his head. *"Tak!* Now I remember. When Larry sent Ziggy to sabotage the competition, Ziggy changed his name to Nelson. Now I remember. But they are brothers, Larry and Ziggy."

"What competition?"

Affanassi Kulagin shook his head from side to side. He didn't know. "All I know for certain," he said, "is the Chekhovs want something that some rich man owns. And they are planning a big heist. That's all I know."

Maritime records showed the *Longitude*, formerly *Dolgota*, had entered from the Strait of Juan de Fuca into Puget Sound on a number of occasions over the past five years. Delivering Chinese goods, containers of hand-carved faux antique tea chests, bobble-head dolls, and rubber Mexican-style huaraches made in China. The *Longitude*'s papers were in order, the ship owned by a Russian company, registered in Kamchatka. When it sailed out of Seattle, having left its Chinese cargo ashore, the *Longitude* usually returned to Russia with legally registered containers of U.S.-made automobiles, RVs, and trailer homes. Everything appeared on the up-and-up. But this Russian sailor, Affanassi Kulagin, had begged to differ. Sure, fancy cars were being smuggled into Russia on the *Longitude*. But worse than that. Kulagin claimed to know Lina, and he insisted that Lina had told him something nasty was happening aboard the *Longitude*. Nasty and evil. Lina had seen it with her own eyes. When pressed for more details, all Kulagin could say was, "Lina didn't tell me exactly what. She was afraid of being killed. Now I am, too."

The man looked like any other guest when he walked into the Edgewater Inn, moved through the lobby, turned left down the hall, and approached Natalia's suite. Rounding the corner, he saw the hall was empty except for one officer posted at Natalia's door. He drew his silenced gun, aimed, and fired. The officer fell to the carpet, clutching his chest. The gunman fired a second shot into the door lock. A few seconds passed, and then the door opened and Natalia came out. They fled out a side entrance into the Edgewater's parking lot, where his car waited. They pealed rubber out of the parking lot.

Half an hour later, Nils Pederson received a telephone call at his office. A woman's voice, heavily accented, said, "We are holding your son, Henry. If you want him back alive, do what we tell you. Put one million dollars in unmarked cash—hundred-dollar bills only—in a suitcase and go to the park at Hiram Chittenden Locks. Leave the suitcase on the second park bench to the right of the entrance. Keep walking straight ahead. Do not look around you or you will be shot. Do this tonight at nine P.M. Do not contact the authorities. Otherwise, your Henry will die."

Nils contacted Rocco immediately. "I'm scared as hell," he told Rocco. "What should I do?"

"Get the money together," Rocco told him. "Leave the rest to me."

"You'll go in my place?" Nils sounded hopeful on the phone.

"Get the cash and meet me at your house at eight o'clock."

"All right. I want my boy back."

"I'm going along," Venus told Rocco.

He was arranging a surprise boarding of the *Longitude*. Rocco said, "Actually, you'll be leading the boarding party. I want this to look like a routine inspection by the U.S. Department of the Interior, Fish and Wildlife Division. We're looking for black-market animal parts. That's all we're interested in, just having a look at the cargo. They'll buy it. You guys are always inspecting vessels from China and Russia."

She said, "Works for me."

They were at Venus's condo in Belltown. On the top floor of a restored 1920's hotel, the condo had seventeen-foot ceilings and a terrace overlooking Elliott Bay. It had wood floors and windows facing north and west. Sparsely furnished, one living room wall supported her butterfly collection, another, an abstract mural Bart had painted. Her bedroom windows faced the Space Needle. She had placed her large bed in the center of the room, an all-white refuge beneath a finely woven soft white mosquito net.

The mosquito net was half a decorative touch, half a paranoid reaction to the malaria. Maybe someday they'd find a cure for the strain she'd contracted. Before the fevers killed her.

She had just showered, her hair still wet, slicked back. In the front loft, on her white couch, Rocco nursed a mug of coffee, his feet resting on the glass table in front of him. He was on his cell phone, talking to the Coast Guard, making final arrangements for the *Longitude* boarding. He cupped his hand over the speaker holes and said to her, "Go lie down. It's going to be a long siege."

She shook her head. When Rocco got off the phone, he said, "The *Longitude* has moved back into Elliott Bay, which makes our job a little easier."

"Why did it come back?" she asked.

"I don't know. But we can't board the vessel until dawn. Coast Guard needs time to maneuver into position. And I just spoke with your boss. Olson says your office needs a little more time to get their act together." Rocco checked his watch. "It's just six o'clock. We've got two hours until we need to be at the Pederson home. After that, all hell breaks loose. So I suggest that you go to bed, take a nap."

She picked up his coffee cup, went into the kitchen, poured him some more, brought it back. He scooted over on the couch, patted the cushion beside him. She sat down and said, "Could be a setup—the *Longitude* moving back into Elliott Bay."

He had thought of that. "We want that kid back, so we don't have much choice. Now, I really think you should rest," he said. "Otherwise, you'll get sick again, and then you won't be any good to anyone."

"I can't sleep. I can't stop thinking about Henry, what might be happening right now. I feel that somehow I goofed up somewhere."

Rocco turned her to face him, his hands gripping her shoulders. His hands felt good there, touching her shoulders, touching her anywhere.

"You can't be doing that to yourself," he said. "You didn't bring this on. You've done a lot of stupid things in your life, but this wasn't one of them. You didn't cause Tim's death, so just get over that guilt crap."

She felt tears pooling in her eyes, but she refused to cry. She blinked slowly, and when she opened her eyes, his face was against hers and then he was kissing her. A long, slow, lingering kiss. Desire. His eyes traveled around her face, and she was acutely aware of the scar on her jawline. As if knowing her thoughts, he reached up and caressed it. She said, "Maybe we should cool it."

"Maybe." He kissed her again, this time a longer kiss, and she relaxed into it, then felt herself letting go. She felt his tongue inside her mouth, felt his hands sweeping over her body, their mutual space electric. Then Rocco held her at arm's length and said, "We don't have to do this."

She stood up, took his hand. "Yes we do," she said, and led him to the white bed beneath the mosquito net. When he touched her, she opened her mouth to cry out, but he gently placed a hand on her lips and said, "Shh. Don't move."

Nils opened the door himself. In the living room, Ingrid, pale as death, sat stiff as a mannequin in a wing chair. Her sister, Cora, stood behind the chair, one hand resting on Ingrid's shoulder. The suitcase was large and had wheels. It lay on a coffee table. It was open, revealing its bounty. Ten thousand one hundred-dollar bills.

"They aren't marked," he said. "I'm keeping my part of the bargain."

Venus said, "You already contacted the police, Mr. Pederson. That wasn't part of the bargain. You're pretty much at their mercy at this point."

Nils Pederson looked at Venus. He had never really looked at her before. She had always been just the famous actress's least-attractive daughter, the runt. Now he saw her for the first time as a woman, and if he wasn't mistaken, she exuded sensuality. He said, "This is totally outside my experience. I'm confused as hell. And scared. So is Ingrid. We're scared that Henry might already be dead."

They left the Pedersons', Rocco pushing the heavy suitcase on its wheels. In Venus's car, they ditched a couple of reporters, drove to the locks, and left the Audi in the parking lot. At 8:30, Venus entered the park and blended in with the usual summer-evening strollers. It was a pleasant dog-day evening; the park was full of people enjoying their evening constitutional, picnics, lovefests. She stayed within shooting distance of the second park bench from the southern entrance. An elderly couple was seated on the bench, holding hands and staring at the bay. Red sails in the sunset. They didn't look like they wanted to move. At nine o'clock exactly, Rocco, wearing one of Nils's raincoats and one of Nils's golf caps, entered the park, pushing the suitcase in front of him.

Rocco walked slowly, deliberately, along the path that bordered the locks. When he reached the second park bench, he stopped. Rocco pushed the suitcase up onto the grass and nodded to the couple. The man nodded back. Rocco said, "Mind if I sit down?" He didn't wait for an answer. He sat on the bench beside the couple, the suitcase in front of him. Across the path, near the fish ladder, Venus checked her jacket pocket. Her gun was ready. She was ready. Rocco was ready.

The couple didn't budge. Rocco wondered if he should leave the suitcase beside the couple. He hesitated too long.

Venus saw the SUV enter the park, edging up the narrow footpath. The same navy blue SUV. No license plate. Windows tinted. She couldn't see inside. The SUV pulled up fifteen feet from the park bench and idled. A man wearing a stocking cap over his face stepped out of the passenger side. He held a gun. Rocco stood up, then walked in the opposite direction, keeping his face hidden. The masked man didn't like what he saw on the bench and he didn't like the looks of Rocco's back. He aimed his gun at Rocco. Venus raised her gun.

"Watch out," she yelled, but too late. The elderly woman had seen the gunman and had jumped up off the bench. She took the bullet intended for Rocco. She fell to the ground. Her husband knelt and desperately tried to help her. The bullet had struck her leg. She lay on the ground, moaning. Rocco fell sideways, wheeled around, and fired his own gun at the car. Then he turned to help the woman. The gunman grabbed the suitcase, then ran back to the SUV as Venus fired at him. But she was too late. The SUV squealed backward out of the park. Rocco got on the phone and called Dispatch. They waited until the ambulance arrived, and then Rocco and Venus ran to the Audi. It sat where they'd left it in the parking lot, only now it couldn't go anywhere. Somebody had given it four flat tires. The SUV had headed east toward the Ballard Bridge. They heard the sirens giving chase, but somehow they knew that the SUV would escape. It blended into the rest of the SUVs, a dime a dozen.

The Coast Guard cutter *Victory* idled in Elliott Bay, a half mile south of the *Longitude*. At dawn, the *Victory* would move up beside the *Longitude*, radio the skipper, and then they would board the cargo vessel. Venus wore her Fish & Wildlife uniform and carried various official documents.

Olson, Song, and two other U.S. F&W agents, all in uniform, prepared to board the *Longitude*. They were calling it a routine check for wildlife contraband. Even so, if the crew of the *Longitude* suspected anything else, they'd be ready. Anything could happen. Venus and Rocco briefed the team. Then they sat in the galley, drinking hot coffee until the first rays of morning light poked through the clouds. The *Victory*'s engine ramped up and Venus got on the radio.

The *Longitude*'s skipper identified himself as Dmitry Rostovich. Venus told Rostovich to prepare for a boarding. The skipper didn't reply immediately, and when he did, he said, "How many in your party?"

Venus told Rostovich there would be five agents from U.S. F&W. A routine check of the cargo. No reason in particular they'd chosen the *Longitude* to check, just a random search. Nothing to worry about. Rostovich said, "You are most welcome to come aboard and check. Ve heff nothing to hide."

"What's your cargo?" she asked the skipper.

He took his time replying, then said in a raspy voice, "I am told we are carrying American-made RVs and some mobile homes. For export to Kamchatka Peninsula. That's all."

"We'll board in twenty minutes," she told the skipper, and got off the radio.

As the *Victory* pulled up beside the *Longitude,* Venus stood near the gangplank and watched the Russian ship's crew scurrying around the main deck. Rocco stood on one side of her and Louie Song stood on the other. She was acutely aware of the tension between them. She could neither prevent it nor try to explain what she felt for each of them. A triangle is a triangle, and no point has more power than the others. Louie Song had blazed deep inroads into her heart, understanding her better than anybody ever had, loving her gently, tenderly, passionately. She could not deny that she loved him, even now, even after her evening with Rocco. But Rocco, too, had managed to burgle her heart, and stake a claim there. Standing between Rocco and Song on the *Victory,* she wondered if Song could tell what she and Rocco had been doing just a few hours ago.

Song said, "Remind me again. What does Ziggy Nelson look like?"

She said, "You can't miss him. Red beard. Pierced like a pincushion. Believe me, we'll know him by sight."

Rocco said, "About five minutes to boarding."

Venus got on her cell phone, called Olson, who was waiting inside the cabin along with the other two Fish & Wildlife agents. "It's time," she said. Less than a minute passed, and then Olson appeared, accompanied by agents Sweetwater and Mandell. Eric Sweetwater, one of F&W's toughest agents, was the kind of agent you send into the big battles. Eric had dragged Venus to safety during the last poacher raid, after she'd been shot in the face. The other agent was a rookie, an African-American named Mandell. Curtis Mandell. Already, Mandell had racked up a record number of arrests of black marketeers, mostly in Seattle's Chinatown International District. Mandell stood six foot six in his bare feet and his face wore a constant grin, which inevitably caught the enemy off guard. Olson had chosen his three toughest agents: Song, Sweetwater, and Mandell. She couldn't have asked for a better team. Maybe for an agent who spoke and understood Russian fluently, but that would be asking for the nonexistent.

Inside the *Victory*'s main cabin, a half a dozen Coast Guardsmen, armed and ready, waited for Venus's signal. She hoped she wouldn't have to call on them. She hoped this would be easy. Board the *Longitude,* locate the boy, take him and his kidnappers into custody, go home. This was the plan, but plans almost never go as planned. Still, it helped to visualize a smooth, successful operation, without gunshots exchanged.

She reached up and touched her jawline. It had become a habit with her, to feel the hole in her face. Venus felt Song's eyes on her; she turned and looked at him. Song placed one of his hands on her face and she felt her skin burn; she wondered if Rocco was watching. Song said, "Hey, beautiful." Then he removed his hand.

When the *Victory*'s gangplank lowered onto the *Longitude,* Venus went first across the walkway, followed in order by Olson, then Sweetwater, then Mandell, with Song bringing up the rear. Rostovich was waiting on the deck.

He was a short and stocky mix of Russian and Inupiat, mostly Russian. He had a handshake like a meat grinder, and when he smiled, no teeth were visible, just a lot of blank space. "Welcome, welcome," he said cheerily.

Venus said, "Do you understand English?"

Rostovich said, "Have to. It's the rules. Have to speak good enough to talk to American harbor pilots."

Venus said, "We'd like to inspect your cargo. We'll start with the main hold, then move on to the engine rooms, the galley, pilothouse, and crew's quarters. We'll need to inspect every inch of the vessel."

Rostovich nodded. "Sure," he said. "I been inspected before this time. Only once, but I know the routine."

Venus introduced the team. Led by Rostovich, they began walking toward the lift that would take them down into the hold. Venus said to Rostovich, "How many crewmen?"

"Five. It's all we need. When we get to Kamchatka, we hire dock workers to unload."

"What other ports do you visit?"

Rostovich stood aside to let Venus into the lift first. Olson and the team followed; then Rostovich stepped into the lift and pressed the button that would take them down to the hold. The elevator sank smoothly. Rostovich said, "Shanghai. Singapore. Vladivostok. That's about it."

Venus said, "How about Hong Kong?"

Rostovich bent his head to one side, as if pondering. Finally, he said, "Maybe two times, or even three. *Da,* we've made port in Hong Kong."

Venus said, "Who owns the *Dolgota?* The *Longitude?*"

Rostovich smiled. "Me," he said with pride.

Venus said, "The Port Authority's documents list the Dolgota's skipper as Igor Kremnyev."

Rostovich smiled. "But he quit."

When they reached the hold, Rostovich held the door and exited the lift last. They were met by a crewmember, whom Rostovich introduced as Uri. Uri was big, almost as tall as Mandell and probably at least as strong, and somewhere along the way, a hard glint had taken possession of his flinty eyes.

Rostovich spoke in Russian to Uri. Uri nodded, then made a sweeping gesture with his arm and said, "*Pashaulsta.*" Rostovich stepped back into the lift and disappeared.

They followed Uri into the hold. It was crammed with floor-to-ceiling stacks of containers, each big enough to accommodate a large car, SUV, or an RV. In the rear of the hold, several small mobile homes were steel crated, their manufacturer's seals still on the crate frames. Uri handed over bills of lading and export papers, all apparently in good order.

Uri said, "*Palshaulsta*" again, and they followed him from one crate to the next, inspecting each one, Venus making remarks into a small tape recorder. An hour later, they had finished in the hold and went back up in the lift to the main deck, where Rostovich met them.

"Time for breakfast," he said, smiling hospitably.

He led them to the galley, where they had smoked salmon, sturdy rye bread with great blobs of butter, goat's milk cheese, and thick, sour kefir. The coffee was hot and bitter. Rostovich ate heartily and entertained them with tales of life on the Kamchatka Peninsula. He'd grown up there, lived there all his life. Still did, when he wasn't on the high seas, that is.

Venus watched Rostovich's animated show. Parts of him seemed genuine. And yet he seemed to harbor a guilty conscience. After the meal, she asked to tour the engine room. They went back down in the lift, then entered the engine room, where the ship's massive engines were being cared for by two engineers, both Russians. Neither engineer spoke English. Half an hour was all it took to inspect the engine room and the surrounding area thoroughly. Back up in the lift, then to the galley, where they had eaten breakfast. The galley inspection took no more than fifteen minutes. The Russian cook spoke bare-bones English, mostly words referring to foods. He could say *cheese, bottle,* and *beefsteak.* The galley held no surprises, no hint of trouble. Next, Rostovich led them through the crew's quarters, a warren of disheveled cubicles that smelled of body oils and urine. Nothing suspicious there.

"We'll go up to the pilothouse now," said Rostovich, obviously happy with how the inspection was proceeding. "And there I must leave you. My navigator, Yevgeny, needs a break. And we need to sail before noon if we expect to make our schedule."

The pilothouse cut a wide and narrow swath across the front of the top cabin. Its equipment was state-of-the-art and surprisingly well maintained. Compared to the rest of the *Longitude,* the pilothouse was pristine and technologically marvelous. Rostovich couldn't contain his pride. "This," he said, "is where I live. Welcome to my home sweet home."

While the others were inspecting the equipment, Venus said to Rostovich, "Where do you sleep?"

His mouth worked, but no words came out. His eyes suddenly grew dark, his gaze distant. Venus repeated the question. Finally, he said, "Poof. I don't sleep much, but when I do"—he swept a hand across a long built-in couch in the rear of the pilothouse—"I sleep right here."

Venus pointed to a closed door in the rear wall. "That must be the captain's quarters," she said.

Rostovich looked at the door as if seeing it for the first time. He shrugged. He said, "Not much used. Maybe when I want to read, or just be alone, I go in there." He shook his head. "Not much used."

Venus said, "I'd like to take a look."

Rostovich sucked his cheek and chewed. He was thinking. He ran a stubby hand across his face, and Venus noticed light beads of sweat forming on his forehead. Over at the controls, Yevgeny was showing Song, Olson, Sweetwater, and Mandell how the depth sounder worked. Rostovich stared toward them, but his stare went through them and traveled a long way out into the bay. Maybe he was thinking of a way to divert her attention from the door. She waited, let him think it over, allowed him to consider the implications. He wouldn't be the first Russian captain arrested in U.S. waters for refusing to comply with the orders of federal agents. Still, that didn't mean he'd like it. Maybe now, Kamchatka Peninsula seemed like a fine place to live and work. Forget the high seas, where pirates and infidels mingle with innocent sailors and singing a Russian sea shanty cuts you no slack. Sailors have a sacred bond. Whatever goes on at sea is confidential, not to be shared with landlubbers, especially not with the police.

Behind Rostovich, the sun rising in the sky had nearly reached its zenith. Venus glanced at her Swatch: 11:17 A.M.

Then Rostovich opened his mouth and said, "We can't go in there."

"Why not?"

"Because my son is in there. He is very sick. He has a contagious disease. Only his doctor can be with him."

"What disease?"

Rostovich rubbed his face. He said, "Malaria. He has malaria."

Venus said, "Malaria isn't contagious, Captain. Humans contract malaria only from mosquito bites. If your son has malaria, he won't spread it. You ought to know that, having traveled in so many exotic tropical ports."

Rostovich's eyes searched the pilothouse, looking for his next excuse, but he couldn't muster one, and so he shrugged and said, "Let me call inside first. Tell them you need to see in there. But only you, understand? I don't want my son disturbed by a lot of people."

"I understand."

Rostovich got on his intercom and spoke softly in Russian. He argued with someone, then said finally, "*Da, kanyeshna. Ya poneemayoo,*" meaning "Yes, certainly. I understand."

Rostovich turned to Venus and smiled ingenuously. "We wait five minutes," he said. "The doctor wants to prepare the boy."

She moved a little to the right, made eye contact with Song. That's all she had to do. They'd communicated like this dozens of times in critical situations. Song blinked, and she could read his comprehension. He'd be ready. The team would be there for her. That's what she and Song believed at that moment.

While they waited, Rostovich said something in Russian to Yevgeny. The navigator kept his back to Rostovich but nodded and said, "*Ya poneemayoo.*"

Yevgeny spoke calmly but rapidly into the intercom. Rostovich hitched up his trousers. Maybe checking for his gun. In the distance, another ship's horn sounded, its mournful melody traveling languidly across the bay. If she looked out to her right, Venus could see Elliott Bay Marina, where the *Caprice* was still docked. She could make out its silhouette. To the left lay the *Victory*, its gangplank still attached to the *Longitude*. Off the stern, the bay and the Seattle waterfront glittered in the sunlight. Straight ahead, the mouth of the bay led into the shipping lanes.

Venus said, "It's been five minutes. Maybe they're ready for us."

Rostovich said, "Okay. You and me. Let's go."

CHAPTER TWENTY-NINE

The door slid open. Rostovich went in first, then Venus. The door slid shut. She was standing in a salon twice the depth of the pilothouse and as wide. It was furnished like a gaudy Vegas penthouse, all throw rugs and plaster statues, filigree touches everywhere. Mirrors across the walls. And in the rear, a curtained-off section. She was looking at the crimson curtain when she felt the cold metal against her right temple. The pressure grew stronger. Asking if he could shoot her now, Rostovich said, *"Mozhna?"*

A voice, coming from the shadows, said, *"Nyet."*

Rostovich lowered his gun. He led her to the crimson curtain and said, "I want to introduce you to my son. His name is Alyexi. Please, don't take too long." And then he pulled the curtain aside.

He lay beneath a black silk duvet, a black bolster tucked behind his head and neck. The coverlet hid his entire torso except for his head and shoulders. Still, she recognized him: his blond hair, the bangs brushing into his ice blue eyes, the full mouth, the haughty expression had faded to a wan stare. She went over to the side of the bed and, containing her rage, said, "Henry, it's me, Venus."

Slowly, he turned his head to look at her. In a weak voice, he said, "What are you doing here?"

"I came to take you home."

Rostovich coughed lightly.

Henry said, "I am home."

"Your home is with your parents," she said gently, so as not to frighten him.

Henry glanced past her toward the shadows. She followed his gaze and saw the silhouette of a man holding a gun.

"I'm staying with Larry and Ziggy," Henry said. "My parents can go to hell."

Venus placed a hand on the black silk coverlet. "Your parents love you," she said. "They want you to come home."

Henry laughed bitterly, "Go away," he said. "You can't save someone who doesn't want to be saved." Then he turned his head and closed his eyes.

She could not resist the urge to draw back the coverlet. He was wearing black silk pajamas. His right arm was heavily bandaged at the stub where his hand used to be attached.

She grabbed Rostovich, shoved him against the cabin. Rostovich shoved her back. The man who had spoken to Rostovich came forward, and she saw Ziggy for the first time. Up close, she could see the family resemblance. Like Kulagin had said, Larry Chekhov's brother. Venus said, "You bastards are going to fry for this."

Rostovich shrank back and whined, "I am only captain of the *Longitude*."

Ziggy shoved the round steel barrel of his gun against Venus's temple. Reaching down, he removed her gun from its holster and her cell phone from her belt, then tucked both guns into his belt.

Rostovich raised his own gun in his itchy fingers and placed it at Venus's head. Once again, he said, *"Mozhna?"*

"Nyet, nyet," insisted Ziggy, and then he said something else in Russian, but Venus didn't understand it. Then Ziggy went out through the curtain. She heard the sliding door open and she could feel the air from outside and heard the voices of the men in the pilothouse.

"Who did this?" she asked Rostovich.

Rostovich said, "It's what they told me to say. They didn't want you to see this boy. I don't know why they did it. I don't know anything. I just take my orders and follow them."

"Who gives the orders, Captain?"

Rostovich shook his head. "Please, don't blame me for this. I should tell you the truth. It doesn't matter now. You see, you won't get off this ship." He bent his head slightly, almost apologetically. He said, "I was Captain Kremnyev's first mate. But Captain Kremnyev had . . . well, an unfortunate accident, so I have taken over the *Longitude*. I am a good man, really I am. I would never hurt a child. Believe me, I have son of my own. I would never hurt any child. Maybe Larry and Ziggy would hurt a little child. Not me. Not Dmitry Rostovich."

She grabbed him by his shirt and shoved her face into his. She said, "Tell me where Larry Chekhov is or you'll wish you were in the gulag."

Rostovich made a tragicomic face and poked a gun in her ribs. "I am sorry to remind you that you will not leave this ship alive," he said.

From the pilothouse came sudden bursts of gunfire. Then shouting, scuffling. Yelling, confusion. More gunfire.

She moved toward the curtains. Rostovich laughed and said, "Too late, miss. It is all finished."

He didn't stop her. The first thing she saw was Yevgeny standing in his usual spot at the controls, a gun tucked in his belt. He had picked up speed and she could feel the ship moving swiftly. At the navigator's feet lay Eric Sweetwater and beside him sprawled Curtis Mandell, both bleeding profusely from gunshot wounds. Eric had taken a bullet through the heart. Mandell had taken several in the torso and one through the head. She knelt over Sweetwater. He was dead. She turned to Mandell. He, too, was dead. Where were Song and Olson?

She heard a soft thud and felt the *Longitude* move. She watched as Yevgeny pulled away from the *Victory*. On the *Victory*'s deck, Rocco and the rest of the team were trying to reboard the *Longitude,* when the gangplank wavered and then, with a screech, dropped, crashing against the *Victory*'s side. The *Victory*'s steel hull absorbed the blow, but the twisted gangplank dangled uselessly. Yevgeny had severed the umbilical cord. Now he flipped a switch. A pinpoint laser beam shot out of the pilothouse and struck Rocco in the face, nearly blinding him. Rocco hit the deck, gun drawn, and fired at Yevgeny, who laughed and aimed the laser again at the *Victory* as he ramped up the *Longitude*'s speed. The Coast Guard cutter was swift and seaworthy and surely could outrun the *Longitude*. But first it had to recover its gangplank. As the *Longitude* gained distance, Venus caught sight of Rocco again, aboard the *Victory,* and then the boats were too far apart to recognize anyone.

Overhead, a police helicopter approached. Yevgeny glanced up at the sky and changed the ship's direction, turning slightly to starboard. The sound of the chopper's churning blades grew louder. Yevgeny flicked the laser switch, aimed the beam at the chopper pilot. The chopper turned on its side flipped over, and fell into the bay.

A second helicopter approached. This time, Yevgeny didn't employ the laser beam. Venus saw the chopper move down and hover above the foredeck. Behind her, Rostovich coughed lightly.

"We'll be gone before anyone finds you," he said. "Anyway, in a few minutes my ship will explode." He pointed out the window. "That, too."

She looked out the window. The *Victory* had finally recovered its gangplank. The cutter was a quarter mile behind the *Longitude,* but moving in fast. "Here they come," she said.

Rostovich seemed amused. "They won't make it this far before they blow up."

"No," she cried. "You've got to warn them."

Rostovich made a sad face. "Too late." He spoke to Yevgeny. The navigator reached for his gun, turned halfway around, and pointed it at her. Rostovich went back into the captain's quarters. Ziggy appeared on the foredeck.

Where were Olson and Louie? They might have gone back across the gangplank before it got detached. Or they might still be on the *Longitude.* Either way, they would be blown up, like herself, like Rocco and the Coast Guard crew.

When the chopper set down on the *Longitude*'s foredeck, the *Victory* was less than two hundred yards away. Rostovich returned, carrying Henry in his arms. Henry's head hung limply over the captain's arm. Groggy, he was moaning. Rostovich said something in Russian to Yevgeny and exited the pilothouse with Henry. She watched through the window as Ziggy and Rostovich lifted Henry up into the chopper, then climbed in after him, followed by the *Longitude*'s other crewmembers. Now, as far as she knew, only she and the navigator were left aboard. Pointing his gun at her, Yevgeny turned around and faced her.

He had the face of an angel until he sneered, and then all the evil oozed to the surface. He licked his lips, hungry to kill. He probably liked the idea of killing a woman. He had evil written all over his face. Why was he taking his time? Why didn't he pull the trigger? He seemed to be relishing her frozen fear.

The ship lurched. Yevgeny turned to check the controls. She dove for his gun, knocked it from his hand onto the floor. It skittered across the pilothouse, ricocheted off Mandell's body. Yevgeny dove at Venus, knocked her to the floor. He was strong, much stronger than she was, and he fought dirty. With one foot, he kicked the gun up to his hand, grasped it. He squeezed the trigger, firing off a shot, but she had delivered a hard blow to his shooting arm, and the bullet went astray. She shoved her elbow into his mouth, jammed it as hard as she could with her body, and pinned his torso down. She used her other hand as a fist and sank it into his diaphragm. He gasped and let go of the gun. She grabbed it.

The chopper was waiting for him. The *Victory* was less than fifty yards distant, bearing down fast. Yevgeny, breathing hard, raised his hands over his head. She kept the gun pointed at him. From the vicinity of the chopper, someone fired a gun into the pilothouse. She ducked. Yevgeny lunged, kicked her to the floor, and pinned her arm with his boot until her hand opened and she let go of the gun. Now he had to choose. Go for the gun or go for the chopper. There wasn't time for both. He ran to the door. Venus grabbed the gun and fired. He stumbled onto the deck, blood flooding his eyes. He stumbled again and then, wrenching sideways, fell overboard just as the chopper lifted off the foredeck. It banked and swung around to head southeast.

The *Longitude* kept moving, but the *Victory* was gaining on her. Venus tried shouting to the *Victory*'s skipper, but he was inside the pilothouse and didn't hear. Where was Rocco? Inside with the skipper. Now she saw him through the window. Then Olson, and then Song. They were all aboard the *Victory*, watching the chopper fly away. Why were they all in the pilothouse? No crew on deck. She yelled, but they didn't hear. She ran to the *Longitude*'s controls. The navigator had disabled the radio. She fumbled around until she found the switches to cut the engines.

In the corner of the pilothouse, she found a wetsuit and diving gear. She dressed rapidly in a suit too large for her small frame. It would have to do. She dropped over the side of the *Longitude* into the frigid Sound. She swam as fast as she could. When the explosion ripped through the *Longitude,* she felt the roiling wake. She swam toward the *Victory*.

The *Victory*'s hull was white, and the hot sun beating down into the cold crystalline water glared off its surface. She moved fast, circling the vessel once without success. She dove deeper and circled again, once again without success. She decided to take one more look, concentrating on the bottom of the hull. She found the explosives attached to the bottom of the propeller.

She had disarmed smaller bombs in the past, and even then had risked her life. This bomb was huge, more complex, and had been freshly attached, likely within the past hour. Someone had gone over the starboard side of the *Longitude,* dived to twenty feet or so, and approached the *Victory* from the depths of the bay. Planted the explosives. Set a timer. Now she read the timer. Three minutes to go.

Her best hope might be to surface and try to warn the *Victory*'s crew to jump ship. Even then, *if* they escaped into the water, the explosion would probably blow them up. There was no time. She had to try to disable the bomb. But how? Frantically, she studied the wiring attached to the intricate metal mechanism. If she could detach the bomb from the hull, and the explosion occurred in a wet vacuum, it would be less powerful. She concentrated on the heavy metal arm that hooked around the prop shaft, fastening the bomb to the propeller, but it was thick and she had nothing to cut it with. Her only choice was to take a chance, try to disable the bomb before the timing mechanism triggered its explosion.

The wires were a rainbow of deadly veins that she couldn't decipher. She had less than two minutes now. If she disabled the timer, that might disable the bomb. She tried smashing the timing device without disturbing the explosives but couldn't give it enough force. She saw the timer's digital readout turn over to sixty seconds.

It's now or never, she told herself. She extended the fingers of her left hand toward the wires and was making a last-ditch decision which to pull first when in her peripheral vision she saw a figure moving toward her. A diver, moving fast in her direction, carrying what looked like a machine gun. She froze.

When the diver got up close, she saw it wasn't a machine gun. It had a saw blade. She looked at the diver's face. When she realized who he was, she showed him where the steel arm looped around the prop shaft. He started sawing. The timer was down to forty seconds. She held on to the device and he sawed through the steel arm. Slowly, slowly, the metal took its time dissolving under the saw's pressure. Thirty seconds. Slowly, slowly. Halfway through. Twenty seconds. That couldn't be enough time. Impossible. The saw worked and worked, grinding away at the steel arm. Ten seconds. The arm was thick and resistant. She waved the diver away, but he kept sawing, and then she was holding the bomb in her hand, free from the *Victory*'s hull. She let the bomb go. It sank beneath the *Victory* as she swam to the water's surface. When her head came above water, she heard a muffled burp from a benign underwater blast.

She was swimming back to the *Victory* when ahead of her she saw a glowing, undulating object on the water's surface. Could it be? Yes. A giant jellyfish. Bigger than she'd ever seen. Big as a car, maybe bigger. At least as big as Tim's bed. Its translucence reflected sunlight. It dazzled and undulated and moved closer to her. She could see its tentacles and its massive curly mane, just as Tim had described. A monstrous lion's mane.

Something touched her shoulder. She swung around and saw Louie Song surfacing beside her. She said, "Check out the j-fish."

Song spit out seawater and looked around. He said, "What jellyfish?"

He was right to ask. The big jellyfish had disappeared.

PART THREE

Henry's hand arrived just before dawn. Tossed from a speeding car, it landed on the Pedersons' parking strip near a bystander who had been hanging around the scene, hoping to catch a glimpse of the famous actress, who lived next door. The hand struck the bystander's ankle. He looked down and nearly fainted. Then he saw Kimberly Forget. Recognized her from television. The man yelled and Kimberly came running. That's what Kimberly and the man told Rocco when he took possession of the severed hand. When it had been sent off to the police lab, Rocco turned to Nils Pederson and said, "I think it's time you bare your soul."

They were in the Pedersons' living room. Venus was standing at the great glass picture window, staring out at the Land of Thrush. Rocco sat on one of Ingrid Pederson's long couches. Ingrid sat in her wing chair. Nils stood near the fireplace, his arm resting on the mantel, looking poised but worried. Cora, Ingrid's sister, had made sandwiches and lemonade, but these sat untouched on the coffee table. No one felt much like eating or drinking—not even lemonade, though the day was hot and muggy, the air close, stifling.

Nils chewed his lower lip. Rocco watched him and waited. Rocco wasn't in any hurry, because he knew that the answers that would lead to finding Henry could come only from Nils now. Everyone else was dead, or in hiding. Nils was the only accessible witness. Maybe not a witness to events as much as the person who was privy to the scheme that had started this wave of evil. And Nils had been stupid. Marked bills had infuriated Ziggy and Natalia.

Someone coughed. Ingrid. And then she hiccuped and broke into a sob. "Oh Nils," she cried, "if you know anything at all, please tell them."

Nils sighed and turned to face his audience. He could work an audience if necessary. And now it was necessary. Still, he wasn't sure how little he could get away with revealing. The less the better.

"I imagine this goes with the territory," he said uncomfortably. "Being prominent, wealthy. Kidnapping is something Ingrid and I have always considered with dread. We've talked about it on numerous occasions. But we never really believed it would happen to us. Then, well, you know how people talk."

Nils went to the coffee table, poured a glass of lemonade, and held it up inquiringly. No takers. Nils carried the glass back over to the mantel and repositioned himself. He drank about half a glassful and set the glass on the mantel. Ingrid stood up, went over to a Danish-modern cabinet, and opened a drawer. She fished out a leather coaster and handed it to Nils, who placed it underneath the glass on the mantel. Protection.

Venus said, "What were people saying?"

Nils shrugged. "You know how rumors get around. I don't recall who it was; one of my employees probably told me. Every major rumor that travels through this city passes through my office at some point."

Venus said, "Why's that?"

Nils said, "I've been considering running for public office. For mayor, actually. So I have my ear to the ground. My employees feed me everything they hear."

"And what did your employee hear?"

"People were saying that Rupert Scree had gone into the car-smuggling business. That he was shuttling stolen cars on the *Caprice*." Nils glanced up at Venus. "I'm sorry to speak like this," he said. "I know your mother was very fond of Scree. It's just what folks were saying after the *Spindrift* was blown up. If I'd suspected any of this before Pearl . . . well, you can bet I would have prohibited my children from boarding that boat."

Rocco nodded. "Go on with the rumor," he said.

"Word was that Scree had placed explosives on the *Spindrift* after learning that someone was using the *Spindrift* to compete with him. That both Scree and someone using the *Spindrift* were delivering stolen cars to the same container vessel and the competition got ugly. So Scree, being a former Coast Guard diver, wired explosives to the *Spindrift*'s hull and it exploded on the Fourth of July, as we all know too well."

Nils drank the rest of his lemonade and went back for a refill. This time, he didn't return to the mantel, but walked over to the big picture window and looked out. The sun beat down into his gardens, and he knew if he touched the sliding window, he would feel the heat from outdoors. Thank God for air conditioning. Who would ever have thought residents of the Pacific Northwest would need air conditioning?

Ingrid had started sobbing again, more quietly now. Rocco picked up a sandwich wedge and bit into it. Venus wondered why he didn't push Nils harder. Time was wasting. Every minute counted.

Venus said, "What's the rumor about Scree's murder?"

Nils kept his back to them. He shrugged lightly and said, "Retaliation."

"The other car smuggler?"

"That's what people are saying."

Venus said, "Who's the other smuggler? According to rumor?"

Nils shook his head. "I never heard a name. But I've heard he's dead. I heard two stories. One that he blew up with the *Spindrift*. The other, that the Russian mob killed him and then they chopped off his hand and delivered it to his wife. His widow."

Venus said, "Where'd you hear that?"

Nils inhaled deeply, exhaled slowly. "Can't recall. Stuff gets around. And then Pearl's hand being missing . . ."

Ingrid cried out. Nils raised a hand. His wife bent at the waist and rocked, sobbing quietly. She murmured, "Nils, you told me sharks took her hand."

"Take it easy, Ingrid dear. We don't know anything for certain. Maybe never will."

Rocco said, "Have either of you heard of Larry Chekhov?"

Ingrid shook her head. Nils hesitated, then shook his.

"How about Ziggy Chekhov, or Ziggy Nelson?"

Ingrid looked at Nils, then at Rocco. "Why, no," she said. "At least I haven't heard any of these names. What about you, Nils?"

Nils shook his head. "Nope," he said. "Never."

Venus and Rocco both resisted exchanging a glance.

Venus said, "One of your children, either Pearl or Henry, may have confided to Tim what was happening aboard the *Caprice*. Something very illegal. Maybe the car smuggling was the secret, but perhaps there was more. And

Tim knew, but whichever of your children told him also swore Tim to secrecy. I think Tim was murdered because he got caught spying on whatever activity was taking place aboard the *Caprice*."

Ingrid sobbed. Nils shook his head. "Pearl drowned. He held her head under the water. Why can't you just accept that that little Asian Kid murdered my girl?"

The room fell silent. Ingrid slowly raised up and stared at Venus. Nils kept his back turned. Rocco flicked his thumbnail. Venus didn't know what he was thinking, but he wasn't stopping her, so she said, "Do you know a boy named John Stark?"

"Never heard of him," replied Nils, speaking curtly.

"Yes, we do, Nils," Ingrid said confidently. "John Stark is that little boy Henry brought home from Westlake Mall. Remember? He's about Henry's age, a very good-looking young boy. But after Henry stole money out of my purse, I thought John might be a bad influence. I told him to never come around Henry again. Remember, I told you about this, Nils?"

"Maybe something. I don't really recall."

Venus said, "John Stark disappeared on the same day Pearl disappeared off the *Caprice*. He was last seen at Hiram Chittenden Locks. He might have boarded a boat there, as it came through the locks. He hasn't been seen since. These children shared a common connection with an adult who recruited them for some activity, though exactly how they were recruited, or for what purpose, we can't yet say for certain."

Nils, still staring out the window, said, "My children were never allowed to use the Internet without supervision. The only other access they've had to computers is at their private school, where the children are carefully supervised at all times."

"Might not have been via the Internet," said Rocco.

"Was it Rupert?" asked Ingrid. "Was Rupert harming our children all along? Nils, do you know anything about this? Please be honest with me."

Nils turned around and faced Ingrid. She placed a fisted hand over her mouth. Nils said, "God, I haven't the faintest idea who would want to harm Henry. I've racked my brain." He seemed to swallow back a sob. "I just don't know."

Venus said, "What do you know about the social worker? The woman calling herself Dr. Lane."

Nils shook his head. "I haven't the foggiest. All I know is what you've told me, that she was posing as a court-appointed social worker. I'm as clueless as you folks apparently are."

"Any idea where we might find her?"

Behind her hand, Ingrid sniffed and cleared her throat; then she reached into her skirt pocket and drew out a business card. Peering over her fist, she murmured faintly, "Try this phone number."

Nils moved forward, reaching out his hand as if to intervene. "Ingrid, please," he said.

Venus stepped in front of Nils, accepting the simple white card from Ingrid, and Nils backed away, obviously irritated.

Ingrid said, "She didn't give it to me. It fell out of her purse and I found it underneath the couch. I had meant to return it to her. Oh, and her first name is Cherry. At least that's what she told me."

Venus read the business card: "Lane Pathogenetics Laboratories, 2922 Western Avenue, Seattle 98121." A telephone number and a fax number were included. No E-mail address.

"May we keep this?"

Ingrid nodded.

Rocco looked at Venus and stood up. They walked into the front hall. Rocco said, "Good work."

"A lot of conjecture. At least we made the connection to John Stark." She looked up at him. He was tired, she could tell, from long hours on the job. Brown circles shadowed his eyes and she noticed the skin on his jawline was sagging. Even so, he made her heart skip a beat. She said, "Why didn't you bring up the red Jetta?"

"That's next on my agenda."

"What do you know?"

"That the red Jetta was sold to Pederson Security Company, that it's legally registered to Nils Pederson, and that it hasn't been seen around Nils's company offices since the day after Pearl drowned." Rocco checked his watch. "I'm going to ask Nils about it now. I'll let you know what lie he spins."

"The woman posing as a social worker was driving it."

"Dr. Cherry Lane."

She looked up at him. "We let our own guys get killed."

Rocco said, "Yeah." He squeezed her shoulder. "You go on. I need more time with Nils."

Venus said, "I'll have a look-see at Lane Pathogenetics."

"How are Olson and Song?"

She shrugged. "Olson's . . . okay. Grief-stricken, like the rest of us, over Eric's and Curt's deaths. And mad as hell that we dragged him into this. Other than that, stable." She reached up and scratched her neck. "Olson told me that during the ambush, he and Song just barely made it across the gangplank alive." She paused, then added, "I haven't spoken with Song since the *Victory*."

Rocco said, "Did they ever explain why they didn't shoot the Russian navigator?"

She shrugged. "Olson told me the gunmen burst out of a ceiling hatch, firing like mad dogs. Took them totally by surprise. They didn't have time to draw their weapons. Curt and Eric didn't even have time to duck. Olson and Song had just enough time to jump out of the line of fire and then run across the gangplank. Olson said they tried shooting the navigator from there. But that sucker was wily and he had that laser beam. You're lucky you weren't blinded, by the way. The gunmen covered the navigator while he ramped up the ship's speed and changed course."

Rocco said, "At least you took care of Yevgeny. Maybe saved our lives, those of us who survived."

"Louie saved our lives. We should be grateful."

"I am, but that doesn't mean I have to like him."

"You should like him. Louie's a topnotch human being."

Rocco shook his head. "Don't tell me whom I should or shouldn't like. I don't care if he's Mahatma Gandhi. I don't like him."

She squinted up at Rocco. She said, "I never noticed your eyes were so vividly green."

"Look who's talking, Miss Traffic Lights."

Both the *Dirty Blonde* and the *Earline* were now in dry dock at the Harbor Patrol's inspection site. Venus stopped on Harbor Island and consulted with the forensics examiner. "Clean as a whistle," said the examiner. "Nothing of apparent interest. Not even a suspicious fingerprint."

"What about that woman Lina's belongings?"

The examiner scratched his beard. "Now, I couldn't tell you much about those. She took them all with her over to the motel where they were staying. She didn't leave anything but her fingerprints aboard either boat."

At the Edgewater, where the room had been sealed off, Venus got the same story. The duty officer said forensics had found nothing of particular relevance. Natalia had left behind some clothing when she fled the Edgewater Inn with the gunman, but that was all. Lina had been wearing only her bathrobe when she was taken to the hospital. She'd left behind some clothing, her passport, and a few worn photo-graphs—probably family pictures.

"Where did they take Lina's stuff?" she asked.

The officer said, "I imagine it's at the main precinct, in the evidence room."

She had to get Rocco to call in permission. He was still at the Pedersons' and Nils had clammed up. She was escorted into the evidence room and watched like a death-row inmate while she pawed through Lina's things. Big, spacious clothing: a fleece-lined overcoat, two bulky sweaters, the flowered dress she'd worn for her big swim, a few more dresses, that one pair of black capris and the white turtleneck shirt she had seen Lina wearing when they first met on the *Dirty Blonde*. Two pairs of gravy-boat sneakers, boat shoes that could hold half of Delaware. A cosmetics case containing three tubes of lipstick, all deep crimson, each a shade different. A powder compact with a magnifying mirror. A metal roach clip, with little alligator teeth. A hairbrush containing gobs of bleached hairs. A comb marked "Made in Mockba." Metal hairpins. Six jumbo hair rollers and twelve medium-size ones. Tweezers and a small nail clipper. A half-empty tube of Plus White toothpaste. One bottle of sparkly red nail polish. A packet of razor blades. The razor itself had been itemized sepa-rately because she had used it on her carotid artery. That was all.

The photographs, all black-and-white ones, apparently had been taken in Russia—the far eastern part of Russia, Siberia. Several were of groups of people set in snowy scenes. One of the photos identified the group as "Vladi-vostok Christian Choir." There was a photograph of a small shorthaired dog, apparently a pet. On the back, someone had written "Fyodor" in Cyrillic letters. The last photograph was the payoff. A picture of Lina and a Russ-ian man whom Venus didn't recognize. On the back of this print, someone had written a caption in Russian: "Captain Igor Kremnyev and Lina Chekhovna Kremnyev. July 2001." Lina wearing a short white veil, holding a bouquet of calla lilies.

Moses had just finished piercing a girl's tongue when Venus walked into his salon. He scrubbed his hands and his arms up to the elbows before he shook her hand. He said, "Have you found that kid yet?"

"Negative. But I think you can help us."

"Anything, man," said Moses.

"I need you to hack into Nils Pederson's employee records."

Moses said, "Which company?"

She said, "Pederson Security. I want to know if someone named Ziggy Nelson ever worked as one of Nils Pederson's security guards, and if so, where he was assigned. I need you to go back in the records as far as possible. Can you do that?"

"Of course. That's simple," said Moses, "but it's highly illegal. Aren't you a cop? You should know that's illegal."

She waved a hand. "Just do it. And hurry. I need to know right now."

Moses turned to his computer while she stood watching over his shoulder. He knew how to hack. Ten minutes later, he had entered Pederson Security Company's employment records.

"What's the name again?" he asked her.

"Nelson. Ziggy, or some form thereof. Zigfeld, Zbignew, whatever. A Z name, with the last name being Nelson."

Moses searched and then shook his head. "Nothing. Nada."

She said, "Keep looking."

Moses searched some more, and she could see little beads of sweat forming on his forehead. "Here's a Nelson," he said. "Ardith Nelson. Female. Hired in 1997 as a dispatcher."

"That's not it." Venus took over the keyboard. Moses moved to give her room. She punched in the letter Z, then "Find all." Dozens of files came up. She scrolled down them.

"Z for *zone*. Zone, zone, zone, they're all zones. Z for—oh my God."

"What is it?" said Moses.

"Typing error. I accidentally typed an 'S'. I got Siggy Nelson. It says here that Pederson Security hired a Siggy Nelson in June of 1993."

He was listed as a Russian national, no green card. He was placed on payroll as a security guard for a downtown restaurant. Over the next four years, he was transferred to several other restaurants, some of which Rocco had said were vandalized or burned down. In January 2001, Nelson was assigned to guard the Pederson family home. That summer, he left the company to go to work for Icyfrost Seafood. His home address was listed as Shilshole Marina. His payroll records showed one dependant, a spouse named Natalia.

The building at 2922 Western Avenue was four stories high, inset from the curb and surrounded by a twenty-foot solid iron fence with an equally solid iron door, on which was a sign painted in twelve-inch letters: NO TRESPASSING. Nothing on the building's exterior identified it. No name, no mailbox, no sign reading LANE PATHOGENETICS. No buzzer system. No entry unless you possessed a coded key card to slip into the narrow slit in the iron fence, just beside the iron door.

Venus crossed the street and looked up at the building. Its windows faced west, out over Myrtle Edwards Park and a view of Elliott Bay. The windows were tinted dark and she couldn't see inside. She had parked the Audi around the corner. Now she went back for it, drove onto Western Avenue, and found a parking spot on the side of Western directly opposite the iron fence. She was suddenly aware she was hungry. She got out of the Audi, locked it, and walked to end of the block, then downhill to the café next door to the Orbit. Chez Gus. Named after the owner's Jack Russell terrier. Chez Gus served the best Dutch Babies in town, but she didn't want a Dutch Baby. She wanted red meat, her body craving protein, a desire she recognized as her body's preparation for a long siege. Pack in the protein, then sit around and wait and wait and wait. Sometimes patience paid off. She possessed little patience.

She ordered a rare hamburger, thought fleetingly about Creuzfeldt-Jakob disease, and changed her order to a sirloin steak, medium rare. No blood. She ordered a Coke with lime to wash it down. During her meal, she heard a distant sound, like an explosion. She chided herself for her paranoia and continued eating. She thought about Tim. Had he come to this little café just a few yards from where his body was recovered, and bought himself a meal before he boarded the *Earline*? Probably not. He would have been afraid of being recognized. He'd been on a mission. But what mission? What had Tim hoped to accomplish aboard the *Earline*? Had he planned to confront Larry Chekhov? Had he realized how dangerous the Chekhov brothers were? She decided that Tim had been very clear about the danger, must have feared that more children like Pearl Pederson and John Stark would die if he didn't do something. But what could a twelve-year-old boy do against the Russian Mafia? How did Tim think he could stop the Chekhovs? Venus might never know what Tim had planned. But she knew for certain that he had intended to prove his own innocence and that he had intended to expose the smut peddlers. "Sometimes a lie is a necessary evil, to protect the vulnerable from a worse kind of evil." What lie had Tim told?

Half an hour later, she paid her bill and walked back up the hill. The spot where she had parked the Audi was empty now, except for a pile of twisted metal and some smoldering ash, all surrounded by yellow police tape.

CHAPTER THIRTY-ONE

At nine o'clock, dusk fell over the city, and with twilight came ponderous clouds across the western sky, looming black and dense, pregnant with moisture. With total darkness came rain. Raindrops the size of marbles splashed off the curb, coalesced, and rampaged in rivulets down the street gutters. Venus stood beneath a burned-out streetlamp, shifting from one foot to the other, shivering in the sudden chill that shocked a city spoiled by weeks of more sun than rain. In the past hour, the temperature had dropped twenty degrees, from seventy-five to fifty-five. She was dressed for sun, not rain, and this was no small summer shower. This was a downpour without mercy, and on Western Avenue, she was the only creature stupid enough to be out in it. Even the fish in the sculpture garden's koi pond had dived deeper to avoid the rain and the cold, humid air. Even the police had abandoned the site of the Audi's explosion.

At 9:45, a black Cadillac Seville with dark-tinted windows pulled up to the iron gate. The driver's window came down and a hand shoved a key card into the compatible slot. The iron gate slowly slid to one side and the Caddy drove into the property. Venus bolted across the street and inside the gate just before it had completely closed. She knew security cameras might spot her, but she'd take the risk. The Caddy pulled into a garage. Venus ducked low and followed it into the building's interior. The Caddy's engine idled, then went silent. A moment later, the driver's door opened. A high-heeled sandal on a pale foot attached to a shapely pale leg emerged, followed by a twin, and then Cherry Lane stepped out of the Caddy. No one else. Just Snow White. She wore a tailored summer suit and the backless high-heeled sandals. Her dark hair was pulled back into a severe knot, not a strand out of place. She locked up the Caddy and walked toward an elevator. She put the key card into a slot and pulled it out again. The elevator door opened. She stepped into the elevator. Venus watched from behind the Caddy. The woman hadn't seen her. The elevator door shut. Venus watched the floor numbers light up above the elevator: 1, 2, 3, 4. The elevator stopped on the fourth floor, the building's top floor.

Venus wanted to talk to the woman, yes. But first she wanted to know more about her. Dr. Cherry Lane of Lane Pathogenetics Laboratories. Who was she and why had she impersonated a court-appointed social worker? Why had she tried to murder Rupert Scree? And then tried to kill Venus? She could be arrested; she could get, if not the death penalty, life imprisonment. She'd taken big risks. Why? Did she have a scheme for getting away without being prosecuted? If so, who would arrange this?

Of course. The parents.

The realization swept over Venus like a warm blanket. Might Nils have hired Cherry Lane to impersonate a court officer? Dr. Lane—whose doctorate might actually be in science instead of medicine—was certainly a smart cookie, smart enough to play at being a child psychologist. Smart enough to influence Henry's testimony, to implant false memories in his vulnerable brain. Even smart enough to win Tim's trust. Had Nils convinced Cherry Lane to poison Rupert Scree? Why? Because Rupert had seen something, or done something? But why would Cherry Lane do this for Nils? What was their connection? What bond did they share? What evil thing?

Nils hadn't counted on his kids being harmed. He hadn't counted on Pearl's drowning and he hadn't counted on Henry being kidnapped, his hand severed, maybe as punishment for trying to pawn off marked bills on the boy's captors. Nils hadn't counted on trouble of any kind. But he got it in spades after spreading his tentacles as wide as his privilege and power would allow, sucking in and devouring anyone who tried to compete. But who, really, was competing with Nils?

What had Kimberly Forget said? "Watch out for Nils." Kimberly Forget, the investigative journalist, a clever girl, ambitious perhaps, beyond scruples.

Venus looked around for a stairwell, found it. The door was locked. This door also required a key card. Venus took out the wallet she kept her badge, cash, and credit cards in, fished out the Visa card. It was the same size as the key card and fit into the slot. It'll never work, she told herself. She shoved it most of the way in and wiggled it. Nothing happened. She tried several times in vain, then turned the card over and tried again. A green light blinked on. She was in.

A huge overhead skylight invited some gray pall into the stairwell, illuminating it. When she reached the second floor, she thought she heard screeching. She stopped, listened. Yes, screeching. On the third floor, she heard the same sounds. The fourth floor was silent as a tomb when she entered the long hallway. From the stairwell, the hallway ran due west and branched out halfway across. She stood at the intersection and listened. Silence. She waited. God, she hated standing still. But she waited and it paid off. A woman's voice floated out of a door at the very western end of the hall: Cherry Lane speaking to one of her employees.

"Haven't I told you before, Edward, that you are never, and I mean never, under any circumstances whatsoever, allowed to dump waste materials into the drainage system? Do you understand?"

A low murmur from a man's voice. A youngish voice, saying, "Yes, Dr. Lane." Maybe an assistant, or a technician.

Cherry said, "Now that this has finally seeped into your idiot's brain, I want you to go down to the second floor and bring Babs up to me."

More muttering, then a sound. Edward was heading for the door. Venus ducked stage right and flattened against the wall. She heard Edward's feet padding along the hall, then saw him as he passed, turning to his stage right. A hefty young man, Amerasian maybe, built like a tractor. He walked a little way and pressed a button for the elevator. If he glanced up to his left, he would see her standing pressed against the wall at the hall's intersection. She froze. The elevator took its time coming. Edward was working his mouth, silently holding a conversation with an imaginary adversary. Maybe Cherry.

He glanced up once, just as the elevator arrived, its pinging diverting his attention even before he could focus down the hall. He stepped into the elevator and the door closed.

Venus walked down the hall toward the room she was sure must be Dr. Lane's office. She was standing outside the door when Cherry's cell phone rang.

"Nils, where are you?" said Cherry. A few seconds later, she said, "I have to check on Babs first. It'll only take a few minutes. Then Edward can go home. Can you be here in, say, half an hour?" Silence, then: "I know, I know, but it's okay. Just stop worrying so much." A pause, then Cherry said, "Look, Nils, I've tried my damnedest to help you. I could have been arrested any number of times. I risked everything for you."

Silence, then Cherry said, "Maybe I never should have fallen in love with you, Nils. Maybe we should have kept this all business and no romance. I have to be honest with you. Your wife told me about your plans to run for office, how you made her change her last name to yours to look better for the campaign. You have no intention of leaving Ingrid, Nils. Everything you've promised me has been a lie. All you ever wanted from me was the product rights, half of the profits. Now I see it, Nils. It took Ingrid's slip of tongue to open my eyes, but now I see that all along you never intended to leave Ingrid and marry me."

More silence, then: "Well the sex part is over, Nils, unless you can manage to find your cajones and leave Ingrid." A beat, then: "Don't shout at me. And stop calling me names. I'm sick and tired of your abuse, Nils."

Another beat, then Cherry sighed and said, "All right, you've had your say. Now you listen to me. This business transaction has nothing to do with your children. That's an entirely different matter. I don't know who has your boy, but it has nothing to do with me. I realize that your life is one living hell right now, Nils, and I'm doing my very best to help you. I've taken risks for you that I would never have taken for myself. Nils, I almost murdered two people for you! If Rupert Scree had died from the fentanyl, I shudder to think what would have happened to me. By the way, I had the distinct impression that Rupert was a pretty decent guy."

Two beats, then: "I don't *know* how the Chekhovs found out about the toxin. But I'd bet my life that they killed your kids. Larry's ruthless. I should know."

The door to Cherry Lane's office opened outward. Venus slipped behind it, pressed herself hard against the wall, and waited. A few minutes passed. Cherry was opening something, maybe the wrapper on an energy bar, or a candy bar. Venus could hear her chewing. Then the elevator pinged. Cherry Lane said, "Nils, this product is worth all the risks we've taken so far. If the negotiations with our client work out, you and I will walk away from this free and clear, and richer than we ever imagined. But if the Chekovs locate and steal our product, we've lost it all. So you better pay attention to their demands. I don't care if it is blackmail."

Footsteps sounded along the corridor. Venus held her breath. Edward wouldn't see her hidden behind the door, unless he tried to close it for some reason. He didn't. He walked into the office and set something down.

Cherry said, "I have to go now. I'll see you in half an hour. I'll wait in the garage. Honk when you arrive at the gate and I'll let you in."

A chattering sound, then Cherry said, "Edward, Edward. I meant take her to the lab and put her in with the others. Not bring her to my office."

"Yes, ma'am."

"I'm coming along. I need to finish up this test and get out of here."

Venus heard sounds as the two prepared to exit Cherry Lane's office. What if Cherry decided to shut her office door?

Cherry Lane and Edward came out of the office. They did not stop. They walked down the long hallway. Venus peered around the door and saw them turn left. Edward was holding on to a macaque the size of Zen, Liu Ping's dog. The macaque looked over Edward's shoulder, pointed at Venus, and made a squeaking sound as the trio turned into a doorway.

Venus moved quietly along the hall until she reached an inward-facing window. The window was either tinted or the room inside was in total darkness. Which? A second later, Venus had the answer as an ultraviolet light flooded the room. Carefully, she peered into the window. The room was full of macaques, and they were glowing fluorescent green. The color of some jellyfish at night.

Venus had heard about this medical breakthrough. Bioluminescent and fluorescent proteins harvested from *Aequorea victoria,* a jellyfish common to Puget Sound, the Strait of Juan de Fuca, and the Strait of Georgia in Canada. The proteins were used in medical research as trackers. But the protein had been cloned, eliminating the need to harvest more jellyfish. These macaques had apparently been genetically altered to include the gene that made some jellyfish glow. But this experiment had been done years earlier. Why bother to do it again?

The fluorescent monkeys skittered around the room, chasing one another's tails. They glowed only under special lights, but otherwise, they appeared perfectly normal. After a few minutes, the ultraviolet light went out and an incandescent light came on. The macaques looked perfectly normal, their fluorescent marker invisible. Venus ducked into a small utility closet and waited as Dr. Lane and Edward left the laboratory, turned right, and walked back down the hall.

"I'm delighted with Babs, Edward," said Cherry. "Very impressed. You did good work."

Edward laughed self-consciously and said, "I guess that gets me off the hook, eh?"

"This one last time. The next time I catch you dumping waste materials down the drain, I'll fire your big ass. That stuff drains straight down into Elliott Bay. I've told you that for the last time. It's potentially toxic. We're breaking the law here, sonny boy. I could be permanently shut down and fined within an inch of my life. Do you understand?"

"Never, ever again. I swear, Dr. Lane."

Venus waited in the utility closet until she heard them step into the elevator. She waited five more minutes, then stepped out into the dimly lit hallway. Someone had turned off the regular lights and turned on the night-lights.

Bella Diamond spent her days seated in a broad wing chair, much like Ingrid's chair, staring out the picture window at Elliott Bay. Where her stepson, Tim, whom she had loved more than anyone in her life, had been brutally murdered. Elliott Bay. Where the *Caprice* sat in the water, under a police watch. She was sitting in the wing chair, thinking about the *Caprice,* when Rocco stopped by to pay his respects.

"I wish they'd blow it up," she said to Rocco.

"You might want to sell it once we've released it. I have a broker friend who would love to get his hands on this sale."

"In that case, you may tell him to make an appointment with me. I don't trust Sotheby's anymore. They've fixed prices, you know."

Rocco said, "Speaking of cheating, what do you know about the Pedersons' scruples?"

"Nils and Ingrid are my neighbors, and my friends," said Bella. "Even if Nils does blame Tim for Pearl's death. I do not gossip about anyone, especially not about my friends."

Rocco hadn't told her the truth about Nils. In fact, he

still didn't know the whole truth. He had to hold out until he was sure. He said, "Let's just say I question Nils's personal value system."

"I won't have this discussion," snapped Bella. "If you wish to rehash all this trouble, why don't you find Venus and speak with her? Venus is always ready to jump to conclusions, much like yourself."

"I'm in love with Venus."

The actress's eyes bulged. She made a snorting noise. She said, "You must be joking. You are far too handsome and savvy for Venus. You should meet my other eligible daughter, Echo. You and Echo would make a fine pair."

"You're talking to a man who's passionately in love with Venus. And I've got some news for you."

"What news?"

Rocco leaned forward in his chair, stretching across the table that sat between them. He placed an index finger in Bella's face and said, "If you ever—and I mean ever—say an insulting word about Venus again, I will turn you over my knee and spank you harder than you've ever been spanked in your long, spoiled-rotten life. And I bet you'll love every whack."

For the first time in her life, Bella Diamond found herself speechless. Rocco stood up, bowed gallantly, and left. In the front hall, he encountered Stephen, the lurker.

"I was just coming in to relay the Mariners score," said Stephen. "Anything to divert, you know? Twelve to three, Mariners. In case you're interested."

"I am," said Rocco. "Very interested."

Stephen held the door for him. Rocco stepped out into the nighttime glare of newscasters' spotlights, shaded his eyes with his arm, and pushed through the crowd. He walked a half a block to his car, unlocked it, and slid behind the wheel. He turned the ignition key, his last act. The car exploded into flames.

Dr. Lane's computer certainly held some information, but Venus couldn't hack into it. She called Moses and he walked her through several maneuvers, until finally she was able to access the files. She searched until she found what she'd thought might be there; "Correspondence with Mayor Barstow." Venus opened the file and read through several letters Cherry Lane had written to Mayor Barstow. The first letter provided the key to all the others.

Dear Mayor Barstow,

This morning one of your EPA officials visited my laboratories on Western Avenue and informed me that you had signed a "shutdown" order for my facility. The official informed me that the order came straight from your office and was based on an undercover investigation that the EPA had conducted on Lane Pathogenetics. I must take exception with their findings, and therefore protest your unfair order.

Lane Pathogenetics, the EPA official charged, was guilty of dumping toxic-waste materials into Elliott Bay. The official cited six separate occasions over the past year in which, he claimed, toxins originating from my building on Western Avenue drained one city block downhill, flowing westward through the groundwater drain system, and thence directly into Elliott Bay. I, of course, asked the official for evidence of this alleged infraction of EPA regulations. He told me that he was not at liberty to divulge any evidence and said that if I wished to fight the shutdown order and subsequent prosecution, I should contact you directly. Please consider this my official protest letter. Should you have any questions that I may not have addressed in this letter, I suggest that you discuss this matter with my business partner, Nils Pederson, with whom, I understand, you are acquainted.

Sincerely,
Cherry Lane, Ph.D., M.D.

So she was also a physician. Of the healing profession. Venus printed a copy of the letter and went to the next file. The folder was named simply "NP." Venus opened it. Bingo. A letter from Nils Pederson to Mayor Barstow, in which Nils pleaded with the mayor to drop all charges against Lane Pathogenetics. He ended by reminding Barstow that they had a golf date coming up soon and that he hoped Barstow would keep it.

Nils Pederson had saved Lane Pathogenetics from EPA violations charges.

The second item in the "NP" folder was a copy of a letter to Nils from Cherry, informing Nils that she had ended her contract with L&Z Security Company and had hired new security guards from Nils's company.

L&Z. Of course. Affanassi Kulagin had referred to "the competition." L&Z. Larry and Ziggy. The Chekhovs must run a rival security company, she realized.

The third item in the "NP" folder tied it up into a neat bow. A brief, almost terse letter from Cherry Lane to Nils Pederson, confirming their business partnership and accepting Nils's investment of $4 million, which was earmarked specifically for what the letter referred to simply as the "Toxin Trials." Venus printed out a copy of the letter and kept searching from one file to the next. Half an hour went by before she found another item of interest, a file titled "*Cyanea capillata,* Accidental Hybridization in Elliott Bay with Australian Box Jellyfish DNA. An Anomaly." She opened the file and printed it. The last page was rolling out of the printer when she heard the elevator bell ping. From

down the hall, came voices. Someone coughed. Then
Cherry's voice, and Nils's. Venus snatched up the printouts,
turned off the printer and computer, and doused the office
lights.

Footsteps. The voices sounded closer. Venus looked
around for a place to hide. The room was a square box,
sparsely furnished. No closet or cupboard, no place to
hide. The footsteps grew louder, and she heard a light
cough, like someone clearing his throat. The footsteps
paused. From underneath the door, Venus saw lights
stream into the corridor. She heard Cherry say, "I'm sure I
didn't shut this door when I left. Now my keys are locked
inside."

Another voice said, "Not to worry, ma'am. I can let
you in."

A security guard must have accompanied Cherry and
Nils. The door handle turned.

Venus stuffed the papers down her shirt and tried the
window latch. It was stuck. She struggled until it opened,
and then she rolled out onto a narrow rooftop ledge. Rain
fell in sheets. A high wind whipped at the rain. Venus got
to her feet and peered over the ledge. Too far to jump to the
ground. Six feet away, the top of the iron fence joined the
building. On the other side of the fence was a small courtyard belonging to the next-door property. Maybe condos.
A large rhododendron bush had grown up against that side
of the iron fence. If she could jump that far, over the fence,
she might land safely in the rhododendron. But it was a
long jump, and she had short legs.

The lights went on in Cherry's office. Venus flattened
on the ledge and waited.

A Pederson guard stepped into Dr. Lane's office and
looked around. He noticed the open window. He walked
over and peered out. He saw rain, and then Venus. He

shouted. "What do you think you're doing?" Cherry and Nils rushed to the window.

Venus scrambled to her feet. The guard climbed out the window and came after her, shouting. She ran to the ledge and jumped.

She landed in the big rhododendron. She lay still and listened. She could hear the security guard speaking into his cell phone. She struggled out of the rhododendron and was letting herself out the courtyard gate into the street when someone fired a gun. Once, twice, three times. The third bullet zinged past her ear. She ducked behind a telephone pole, drew her Glock. Her trespass into the courtyard had triggered a security alarm, which blared into the night.

She could see the Pederson guard on the roof of Lane Pathogenetics, silhouetted against the streetlight glow. His gun was drawn and he was stretching his neck, trying to locate her in the street. In the condo courtyard, a security guard had come out of the lobby to investigate. He yelled up at the Pederson guard on Lane's roof. Venus used the distraction to run.

She ran through the rain, up the steep Broad Street hill, turned right on First Avenue, and ran four blocks to a hotel entrance, where a valet hailed her a taxicab. She gave the driver her home address. Her cell phone rang. She placed it to her ear, saying nothing, just listening. A voice said, "Next time, we won't miss."

She was soaked to the skin, shivering, and in a hurry. When the cabdriver pulled up in front of her building, she saw a man lurking behind a cedar tree, standing in the rain. Waiting for someone, maybe for her. She told the cabbie to drive around the block and enter the alley. From the alley, she could enter her garage. She told the driver to wait, then got out and used her key card on the garage door. Inside the garage, she ran to her storage unit and opened it. She pulled out her scuba-diving gear and returned to the taxi. She tossed the diving gear into the taxi and got in. "A hundred bucks," she said to the driver, "if you can get me to Pier Seventy without being followed." The driver pealed rubber out of the garage and through the alley, not stopping until he reached the foot of Broad Street. She offered him another hundred dollars to wait half an hour. The driver turned on his OFF DUTY lights and settled back in the cab.

In Orbit's parking lot, Venus pulled on the diving gear. She walked to the end of the pier. Orbit's outdoor terrace was closed because of the rain. From here, she could look up at the shore and see the Lane Pathogenics building two blocks uphill from the Orbit. She crossed the terrace, where Alexis Anders had claimed to have been stung by a jellyfish, and slipped over the pier into the water.

Ten minutes later, Venus emerged from the water. She had found what she was looking for. In Orbit's parking lot, the taxi was waiting. She pulled off the diving gear and got in. She gave the driver Bella's address. They were crossing the Magnolia Bridge when her phone rang. It was Bart, with news about Rocco. Very bad news.

Kimberly Forget bribed the security guard with a one-hundred-dollar bill, which he stuffed into his shirt pocket before letting her inside the gate. Kimberly strode confidently up to the front door, pressed the bell, and heard chimes. A moment later, the actress's personal assistant answered the door. Kimberly asked to see Venus Diamond.

"Ms. Diamond is not available," Stephen said curtly, and started to shut the door.

Kimberly stuck her foot in the door and said, "I don't want to interview her. I have some information that she wants."

"How do you know she wants it?" asked Stephen, growing impatient.

Kimberly held up her right hand, as if taking an oath. "Believe me, she wants to hear what I have to say. Just tell her it's the investigative reporter from KIRO. The reporter who broke the Alexis Anders jellyfish story."

"Whom might Alexis Anders be?" Stephen really wanted to shut the door in her face, but her power was greater than his.

"The woman who claimed to have seen a giant jellyfish and said that it stung her. Down at the Orbit Restaurant. Then she was murdered in cold blood."

Stephen regarded her with contempt. "I saw that in the newspaper. The husband has been arrested for his wife's murder. At this point, Ms. For-zhay, I don't see what relevance you have to anything."

Kimberly placed the palm of her hand against Stephen's chest and pushed hard. He struggled backward and Kimberly sidestepped him into the house. She yelled, "Venus Diamond!"

"Shut up," grumbled Stephen, recovering his balance. "I'll go find her." He gestured toward the living room. "Just go in there and sit your fanny down."

Kimberly sat on the couch, staring out the famous actress's big picture windows, marveling at the villa's grand view, its lush gardens, and at the Pederson gardens next door. Kimberly suddenly realized that for the first time in her short journalism career she had managed to get inside the house of a rich and famous person. Not that she cared much about Bella Diamond the actress; Kimberly came from a younger generation than most Bella Diamond fans. It was the aura of success that Kimberly felt in Bella Diamond's home. Someday, Kimberly thought to herself, I could be this rich, this famous. After the Pulitzer.

Stephen had warned Venus about the guest, the KIRO journalist, a Nosey Parker. When she entered the room, Venus noticed that Kimberly Forget, like most people who visited her mother's luxurious home, had been bitten by the opulence bug. She could see it in Kimberly's eyes; sparkling acquisitiveness.

Venus hadn't slept since Rocco's murder, and she had no desire to see anyone. She spent her time mourning Tim and Rocco, wondering why they had to die. Rocco hadn't had children, and for that she was relieved. But why did all the good people have to die so violently? She had already moved past denial into grief when Kimberly Forget came calling, and when Stephen came into the sunporch to announce Kimberly's presence, Venus felt her grief turn to anger, and the anger felt good. Now she sat across the coffee table from Kimberly.

"It's about Nils," Kimberly said. "And Ziggy Nelson."

Stephen came into the living room to inquire if anyone wanted refreshments. Talk about Nosey Parkers. Kimberly said, "Lots of sugar and no lemon, please." Stephen went away and Kimberly continued. "It all started when I came across a court document naming Ziggy Nelson as a witness for the prosecution in a case involving Nils Pederson's security company, Pederson Security. This was from three years ago. Some Young Turk junior prosecutor wanted Pederson's ass and wanted it bad. Guy named Karp. He had uncovered evidence that a guard from Pederson Security had committed a restaurant arson, during which a competing security company's guard was shot dead. Karp wanted to press charges, go to trial, but the chief prosecuting attorney nixed the case, saying there wasn't enough evidence to prove that the Pederson guard had committed the arson and shot the other guard. Karp, the junior prosecutor, stayed on the case for two years; then last year, he filed a court document asking for a judge to overrule the chief prosecutor and to order the case to trial. If Karp had gone to trial and proved his case, Nils Pederson's ass would have been thrown into prison. Somebody in City

Hall found out about Karp and must have tipped Nils off. Two weeks after Karp had filed the court document, he was found dead. The medical examiner who performed the autopsy on Karp determined that he had died of poisoning from an unknown toxin. His body was found in the water off Pier Seventy, below Orbit, the restaurant, you know? The place where Alexis Anders claimed to have seen and been stung by the monster jellyfish? Karp's death was ruled a suicide.

"The ME's conclusion ended the whole investigation into Pederson Security Company. Later on, I got hold of the ME's assistant. She had worked on the Karp autopsy. She remembered that one of the toxicology reports stated that Karp had had a high level of this unknown toxin in his digestive system, and that inconclusive tests had suggested the toxin came from jellyfish venom. When I asked her to show me the report, she said that shortly after the official cause of death was announced, she was closing up the file and discovered that the toxin evidence had been removed from the file."

Stephen shimmered into the room, set a tray with iced tea and cookies on the coffee table, and took his time fixing Kimberly her drink.

Venus said, "So Karp may have been murdered."

Kimberly nodded emphatically. Stephen lingered, pretending to straighten up the magazines on the coffee table.

Kimberly said, "After I discovered the Karp papers, I arranged to meet both Nils Pederson and Ziggy Nelson. First, I met Nils. He's a real jerk, in my opinion, but I never could uncover any evidence to link him to Karp's death. Then I caught up with Ziggy on his boat, the *Dirty Blonde,* over at Shilshole Marina. Ziggy wouldn't talk to me. He just clammed up. His wife threatened to shoot me if I tried to get near Ziggy again." Kimberly leaned forward. "So here's what I think happened. I think Karp was put in the water, meant to drown, or else poisoned first and then dropped over the pier."

"Why?"

"You probably have heard that Pederson Security's competition was L and Z Security?"

Venus nodded. "Larry and Ziggy Chekhov's company."

"Right. Russian mob."

Venus said, "I know. Before Larry Chekhov's brother Ziggy went to work for Pederson Security, he had his last name legally changed to Nelson so Nils wouldn't make the connection. But why?"

Kimberly said, "Ziggy was a plant for the Russians. See, Ziggy was supposed to set Pederson Security up for a big fall."

"By doing what?"

Kimberly said, "Probably just sabotage at first. To put Pederson Security out of business. But then the Karp investigation got rolling, and Karp had come across something really hot, something involving Nils. And that's why Nils wanted to kill him. Problem was, Nils made the mistake of trying to hire Ziggy Nelson to kill Karp."

Stephen was still fussing. Venus said, "Thank you, Stephen." He snarled and left the room. Venus said to Kimberly, "Then what happened?"

Kimberly sucked an ice cube as she spoke. "I only meant to extract information from Ziggy, to figure out how much he knew about Nils's shady dealings and get him to confide in me. But then I started wondering if maybe Ziggy had killed Karp."

"But why? If Ziggy Nelson was going to testify for Karp, why would he murder him?"

Kimberly shrugged. "I'm thinking Nils bought him off with a bundle of U.S. dollars and a promise not to go after his ass again."

Venus said, "After Karp died, what happened?"

"Pederson Security thrived, while the competition floundered. The Russian mob has been after Nils's ass ever since. So when Nils's daughter drowned under suspicious circumstances and one of his ex-employees, a Russian illegal named Ziggy Nelson, was reported to have been on the scene, I got mighty suspicious. Especially since I already knew that Ziggy was Larry Chekhov's brother. And Nils eventually figured it out for himself. I've heard rumors that Nils has access to a lot of public records because his security company contracts out guards to city and county buildings. So any information Nils needs, any prosecutor's records or other court documents, he can easily acquire."

"You never bought the line that Ziggy Nelson tried to save Pearl from drowning?"

Kimberly said, "Heavens no. I'm too much of a cynic. Anything that happens around Ziggy Nelson has to be deliberate. He's a cunning SOB. And those rumors about him blowing up with the *Spindrift*? He planted those himself."

"You got proof?"

Kimberly set her tea on the table, sat back, and sighed. "Not yet," she said. "But I feel it in my bones. Only at this point, I can't figure out if he's working for Nils or if he's out to destroy Nils. Either way, Nils is up to something that Ziggy wants a part of, maybe some business transaction. . . ."

Stephen appeared. "Miss . . . ah . . . For-zhay. Your boss is standing outside at the front gate, demanding to see you immediately."

Kimberly sighed and stood up. "He's threatening to fire my ass if I don't get back on the stupid jellyfish hysteria story and quit scrutinizing Nils. You know, Nils looks so darn pristine from the public perspective. My boss is just naïve enough to buy that liberal do-gooder facade."

At the door, Venus said to Kimberly, "Ever hear anything about the Russian Mafia and children?"

Kimberly made a face. "Like what?"

"Child pornography?"

Kimberly's eyes popped open. "Good grief, no," she said, reaching into her purse. She fished out a business card and handed it to Venus. "But if you know something, please call me first."

Venus waved the card away. "I've got one of those," she said, and then Kimberly walked down the path to the front gate. Venus watched as a security guard left her out.

A security guard.

Venus walked down the path to the front gate, which the guard had just closed behind Kimberly Forget. Venus looked at the guard's uniform. No company identification. Just PRIVATE SECURITY on a patch on his shirtsleeve.

She said, "Who do you work for?"

The guard said, "L and Z Security. Why?"

Venus said, "You're fired."

Stephen went ballistic when she told him she had fired Bella's security guards. She let him rant as she phoned another security company and arranged for some new guards to take over the watch.

"You have no right to involve yourself in your mother's affairs," snapped Stephen. "She will be absolutely livid when I tell her what you've just done."

"Go ahead. Tell her everything. Maybe she'll finally grow up and face reality. Although I doubt it."

"Get out of this house," Stephen said, fuming. "Immediately. Get out or I will have to throw you out."

Venus scratched her neck. Stephen was back to his old power games. "How much longer do you want to live, Steve-o?"

"Stop calling me that."

"Then get over your imperious bullshit and listen to me. If you know anything at all about Tim and Henry and Pearl that might help us find Henry, you'd better tell me right now. Otherwise, maybe I'll let you go ahead and commit suicide."

"I would never kill myself."

"But you'd let a security guard do it for you."

"I don't understand," he said huffily.

"You don't need to," she said. "Now think. What do you know about the kids that might help find Henry?"

"There is one thing," he said. "I don't know why I didn't think of this earlier."

He led her to his room. She stood in the doorway and waited while he rummaged through some DVDs. He pulled one out and handed it to her. Inside the plastic case was the typed note: "For Venus." Stephen said, "I found this a couple of days ago. In the gravel area between your mother's property and the Pedersons'. The area you and your siblings refer to as the Land of Thrush." He gestured at his computer. "I meant to give it to you, but then I just forgot."

They fed the DVD into Stephen's computer. Stephen stood behind her, looking over her shoulder. She said, "Where's Bart?"

"With your mother. I believe they are both in the pool."

"Go get him. Do not, under any circumstances, allow my mother to come in here."

Stephen went away and returned a few minutes later with Bart, who was still wet from the pool, a towel wrapped around his waist. Venus punched the play button and the DVD started spinning.

A ship's berth. Three children sat side by side on the edge of the bed. Pearl, Henry, a dark-haired boy. The lighting was good, almost expert, and the *Caprice*'s teakwood paneling made a fine backdrop. As the action started, Ziggy appeared in the picture. Pearl cried out, "No, please, don't hurt me!" Ziggy laughed. Pearl began to weep.

Bart said, "Oh God, Venus. Shut it off."

Venus pushed a button and the computer screen went dark. She turned around. Bart had turned ashen. Stephen was trembling violently. Venus said, "I'll take it to my office. We'll have to look at the whole thing."

Bart half-whispered, "Timmy . . ."

Venus said, "Let's hope not."

Olson and Song were in Olson's office. She didn't hear what they were talking about but imagined it was the Tran trial. Tran, the bear poacher, who last spring during a raid on his jacklighted camp, had shot Venus in the jaw. Tran, whom she hoped would languish in prison until he rotted to death. Tran, whom she hoped would suffer more than the black bears he had captured and tortured the lucrative gall out of by slowly draining it through permanent catheters, until finally the shackled, exhausted creatures expired. Tran and his men would chop off their paws, harvest their organs and claws, sell them on the black market, make a tidy profit, and then go after more bear. May he slither into hell.

Olson motioned to a chair. Venus said, "We need a private place. More private than your office." She showed them the DVD.

Song said, "Let me look at it, Venus. You don't need to see it."

"We need to see this."

They went into the conference room. Olson gave the word that they were not to be disturbed. The image came up on a large flat screen mounted on the wall.

Olson stopped watching halfway through, buried his face in his hands. Song forced himself to watch, his jaw clenched tight, his fury mounting. Venus felt a similar rage, and when Ziggy appeared in the picture, she knew that Tim's hunches, if they were only hunches, had all been right. And then Larry Chekhov appeared. Heinous, sick, perverted acts. An hour later, the sadistic drama ended with a slow fadeout and Pearl's soft sobbing.

Olson stood and walked over to a window, wishing it opened, needing fresh air. Song slammed a fist into the wall. Venus could see his tightened jaw muscles twitch. She said, "We need to find their Internet Web site."

Song agreed. "They're making a pile of money from some goddamned perverts out there who actually enjoy watching this crap."

Venus rebooted the DVD. "Now watch carefully," she said. Olson came back and sat down. Venus fast-forwarded the DVD until very near the end, then stopped the action. "Look in the background," she said. "Focus on the clothes cupboard."

Olson and Song looked. Olson said, "My God."

Song said, "That's Tim."

"Right," said Venus. "He was spying on them that day. This DVD was made the day Pearl went overboard. See? Both she and Tim are wearing the same clothing they had on that day. Tim must have stolen this master DVD and then planted it in the garden grove for someone to find." She ejected the DVD and handed it to Song. "We need it checked for Tim's fingerprints."

Song shook his head. "Tampered evidence. You've touched it. Stephen touched it. Not admissible."

"Screw admissible. Tim left this for me to find. He knew what was happening to Henry and Pearl and John Stark. He was probably the only person other than the

adults involved who knew what was going on. He was trying to honor a secret between friends, but at the same time,
he wanted to stop it. He was scared, afraid someone might
get hurt. And yet he had promised Pearl or Henry, whichever
told him about the secret, that he would never tell. Tim was
in a tough spot."

Olson returned to the window and stared out. A sunny
day, the sky pure and clean. "You know how I felt about
Tim," he said sorrowfully. "Still, he was a chronic liar."

Venus said, "He might have lied about some things. But
he had seen a giant jellyfish. I've seen a jellyfish exactly like
the one Tim described. He wasn't lying about that. Nor
was he lying about how he tried to save Pearl. His lie was
covering up what actually happened to Pearl. I'm willing to
bet that Ziggy had suggested the pirate scheme to Tim and
Henry, and that when Pearl stood at the end of the plank,
Ziggy had been in the water below and had ordered Pearl to
jump in. She was terrified of the water, but more terrified of
what Ziggy would do to her if she refused. Ziggy probably
promised that he'd catch her when she landed. So Pearl
jumped in, and then Ziggy held her head under water until
she drowned. After she drowned, he dragged her away
from the boat and cut off her hand."

"But why, for crying out loud?"

"She went overboard shortly after this film was made.
On the same day. She had wounds. They couldn't let her go
home looking like that. She had to be killed."

CHAPTER THIRTY-THREE

Liu Ping might have been attached with Super Glue to the counter in his Chinese Apothecary. His hands, where they gripped the wood countertop, had worn valleys into the grain. He smiled when Venus walked in. "You bring jellyfish for Liu?" he asked.

"Not this time," she said. "Next time, I promise." She told him why she had come, what she needed him to do.

Liu Ping listened closely, then said, "Why should I help you cops?"

"Because as we speak, Liu Ping, your pal Tran is on trial for poaching black bears and selling parts on the black market. I happen to know that you've done business with Tran in the very recent past. You'd make a fine coconspirator, Liu Ping."

"What is coconspirator?"

She explained.

Liu said, "You can't prove nothing."

"I can prove everything," she said, lying.

He fell for it. "Okay. This one time. But you never tell nobody I help you."

He always said that, and she always agreed. "Not a soul," she promised.

"When?"

"This afternoon. In a couple of hours."

Liu Ping shook his head and gestured at his dog, Zen, asleep now on his silk cushion, an open book beside him. "I take dog to vet this afternoon."

"Zen can wait," she said. "This afternoon."

"Zen need shots."

She said, "Liu Ping need lawyer."

Liu ping sighed. "Okay. But then you bring jellyfish."

Rocco's replacement was the young homicide detective Sanchez. "I'm sorry as hell about Rocco," he said to Venus. "We all loved him."

They talked for a while about Rocco, shared memories, laughed about his perpetual dieting. She didn't share all her memories of Rocco. Never would. Not with anyone. Not even with Song.

"We'll need two teams," she said to Sanchez. "One for the sting at Liu's Apothecary and at Myrtle Edwards. The other for Shilshole Marina. And I want my Fish and Wildlife team on both jobs."

Sanchez frowned and said, "Can we do that?"

"If it involves capturing the men who killed two Fish and Wildlife agents, yes, we can."

Sanchez nodded. "Okay. Let's do it."

"Just one thing."

Sanchez looked at her inquiringly. She said, "The SPD

can have Nils Pederson and Snow White. I want Ziggy Nelson and Larry Chekhov for myself. Deal?"

Sanchez didn't have to think long. "Deal," he said. "What time?"

"Four o'clock this afternoon at Liu's apothecary. Ten o'clock tonight at Shilshole Marina. Then immediately afterward, eleven o'clock, at Myrtle Edwards."

Sanchez said, "What if the sham in Chinatown tips off the Russians before they arrive at Shilshole?"

Venus shook her head. "Not to worry, Sanchez. They aren't on speaking terms."

Sanchez frowned. "I don't get it."

"It's like this. Dr. Cherry Lane is Nils Pederson's business partner. And they've been lovers for some time. What she does for him is part of an agreement between Cherry and Nils. At Nils's command, Cherry tried to eliminate all but Tim as being responsible for Pearl's death. Nils was terrified that Henry had actually killed Pearl. So he enlisted Cherry, who owes Nils big-time, to masquerade first as my mother's chef. Nils was worried that Rupert Scree might know something that would damage Henry's alibi. Cherry's an expert in toxicology. Cherry laced a tasty dish with fentanyl and served it up to Rupert, under the pretense of being Bella's new chef. By some miracle, Scree didn't die from the poisoning. Ironically, he was murdered by the Chekhovs because they suspected he blew up the *Spindrift* in revenge for the car-smuggling competition. Anyway, Rupert got nailed. That must have pleased Nils immensely."

Sanchez snorted. "Go on," he said. "I'm still listening, even if my tongue's in my cheek."

"Then Nils put Cherry on the scene, having her pose as a court-appointed child psychologist. Cherry did to Henry what any smart adult can do to vulnerable kids—win trust and then manipulate their memories. In the chaos surrounding Pearl's death, Cherry easily blended into the scenario. Henry was already lying, blaming Tim to protect the Chekhov brothers. She won Henry's trust and manipulated his memory, reinforcing the lies he had made up. With Tim, she had more trouble. He never let go of his own interpretation of what happened on the *Caprice* that morning. Even though he lied about it, he never changed his story."

"Have you found the Web site?" Sanchez asked.

She said, "I've asked Moses Freeny to locate it. It shouldn't take long to identify it, and then it's just a matter of tracking down the address where the money for the DVDs is received."

Sanchez ran a finger along his pencil-thin mustache. He said, "Why would the kids cooperate?"

"Maybe it was just as simple as getting attention from adults, feeling loved in a perverse sort of way. But don't confuse this with how Pearl felt about Rupert. I think she truly loved him, that he was the only adult who really paid her any attention, and I'll bet he was kind to her. Rupert might have been smuggling cars, but nothing points to him molesting children or harming them in any way. Pearl and Rupert had a secret, but it might have been an innocent one. And Pearl would never have given up their secret. I think the attention the children received from the Chekhov brothers was what terrified them. Maybe Rupert knew, and turned his back, I don't know. I'm guessing Pearl went through stages. First, it confused her. Then, when she was being physically abused, she got scared. Ziggy threatened to kill Pearl if she told Rupert that he was hurting her. Then, I imagine, gradually the violence escalated. Then Pearl reached the last stage."

Sanchez looked at Venus. "Go on," he said.

Venus said, "Ziggy had hurt her more than usual. You've seen the autopsy results on Pearl. You know that her body was covered with welts. She had been severely whipped."

Sanchez nodded. "And molested. Unfortunately, we have no DNA samples."

Venus nodded. "I think at the end, Pearl wanted to tell someone. I'm guessing she told Tim, not Rupert. And she told him Henry was involved, too. Tim confronted Henry about the game, and then Henry told Ziggy that Pearl had squealed. Now it was time to get rid of Pearl. And Tim."

Sanchez stood up and stretched. "Speculation," he said. "Too complex."

"Speculation, partly. Complex? I don't think so."

"What about Rupert? Are you sure he didn't know the kids were being harmed?"

Venus shrugged. "He probably had an inkling but wasn't sure until the last day, when Pearl went overboard. He might have figured things out too late. I realize this part is guesswork."

Sanchez leaned forward and touched her lightly on the shoulder. "Rocco loved you," he said. "He trusted you. I'm going to honor him like this: I'm going to go with your female intuition."

"Try logic," she said. "I think we'd better get moving."

Sanchez said, "So, if I understand your plan correctly, I'm going to impersonate a biologist?"

"If Snow White can impersonate a child psychologist, you can do a biologist. Trust me. This will work. If we're smart, we'll catch all of them."

Edward was feeding the monkeys when Dr. Lane entered the room where she kept her research monkeys caged. She was accompanied by a Latin-looking man with a thin mustache. "Edward," said Dr. Lane, "I'd like you to meet Dr. Sanchez."

Edward wiped his right hand on his lab coat and shook the man's hand.

Dr. Lane said, "Dr. Sanchez tells me that he's with the university. He is working on a research paper about the living conditions of research animals. I have granted him permission to inspect the facilities."

"I haven't poured anything down the drains," said Edward defensively.

Dr. Lane laughed. "Don't be obnoxious, Edward. Dr. Sanchez is merely conducting a routine inspection of our research animals' living conditions."

Dr. Sanchez smiled at Edward.

Dr. Lane said, "Dr. Sanchez has invited Mr. Pederson and myself to view a most unusual specimen. I'll be going out with Dr. Sanchez now, Edward. Can you manage the rest of the staff this afternoon?"

Edward said yes, he could manage things in Dr. Lane's absence. After they left, Edward finished up the feeding, paying special attention to his young prodigy, Babs.

Liu Ping smiled when the trio entered his shop. As they looked around at the jars and bins, Liu stroked his long beard and pretended not to watch them. He had locked Zen in a cage in the back room. Liu wanted things to go smoothly because he stood to gain a fine jellyfish and, too, freedom from prosecution. He waited five minutes and then said to the two men and one woman, "Looking for something?"

Sanchez approached the counter. "I heard about this jellyfish," he said to Liu.

Liu feigned puzzlement. "What jellyfish?"

"It's a hybrid," said Sanchez.

"What is hybrid?"

Sanchez explained, speaking loud enough for Dr. Lane and Nils Pederson to hear, then added, "This particular jellyfish is a hybrid between a lion's mane and an Australian Box jellyfish. I heard you have it here, in a tank."

Liu pretended some more. "Can't help you," he said.

If Cherry Lane had resembled Snow White before, she now looked white as a freshly laundered sheet. She moved away from Nils and up to the counter. "Dr. Sanchez," she said in a low voice, "did I just hear you correctly?"

Sanchez said, "What did you hear?"

"Did you just say something about a hybrid jellyfish?"

"I did."

"That . . . that this Chinese man has a hybrid lion's mane and Australian Box jellyfish?"

Sanchez showed her an open palm. "That's what I wanted to show you. But first, we need to convince Mr. Ping that it's safe to show us the jellyfish."

Cherry scowled and said, "But is this really possible? I mean, this hybrid couldn't have occurred. It's scientifically . . . well, impossible."

Sanchez, no genetics expert, rubbed his beard and took a chance. "Genetic engineering has come a long way, hasn't it, Cherry? We scientists are doing some amazing things."

"But . . . this Chinese man, he isn't a scientist, really. You aren't telling me that this man has successfully crossed an Australian Box with a lion's mane?"

At this point, Liu Ping said, "No jellyfish."

"Aw, c'mon, Liu Ping," said Sanchez. "What say I give you a hundred bucks, mon? Show my friends the sea monster."

Liu gripped the counter tighter and shook his head. From the back room came a long, low growl. Zen wanted

out. Liu said, "Please excuse me. My dog needs attention."
He disappeared behind the curtain, where Venus was trying
to quiet Zen.

At the counter, Cherry said to Sanchez, "Is this some
kind of joke?"

Sanchez looked surprised. "Would I joke about this?
Would I take up your valuable time with a stupid joke? I
tell you, I've seen this monster jelly, and he's incredible.
Liu's maybe a little afraid."

"Of what?" Nils had joined them at the counter.

"Maybe being charged with doing something illegal.
Maybe he thinks you two are cops, that I've brought a couple of cops in to have him arrested."

Nils said, "Why would anyone arrest a person for conducting a scientific experiment?"

Sanchez ran his finger across the thin black mustache.
"Maybe not for the experiment, but maybe for how the
results were used."

Cherry's jaw was set tight. She gripped the customer
side of the counter and said, "Something's wrong here."

Nils looked at her and said, "What do you mean?"

Cherry said to Sanchez, "What is the Latin name for a
lion's mane jellyfish?"

Sanchez could feel sweat forming on his forehead. He
didn't know one jellyfish from the next. Then Liu Ping
came back through the curtain, brushing his hands
together.

Liu said, "The dog is better now."

Cherry persisted. "Dr. Sanchez, kindly tell me the Latin
name for a lion's mane jellyfish."

Venus whispered into Liu Ping's back.

"Easy," said Liu Ping, breaking in. *"C. capillata."*

Sanchez relaxed. Cherry snapped, "I was speaking to
my colleague, not to you."

Liu shrugged and poked one long fingernail into his yellowed teeth. A tense silence settled over the shop. From the back room came snoring sounds. Zen had fallen asleep. Venus waited. Liu Ping had perfect timing, and now he said, "Jellyfish too big for tank. I keep him somewhere else." He pretended to think it over and added, "Tell you what, Dr. Sanchez. You meet me late tonight. I show you jellyfish."

Cherry and Nils exchanged glances. Sanchez said, "Can I bring my friends along?"

Liu studied Cherry and Nils, then said, "He is famous man. I know his face."

"He's okay, really, Liu Ping," said Sanchez. "You're right, he's a very prominent businessman. He's very interested in scientific experiments involving genetics engineering. This could mean a lot of money to you, Liu Ping." Sanchez leaned in close to Liu's ear and whispered loud enough for Nils to hear. "He might even make you an offer. He might pay good money for the jellyfish. You could do worse, Liu Ping. Trust me."

Cherry jumped in. "Ten o'clock. In Myrtle Edwards Park. Meet us at the south entrance to the park. From there, we'll take my car."

Nils started to balk, but Cherry persisted. "You be there," she said to Liu Ping, "You take us to your jellyfish, and somebody might have a nice present for you."

Liu Ping said, "Ten o'clock too early."

Cherry frowned. "It has to be ten. No later."

Liu Ping folded his arms and shook his head. "Eleven," he said firmly. "Can't come before."

Cherry said, "Eleven, then."

Liu Ping nodded. "You bring diving gear."

Cherry and Nils exchanged glances. So the Chinaman knew where the jellyfish were kept.

"I dive," said Cherry. "Nils doesn't. I'll bring my gear and you can take me to see the jellyfish."

Liu Ping nodded solemnly and said, "You bring cops, I kill you."

Nils held out a hand. "Hey, don't worry about a thing, Mr. Liu."

Liu Ping smiled benevolently. He wasn't worried at all.

CHAPTER THIRTY-FOUR

Another sultry July evening, the sun still high in an indigo sky. At 5:00 P.M, Venus surfaced from the frigid waters of Shilshole Bay. Climbing aboard the dock at the opposite end of where the *Dirty Blonde* used to sit in the water, she walked into the boathouse. In the bathroom, she changed out of her diving gear into a pair of black leather pants, white shirt, and a bulletproof vest. When she emerged from the bathroom, she saw Olson holding a large canvas bag, speaking in a low voice to the harbormaster. Briefing him. When Olson had finished, he turned to Venus.

"All set?"

"We'll need at least two sets of headphones."

Olson reached into his arsenal and pulled out one headset, then rummaged some more and found a second. She hung them around her neck. "Wireless," Olson explained.

"They'll pick up the signal if you got the bug secured correctly."

"Check. And I had one installed on the *Dirty Blonde* over at Harbor Island."

"This is entirely illegal, you know."

She said, "But it works." She donned one set of headphones, listened, then handed the headphones to Olson. He put them on, listened.

He said, "Someone snoring?"

"Sounds like it. Sooner or later, he'll wake up. You better send the translator down."

He handed Venus the headphones and left. Fifteen minutes later, Venus's cell phone rang. Olson. "The translator still hasn't arrived. She's held up at the Ballard Bridge. The bridge is stuck open. She says she'll get here as soon as she can."

At 6:00 P.M., the *Dirty Blonde* appeared in Shilshole Bay. At the helm was a plainclothes police officer. He steered the *Dirty Blonde* into its slip at Shilshole Marina, beside the big Chris-Craft. On the dock, another plainclothes officer waited, caught the tie-line, and secured the boat to the dock. The two officers drove away in an unmarked patrol car. The *Dirty Blonde* sat in the water, bait waiting to be nibbled. Inside the marina's boathouse, Venus watched through binoculars.

Two minutes after the officers drove away, Venus saw activity on the Chris-Craft. A figure inside moving about, speaking into a cell phone. She couldn't identify the figure as male or female. A large person. Maybe the Russian. Then the large person got off the cell phone and stepped down off the boat onto the dock and Venus saw it was him. The same man who had been on the Chris-Craft the first time she came looking for the *Dirty Blonde,* the man who told her that the *Dirty Blonde* had sailed to the San Juan Islands. So he was one of them. He held the cell phone as he walked over to the *Dirty Blonde* and peered down into its open hatch. He walked around the sailboat, inspecting it carefully. When he finished, he got on the phone again, punched in a number, and spoke into it. Now he turned his back to the dock and the boathouse, and Venus couldn't see the expression on his face. When he had finished his telephone conversation, he shoved the cell phone into his pocket and reboarded the Chris-Craft.

Half an hour passed. Venus called Olson. "Any word from the translator?"

"She's still on the wrong side of the bridge. She tried to back out of the traffic and go around to the Fremont Bridge, but she can't move an inch. She's locked in."

"It might be faster to find another translator. Maybe over at UW."

"I've tried that. Nobody's answering their damn phone. I hate voice messages."

Venus said, "Team together?"

"*Da,*—" he replied sardonically.

Olson was out for blood and had pulled together his meanest agents, guys who knew forty-five different ways to make a victim suffer before he died. Olson had lost two of his best agents, and he wanted revenge so bad he could feel it coursing through his veins, throbbing at his temples, his blood pressure reaching dangerous heights. Olson and his team waited in the marina's parking lot. Half a mile away, near Old Ballard, Song sat at the controls of a Fish & Wildlife chopper, waiting for Venus's signal. Venus and Song were talking now by phone.

Song said, "I thought you'd like to know. Moses Freeny found the Web site."

"As bad as we feared?"

"Worse. One consolation is that Tim doesn't appear anywhere."

"Tim was too smart for the Chekhov brothers."

Song said, "We've got one actual murder scene. Ziggy choked a kid to death. I think it was the missing boy, John Stark. I tried to find his mother, to verify his identity, but she's in a lockup. Cops picked her up soliciting on Aurora Avenue. But I'm positive the victim was John Stark. If Ziggy isn't already dead, he's gonna fry."

"He's not dead yet."

"You seem so sure of that. I'm not convinced yet," said Song. "What did you find in those lab documents?"

"It's not related. But it's good stuff. Dr. Lane kept a detailed account of how the jellyfish toxin was discovered. It started by accident, when one of her assistants dumped some lab waste down the drain. It ran for two blocks straight downhill through the groundwater drainage system and into the bay. Not the sewage system, but the groundwater system that feeds directly into Elliott Bay. The waste materials apparently seeped into the algae that formed around the drainpipe. A lot of jellyfish hang out there. Some of them fed on this contaminated algae. The waste materials had come from an experiment Dr. Lane was conducting with Australian Box jellyfish toxins. A smack of lion's mane jellyfish fed on this waste material and—"

"Wait, wait, wait. Did you say a 'smack of jellyfish'?"

"Check. Look it up if you don't believe me. So in that muddled biological milieu was born the hybrid. The toxin produced by the hybrid has very special qualities. It causes anaphylactic shock, killing its subject instantly. The nice thing about it is that it's a new toxin, an unknown substance. An autopsy on someone who died from this toxin might reveal that a toxin was present in the blood. But since it's new and unknown, it hasn't yet been classified. So far, Dr. Lane hasn't succeeded in reproducing an artificial replicate. So she needs all the hybrid lion's manes she can capture to continue her research and experiments. And tonight, if things go as planned, she'll lead us straight to her stash. I've already located it, by the way, though I haven't seen the whole collection yet."

Song said, "What's the value?"

"In the toxin? Worst-case scenario? Biological warfare. Any number of power-hungry demagogues would kill for it. Cherry and Nils could make a gazillion bucks selling it to the right person, or government. The report indicates that she has nearly figured out how to reproduce the toxin synthetically. If so, she's got an endless supply of a secret toxin worth a despot's fortune. And the Russians want it so bad, they can taste it."

"How are you feeling?" Song asked her.

"Peachy."

"Don't give me that stoic shit. How are you holding up?"

She didn't know what to say. She had perfected a tough facade. She could hide all manner of emotional pain—grief, loss, lost love. For Tim. For Rocco. She could hide any of her feelings, except from Song.

He said, "I asked you a question."

"Look, Louie, this isn't a good time to talk."

She heard him snicker over the phone. After two beats of silence, he said, "You're a wimp, Diamond. A true wimp."

"I've always wondered," she said coolly. "What's a wimp?"

"Depends on usage. Sometimes it's an acronym for 'windows, icons, mouse, and program.' Sometimes it means a gutless, timid individual. And sometimes it's an acronym for 'weakly interacting massive particle.' You choose."

She felt tears welling in her eyes. "You're cruel," she said.

"Cruel in love."

The tears came freely now. She stood facing out the window. Behind her, the harbormaster sat at his desk, reading a magazine. He couldn't hear her telephone voice and he couldn't see her tears. She let them fall, and though she felt no emotion, only numbness, the tears fell like soft summer rain.

Louie said, "You still there?"

"Yeah."

"Did you hear what I said?"

She put her arm up over her eyes, dried them on her shirtsleeve. More tears followed. More soft summer rain. She was afraid that if she spoke, she'd lose it, break down. Like a wimp. Instead of answering him, she pressed the button on her cell phone to end the call. It rang almost immediately. She let it ring a second time, checked the caller ID. Song. She let it ring until it stopped. In the window reflection, she could see the harbormaster glance up from his magazine as if to say, Why aren't you answering that damn thing?

At 7:00 P.M. Olson checked in. "What's going on down there?" he asked Venus.

"Nothing." The soft summer rain had ceased, leaving an empty well, a shell of herself, and a bruised heart.

Olson said, "Maybe they're smarter than you gave them credit for. Maybe they won't take the bait."

She said, "They will."

"We're sitting around in this parking lot, baking in the hot sun and starving. I'm sending out for dinner. Want anything?"

"No thanks. Where in hell is that translator?"

At 8:00 P.M., the sun still riding the sky, the man in the Chris-Craft stepped down onto the dock and once again walked around the *Dirty Blonde,* inspecting it. Then he stood on the dock and used his cell phone. Now he gestured with his arm, his hand; his head moved right to left, right to left, vehemently. He looked up at the sky. Then Venus heard the helicopter.

She put her phone on conference, got Olson, Song and Sanchez on the line.

"They're coming now. From the northwest. I haven't seen them yet, but I can hear them. They'll have pontoons on the chopper. We want to let them put down and board the sailboat or the Chris-Craft. Then we need to start the cameras rolling. This is a good viewing spot in the boathouse, and the window opens, so the camera can pick up a clear image." She turned to the harbormaster and said, "It might get ugly."

The harbormaster nodded, rolled up his magazine, and stood. "Have a nice night," he said, and then he left, taking the dockside exit and walking to where his boat was moored, like any other evening.

Olson said, "I'm sending Cooper down with the camera." Cooper, a rookie agent. He'd trained in the same class as Curtis Mandell. "And guess who just arrived."

Venus said, "The Russian translator?"

"I'm here. I am Alma."

"Hi, Alma. Come down with Cooper. Walk single file straight from the parking lot onto the dock and into the front entrance of the boathouse. If you walk a straight line single file, they won't see you."

Olson said, "Check. They're coming down now. Song, are you there?"

"I'm here, Chief."

"Sanchez?"

"I'm here. My team's hot to trot."

Venus said, "Let's let them play this scene out before we move in."

The chopper sounded louder now. Venus peered up at the sky. Still not visible. Sanchez said, "I don't want to wait too long. We can't risk another escape."

"Not to worry," said Song. "I'll be on their ass so fast, they won't know what bit them."

The chopper came into sight. Venus said, "Okay, she's got pontoons and is setting down in the water about fifty yards from the slip."

Olson grunted. "Good call, Diamond. You guessed this one right."

"Why is it always intuition or guessing with females? Why can't I have deduced, like you guys?"

"Tut-tut, Wimpy. No whining."

She didn't bother to respond. There wasn't time. The chopper had cut its engine and stopped about twenty yards from the bow of the *Dirty Blonde*. The chopper door opened. Cooper and the Russian translator, Alma, entered the boathouse just in time, Alma apologizing profusely, as if it were her fault the bridge had gotten stuck open. Venus handed Alma a headset and Alma stood beside her at the open window. Cooper set up a monitor, wired it to his camera, and got his camera rolling. She saw the Russian skipper, Dimitri Rostovich. He held the door open while someone else slid an inflated dinghy into the water. The dinghy had a small outboard engine. In the stillness, Venus heard their voices, and so could Alma. The microphone planted on the dock was picking them up loud and clear. Alma translated.

"Chekhov goes first," said Rostovich.

Larry Chekhov stepped out of the chopper. He hadn't changed. Still a burly fortyish bear with a thick head of brown hair, a florid face, and eyes that gave frogs a good reputation. Larry Chekhov, Mafia boss. A man without a conscience. A man who had a fetish for collecting his victims' right hands.

Chekhov said, "Give me the box."

Rostovich reached into the chopper. Someone inside the chopper handed him the box. A large ice cooler. Rostovich handed the box down to Chekhov, who struggled with it as he sat in down the dinghy.

"Now tell Yevgeny and Natalia to get ready for take-off," said Chekhov. Rostovich spoke into the chopper, then dropped down into the dinghy and sat beside Chekhov. Rostovich started the outboard engine and the two men puttered a few yards toward the dock.

Behind the camera, Cooper said, "Got it."

"Keep her rolling," said Venus.

Cooper checked the monitor and said, "You'll get a better view on the screen."

Venus looked at the monitor. Now she saw Larry Chekhov and Rostovich close-up. Larry Chekhov still wore that perpetual grin born of a total lack of scruples. She remembered the same expression had been on his face as he went down into the Strait of Juan de Fuca off that floatplane pontoon. A blissful sneer. How could anyone—even a Russian bear like Checkov—survive those icy waters?

Rostovich pulled the dinghy up beside the Chris-Craft. Chekhov stepped onto the boat's swimming ladder, ascended two wooden steps onto the stern deck, and tied the dinghy to a cleat. Rostovich cut the motor, handed the ice chest up to Chekhov, and went aboard the Chris-Craft. The man inside the cabin came out and helped Chekhov carry the ice cooler into the cabin.

Venus turned to Alma. "You ready?"

Alma nodded, adjusted her headphones, and, when the men began speaking, translated.

"They brought it back around six-thirty P.M.," said the man from the Chris-Craft.

Chekhov said, "It's a trap. They're watching us as we speak."

Rostovich stood aside and let the two other men talk. Cooper's camera had limited access to the boat's interior. The monitor showed shadowy figures moving about the cabin. Someone went into the galley and brought a bottle back to the salon. Glasses appeared. The men drank as they conversed.

Chekhov said, "At the most, we have thirty minutes. Bogdonov, you'll do the explosives. Once these two vessels are gone, we're covered. They'll have nothing to go on. Nothing."

Bogdonov, the man Venus had seen on the Chris-Craft, spoke. "I've already prepared this boat. The sailboat will only take a minute. But I have one request, Chekhov."

"What's that?"

Bogdonov said, "I want Natalia to go along with the boats."

Chekhov gave a deep, rolling laugh. "Why in hell do you want that, Janis?"

Janis Bogdonov said, "You can't trust her. Did you know she was sleeping with the skipper of the *Caprice*?"

Chekhov said, "Scree? I'm not surprised. Did Ziggy know about it?"

Bogdonov said, "Yes, certainly. They shared her. At least that's what Natalia told me."

Alma turned to Venus and said, "Janis Bogdonov is Latvian, at least partly. I can hear his accent."

Chekhov said, "Poof! I don't believe her. She's a liar."

"I am serious, Chekhov," said Bogdonov. "She makes trouble where there isn't any. She's dangerous. I want her out of the picture altogether. If we don't get rid of her now, I'll do it later. But now is better."

Chekhov sighed and said, "Okay. Rostovich, take the dinghy and bring Natalia back here. And hurry."

Rostovich came out of the cabin and untied the dinghy, stepped down into it, and puttered back to the chopper. Fifteen minutes later, he returned with Natalia. She boarded the Chris-Craft, stepped into the cabin. The monitor showed her enter the main salon.

"Where is Ziggy?" she said, looking around the salon.

Silence.

Natalia said, "Rostovich told me Ziggy wanted to see me."

Silence.

Natalia said, "What's going on? Something is going on. What? Where is Ziggy?"

Janis Bogdonov pulled out a gun and shot Natalia through the head. She fell across Chekhov's legs. He twitched and her body slumped to the floor.

The men worked quickly, emptying several boxes into the dinghy.

Venus spoke into her cell phone. "Song, are you there?"

"Check."

"Power up. Olson and Sanchez, teams forward."

"Check."

"Check."

Venus turned to Alma and Cooper. "Get out of here. Now. Move single file and fast. Go to the parking lot. Hurry."

Cooper said, "I want this on film."

Alma fled. Venus said to Cooper, "You might get blown to smithereens."

Cooper grinned. He said, "I trust you guys."

"Fool," she said, placing a hand on her gun.

The men had boarded the dinghy and now Rostovich started up the motor. Venus made her move, sprinting out of the boathouse, across the dock. The dinghy was twenty yards off the Chris-Craft's stern when she reached the larger boat. As she stepped inside the *Chris-Craft's* cabin, Olson's team emerged on the opposite side of the *Dirty Blonde*. Sanchez and his team ran directly down the long dock to the end, where the dinghy had been tied up. She heard someone fire the first shot and then she heard chopper blades whirring. The chopper? Song? More gunfire. Venus stepped over Natalia's body, heading for the ice chest. It was heavy and she struggled to raise it off the floor. She had reached the cabin door when the *Dirty Blonde* exploded in flames.

The heat seared her face and burned the hair off her arms. She crouched with the ice chest, using it as a shield against the roaring flames and flying shards of what used to be the *Dirty Blonde*. More gunfire, coming from the dinghy. She looked up over the melting ice chest and saw the dinghy pulling up beside the chopper. Had she been wrong? Had she heard this chopper, not Song's?

Rostovich hadn't made it out alive. Chekhov and Bogdonov climbed aboard the chopper. How had they survived the shower of bullets from Olson's and Sanchez's sharpshooters? But they had and were climbing into the chopper. The chopper lifted off, straight up over Shilshole Bay.

A crowd of boaties had formed along the docks, milling about, frenzied, as police officers tried shoving them back away from the Chris-Craft. People screamed, shouted. What the hell was happening at their peaceful moorage?

Venus lowered the ice chest onto the dock, placing it behind Sanchez's men. They were firing now at the chopper and she heard a bullet zing off the chopper's metal side. Then another, but when she looked, she saw the chopper had survived the hit. It rose thirty feet off the water, tilted, and turned to the northwest. As it flew off, the noise from its engine faded. She could see it in the distance, heading toward the horizon, but she could barely hear it.

"Song," she barked into the phone. "Where in hell are you?" No answer. "Damn it, answer me," she said, and then she heard Song's chopper.

He put down in the water about fifteen feet from the dock where she stood. He waved to her. She left the ice chest with Sanchez and borrowed the harbormaster's dinghy. In two minutes, she had reached the chopper. She pushed off the dinghy and climbed in beside Song.

"Pretty good," said Song. "For a wimp."

"Shut up and fly."

They caught up with the Russians two miles out at sea. Chekhov's chopper was apparently heading for a cargo vessel now visible on the horizon. Venus would bet her new porcelain teeth that Ziggy Nelson was aboard that cargo ship. Ziggy, and, if he hadn't already killed them, the crew he'd bought off, or taken hostage. Ziggy was the real pirate.

Song pointed behind her. She reached back and brought up a Mac 10. She mounted it and looked through its scope. Song lifted up above the Russians' chopper, flew directly over it. From the lower chopper came gunshots. A bullet zinged off Song's blades. Venus leaned out the window. Song lowered the chopper and Venus fired. The first hail of bullets hit Yevgeny. The *Longitude*'s navigator had been flying the helicopter. But he couldn't manage it very well with several bullets through the head. The Russians' chopper lurched. Chekhov grabbed the controls and brought it back upright. Venus aimed, fired, missed.

"Lower," she shouted at Song.

"I'm sitting on their goddamn blades," he shouted back.

"Just a little lower. Do it!"

Song lowered the chopper slightly. Venus said, "Now tilt to starboard." Song tilted the chopper. "Get ready to rock and roll." She fired into the Russians' chopper before Song pulled up on the throttle and sped forward. The Russians had dropped down to twenty feet and were firing an Uzi upward at them. The bullets struck Song's windshield. Venus leaned out the side and fired one last time. The Russians' chopper burst into flames, its seared pieces falling in slow motion into the sea, matching in color a brilliant red-orange sunset.

Song said, "Hang on." He made a sharp turn and headed back to the marina.

CHAPTER THIRTY-FIVE

The ice chest had contained young Henry Pederson's remains, wrapped in black plastic trash bags. She had suspected as much, but when she saw the boy's dismembered body parts, Venus leaned over the side of the dock and vomited. Somebody took the ice chest and its contents away. Five minutes later, she was speeding across the Ballard Bridge, headed for Myrtle Edwards Park.

At 10:15 P.M., Venus sat on a park bench in Myrtle Edwards Park, her feet dangling, waiting for Song. He was late. They needed to be ready now. Where was he?

So all these years, Larry Chekhov must have retained his status as local Russian Mafia boss. Captain Kremnyev, Lina's husband, had been the *Dolgota*'s or, *Longitude*'s, captain, until he had been murdered. Kremnyev had told Lina too much. More than about smuggling stolen luxury vehicles. Much more. Kremnyev hadn't liked what Lina's cousins, Ziggy and Larry Chekhov, were doing to little boys and girls on his boat. And maybe Natalia, too. Captain Kremnyev must have confided everything to Lina, and Lina had taken some secrets to her grave. What grave? Where do you bury the body of an illegal Russian immigrant whose husband has been murdered and whose cousins are wanted by the law? Venus wondered where Lina's body lay now. In the ME's cooler, no doubt. Only not dismembered like Henry's.

Why had the Chekhov brothers targeted Nils Pederson's children? Was it the rivalry between Pederson Security and L&Z Security? Or just that Henry and Pearl were conveniently available on the *Caprice*? Was it just for sheer perverted pleasure, for twisted satisfaction, for profit? Ziggy had had easy access to Nils's children. Even easier after his onetime friend Rupert Scree had hired Ziggy as the *Caprice*'s engineer. As long as Tim brought the Pederson children aboard the *Caprice*, Ziggy could enjoy their company, film them, and, ultimately, deliver them to his brother. But then Ziggy hadn't been able to put on the brakes. His needs grew more and more perverse and cruel. How many children had the Chekhov brothers murdered, off- or on-screen? When Rupert wouldn't go along with the program, Ziggy'd had to get rid of him. And, too, there was the car-smuggling competition.

But there was more. The Chekhov brothers were after Nils's and Cherry's product. A deadly toxin, so far with unidentifiable origins. A perfect weapon. A weapon almost any national government would covet. A ticket to more power and fortune than the Chekhovs had ever imagined when they had taken over control of Seattle's Russian mob.

At 10:30, Venus saw Song drive his van into the parking lot. She watched him unload the diving gear—his set, hers. She hoped he'd remembered the Firefly Plus ACR dive lights, and hoped the flashlights' batteries were fresh. She watched Song don his diving gear and walk across the parking lot to the concrete railing that ran from Pier 70 along a sidewalk to the park's south entrance. She watched him climb over the railing and slip down into the water. She knew where he was headed—for the wood pilings underneath the Orbit. Fifteen minutes passed, and then at 10:45, Liu Ping arrived at the park entrance. He'd brought Zen along. Entering from the south, Liu Ping could certainly hear the restaurant patrons on Pier 70. She watched as Liu passed the Orbit. Beneath a generous moon, Zen shone like a white bone. He trotted dutifully at Liu's heels, maybe the only loyal friend the old Chinese man could claim after forty years of black-market shenanigans.

Liu saw Venus seated on the park bench, the second one in from the entrance. She pretended not to notice him and he walked past her without acknowledging her. But Zen, that obdurate dog, stopped on the path, growled, and then barked like a sick seal until he'd worked up a mouthful of foam. Liu tried calming Zen, but the dog wasn't having it. Venus had prepared for another attack, and when Zen rushed her, she tossed out a fresh raw sirloin steak she'd bought at the Orbit a few minutes earlier. Zen stopped in his tracks, sniffed the air, located the meat, and padded across the grass toward the bloody flesh. Venus watched him devour the meat. On the path below, Liu stood waiting, studying his four-inch-long index fingernail. When Zen had finished his meal, he turned and gazed at Venus. Then he padded over to her and very gently licked her ankle. Venus reached down and petted his head. He made a purring sound in his throat. She said, "Nice boy." Zen sat down on his haunches and wagged his tongue. He didn't crave ankle flesh now.

Liu said something in Chinese. Zen turned and lollygogged back to his master. Master and dog trotted along the path, deeper into the park.

Venus sprinted to the van. Her diving gear was on the ground at the van's rear. She donned it and shoved her clothing into the van's rear hold. Song had remembered the Firefly Plus dive lights. She snatched hers up, crossed the parking lot to the concrete balustrade, climbed over it, and slipped down the other side into Elliott Bay. She stayed on the water's surface, watching Liu Ping standing beneath the moonlight, bent like a withered willow tree. She watched him and she watched the park entrance.

At 11:00 P.M., the black Cadillac Seville drove into the park's south parking lot, pulled into a space, and then its headlights went off, followed by the motor. A few seconds later, Venus saw Cherry and Nils exit the Caddy. Cherry wore a diving suit, and now she strapped on an oxygen tank. She held her flippers in one hand. Nils was holding a large briefcase by its handle. Venus would bet her best Doc Martens that the briefcase contained cash. Cash to try buying Liu Ping off. Because the old Chinese man obviously knew something that he shouldn't.

Venus wrapped her lips around the oxygen tank's mouthpiece and slid downward into the bay.

She found Song waiting underneath the pier, a black shadow half-illuminated by moonlight. She joined him there, and they waited.

Liu Ping was a clever man and everything he did was motivated by self-interest. Earlier in the day, he had seen a news broadcast about the Tran trial and had heard a KIRO news reporter mention his name, his shop. "The prosecutor refuses to confirm or deny a report that Liu Apothecary in Chinatown's International District has been used by Tran as a conduit for selling poached animal parts." That's what the reporter had said. Liu suspected that Agent Diamond had planted that little tidbit just to make him nervous, to emphasize how important it was that he cooperate in this scheme to trap the city's most prominent businessman. Liu

Ping hated the police, but he hated the idea of prison more, and he was a pragmatic man. And so when the man and woman approached him in the park just after 11:00 P.M. on that moonlit night, Liu put on his best performance yet. He picked up Zen and stroked the dog's smooth back. Zen purred. When the couple got up close, Nils said to Liu, "Does he bite?"

Liu stroked Zen some more. He said, "Only cops. He only bite cops."

Cherry said, "Are you going to show us the jellyfish you claim to have?"

Liu cocked his head toward the pier. "My hybrid down there," he said to Nils and Cherry. "Underneath Pier Seventy. Underneath restaurant. In net, so it won't escape."

Cherry and Nils exchanged a glance. Nils said, "Will you show it to us?"

Liu Ping shrugged. "I don't dive. My grandson takes care of that for me. You want to see jellyfish, you go down."

Zen began whimpering and wriggling in Liu's arms. He'd caught a whiff of something in the air. He wanted down, and fast. Liu leaned over and set the dog down on the path. Zen raced across the grass to the boulder jetty.

Liu said, "We have mutual friends."

"Who?" said Nils.

Liu's eyes sparkled. "Chekhov boys."

Nils said, "How do you know the Chekhovs?"

Liu shrugged lightly. "Contraband take same path no matter what. Drugs. *xiong dan*. Ivory. Mercedes-Benz. Humans. All black-market product take same path. Chekhovs sell me *xiong dan* and paws."

"What's *xiong dan*?"

"Gallbladder of bear. Very good medicine. Very expensive."

Cherry said, "Nils, let's just forget this."

Nils placed a hand on her arm. "Just calm down." To Liu, he said, "So what if I know the Chekhov brothers?"

"We have common interest, too." Liu showed his yellow teeth.

Nils sighed. The old Chinese man was playing verbal cat and mouse and Nils was growing nervous. He said, "What's that?"

Liu said, "Larry Chekhov. He want my jellyfish. He say he kill for jellyfish."

Cherry said, "I told you, Nils."

Liu said, "Now you got it right. Good black-market product, too."

Cherry's patience had run out. Liu Ping was lying through his teeth. She knew it and he knew it. Maybe he wanted her to call his bluff. She said, "Mr. Liu, it occurs to me that you are bluffing."

Liu squinted. "What is bluffing?"

"You are cleverly setting us up for a bribe."

Nils placed a hand on Cherry's arm. "Don't," he said.

Cherry shook off Nils's hand and persisted. "You and I both know, Mr. Liu, that the jellyfish down there belong to me. And that they are very special specimens. Somehow you found out about the hybrid and now you are trying to bribe me for your silence."

Liu Ping made as innocent a face as a perpetual liar can manage and said, "Why would I do that?"

"Because you have learned through whatever source told you about the hybrid that it is extremely valuable, and that its development has so far been kept secret."

Liu waved a gnarled hand. "Who care about jellyfish anyway?"

Cherry steamed and Nils tried to intervene. He said, "I am prepared to offer you any amount of money, cash."

Liu showed interest. "For what you do that?"

"Your silence," said Nils. "You see, this is a secret government project. . . ."

Liu Ping opened his mouth and let out a raspy chortle. "Ha-ha. Can't fool me. Government don't know nothing of jellyfish."

Nils set the briefcase down on the path, squatted, and clicked the case open. In the moonlight, Liu saw the cash. Hundreds of bills, maybe thousands. He could feel his mouth water. Nils took out some bills and counted them, then held them out to Liu Ping. "Ten thousand," he said. "For your silence."

Liu sucked his cheek. Ten measly thousand. Who did they think they were dealing with? He said, "You go to hell."

Nils counted out more cash, held it out. "Twenty-five thousand. That's the highest I can go."

Liu laughed. "You are very rich man," he said. "You can pay more."

Nils grew surly. "That's it, I'm telling you right now. That's all I can manage."

Liu said, "What if I say go to hell?"

Nils said, "Then, Mr. Liu, I will make damn sure your business is shut down and never opens again."

Zen came back, carrying something in his mouth. Liu leaned down to inspect it. A wharf rat. Zen dropped it proudly at Liu's feet. Liu said something in Chinese. Zen barked once. Liu said something else. Zen picked up the wharf rat and trotted off toward the jetty.

Liu smiled. "Maybe I bluff. Maybe no jellyfish down there. Maybe I made up story."

Cherry said to Nils, "He's stolen them."

Nils said, "Now, Cherry, just calm down."

"I'm going down there," Cherry said.

"He might have the grandson down there."

"There is no damn grandson," Cherry said huffily. "The man's a blackmailing son-of-a-bitch liar." She slipped on the flippers and entered the water from the jetty. Venus ducked underwater and waited while Cherry swam toward the pier pilings. The odor of creosote off the pilings had made Song dizzy and he motioned that he needed to move away from the pilings. He went underwater silently. When Cherry had reached the pilings, she switched on a flashlight. Not as powerful as the Firefly Plus, maybe a twentieth of the illumination power of Venus's flashlight. Cherry swam through the warren of pilings until she reached the center of the dock's underside, about twenty yards from where Venus waited behind a piling. Venus hoped Song was nearby.

Cherry's flashlight illuminated only a small underwater area, about the size of a telephone booth. Along the dark perimeter, lit only by an eerie phosphorescent glow, lay the huge net Venus had discovered when she first had dived down here, when a taxicab had waited for her in the Orbit's parking lot. The net had been attached to the pilings. Venus watched it now. Inside the net, huge golden jellyfish, dozens of them, billowed and floated, trapped.

Now Venus's flashlight beam washed across the pilings with a light so bright, it might have been high noon underwater. Startled, Cherry turned and saw two figures swimming toward her. She turned and swam away, Song swimming after her, aiming his high-beam flashlight.

Cherry was an expert swimmer, but the power of Song's flashlight caught her in a wash of illumination that must have terrified every swimming thing in its path. Song sped up, reaching Cherry at the end of the pier. They struggled underwater. Venus swam forward toward them. Cherry fought like a wildcat, and she was strong and resourceful. She got her hand free and used her knife to cut Song's air hose. Song continued struggling until he had to surface for air. Venus moved in, her own knife ready.

Cherry turned and saw Venus coming at her. Cherry brandished her knife and moved in to attack.

Cherry was even stronger than Natalia. She grabbed Venus's arm and yanked hard. Venus rolled, then kicked at Cherry, striking her in the stomach. Cherry let go. Venus didn't wait for Cherry to recover; she grabbed her wrist and pressed hard until Cherry's hand opened and her knife floated out. Venus backed off to check her oxygen supply, Cherry moving in again. Suddenly, Song appeared, tankless, and though Cherry fought hard, she could not escape his grasp. He dragged her upward to the surface. When they emerged near the jetty, Song waited until Cherry quit struggling, then turned her over to a police officer who had been waiting on the pier with handcuffs.

Underwater, Venus was swimming back toward the pier when the Firefly Plus failed. The underwater drama dissolved momentarily into darkness. Then the moon came out to illuminate the depths, and as she moved toward the pilings, she saw glowing jellyfish ahead of her, reflecting moonlight. She reached them just as a spear pierced her wet suit, striking her torso.

CHAPTER THIRTY-SIX

Venus felt her energy drain, her body sinking fast. She curled into a crouch, grabbed the spear's end, and yanked as hard as she could. It came out, tearing a hole in her wet suit. She checked the spot. It was too dark to see, but she could feel the hole where the spear had pierced her wet suit. She knew he was nearby, but in the darkness, she couldn't see him. She clung to a piling.

She had plenty of oxygen. The wound seemed superficial. She was disoriented, though. Which way was up? She went limp and let the force of gravity guide her, then propelled herself against it, surfacing at the end of the pier. The moon played cat and mouse with some high striated clouds, its light now dimmer than before. She stayed very still and listened. He was somewhere nearby. Where? What weapons did he carry? Her body began shivering and she couldn't control it. Her breathing felt shallow, insufficient.

Where was Song? A single ponderous dark cloud raced across the sky and the moon slid behind it. Total darkness. The air took on a chill, her body losing blood. Now she could feel it. Definitely losing blood. She should take a chance, swim to shore. She quietly pushed off from the piling and tried to swim, but she had grown too weak. She was stuck out here at the end of the pier. Above her, she could hear music and people laughing. They seemed millions of miles distant, yet they were maybe fifty or sixty feet over her head, dining alfresco on the pier. Could she yell for help? He'd hear her. She had no choice. She had to flush him out while she still had enough energy to fight back.

She yelled, "Man overboard!"

Above her, the laughter ceased, but the music kept on playing. The Orbit's alfresco diners probably thought they were just imagining that they heard someone yell. But Ziggy had heard her, and now that he knew her location, he moved toward her through the dark, silent water. She could hear his slow breaststrokes coming closer. Then she heard his breathing. She turned toward the sounds. Ziggy Nelson was ten feet from where she clung to the piling. Close enough to see his dripping beard, his broad chest, his Popeye biceps. His spear gun.

He moved in slowly, aiming the spear gun at the space between her eyes. When he fired the gun, she had already ducked behind the piling. The spear landed in the wood piling. He reloaded. She ducked underwater and swam, feeling her way through the warren of wood pilings. She knew she must have found an opening, because she felt no more pilings, only open water. She swam, but inefficiently, her wound taking its toll. And then he was on top of her, holding her head underwater. He reached down and yanked at her oxygen hose. She struggled, but Ziggy was stronger, and she felt herself losing consciousness. Then the sun came out, or seemed to, and the deep waters were bathed in light. She felt his grip loosen and she took advantage of it, wrestling out of his grasp. When she had swum a few yards, she looked back. The illuminated bay was teeming with frogmen.

The Coast Guard divers wore huge insignias on their backs, which was the only way to distinguish them from Ziggy's men. Ziggy must have had ten or more accomplices, for his attempted jellyfish heist, spread out among the dock's wood pilings. The Coast Guard frogmen moved in, surrounding the dock. Venus surfaced long enough to reattach her oxygen hose, then joined in the fray, going straight for Ziggy. She could recognize him now by his shape. She saw him swim behind a wood piling and aim his spear gun toward a Coast Guard frogman. She swam around the pilings and came up behind him before he realized that she was there. She felt another surge of energy. She grabbed Ziggy from behind, around his thick neck, and pressed hard. He raised his arms to pry off her grip but lost his spear gun in the process. He struggled like a crazed carp. All around her, a bloody ballet played out against the illuminated waters. She squeezed Ziggy's neck as hard as she could, but then she felt a large hand wrap around her neck. Not Ziggy's hand. Her grip on Ziggy loosened and now he broke free. The hand around her neck squeezed tighter. She twisted suddenly, gave her captor a knee in the groin, and swam through the pilings toward the big net. The man followed, swimming fast.

Like Tim had said, they were the size of his bed. Counting the kelpy manes and the tentacles, the size of his bedroom. The moon reappeared and suddenly the jellyfish were undulating golden luminescent blobs, a thousand tentacles waving their lethal tips. Venus reached into her belt, pulled out her knife, and slashed the net. It bloomed open and the smack of lion's manes floated out. The man swimming after her had almost reached her side. He paused, treaded water, stared at the jellyfish, and then went after Venus. As they struggled, a massive golden blob floated above them and dropped its kelpy feeders over both divers. Venus struggled to untangle from the lion's mane, ducking each time a poisonous tentacle swooped in her direction, ready to stun its prey. It didn't have a brain, but it knew how to kill.

The man had broken loose from the lion's mane and was swimming away when one of the medusa's tentacles struck him across his face and neck. It must have found flesh and made contact. He jerked away and swam fast toward shore, but the poison had triggered anaphylactic shock. Fifteen feet from the jetty rocks, he went rigid and then sank.

The feeders had a good grip on Venus and its tentacles kept waving toward her. She slashed with her knife, finally cutting free from the tangled mane. The golden blob undulated out with the tide. Freed from its hold on her, she could probably swim above it, slash it with her knife. How do you kill a jellyfish? In the end, she decided to let the thing go free.

Ziggy was fleeing now, swimming toward land, approaching the rock jetty in the park. She went after him, leaving the lighted space, entering the black unknown. She could hear him surface, and she surfaced, too. Thin moonlight revealed him to her. He had reached the jetty and was crawling up onto it. She made landfall five seconds behind him. Ziggy was dropping his flippers. She yanked hers off and went after him. He ran up into the park, Venus in pursuit. He disappeared in a grove of birch trees, then reappeared on a grassy knoll. There was a cyclone fence that divided the park from the railroad tracks. Ziggy ran down the other side of the knoll and had almost reached the fence, when a terrible sound stopped him in his tracks.

Vicious barking.

The dog leapt at Ziggy, taking Ziggy's leg in his mouth and biting down hard. Ziggy tried fighting the dog off, but the dog had a solid grasp. Ziggy howled. The dog refused to let go. Then Venus saw the figure standing in the shadows of the birch trees. He was stroking his long beard, smiling. She went over to him and Liu Ping handed her a set of handcuffs. She handcuffed Ziggy Nelson to the cyclone fence, Zen holding on tight until she'd secured the cuffs. Then Liu Ping called to Zen and he let go. Ziggy said, "You'll never get Larry. Never." Maybe Ziggy hadn't heard about the chopper crash. When she turned around, she saw police officers leading Nils Pederson away. He wasn't wearing handcuffs. Not yet anyway.

Venus didn't see the great golden blobs again, the monstrous jellyfish that some diners claimed they saw that night in the bay waters off Pier 70. The clouds had retreated and the phosphorescent globes glowed in the moonlight as they rode the outgoing tide. Many of Orbit's diners saw them. They were big as trucks, hysterical witnesses claimed, and they undulated on the water's surface. One witness said she saw a harpoon stuck in a blob's golden dome. Another witness swore he saw a man's body inside a golden blob, as if he had been swallowed up for dinner. And the story grew stranger and stranger. By the time it reached Internet chat rooms, it had taken on a life of its own.